MIDNIGHT'S PARK

MIDNIGHT'S PARK

by brandon spacey

Copyright © 2013 by brandon spacey
and SpaceBrew Publishing.

All Rights Reserved.

spacebrew

publishing

publishing.spacebrew.com

Cover art by brandon spacey.

Midnight's Park is a work of fiction. All characters
appearing in this work are fictitious. Any resemblance to
real persons, living or dead, is purely coincidental.

Second Edition

This is for my dad, Paul,
who is the biggest fan of this book.

Midnight's Park

"At once I saw her calling out,
    and fear within her eyes.
Upon her legends coming clear,
    she'd whispered her goodbyes.

"I came upon a winter's ground,
    in search of my love true.
For she led me to eternal dream,
    but my love had just passed through.

"I sang and cried my life away,
    but had gotten there too late.
Amidst my passion complacent me,
    I'd fallen for my fate.

"I searched for years and found my love,
    interred within her hunger.
I wept for though the time had passed,
    my love had grown much younger.

"But deep within the walls of time,
    and void with perfect dark,
I woke to find my dreams were real,
    at home in Midnight's Park."

S he sat hunched over the keyboard, scratching her head with one hand and pounding the enter key with the other. The terminal was lagging, and her commands were processing in slow motion. Someone was here – interfering. She could feel it. It was not possible, they had said. These computers and this network were impenetrable from the outside world. But what else could be causing this lag?

The small room was dark – a darkness so complete she could not see anything beyond the screen of her laptop computer. Her fingers rested on the keys as her eyes focused on the LCD screen. The computer's processor grinded and the hard drive clicked madly as it tried to handle all the data flowing across the screen. The four gigabytes of memory within could not curtail the lethargy that came with processing this much data. She would simply have to be patient.

After several minutes of grinding, she finally noticed some improvement with the performance of the machine, and then it happened.

An alert box popped up in the corner of the screen. It read INTRUSION ALERT.

She froze, her eyes wide with fear, and her fingers trembling above the keyboard. The application in which she worked was proprietary, and top-secret. Whoever was in her system had access to directories, files, and power they could not begin to comprehend. She tried to exit the application, the only way to keep the intruder from getting his hands on the company's most important asset. The program was hard-locked and spiking the CPU, relentlessly grasping for processing power it did not have available.

Dialog boxes popped up in rapid succession, asking her if she wanted to proceed with the actions she was commanding. She kept hitting the enter key – answering yes, that she was sure of her intentions. She had been schooled by the best, and had worked with the most advanced technology available. She did not need some software application second-guessing her every command – but still, it persisted.

When some memory finally became available, she hit the exit button again, and saw a whole batch of data turn dark blue. A portion of the data string she had open within the application was now highlighted. The intruder was trying to copy that data. She hit the escape key. Nothing happened. She hit it again several more times, all to no avail. Then slowly, the data started disappearing. It shifted up and to the left, as the data after the highlighted area moved to fill in where the missing bits had been. And she couldn't stop it.

She pounded the keys furiously, cursing under her breath and biting the inside of her lip. Nothing was working. Since this was an "impenetrable network", the company had no intrusion tracing software loaded. Intrusion detection was built into the platform, but she had no way of immediately knowing who had hacked in. With no power over the hacker, she could not exit the program, or deselect anything he had highlighted to copy. Her only solid choice of action was to shut off the computer. So that's what she did.

It was suddenly bright in the room again. She leaned back in her seat and ran her hands through her hair. She sighed heavily, shaking her head. This was not supposed to happen. Now they had lost a ton of data. This was bad. This was grave. The magnitude of the repercussions they would face could be inexplicable. This was beyond grave; this was catastrophic. And now she would have to wait years to see what had really happened.

CHAPTER ONE
Evanescence

The wheels of the shopping cart squeaked loudly and objected to any kind of physical control Daniel tried to administer on it. Daniel, frustrated and tired, leaned on the handle while Anna read the sides of boxes, looking for the perfect combination of ingredients. Daniel's sighs were growing a little more pronounced, and Anna was beginning to get jittery. "It has to be right, Dan. My world-famous banana pudding only works with the perfect ingredients."

"It's pudding, Anna. No one cares what brand of flour you use."

"Flour?" she said. She stared at him, dumbfounded.

"Look, will you just hurry up so we can get this over with?"

"You really don't want to go, do you?" Anna asked. She finally dropped the pudding mix into the basket and ran her hair back behind her ears.

"You know I don't want to go. It's always pins and needles when I'm over there. Your dad won't even talk to me."

"Daniel, he doesn't talk to anyone."

"Yeah, you know how uncomfortable that is for me? He just sits there glued to his TV. Any comments I make are answered with blank looks and scoffs."

"I told you, just give it time, baby. He'll come around." She walked around and put her arms around his neck from behind him, leaning in to get close to his ear. "I'll make it worth your while," she said.

Daniel smirked and stood up straight, turning to look at her. "Hmm. What does that mean?"

"You'll just have to wait and find out. That is, of course, assuming you don't drink too many beers tonight."

"I'm not drinking at all tonight. I'm on-call."

"Well good then. There shouldn't be a problem, should there?" she said, taking him by the chin like a child. She stood up on her tiptoes and kissed him on the lips.

"Yeah, I just hope I don't get called in tonight." Being a systems engineer for his company, he was almost always on-call, and got work-related pages almost constantly. And secretly, he hoped he would get called in tonight. Anything to escape spending time with her parents.

After checking out and loading up the groceries, Daniel took his place in the driver's seat of the Jeep Wrangler and backed out of the parking spot. He was trying to get in a better mood about going to her folks' house. Ever since their first date, he had felt resistance from her father. Daniel had had to pick her up from her parents' house, and her father had answered the door. The dislike had been almost instant.

"Cheer up, Dan. We don't have to stay long!"

"Any amount of time at your parents' house is a beating for me."

"Thanks." Anna pulled her seatbelt, then sighed again, crossing her hands in her lap, flicking the grocery list she had been checking off in the store.

"Hey, I only go because of you. You know I can't get enough of you, baby," Daniel said, leaning in to kiss her cheek. She half-heartedly reached up and tousled his hair with a half-smile.

"You know when we get married, you're marrying my family, too," she said.

Daniel made a face and nodded. "Yeah. I know. Why do you think it keeps getting postponed?" Anna stuck her tongue out at him.

She shrugged and dropped the outdated grocery list in the cup holder. "Well, my parents haven't seen us in two weeks. So thank you for 'enduring' it for me," she said, making quotes in the air.

Daniel pulled out of the parking lot and into the busy street that would take them across town to the highway. Anna tightened her ponytail and rolled up her window.

"Can you grab my smokes from the glove box please?"

Without looking at him, she fetched the cigarettes and tossed them toward him. They sailed right past him and out the open window. Daniel sat staring at her for a moment before she finally turned and looked at him wide-eyed. A mischievous mouth completed the picture. *Oops!* it said, but did not betray even the slightest amount of guilt.

Her smile finally broke, then she reached in and grabbed another pack from the glove box and did the same thing. He snagged them out of the air this time, giving her a fierce look. "Bitch, you keep tossing my smokes out the window, I'll push you out the doe."

Anna wrinkled her nose and punched him hard in the ribs. He shouted out in pain, laughing as he tried to recover the wheel, having almost lost control of it. "You so violent, tiny gangsta!" he said. He opened the fresh pack and threw the plastic at her, then pulled out a cigarette. Anna sat staring out the side window, hand on her chin, and ignored it. It finally blew out the opposite window.

The sun was on its way down, casting a funeral of shadows on the road, and a dazzling array of blue and purple spots on the windshield. Daniel cupped his hand over the cigarette and touched the car lighter to it. "Mmm, don't you love the smell of a fresh lit cigarette?"

"God, are you kidding?" she said, screwing up her face again. "It's disgusting Daniel!"

"Well just those first few seconds when a cigarette is lit in a car. I love that smell. You don't think it smells good?" He tapped the lighter on the ashtray before pushing it back into its socket. "You gotta admit," he looked back at her. And with no sign or warning, she disappeared.

"Oh my God!" he shouted. Daniel slammed on his brakes and swerved onto the shoulder of the narrow road. The mini-van behind him slammed into his back bumper. "Holy shit! Anna!" Daniel screamed. The Jeep lurched forward as he lost the clutch, and died.

Quickly, he unbuckled his seatbelt and twisted wildly, in search of the woman who had been sitting in his passenger seat just seconds before. She was gone. Daniel was immediately trembling and white with fear. "Anna! Anna!"

Finally, Daniel popped his door open and stepped out onto the street. Just ahead of him, another car slammed into a speed limit sign and spun out, coming to rest in the grass, smoking and leaking radiator fluid. His eyes were wide with fear, and his heart was slamming in his chest. There was no driver in the other car.

Daniel stood on the street by the Jeep, hands in his hair, shaking his head, staring dumbly at the chaos around him. "What in the hell. What in the hell is going on?" he kept saying. But no one would answer. No one was there to answer. And his girlfriend was nowhere to be found.

After the police officer had taken Daniel's statement, he had returned to the cruiser to run his license. Daniel waited patiently beside the Jeep, still trembling and perplexed. After several long minutes, he had finally looked back to the cruiser to discover the officer was no longer there either.

Daniel approached the cruiser carefully, and looked in the windows. There was no one there. The radio handset lay in the driver's seat next to Daniel's driver license. Daniel's stomach sank even further. He feared he was about to hyperventilate. Having no other immediately visible option, he pulled the door of the squad car open and retrieved his license, then returned to his Jeep, hurriedly pulling away from the scene.

His hands trembled badly as he drove home, and he chain-smoked all the way.

Daniel sat staring dejectedly at the television, hoping for some kind of explanation. The news crews, and everyone to whom they spoke, were just as lost as he was though.

This inexplicable phenomenon has baffled scientists and clergymen alike. No one can explain away the sudden disappearances.

The news reporter looked scared and unsure of herself as she tried to maintain composure in front of the camera.

We have talked to several people who have been affected by this – well, incredible occurrence. We spoke to Nick Riggola earlier, a 757 pilot. He said, "About forty minutes outside of Dallas, my copilot just vanished, clothing and all. I damn near crashed the plane trying to land."

Another man said his two children and wife vanished directly before his eyes in a shopping center. He said, "I was tying little Steve's shoe and he just disappeared. I turned and my wife and daughter were gone as well. Even the shoe was gone."

Daniel shook his head again. This was beginning to look like something out of one of his science fiction books. His phone buzzed again. He cleared the page and dropped it on the messy coffee table among overflowing ashtrays and computer components. His entire living room was overwhelmed with computer equipment, laptops grinding away, circuit boards collecting dust and monitors running cheap screen savers. It was a typical hacker's pad, complete with empty pizza boxes and half-empty soda bottles – cigarette butts floating in the flat leftover syrup within.

His phone rang, startling him. It was his ex-girlfriend, Priscilla.

"You seeing this shit?" she said.

Daniel could barely answer. "Yeah, I'm seeing it."

"Where are you?" Priscilla asked. Her voice shook with fear.

"I'm at home. I just got back."

"Want me to come over?" she said.

"No. Don't leave your house, Pris. It's effing mad out there."

"I know. I'm scared, Daniel! I don't want to be alone. Can I come hang out with y'all?"

Daniel breathed in sharply. He considered very briefly letting her know Anna was gone, but decided he wasn't ready to get into it. "I don't think it's safe, Pris."

"Yeah, well, okay."

Daniel was beginning to feel sick at his stomach again. "This is like some bad novel."

"You know what it looks like to me?" Priscilla said. "It's like the rapture."

"Uh huh. I don't much buy into that whole rapture bit."

"Why not, Daniel?" she said. After a long pause, she said, "You know I read that rapture series by those two guys, and it was much like this."

People have been disappearing since early this morning. A map of the United States appeared on the screen, with red spots over the affected areas. There were red spots in almost every state, and very heavy in a lot of them. *The red spots on the map indicate the areas affected based on phone calls to police and news stations.*

"It just sounds too hokey to me, that's all," he said. Daniel leaned back and sunk down into the couch again. "I can't see a bunch of people just 'blinking out of existence'. And that's what the whole rapture thing is about. A whole series of people just disappearing."

"Look at the telly, dumbo! That's what happened!" Priscilla said. It sounded a lot more like sarcasm than it did joking.

Daniel sat in silence again for a few long moments. Every time his mind went back to Anna, his stomach would sink again. He tried to push it out of his head. He was afraid the fear was very close to consuming him. And he did not know how he would handle that. But it was pretty evident that it was imminent.

"Isn't the rapture supposed to happen in one fell swoop? Because this has been happening sporadically. Throughout the day." Somehow, Daniel thought that if he gave her a logical explanation, it would make his point true. Subconsciously, maybe he even believed that he could make it all disappear in a puff of logic.

"I don't know," Priscilla said after another long silence. Her voice was almost inaudible now. "I'm scared to death though, Daniel."

"Yeah, me too."

The news reporter continued, *Our rough estimate is somewhere close to fifty thousand at present, and seems to be climbing by the moment.* The reporter was trembling visibly. The camera panned around to capture the damage, and two people on the side of the screen vanished. *Oh my God! Two people just disappeared right over there…*

"Holy shit! Did you see that?" he cried. Every time he thought he was beginning to get used to the idea that people had just vanished, he found himself surprised again, and that familiar ball of dread would reappear in his stomach.

Priscilla just kept saying, "Oh my God," quietly.

Rapture or not, if Daniel could not explain it, he did not believe it. Admittedly, it did sound like a rapturous event, and he was forced by reason to consider it now. Was this what it was all about? Surely, there would be more than fifty thousand people gone. Whatever it was, it was happening right now, and apparently all over the world. He had always been a 'see-it-to-believe-it' guy, but now he thought he'd have to reconsider. He had seen it. But he still didn't believe it.

Daniel's eyes returned to the television, which was replaying the disappearance in slow motion. The effect was like a cheap movie. The people were there in one frame, and gone completely in the next. There was no transparence or fading, they were just very simply gone. Over and over it was played, as a commentator pointed out things like passing leaves in the breeze, and people in the vicinity of those who had disappeared. The leaves were blowing toward the people, and then went right through the spot where they had been, with no visible skip or flaw. The couple behind those who disappeared visibly flinched when it happened.

"Fifty thousand people?" Daniel said, shaking his head. "Son of a bitch. This is bad, Pris."

"This is bad, Daniel." Then his phone went dead.

"Priscilla?" He pulled the phone away from his face, fresh fear filling his veins again. "What the hell?" His phone had no signal. Had Priscilla disappeared too? Now he could not be sure.

Two days later, Daniel was beginning to feel human again. He had not learned to manage the grief to a tolerable level, but its visitation had become less frequent. Had his experience been unique, he would surely have thought he was crazy, but the disappearances had been worldwide. They had labeled those who disappeared as 'ghosters'. Investigations were ongoing, but unproductive. For one, nobody knew where to start. Daniel often found himself glued to the television watching the news in hopes of some explanation, one that never came. An emptiness had filled his chest, as he had no opportunity for closure of any kind with his missing girlfriend.

His only consolation was that only about two hundred thousand people worldwide had disappeared, and most of the clergy who had taken interviews on television had dismissed the plausibility of a rapture, saying there would have been millions gone. Furthermore, they had all seemed to say, it would have all happened at once. The disappearances all happened on the same day, but at different periods throughout the day – and inconsistent with any explanation rendered by time zone separations. Some had gone early in the morning, while others went late on into the night. But by midnight that night, the disappearances ceased, just as mysteriously as they had begun.

Mysterious they were, though, and every instance seemed set apart from the rest by its own distinctive properties. Many people had claimed to lose someone to the evanescence as a means of swindling money. Insurance companies investigating claims had no leads or proof whether or not someone had disappeared, or if they had just taken a vacation. There were no policy clauses for rapturous events. There would be though.

A man in Dayton, Ohio had filed a missing person's report in addition to his insurance claim. He had been boating with his wife when she had suddenly disappeared from the boat. His insurance company had suspended all payouts pending resolution to the global phenomenon, but they had conducted their investigations nonetheless. This man's case had not taken long to track, as they found record of a credit card transaction where he had purchased a single one-way plane ticket to Miami, Florida, and another transaction for hotel accommodations. His wife was down living the good life until he collected the cool four-hundred-thousand-dollar settlement, whereupon he would move down there with her and they would drink martinis on the beach for the rest of their lives. He was disappointed to find they did not serve martinis in prison.

There were many who tried to pull off such scandals, trying to cash in on huge fortunes, but with little success. Most people were just so stupid about the way they arranged their claims that most were dismissed within a few hours. One man in Los Angeles had locked his entire family in the cellar in the backyard, and claimed they had disappeared. When the insurance adjustor had come to conduct the interview and investigation, he heard muffled screaming coming from the back yard. It turned out a rat in the cellar had scared the children into screaming, and muffed the man's plans for sudden wealth.

Then there were those legitimate claims, from people who had really been affected by the disappearances, and most of those cases involved people just looking for answers. Most of them were genuinely concerned for the welfare of their loved ones, and had no interest in the money. Women calling in saying they had lost their husbands, and how could they survive now, taking care of three kids as a stay-at-home mom? Elderly people who had lost their entire family to disappearance, who were too old to take care of themselves, stepchildren who had lost both parents, and classrooms full of kids who'd lost their teachers. First instinct for some was to call 911. The phones were ringing steadily, the calls and reports flooding every official desk in the nation as people tried to deal with the mass disappearance. In some way, it affected nearly everyone.

Police officers were finding abandoned homes and cars, people wandering the streets absent of thought and cognition – as if they had lost their very minds with the disappearances. Thus, there was looting of stores for food. And on the tail of the tragedy, there was the looting of stores for televisions and electronics and computers and appliances.

Authorities had questioned several people arrested for looting pawnshops. Most of them said it just seemed like the thing to do – the perfect time to do it. The disappearances had not even directly affected them. They had lost no one. They just felt it was high time to pick cotton from the neighbors' patch.

Daniel was sick to death of all of it. If the world ever did return to some sort of normalcy, he would be full of contempt for those in it; his faith in humanity had plummeted. He felt this was something people somehow would not get over, though. At least he knew he certainly would not. He found himself worrying day-in, day-out, about disappearing himself. It seemed the constant looming threat that at any time, without warning, more people would disappear. And who knew, maybe it wouldn't stop until everyone was gone. And who knew, maybe he'd be in the next batch.

Daniel had become depressed and lazy. His Jeep had sat in his driveway ever since Anna's disappearance, and he had taken a leave of absence from work. They made do without him. Not that he was not important – in fact, he was vital – but he was able to work from home on a VPN, and his presence at the office was only required to assist colleagues, not customers.

He wanted badly to get back in touch with Priscilla. She understood him better than anyone else alive, and he knew she would be able to offer him the consolation no one else could right now. But ever since her line had dropped out, she had been unreachable. There were certain numbers that still did not work when he dialed them. Apparently, the catastrophe had brought down a series of cellular networks. Daniel could not begin to understand the connection.

He and Priscilla had started dating about five years back, and were the hot topic at the time. One was not seen without the other, and they were treated like deities. Daniel had never really understood it, but a rise in popularity had been evident at the time of their courtship. They were like the prom king and queen. Everyone loved them together.

They had mutually called it quits when she learned she was going to have to move to New York. They had been together for about three years when it happened, thus in spite of their mutual resolution, they were both badly burned by the breakup. Now, with Anna in the picture, Priscilla had gladly stepped back and allowed him his space. She had been happy to call him a friend if ever he needed one. He had not seen her in several months though, and when he finally picked up the phone to call her, he got a 'disconnected' message.

He stood in the doorway of his office, staring at the wreckage his life had become. The normal chaos littered his office, papers and trash piled high on his desk. Even his physical appearance had suffered. Daniel had not shaven in two weeks, and his showers had been rare. He was the portrait of laziness and depression.

I'll go back Monday. Two weeks was pushing the limits, he thought. Daniel was the only one at his company who had lost a loved one to the worldwide phenomenon, but he was still capable of doing his job. Occasionally showing up was not a bad idea either. He would just have to get used to living again. Somehow, he would have to overcome, to persevere, and to rise above. And ultimately, that meant going back to work. He was not excited about going back to work.

The rain was beating heavily down on the hood of a black Mustang, creating a symphony of sound in the interior that mixed with the weather warnings constantly blaring from the radio. *It's going to be a rainy day. Flash flood warning. Stay inside if you can!* The inside of the car was cold as the outside. The heater had gone out at the end of last winter, and there had been no reason to have it repaired. Not until now.

Amalie London was behind the wheel, and was driving a lot faster than the rest of the traffic on the road. Her need to find Daniel Brandt was exceeded only by her devotion to get to him. She had not even met him, and was seeking him out like a treasure.

Traffic was sparse on the narrow two-lane road, and only half of those driving had intelligence enough to turn on their headlights. Thus driving was not only rough, but also dangerous. She ran her fingers back through her wet hair, fighting to keep it out of her eyes.

The dark clouds hung maddeningly close to the earth and gave the impression that there was no absolute separation between the two. They were dark, menacing clouds – clouds that looked serious. An occasional flash would light up behind them as if they were pulsing with anger. Heat lightning she thought, and smirked at the phrase.

Amalie tapped her gas gauge, hoping it was just stuck – that she really wasn't almost out of gas. But she was. It was right on the E, and there were no gas stations in sight.

The rain was coming down like the wrath of an angry god now, and it finally defeated her. Heavy rain she could handle, but this stuff was coming down by the dump truck full, and she had to pull over. The windows were fogged up so badly that she couldn't see the other side of the glass, so she pulled the car over and parked in the gravel. Maddened, she opened the door and stepped out into the freezing rain. In less than an instant, she was soaked as though she had been thrown from a frigate at deep sea. But God, did it feel good. Amalie could see the steam rising from her hood and she threw her head back and let the rain pound on her face like steel pellets.

She could hear the stereo through the closed door, vibrating the window with every beat. The rain appeared as though it would never ease up, much less go away. She noticed a bridge about a quarter of a mile up the road. It was barely visible, but almost certainly there. She decided she would try and go for it. If she could make the bridge, she could wait the storm out. She got in the car and took off her drenched white T-shirt to wipe some of the fog off the windshield. It did that, but left streaks of water that dripped onto her dashboard in small shimmering puddles. She put a cap on her head backwards and shifted into first gear, wondering where that cap had been a few moments before.

It seemed as though the second she shut her door, the rain started coming down even harder, making the short trip to the bridge more perilous. The consistent roar of rain on the hood and the roof of the car ceased immediately and was replaced by a more comforting, lighter roar of rain being pounded onto the bridge above. She pulled the parking brake and looked at herself in the mirror. Then the car died. She had made it under the bridge, but to what end? Now out of gas, she would be hitching a ride if she wanted to get anywhere.

Amalie climbed back out of the car and wrung her shirt out. Her black miniskirt was riding up her thighs, and her sandals were killing her feet. Her near-black hair was a mess of tangled locks, and now her car was out of commission. "Ahhhhrrr!" she growled, grabbing handfuls of her hair. "Can anything else go wrong?" She pulled her shirt on and walked around the right side of the car to sit on the concrete and wait for a car to pass. Can it get any worse?

A pickup came screaming under the bridge, but did not stop.

This happened several times, and she began to reckon she would have to sit here in the cold wind and rain, waiting for a police car or a taxi. She shivered as she sat waiting, and it seemed like forever had passed when she finally heard the sounds of sirens. They were loud and getting closer. She stood up and ran to the edge of the bridge, and saw the lights in the distance.

An ambulance blew by, spraying her with mist from the concrete, and she shook her head. She kept looking at her cell phone, hoping for bars, but alas – had no service. No way to call anyone.

After an hour of waiting, a beat-up old Dodge came rumbling under the bridge and pulled to a stop beside her. "Need some help, young lady?"

$$* \qquad * \qquad *$$

Daniel stood on the sidewalk outside his house, looking at the street. His hands were in his pockets – the only place it seemed they would not tremble. Tears fought their way to the surface again. He sat down on the curb and let them drip on the dirt in the gutter where they mingled with the sparse rain droplets. The storm was moving in fast.

If he could have just gotten to say goodbye, he felt he would be able to handle it a little better. Anna would still have been stripped from him all the same, but at least he would have had some closure. But alas, he was forced to reckon with reality, which made absolutely no sense. He had at one time put faith in what he thought of as reality – a separation of everyday life from science fiction, but now they seemed intertwined, a seamless marriage of real and unreal.

With a sigh, he rose to go inside. There was nothing new for him to think of. Nothing worth saying to himself. He had said it all and thought it all. She was gone, and he was lost. He had no idea where to begin. If he were to look for her, where would he look? All his Internet news searches about the disappearances had been fruitless. Everyone else was just as baffled and perplexed as he was. Besides, if he were to ask about her who would he ask? Perhaps he would finally break down and put in a call to Anna's father. Daniel had only ever called him once, and dreaded the thought of having to go through that stress again. Would Aaron blame him? Would he even answer? It was all Daniel had.

*　　　*　　　*

Amalie stepped out of the pickup and thanked the man for his assistance. Now armed with a plastic gas tank and two gallons of fuel, she could get back on her way. The old man nodded and wished her well, then she slammed the rusted door and he pulled slowly away.

She found she was trembling slightly as she poured the gasoline into her tank. The rain had finally subsided a little. As she pulled away from the bridge, she felt empowered. Amalie was back on her way to finding Daniel Brandt. It had taken her two years to locate him, which was the hard part. Now the finding him within that location was supposed to be the easy part. Yet somehow, everything that could stand in her way seemed to be growing legs.

The growling Mustang would surely eat up the two gallons of gas before she was able to pull into his driveway – but at least it might get her to a gas station. The thought of having to stop even just one more time on her way to finally reaching him was more than just a little annoying. In fact, to Amalie, who had spent the last two years almost incessantly trolling databases and weblogs in search of a ghost, it was downright maddening. To be so close to the prize, all the little things that started popping up and slowing her down seemed so trivial. Yet they were necessary steps on her way to finally meeting him.

And a ghost he was. Daniel Brandt was a hard man to find. And these days, with the power of the internet, there was almost nothing stopping someone from finding anyone or anything he wanted to find. But someone well versed in the art of incognito – someone who truly did not want to be found… Well, Daniel Brandt had taken all of her resources. But now she believed she had him. Up ahead, a 7 Eleven sign crept into view, easily distinguishing itself from the dark gray sky behind. She would make her final stop there for gas, then Amalie London would finally shake hands with destiny.

∗   ∗   ∗

As Daniel hung up the phone, he sat back against the wall in the small kitchen, his jaw slack. His conversation with Aaron Nicholas had been quick and complex, and there had been a lot of silences. Daniel had been quick to ask if Aaron knew of his daughter's disappearance.

"Yeah, I figured as much. Anita is gone too," Aaron had said. Anna spent most of her nights at Daniel's house, thus Aaron seldom saw her these days.

This had been as much a shock to Daniel as Anna's disappearance. Anita, Aaron's wife – and Anna's mother – had disappeared at almost the exact same moment as Anna, they had discovered. Initially, Daniel had thought that only entire families had disappeared, not just certain members of those families. But that thought had crashed upon Aaron's answering the phone. The only one left in the Nicholas family was Aaron.

Daniel had called in hopes of getting some answers, but had instead hung up with more questions. Aaron, surprisingly, had not blamed Daniel, and furthermore had been very civil on the phone. Perhaps they would find some way to bond over the disappearances. Now there was a thought that almost made Daniel smirk. He no longer had any reason to prove himself to Aaron. With Anna gone, they had precisely no common ground.

Daniel shoved his hand in his jeans pocket to retrieve his cigarettes, but found an empty package. "Shit," he said aloud. "Off to the nevele neves." He swiped his keys from the countertop and was out the front door.

CHAPTER TWO
Recruitment

As Daniel hopped out of the Jeep he heard a loud squealing of tires and turned in time to see a black Mustang pulling dangerously fast into the parking lot of the 7 Eleven. The GT squealed once again as the driver slammed the brakes on and slid the car into the spot just adjacent to Daniel's. "Damn, easy on the brakes, dude."

But it was not a dude who stepped out of the car. It was a woman, and she was soaked like she had been thrown in the sea. Daniel kept walking, trying not to stare, but could not help notice the girl's skimpy miniskirt, and her damp white t-shirt. Aside from her soaked condition and stringy hair, she seemed almost pretty.

"Excuse me!" she cried as Daniel reached the door.

Daniel turned to face her, raising his eyebrows.

"You're Dan Brandt, right?"

"The very one." He was more shocked than his answer had let on. *How the hell does she know my name?*

"Holy shit I just got so lucky," the woman said under her breath. Daniel had caught every word of it though. Maybe if she had not been so *out of breath,* she could have hidden it better. "Thought so. Can I talk to you for a moment?" She was almost smirking at him.

"Sure, but hang back a second – I'm outta smokes," he said, pulling the door open.

"That's okay, I don't smoke."

"Yeah, but I do," he said, raising a finger. "And I don't have any. So if you can wait, I'll only be a minute." He finally stepped into the overly cool store and approached the counter. The woman waltzed right in behind him and leaned back against the counter as Daniel addressed the clerk.

"Box of Ranch Hand Deluxe, please," he said, and looked at the woman again. She was staring at him.

"How long have you smoked?"

"Rough Cut or Slicks?" the clerk interrupted.

"Rough," Daniel said, never removing his eyes from this strange, damp woman.

"Who cares? You writing a report on me?" At his close proximity, he saw at last how pretty she really was. It was not 'almost' as he had thought before. It was a running vault above and beyond just pretty. And made up and dressed, she was probably a knock-out. Daniel turned to look away before he got too attracted.

"Nah. Just curious. You don't have to answer, you know." She smiled.

"Since I was seventeen," he said, and placed a five on the counter.

"So that's what – about ten years? Bet I can get you to quit." It got his attention, and he turned to face her.

"Who are you?" He wanted to ask her how the hell she knew all this about him. But he also did not want to bely his cool posture. He didn't like people to get the best of him.

"Amalie." She gazed at him through huge brown eyes. Daniel found the weight of her gaze almost unsettling – she seemed powerful.

"Amalie what?"

"London."

"I see. And what was it you wanted with me then?" He took his change and pushed the door open.

"I need to speak to you about something. Can we talk somewhere?" she said, tilting her head.

"What's wrong with here, Amalie?" Daniel lit a cigarette and felt the relief pump through his body.

"Well, it's kind of public, don't you think?" she raised her eyebrows.

Daniel shook his head and his hands, backtracking on his thought process. "Wait, wait, wait. Who are you?"

"Let's just go somewhere private," she said, raising her hands. She appeared to be losing patience quickly.

"Private? Are you trying to sell me something?"

She shook her head.

After a thoughtful pause, he said, "Well, I guess you can follow me back to my house. It's private there."

"Good. That would be fine."

Daniel took a drag of his cigarette and explored her one more time.

"Look, you've made your point, okay? I don't always dress like this."

"I didn't say anything," he said. Now he was smirking at her. "I quite like your style, Amalie."

Daniel climbed in his Jeep and pulled the door closed. "You coming?" Amalie shook her head, then turned and got back into the Mustang. *What the hell is her deal?*

As he pulled into his driveway, he let the name roll over his tongue a few times. *Amalie London. Amalie London.* He shut off the engine and sat staring at his gauges. *Amalie London.* Then he got out and flicked his cigarette into the street as he let himself in the house. He stood in the doorway as Amalie made her way up the walk.

"So this is your place?"

Daniel looked at his keys, then frowned. "Oh shit, I've gone into the wrong house!" Amalie didn't smile. "Yes, it's my house." She stared at him stoically.

They walked into the living room, and Daniel turned on the television, then offered her a seat. On the television, a reporter was covering the latest developments in the disappearances. There were no developments. All they knew was that it had in some way affected every religion, creed, color, class, and race. *There were no boundaries to how far it reached. People from every side of the globe, from every country, from every race have lost loved ones. People here in Dallas are starting to file for death certificates, as I'm sure they are in most cities.*

Daniel shook his head. As the dread began to creep back into his stomach, he quickly turned off the TV. He found it easier to deal with if he avoided thinking about it. Seeing it on the news did not help either. There was no consolation. No answers. No evidence. No trace. In retrospect, Daniel realized he would have at least liked Anna's clothing to be left in his passenger seat. Then he would know he was not just crazy. In spite of the fact that the entire world was reeling from the same traumatic incident, he still felt alone. He still felt like it should not have happened to Anna.

He twisted around to look at Amalie. "What do you make of all this?"

"Well, that's kind of what I wanted to talk to you about."

Daniel frowned again, then pointed at the television. "What, this?"

"Yep. Your girlfriend – Anna, right? Annabelle Nicholas? – she ghosted. Right?"

Daniel reeled, and he felt his chest tighten up. "Yeah, you know her?"

"No, I don't. I'm just…" Amalie adjusted uneasily on the couch. "Look. I know why they disappeared."

Daniel surveyed her from head to toe in an obvious gesture of disbelief before speaking. "Is this some sort of joke?"

"Do you know what happened to her?" she retorted quickly. Daniel shook his head. "Then I could assume that you don't know how to bring her back, right?" Daniel once again shook his head. "That's what I'm here for." She stared hard at Daniel, who didn't know whether he wanted to slap her or kiss her.

After a moment, Daniel got up and went into the kitchen to get a Zack's. Zack's was hands-down the best cream soda available. And if he had a can in his hand, maybe Amalie would not notice his trembling. "You want something to drink?" Amalie declined.

She folded her hands across her lap. Daniel watched from the kitchen doorway as Amalie looked about the room, taking note of his messy lifestyle. Brushing away ashes and magazines, Amalie uncovered a thick book by Stephen King on the stained wooden coffee table. She quickly lost interest though, and picked up a single cigarette butt off the cover, and dropped it in the large, overfilled ashtray.

Daniel popped open the Zack's, which shook Amalie back to attention, then he lit a cigarette. He sat on the couch opposite her and slouched back as far as one could slouch without lying down, his arm up on the back. Amalie was the exact polar opposite, sitting with perfect posture on the edge of the love seat, her knees together.

"You aren't wet are you?" he asked, pointing at her. She stood up so fast it looked like she had sat on a hot stove, and spun round to look at the love seat. A heart-shaped wet spot contrasted sharply with the rest of the off-white sofa. Amalie looked back up at Daniel, covering her mouth.

"I'm so sorry. I didn't even think about that."

"No. I don't care about the couch. Look at it." She did. There were a few clean spots on it, but mostly it was dirty and covered with cigarette burns. "Just wondering if you're cold."

"Oh. Yes. A little."

"Let me get you a towel." Daniel stood and dropped his cigarette in the ashtray as he started for the hall. When he reappeared through the doorway, he tossed the towel at Amalie. She sat back down and spread it over her legs.

"So what great revelation do you have for me, Amalie London?" he asked, pulling from his cigarette again.

"Well, like I said, I want to help you get your best girl back. I think I can help you. But I'm going to need your help too."

"Okay, hang on… So you know what happened?"

"Yes," Amalie said nodding.

He gulped from the soft drink, then ran his tongue over his teeth. "You can fix it? So where are all these people?"

"Slow down, Daniel!" she held her hands up to stop his words. "Well… I think I have a solution. But I'll need your help with some technical parts. And since you're good with computers…"

Daniel sighed and sat back, rubbing his face. "Now how'd you know that?"

"You are good with computers, right?" Amalie looked about the room at the ghostly remains of hundreds of computer components to illustrate her point.

"Yeah, I'm decent.   But how does that have anything to do with the situation at hand?"

"Well, I need your computer skills," she said.

"Who the hell are you?" She did not answer. She just breathed in deeply. "What the hell made you choose me?" He took a swig of his Zack's and swished it briefly before swallowing.

"I need someone who can code in Harmony." Harmony was the newest, state-of-the-art application language, developed by Bohr Enterprises about a year ago.   It was eating up everything else on the programming market. There was none better.

Daniel nodded. He had been writing in Harmony since before it came out, having been on the beta team for it, and knew it well. "So you think my being able to code can bring these people back? Namely Anna?"

She shrugged. "Well, indirectly, of course. That's what I wanted to talk to you about, Daniel."

"What makes you think you can fix it? Do you *know* where those two hundred thousand people went? And what about her mom?" Daniel said. "You know, her mom is gone too."

"Well, if my little fix works out, they'll all be back."

"Your little fix?" he said, looking sternly at her. He sighed and shook his head. "I can't believe I'm listening to this."

"Daniel, it isn't that strange to think it could happen, is it? I mean, they disappeared, so wouldn't it stand to reason they could be brought back?" Amalie said.

He shook his head again. "Look, you still haven't answered my question. Do you know what happened to them?" He dragged long from his cigarette.

"Yes." She looked at him as if her answer would somehow cover everything.

"And you think you can bring them back."

Amalie raised her eyebrows. "Is that so far-fetched?"

He shrugged nonchalantly. "No, I guess not, if you really do know what happened. I just don't understand what I have to do with any of this."

Amalie remained perfectly calm while she said, "I'll tell you what you have to do with it. You caused it, Daniel."

Daniel frowned, then laughed. "The ghostings? You think I caused the ghostings?" He stood up, shaking his head, and put the cigarette in his mouth, then fumbled with the soda can. He might have been fidgeting a little. "How the hell could I *possibly* have anything to do with it?"

"Can it, Daniel. I know you. I know who you are. I know all about you."

Daniel stared in disbelief at her, his jaw slack. *This is incredible! Who the hell does she think she is?* He could not find words to put to his feelings, nor did he know what he would say if he could. Amalie stared right back at him, her good-natured smile now just a rumor on her stolid face. He found himself shaking his head, at a total loss for words. He drained the rest of the Zack's, then dropped the can on the pile on the coffee table, making his way around to the opposite side of the table. He wanted a better vantage point. He wanted to seem in charge somehow.

"You know me. What is it you think you know about me, Amalie?"

"You've got some gall, Daniel. You're the one that hacked into the Royal systems."

Daniel's face went white, and his eyes widened. He felt like his heart might have stopped beating, too. If he wasn't numb from the neck down, he might have known if it had. After a long moment of silence, he finally said, "How in the world do you know that?"

"I told you, I know a lot of things. To me, you're nothing but a scrub hacker. An amateur. And aside from my lack of programming abilities, I have no need for you whatever. But seeing as how your hands are all over this, you shall share in the responsibility. And you shall help me bring them back. When this is all over, I'll let you walk away, and I'll forget it ever happened. But no sooner." Amalie still sat calmly on the love seat, looking at him with her hard brown eyes.

"I *shall*, huh?" he said, smirking at her. Amalie took a deep breath in, clearly controlling her patience. But she remained silent. Did this woman work for Royal? Not likely. Royal employees were untouchable. And they did not dress like this woman – wearing a cheap miniskirt and a plain white shirt. Royal employees had money. Daniel crushed his cigarette out, then sat back down on the couch, resigning his implied position of power. It had not quite gotten him what he wanted, and he did not want her to see him betray something with his face. Suddenly blanching was not a good component in his defense.

"So do you have any questions Daniel? Are you going to try to fight me on this?"

"What can I say?" Daniel said, raising his hands.

Amalie smirked. "There's nothing you can say to get out of it. I caught you, Daniel Brandt. And you either pay me by doing this for me, or you do time."

"What do I have to do for you?"

"We'll discuss that later. I just want to make sure you're with me. That we have an understanding. If you run – if you don't help me, I'll-"

"Yeah, whatever Amalie," Daniel said quickly, shaking his head. "I'll help you. But it's not because I'm afraid of your lame ass threats."

Amalie finally stood, hands on hips. "Lame ass threats? You think this is a game, Daniel? I know how you like to live your life! Everything is a game to you! You don't take anything seriously!" She paused and recomposed herself, taking a deep breath and standing up straight. It was a posture askew from the leaning over and shaking her finger at him that she had taken before. She swallowed and carried on. "But this is serious. This is two hundred thousand people we're talking about. And if you wouldn't have been fucking around inside my computer, it wouldn't have happened!"

"I don't know what you're talking about," Daniel said, trying to backtrack.

"I know it was you, Daniel! I caught you!"

Daniel closed his eyes and raised his hands in defense – suddenly feeling very guilty. "Look, that's not what I meant. I'm not saying it wasn't me. I'm just saying I don't know how my hacking into Royal's network could have caused the ghostings."

Amalie nodded, crossing her arms. "That's not for you to know. Not yet."

"Hah. Okay, so when will you tell me, Mystery Woman?"

"Once I know you're on board. Once I know you aren't going to go turncoat on me. I need to know that we have an understanding here. I need to know that you know that *I know* it was you. And I'm the only chance you have to salvage your freedom." She was pointing at him again, and he realized he had been staring at the jiggle of her breasts beneath her shirt as she shook her finger. It was second-nature for him, and he scarcely realized he was doing it.

Daniel nodded somberly, pursing his lips. "Okay. I'm in."

"We have an agreement?" Daniel tried to speak, but she stopped him, raising her hand. "Because I'll be telling you some things that are top-secret. And I'm not talking government cover-up shit. This is real. And it's dangerous."

"Yes, Amalie. We have an agreement. You're wanting me to keep quiet. I will," he said with an air of exhaustion.

Amalie seemed to lighten a bit. She sighed and relaxed her tensed shoulders. "Good. I won't threaten you, because you don't want to hear it. But just know that I can make you disappear if you go blabbing about this."

Daniel stared at her for a moment, then said, "Disappear, huh?" She nodded. "All right. You've got my interest." He smiled. "So you're saying you work for Royal."

She stood up straight and frowned, as if that should have been obvious. "How else would I know it was you?"

Daniel stood up, nodding, his lips pursed again. "Fair enough." He pulled up on his belt loops and stepped forward to shake Amalie's hand. "Okay. We have a deal."

"Very well. Is there a bar around here? I need a stiff drink."

"There is," he nodded. "The Sour Apple. Just off Bermuda Blvd and the Tollway." It had been a favorite of his for several years now. It had an old medieval feel to it, dark and torchlit, cool and full of soul.

"Good. Be there at nine?" She looked at her watch, then looked at him.

Daniel nodded again. After another long moment of staring at Amalie, he said, "Nine it is."

∗   ∗   ∗

There was the usual crowd of people about the pub that evening. Daniel pulled his collar up high and slipped onto a stool at the bar. He looked around the smoke-filled room again, wondering when Amalie would show.

Stevie Ray Vaughan played on the jukebox, singing about his sweet little baby. People laughed and joked, all seemingly having forgotten about the ghosters. It was like it had never happened. The world was back to its apathetic state.

"Hey Skip," Daniel said as the bartender approached.

Skip slid an icy bottle of Pirate Flag across the bar to him. "How goes it, Dan?"

"Well, I suppose. Yourself?"

Skip stood with his hands on the edge of the bar, occasionally glancing at the World Series game on the television. "Hey, forget about it."

Daniel chuckled as he slipped away from the bar. Scanning the smoky room, he thought he saw Amalie in the dark corner. Why had she not come to get him though? Daniel walked casually over to her and looked more closely. It was she, all right. She was soaking wet with fresh rain now, and she still had not changed clothes. Not that Daniel had a problem with the skimpy t-shirt and miniskirt, but he thought she must be miserable soaking wet like that. She sat hunched over the small, round table with her hands hidden beneath it. Her table was bare except for a tall glass of water, which stood on a square white napkin.

Her t-shirt was as wet as her hair, and he felt confident that if she were to sit up straight, he would get a pretty good idea what team she played for. His buddies and he assigned women they saw to different baseball teams, based on the quality of the woman's breasts. If she had a perfect rack, she probably played for the Yankees, for instance. "Amalie," he said nodding. She smiled back at him. "You need my jacket? You look a little shivery."

"You are a god, sir. Thank you kindly."

"You play the part, don't you?" he said.

"What do you mean?"

"A god? You fit in well here in the medieval." Amalie showed him a well-practiced fake smile.

Daniel swung his coat around her back and pulled it together as she sat up straight and looked him in the eyes almost mischievously. Daniel's eyes locked on hers in an effort to avoid looking down at her chest when she sat up. Typically he didn't mind being caught looking, but this was different – as if she had been expecting him to gawk. He didn't want to give her the satisfaction. He had put her on the Orioles for now.

"Go ahead, sit down." She pushed the chair out with her slender leg, and Daniel noticed it was chilled. He pulled the chair around and took a seat at her right.

"Aren't you freezing? I can't imagine wearing a miniskirt in October."

"I'd like not to imagine you ever wearing a miniskirt, Daniel."

Daniel smiled. "Well why don't you go get some fresh clothes from home? We can talk later."

"Well, let's have some cocoa first." She moved her hand to his knee and patted it.

Daniel lowered an exhausted gaze on her. "Cocoa? Do I look like the type who drinks fucking cocoa?"

She shrugged. "Well I didn't say you had to drink it. You can get me some though."

"You want some cute little baby marshmallows in it too?"

"F off. Just get me the cocoa."

"Fair enough." He stood up from the table and turned to make his way to the bar, but slammed head-on into a waitress. A fresh bottle of beer popped as it hit the floor alongside her hard plastic tray. She fell back with the momentum and landed square on her rump in embarrassment and beer. Daniel apologized as he squatted level to help her to her feet.

"I'm so sorry. I should have paid more attention. It's my fault." Most of the bar had their attention on the couple now, and made no effort to hide their interest in the laughable spill of the poor waitress. Some of them clapped, to which he shouted aloud, "Oh, go on!

Mind your damn business!" Some turned away in direct compliance of his command, others ignored, but all were at least silent. Courtesy, as he noticed, was not in abundance within the walls of the Sour Apple.

He helped the waitress establish firm footing again before he let go of both her hands. She leaned in closely and whispered a thank you in his ear, her breath warm against his face. It was more a gratitude for his defense than his helping her up. He smiled and patted her back. Daniel tipped the waitress and paid for the broken beer, and offered repeatedly to help her clean it up, but she refused steadfastly, claiming her own responsibilities. She rushed back into the kitchen, where she emerged only a moment later with a mop and a broom and dustpan.

As he approached the bar, Skip looked up at Daniel. "What'll it be, friend?"

"You have hot cocoa?" Daniel said, feeling slightly foolish. After a moment, he added, "It's for the girl."

Skip nodded, a slight smirk painting his features. "Yeah, we have hot chocolate. I'll have it brought out."

Daniel thanked him and returned to the darkened table. Amalie was smiling politely as he sat down. "That was pretty noble what you did there, Daniel."

"I can't stand that shit," he whispered, leaning in closely to her. "I bet none of them fucks could even carry a tray with beers on it. Then I come along and plow into her and they *applaud*? *That* shit ain't right." He leaned back shaking his head.

"You feel quite strongly about this, I gather," she said. He did not reply, but shook his fist as if to say *damn right*. Another waitress brought the steaming chocolate and placed it neatly on the table beside Amalie's white napkin. Amalie thanked her and sipped from the heated cup and cooed quietly to Daniel.

"So who are you? Really."

"Amalie Gray London." She sat up straight and held her hand over the table as if to swear by it. As she raised her hand, the coat fell from her shoulders, and Daniel glanced down at her chest. When his eyes met hers, she again had a mischievous look about her. He smirked, feeling proud to be caught.

"See anything you like, mister?"

He nodded as he pulled a smoke from his shirt pocket. "Lady, I've never seen some I *didn't* like." She allowed herself to smile, and he lit his cigarette. *Someone just got traded to the Red Sox,* he thought.

"Are we in the smoking section?" Amalie said, looking around.

Daniel ignored that and spoke. "So you already told me your name. I wanna know who you are. You think you can bring them back. And I want to know how." He pulled from his cigarette, trying to maintain his cool.

"Well," Amalie replied, running her finger around the rim of the cup, "let's take our time, Daniel. You'll know everything soon enough. I don't want to talk about it in a bar."

"Do what?" he said, spreading his hands. He was beginning to lose his patience with the strange woman. "You said, 'Let's go somewhere we can talk!' You said you wanted to come to a bar! Speaking of which, why the hell are we in the bar? I thought you said you needed a stiff drink."

"I had one already. Your friend Skip there poured me a glass of bourbon."

"He pours a good one." Daniel sighed then shook his head. "So if not here, then where?" He looked at her again.

Amalie sighed audibly and looked about the place. "It's just so smoky."

Daniel rolled his eyes. "Get used to it. It's a pub. So can you at least tell me what you need me to do?"

"I need you to write a program. You are a programmer, right?"

Daniel laughed. "Well that's like calling a whale a fish. Yeah, I'm a programmer, but that's not all I really do."

"Ahem. You do realize a whale is *not* actually a fish, right? It's a mammal."

"All right, smart ass," Daniel said.

"But you know how, right?" The waitress returned to the table and Daniel motioned for the check. She simply patted the table and smiled at him, walking away. The cocoa was free.

"It really depends. That's ambiguous. There are so many different facets to programming, and I-"

Amalie cut him off sharply, slapping her hands on the table. "Can you write a program?" If she didn't have the slightest smile at the corners of her mouth, Daniel would have thought she was mad.

"Well, yes. We already established that, though! I've been writing in Harmony for almost two years." He sat back and took a drag from his smoke. "Damn, chill out, woman!"

"You are so dense sometimes!"

"You don't even know me!" He sat staring in amazement at Amalie as she sipped from her cocoa cup. Her eyebrows rose. "Okay," he added. "So you do know me. I just don't know how."

*　　　*　　　*

Walter Watson sat hunched over his keyboard, his chin resting in his hands, squinting hard at the computer monitor. His deduction inference program was parsing the names of the two hundred thousand souls who had mysteriously disappeared off the face of the earth on October fifteenth. His eyes straining and red, he rubbed his forehead and leaned back in his chair. The chair fell backwards, and Walter landed hard on the linoleum floor, for the second time in the last hour.

"Son of a bitch!"

Callie Simmons laughed uncontrollably. "I figured you would have learned your lesson by now, Walt!" She laughed so hard no sound was actually coming out now. Her hands wrapped hard around her stomach trying to keep the pain out as she gasped for breath.

"Yeah, yeah, yeah. Laugh it up, blondy. Why don't you try sitting in this fucking chair." Then suddenly the monitor cleared and the cursor blinked ready at the end of a line of simple text, which read, "Parse complete. Commonality attained."

"Well I'll be a retarded eggplant," Walter said as he clamored back into his chair, steadying himself against the desk.

"What? What did it find?" Her face was flush from laughing, but all humor had grabbed its coat and left the room in a rush.

"They all have something in common." He pounded a quick command into the terminal. The screen poured out a list of deductive reasoning results that closely resembled a statistics report. The names of all the 'ghosters', as they had been labeled, were indexed down the screen, with branches interconnecting them all.

"What is it?" Callie said frowning. She was now crouched behind Walter, staring at the screen over his shoulder. Her hair was pulled back tightly into a messy ponytail, and her ten-gauge brown eyes reflected the text on the monitor. Thick-rimmed glasses sat atop her head, unused. She wore them sometimes but Walter still had not learned the rules that decided when she did and did not wear them. Seemingly, vision had nothing to do with it.

Walter turned to look at her and realized she was directly over his shoulder. He flinched, pulling his head back when he realized his mouth had come within an inch of hers. Callie completely failed to notice this as her eyes were locked hard on the monitor, which now began to spark evidence of some recognition deep within the recesses of her pretty head.

"You see it?" Walter had short-cropped black hair that sprouted from his head in every direction, giving the impression that either he did not care, or he immaculately tended to his hair with the thick gel that held it in place, desiring absolute cranial chaos.

Callie nodded faintly, still staring. "I think so. But I don't understand the significance." She turned her head to look at him, and kept talking, despite the fact that her mouth was again within a couple of inches of his. It either did not dawn on her, or she simply had no reservations about the boundaries of intimacy. "It seems to make perfect blaring sense, but yet – at the same time – it doesn't make any." She turned again to face the monitor.

"That's it exactly. I see the relationship, but I'd bet fifty cents no one actually knows what the hell the significance is."

Callie frowned. "Fifty cents? Big bettor, are you?"

"We all see the dirty turtles, we just don't know why they're in the soup." He leaned back in his chair. Callie stepped delicately aside and covered her mouth

as she watched Walter fall over backward again. To
think that she could hold it though was futile. Before
she could take a breath she was laughing so hard again
that tears filled her eyes.

CHAPTER THREE
Distinction

Daniel stood up and looked around the smoky bar. The crowd was beginning to thicken as the Friday night drinkers began making their way in and seating themselves as standard weekend routine dictated. He stretched his arms above his head and looked back down at Amalie. Seated hunched over behind the round table with her hands folded in her lap, she looked fragile and vulnerable.

"So now that we have established that 'yes, I am a programmer', let's move on. Why exactly did you need to know that?"

Amalie took the last sip of her cocoa and scooted out from the table. "Well, I was hoping you would write me a program, Daniel!"

Together, they slipped quietly out of the bar and into the cool night air. The rain had slowed to a drizzle, and hazy reflections from the streetlights were visible on the road. Daniel stuffed his hands deep into his jean pockets and looked at Amalie as he approached his Jeep.

"Where are we going, by the way?" she asked, the fog of her breath dissipating in the crisp air. The roar of the nearby highway was the only sound aside from their breathing.

"Well, I was going to go home and get comfortable. You can come, but you better start talking to me about what's going on," he pointed at her as he opened his door. "And if you aren't coming, could I get my coat back?"

Amalie sighed and furled her lips, stuffing her hands deep into the coat pockets. "Too cold. You're not getting your coat back. At least not yet."

"Well you need a stiff drink then!"

"Already had one." Amalie pulled open the passenger door of his Jeep and climbed in, cursing the Jeep's insipid stance on its big tires.

"Need a hand?" he said, watching her struggle to get in.

"No. I'm a big girl." She pulled the door closed as he walked around to the driver's side.

Daniel lit a cigarette and rolled down the window a few inches. He looked at her, and she occasionally looked back at him, but for the most part, stared at the streetlights across the parking lot. "So how'd you get so wet today?"

"Well my windshield fogged up so badly I couldn't see this morning." Amalie breathed in deeply. "I pulled under a bridge to wait out the storm and ran out of gas." She shook her head, then continued. "I waited under the bridge for over an hour before someone finally stopped to help me. So I've been wet all day."

Amalie spread her arms looking down at her soaked and shrinking clothing.

"Damn. Sounds to me like you need a stiff drink."

"Already had one." She shrugged, then looked at her watch. "I guess we can get started tomorrow."

Daniel nodded slowly, taking a pull from his cigarette. "So you want me to take you home then?"

"Well, I guess I lost my house key today somehow," Amalie said, digging through her purse.

"How do you lose your house key off your key ring?"

She looked at him across the darkness of the Jeep. "Who said it was on my key ring?"

"Well why *wouldn't* it be on your key ring?"

"I keep it on a separate key ring."

Daniel chuckled. "Why are you so weird?"

Amalie raised her eyebrows at him. "You don't know the first of it."

"Well I can probably get you into your house," Daniel said.

"I live in an apartment. Third floor. Not a chance." She smiled wanly.

"Well, I may have something you can slip into at my house. And I have a hot shower if you like." Amalie's eyes widened considerably, and she smiled, showing a row of perfect white teeth.

"Oh God, that would be so great right now. A hot shower. I have been shivering all day." Daniel turned the heat on as he started the Jeep and backed out of the parking spot. Amalie sat in the passenger seat, hands beneath her knees, leaning forward and shivering. She was staring at Daniel with chattering teeth. "Mmm… Heat."

"Yeah. Hot shower, and a stiff drink."

"Already had one."

"So I hear."

*　　　*　　　*

After she finally couldn't laugh anymore, Callie sat down on the rolling stool that stood near Walter's desk. "Okay, so let me get this straight: what the results are saying is that everyone who disappeared was a descendant of someone born on that date?"

"Yeah in a sense. But I don't think it's that simple. See check this out here," he said, scrolling up the screen a little ways, and highlighting a name. "Victor Castillo was born on January 16, 1897. So he doesn't quite fit the formula." Walter leaned back slightly and scratched his head. "All the bold blue dates are the same, but there are some stragglers."

"April 21, 1896," Callie rattled off. "Most of them were descended from someone born on that date. Right? Everyone else was descended from someone born on or around January 1897."

"Yeah, we have a December 3, 1896, and a November 29, 1896, but all close to January."

Callie straightened her back and pointed, leaving a smudge on the computer monitor. Walter knocked her hand down, cursing and wiping at the smudge with a napkin.

"So what is the significance then, if only twenty-five percent of their ancestors were born on that date?" She frowned and rubbed her head.

"I don't know. That's what's got me whipped. I'm not sure this ancestry angle has anything to do with it."

"Well, wait a minute Walter. Sort by date," Callie commanded. Walter clicked. The names all switched places and the screen refreshed, with the earliest date at the top of the screen. No one was born after January 19, 1897 from that batch, nor was anyone born before November 11 of 1896.

"So why did it even parse those names? No one born on that date even disappeared?"

"Well, duh," he said, scientifically. "That's the commonality using the ancestry angle, Callie. If you take that out of the equation, no commonality is attained. I doubt anyone born in 1896 was still alive when it happened anyway."

Callie sat heavily on the stool and sighed loudly. "Okay, maybe I am missing the entire point here, but I don't see the significance of commonality in ancestry if not everyone has it in common." Walter stared blankly at her. "You see what I'm saying?" Callie pointed at the screen. "It's telling us that their ancestors have that date in common, right? So why is it telling us that? Not all of them have that date in common!" She waved her hands around, then put them against her cheeks, burning with frustration. "Is this thing retarded or what?"

"Wait, wait, wait!" he said, standing suddenly. His legs knocked the chair over backward as he stood and pointed at the screen. "Nine months average… Is it possible all these people were conceived on April 21, 1896?"

"Who?"

"All of them! Everyone was born an average of nine months after the date they all supposedly have in common. Could they have been conceived on April 21 then?"

"Yeah, that's it! That's gotta be it!" Callie was now standing herself. "Whoa, that is weird."

"You're telling me… So everyone that had ancestry *conceived* on April 21, 1896 – and all of their descendants – has vanished." Walter walked away from the terminal and paced, his arms crossed, scratching his chin.

"My God this is incredible." Callie covered her mouth.

"Well, we have no way to confirm that's when they were conceived. That's guesswork."

"Yeah, but come on! The system parsed them saying 'commonality attained'! That's surely what it had to mean!" He had been the one who had discovered it, and now he was trying to back away while Callie was in favor of his find.

"The system uses virtual reasoning, Walt. Tell me. What else could they possibly have in common? It would have told us if there was anything else. Heck, it even checks their blood types," she said, waving fingers at the screen.

"Yeah, you're right. For those whose blood type it knows, at least. That's gotta be it."

"Besides, we've waited four days for this scan to finish, and if it ran any tighter a scan, it would take weeks to parse. It's like opening a thousand-meg text file with notepad."

"I don't think notepad will open a file that big," Walter said.

"That's the point, Walt. But hey – we can't all be kings of analogy, you know. At least my analogies make sense."

Walter did not return the smile, but stared perfectly serious into her eyes. "About as much sense as an empty gumball machine."

"Whatever," Callie said, rolling her eyes and walking away.

*   *   *

Daniel turned his key in the deadbolt and swung the door open sweeping his hand through the entrance as an invitation for Amalie to come inside. She crossed her arms over her chest as she entered. The cold wind had made certain parts of her more visible through the thin t-shirt.

"Home again, home again," he said, and led her through the master bedroom and into the bathroom, motioning for her to follow. She followed quietly, as if someone was sleeping and she did not want to wake them.

"Nice house, Daniel," she whispered.

"Why are you whispering?" His question was more audible than she had been all night.

"I dunno. I guess I assumed there would be someone here. You live alone though, right?"

"Yep. For now, anyway. I'll get you something to wear. Here's the shower." He reached in and turned on the hot water for her.

"Thank you so much, Daniel. You are too good." Amalie looked in the mirror as Daniel went back into the bedroom to fetch some clothes. "God, I look like hell," she said, wrinkling up her face. She then checked the water and let the skirt fall at her feet, whipped the shirt off and stepped in the shower. The bathroom door was still wide open.

As Daniel put some fresh clothes on the vanity outside the bathroom, he pulled the door closed. All he had seen was a blur of pink skin hopping in the shower, but the thought of her naked in his house affected him more than he would have imagined. *What the hell is she trying to do?* Anna was still too newly gone for him to seek out another potential partner, but what if she walked right into his house? He didn't know yet how he felt about that – he had not had a chance to consider it until now. And at the moment, the prospect of her coming out of the shower and straddling him on the bed was not something to which he objected wildly.

Daniel sat staring at the television, clicking the channel up button every three or four seconds. Amalie walked in wringing her hair behind her head, looking refreshed and awakened.

"I feel a hundred times better, Daniel. Thank you for the clothes, too." She sat on her leg on the other end of the couch. He had given her some gray wind pants and a maroon fleece shirt with a large black number 23 on the front.

"Good. They fit all right?" He turned to regard her.

"Yeah, these are a little spacey," she said, pulling out the waistline of her pants, "but I'll make do." She could have fit in them twice. Daniel got a glimpse of her belly as she pulled the drawstrings, tightening them around her waist again. She had a thin silver ring through her navel with a lightning bolt hanging from it.

"Sorry, I don't have a bra laying around either."

"That's okay." Amalie grabbed her breasts through the fleece shirt and said, "I can go without. Anything good on?"

"Come again," Daniel said, wide-eyed. He looked more closely at her, thinking her visage would betray her thoughts.

"I asked if there's anything good on the tube."

"Oh. No. Just Discovery Channel reruns. Not that that's inherently bad, but I've seen them damn zebras get their stomachs ripped open by the alligators like fifty times now." He aimed the remote back at the TV.

"Yuck," Amalie said as her face went sour. "Well let's talk about this program."

"Well the zebras keep trying to cross this swamp," he said, moving the remote around as he spoke, "but it's full of alligators. They never learn."

"No. The computer program I need you to write."

"Oh. That program. Well I still have to know what you want me to write before I can actually say I'm writing it for you, wouldn't you think?"

Amalie sighed and twisted her mouth. "Mmm hmm. Well, it shouldn't be that complicated. I just need a quantum mechanical representation of about twenty seconds."

Walter flicked the ash off the end of his cigarette and leaned back against the railing, just outside the back door of the lab. Callie leaned against the rail directly opposite of him, but did not smoke.

"It feels so good to finally be relieved of this shit," he said, turning his head to blow smoke.

Callie agreed, nodding delicately. "It just sounds so science fiction." Beyond all the statistical analyses they had ever calculated, this one leapt and bound. Walter and Callie generated statistical analyses for almost every event that took place in the last several years. Their job was generating these reports for the media and the government authorities. When talking about a particular subject, people always wanted numbers. Their division of the company provided people with these numbers.

"Yeah it does. But that's okay! I like a little fiction in my science." He grinned mischievously.

One of the primary functions for statistical analysis was to trend weather. If there were a common trait or characteristic between two tropical storms, they would find it. Trending and analysis provided a good report for what may happen in the future, as well. They could create an event sequence that seemed reasonable based on past events through trending graphs. Criminology trending was another of their markets.

"I know you do," Callie said. She stared off at the highway beyond the parking lot.

The technology Callie and Walter were using was primarily self-developed applications and systems. Even with Callie and Walter designing the software applications that deduced the commonality from separate events, the company still owned the rights to all of it. They had been asked to sign a non-disclosure agreement upon hire to protect the company's technology, and furthermore, they were to sign a creative rights contract stating any new technology or ideas conceived during the tenure of their employment would belong to the company. Had this not been the case, Callie and Walter could have effectively made themselves rich by the sale of that software alone. Any number of media relations companies would have paid millions to get their hands on such a powerful application.

"I just wonder what it all means." She waved the smoke away from her face. "What the heck does that date in history have to do with anything, that all its people would just up and disappear?"

"I know. Weird shit." Walter dragged from his cigarette again.

"Scary stuff too. Makes me wonder. You know, if it can happen to people descended from that date, it could happen to any other date in history."

"Yeah, you're right," he said nodding. "You're right as the twist on a blender."

"Well we've established our commonality. Now we just have to figure out why the heck it happened."

CHAPTER FOUR
Discernment

Daniel stared irresolutely at Amalie and her unyielding expression. He had no idea what she was talking about, nor did he have any clue how to respond. He had heard her perfectly, but it meant as much to him as eleven randomly selected words aligned in a sentence.

"What are you, some kind of physicist?"

"Yes I am. I've been researching temporal delineation and – in an effort to save eons – I've employed the use of a quantum computer," she replied, again with no expression on her face.

Daniel felt as if he had stepped off a strange train in a strange land, and was now being greeted by a stranger. "Okay, wait. Back up. You lost me. Did you say temporal delineation?"

"Yes. It's the act of taking time out of the standard line it is generally perceived as following."

"Yeah I figured that's what it meant, but to think it's an actuality is ridiculous. Well, to me anyway. I don't know enough about it, obviously." He threw his hands up dismissively. "No offense…"

"None taken." She smiled. "You don't really have to accept my theories or my research. I just need you to write a program for me that will translate quantum mechanical equations I provide you into a standard representational schematic."

Daniel shook his head quickly and held his hands up again. "What the hell. Let me get this straight. I don't have to know about quantum mechanics, but you want me to write a program that will – wait. I thought I had it. Start over."

"I will give you all the quantum mechanical equations, and – for that matter – their answers. I need you to write a program that will turn the answers into a schematic. So basically you'd make a three-dimensional chart representative of the information I have given you. Should be pretty simple, really." She took the remote from his frozen hand, then turned and aimed it at the television and clicked it off.

"Okay. Why don't you use your quantum computer to do these equations?"

"Because. I don't need the problems solved. I've already done that. I just need the answers graphed." The low light of the living room fixture cast shadows on her face that seemed to hide her emotions. Either she was completely withdrawn, being a master of separating work from play, or she just masked it well.

"I think I can do that. I've not done anything like it before, but it sounds relatively easy. It's just parsing data that already exists, so I don't have to understand the information as such." After a moment, he looked more closely at her. "Right?"

"You got it. Now we're on the same wavelength." She wiggled herself into a comfortable position on the couch cushion.

"Okay. So tell me about this temporal delineation shit. It sounds cool as hell." He turned and grabbed his cigarettes off the end table and fumbled with the Zippo in his pocket. Clink, flick, burn.

"I can't tell you much if you don't understand quantum mechanics. But I can tell you my project." She leaned back and pulled a small pillow onto her lap. She now sat sideways on the couch, facing Daniel.

"Good enough," he said. "It's not that I don't understand them, but I just don't mess with it much."

"Them? As in physics being plural? That's cute Daniel," she said.

"You know what I meant. You want something to drink?" Daniel rose from the couch and made his way into the kitchen.

"Sure. Anything." She pulled her hair out of its messy pile and rearranged it on her head. It was still wet and dripping on her back. Daniel returned a few moments later with flutes and a bottle of red wine. This got her cooing, and before she could make mention of the romantic situation that seemed to be pouring in around them, Daniel clicked the stereo on and a soft classical symphony came to life behind them, quietly singing through the Master Audio Acoustics speakers set in the wall above the couch.

"So what are all the – uh…" he said, moving his fingers in a circle trying to stir up the words. "The seconds I'm supposed to graph. What're they uh – you know. What are they for?"

She lowered her eyes at him, a slight smile forming across her lips. "Those are the seconds you stole from me."

Daniel leaned in, looking at her. "I don't follow."

"You know that data you swiped when you hacked my system? Those were seconds. And as soon as they left my system, they became useless shells. They dissolved. And people disappeared because of it."

Daniel sat speechless for a moment, then shook his head. "I'm sorry Amalie. I'm not sure I'm buying this. I didn't 'swipe' any data from your computer. I moved some files around."

"You moved them off my computer and onto yours. I don't suppose you still have those files do you?" Amalie said, then sipped from her glass.

He shook his head. "I'm telling you, all I did was move some things around."

"You didn't lasso a whole bunch of the data string on my screen and cut it?"

"Oh. Yeah. Well, I did do that. I wanted some trophy, you know? Hacking Royal is like a pipe dream. I'm entitled to bragging rights. They're supposed to be the 'unhackable company'. I'll tell you though," he said, pointing his smoke at her, "you guys need to tighten your security there."

"It's been handled. When you took that data, you were taking seconds right out of the temporal soup."

"Temporal soup?"

"Yeah. Call it what you want, you broke in and stole seconds from the clock, Daniel. You couldn't have come at a better time."

Daniel sighed and shook his head. "Come on, Amalie. You don't actually expect me to believe this do you?"

She shook her head, smiling at him. "Nope. I don't. Not now. But you will."

Daniel nodded and crushed out his smoke. "Okay. I'll wait." Amalie finished her glass and set the flute on the table, blinking long. She had drunk it rather quickly, Daniel thought. "You okay?"

"Yeah. That's good wine." She stretched her arms out, moving her hands around in circles. "I'm tingly all over."

"Well help yourself to as much as you like."

"You trying to get me drunk?" She aimed her mischievous smile at him again.

"Nah. You don't feel the least bit awkward about our acquaintance?"

"No, why should I? It's not like I'm sleeping over or something. Though I do concede we seem to have clicked rather *expediently*," she said, stressing the long e.

"Oh. So we're friends now?"

"Don't push your luck, buddy," she said, biting her bottom lip. "I'm only using you to get my seconds back. Once I get what I want, I'll be gone." Amalie reached over and poured herself more wine.

"Okay, I'm dying to know what the hell all this stuff about stealing seconds is. I don't believe you now, but I'd like to hear you try and talk me into it."

Amalie laughed out loud. "Okay, try this. You have heard of quantum computers, right?" She pulled from her flute.

"Yes I have. But that doesn't mean I understand them. Frankly, that whole thing has never made sense to me."

"What whole thing?" Amalie frowned. "Quantum mechanics?"

"Yeah. And how they operate."

"They utilize more than just the usual four dimensions," Amalie said, holding up her wine glass and looking through it. "If you draw a line horizontally, and think of it as space, then a line going vertical as time, you have a graph. Put something on that graph. Like a person, for instance. If the person stands still, over time the line just goes straight up. But if he moves, it's angled. At every intersection between time and place, you make a little tick mark. That's an event."

He nodded, squinting.

"Quantum mechanics – as a science – relies wholly on the principal of uncertainty. At least so it would seem." She gulped. "When observed, subatomic particles seem to be occupying more than one space at the same time. So if you take that graph again, which was two-dimensional, and consider all the places the person could go in the next second, and make a tick mark in all those places, you have a much broader graph. You still with me?"

Daniel nodded again, this time more slowly. "Yeah, you mark every place where he *could* potentially go. But what's that have to do with anything?"

"I'm getting to that. If you stack ten more of those same graphs on top of that one, then you have an idea of where the other dimensions come into play. They are like different universes, where every time an event takes place, they split off from that point and start a new graph. The fifth dimension is nothing more than a realm of possibilities, in a sense. So instead of the tick marks representing where you *could* go, they represent whole new universes where others of you *did* go." Amalie leaned back and drank heavily from her glass again.

Daniel shook his head. "You're saying that at every point event on that graph, the universe splits?"

"Science has all but proven it. Quantum mechanics is the only science that has actually survived all the tests we fire at it. While you can't readily prove something you can't sense, nothing anyone has done to disprove it has worked."

"So where does your project fit in, Amalie?"

She swallowed and continued, "We've been exploring the possibilities of using those other graphs. The ones in the next dimension, you know? If we can manage and manipulate an event sequence on another of the dimensional planes, we could – in theory – chart a timeline across that new event string. So technically, time is still a line, but the line is much wider. Three-dimensionally wide."

"So you could move side to side as well as forward through it."

"Bingo." Amalie winked and gave him a thumbs-up.

*   *   *

"I think we have a major find here," Callie said as she scanned over the long results paper she had just pulled from the printer.

"One of a kind!" Walter said, smiling. He leaned back against the printer table, grinning like a madman. Callie looked at him out the corner of her eye. The crowd she generally ran with was not made up of a bunch of lookers, but rather intellectuals. And – she noted – it was rare someone fit into both categories. But Walter did.

There was a difference, Callie had decided, in just being an intellectual and being a class act genius. He was a normal guy in the respect that he still knew how to work on a lawnmower and change a tire, but he also understood physics and statistical science. He was not given nearly enough credit for his findings, or his knowledge, Callie thought. But humble as he was sharp, he would never say anything about it. He was the man behind the curtain, controlling the project, but never around to take the credit for it.

All in all, Walter was one of the most intelligent people Callie had ever met, and she admired his analytical mind. He was always thinking of a different solution, a better mousetrap, and a smoother way to say it. On his desk stood a steel rod with about 75 iron rings on it. This was his collection of puzzle rings. As a teenager, Walter used to go to game stores and sit in the back working the tavern puzzles, and stealing the rings. He became so proficient at it that he could have every ring from all different types of rope and steel puzzles in about half an hour. But he would never steal the ring from two identical puzzles. Every one was unique. More than half of his ring collection had disappeared a few years back, thus in its prime, his collection consisted of around 200 iron rings of several sizes.

People unknowing would point and ask, and Walter would smile proudly. He smiled like this at Callie now. "I think this calls for a celebratory glass of champagne," Callie said.

"Yeah. Cool. I'm on board with that." His answer startled Callie. They had not gotten out together in a couple of weeks.

"You are serious?"

"Well, yeah. Why not? We may be on the cover of Time next week. I would like to think we were prepared for it!"

Callie nodded, biting her lip. "I don't know if I agree with that entirely. We didn't really discover anything that wouldn't have been found sometime."

"Oh, but I beg to differ, Cal! We wrote the deductive reasoning program! I think we deserve a Nobel!" Walter grabbed her shoulders. Again she nodded. Then she allowed herself to be led out for "champagne". Neither of them even drank champagne. It was symbolic of the drinking they had not had in weeks.

*   *   *

Daniel stretched his arms out, bringing them to rest behind his head, staring at the ceiling fan. His mind was reeling. "Okay. So you say you have somehow harnessed the power of these other dimensions, right?" Amalie nodded, pursing her lips. "So what the hell do you do with it?" he said. He realized he was frowning at his own question.

"We use it for bandwidth. Speed. Some of the calculations we use to generate productive formulas and algorithms for our applications require so much processor and memory and bandwidth – much more than we could possibly obtain through conventional hardware – that we need to utilize these other avenues. For instance, when we're tracing a subatomic particle, there are a billion different directions it could take in

just a nanosecond. The only way to keep up with it –
even remotely – is to calculate the possibility that it will
be in a certain place in the next instant.

"Now keep in mind that this probability changes
exponentially, a million times a second. To make that
calculation would take a computer the size of a small
city a trillion times a trillion years. If you have a
trillion different versions of the same application
running in a trillion different dimensions, growing
exponentially, you get the answer back within a period
of a couple of nanoseconds."

"Wow. That's bad ass." Daniel looked around the
room at his antiquated equipment and suddenly felt a
tinge of excitement about the possibility of getting to
touch some new hardware. He finally snapped out of it
when his eyes landed on a picture of Anna amid the
chaos.   That familiar tug of dread and sadness
threatened to whip in over him, so he returned to the
subject at hand quickly. "So to what end? What's the
end result?"

"Time, Daniel," Amalie said softly.   "We are
essentially getting the answer back before we've sent
its request.   If we can come up with a simpler
application, and devise a simple analogous schematic
for an answer, the program would – in theory – be so
rapid as to give us the answer before we asked it the
question. Needless to say, that's pretty significant."

Daniel shook his head slowly. After a pregnant
pause, he said, "Who the hell are you?"   He was
smiling and frowning at the same time. "Why are you
telling me all this?"

"This is what I do, Daniel." She was fingering her
hair and pulling strands of it back behind her ear.

"So I'm going to be helping you go back in time? I
mean, essentially that's what it sounds like in the end.

You want me to write a program that will put these variables in place so that you can use them against your application, right?"

"No. Not at all. Well, yes. But not for what I was just talking about." Amalie stood, but had to grab the edge of the table to keep herself from toppling over onto it. Then she sat back down, hands spread and eyes wide. "Whoa. I drank too fast!"

Daniel ignored that and continued, "Then what were you talking about?"

Amalie sighed patiently and restarted. "You asked why we use quantum computers. So I told you some instances. What I need you to do is write a program that will take some of the answers we have gathered, then parse them, and create a graphical representation of it in four dimensions." She looked solemnly at him, as if it were all common knowledge.

What had started out with what had looked like the potential for a romantic episode had suddenly taken a sharp intellectual left. So seemingly obvious to him was the presence of sexuality, but on she pressed, either never recognizing its presence, or not allowing herself the escape from her professional purpose, regardless of how informal it had become.

He lit another cigarette and shoved his hands deep in his pockets. He needed one more answer to illustrate to him the magnitude of the problem he was about to be faced with. "Why? Why do you need all this?"

Amalie leaned back on the sofa and crossed her ankles. "Good God, I was wondering when you'd ask!"

CHAPTER FIVE
Determination

The cold night air whipped at Callie's hair as she stepped out of Walter's Durango. There were only a few other cars in the parking lot of the Stellar Café. It had a fine selection of beers, foreign and domestic, and a pretty well rounded menu, though most of the items were heart stoppers. People went to Stellar Café for the atmosphere and coffee, not the menu.

Walter held the door open for Callie and she hunched her shoulders against the wind as she ducked under his arm to escape the bitter cold. "Thank you!" She stood shivering once they were inside.

"You know, it's been a long time since we loosened up enough to get out for a drink. I'm glad we came out," Callie said between fits of shivery.

"Yeah what's it been – two weeks? That is uncommon for us." He looked around the place. The vaulted ceiling was painted black and had glowing stars and constellations all over it. Everything down to the fixtures above the tables was space-themed. Even the music was eclectic. A bespectacled woman stood on a small stage reading poetry in front of a microphone while a small crowd huddled around in the tables directly in front of her, soaking it up.

Callie finally frowned, and spoke. "You know what? Wouldn't you rather just go get a movie and do our drinking at home?"

"What? Not into the poetry?" Walter said grinning.

"I forgot it was poetry night. Surely, that's why the parking lot is empty. Plus, it's just going to get colder outside, and I want to get somewhere warm and stay there. We can get more comfortable on a couch, with a movie."

"It's up to you, Callie girl." He lit a cigarette and looked around again. No one had even come to seat them yet.

"Yeah. Every time that door opens a draft blows through here. It's like absolute zero outside!"

"Good one." Walter smiled easily.

Just then, a hostess approached and picked up two menus from the podium. "Hi, I'm Mandy. Smoking I assume?"

Walter looked down at his cigarette. "Actually, yes I am. Do I need to go outside with it?"

Callie slapped his shoulder. "Smart ass."

Mandy sighed.

"Actually, I think we're not going to stay," Callie said. "Right, Walter?"

Walter smiled apologetically at the hostess, then shrugged.

The hostess just stood staring at them while they decided.

Callie sighed heavily, then pulled up on the waistline of her pants, looking over at Walter. "All right, let's go."

They headed back to the truck, Callie chewing her lip and frowning.

"What's wrong?" he said, unlocking the doors with his key fob.

He opened her door for her, and Callie climbed in. "Nothing. That girl just looked familiar." Walter got in and started the truck, then pulled out of the parking lot.

"Okay, here's the deal," Amalie said. Daniel had even sat back down with curiosity burning him from the inside. Amalie looked amazing in the low light with a slight buzz painting her motions in slow speed. "I've been experimenting with quantum reordination. This is a casual way of saying temporal delineation."

Daniel laughed out loud. "I see."

She smiled and continued. "So anyway, I have been delicately close to discovery, at least so I would believe. But then the other day, I stumbled upon something that totally redefined the way I think about physics." Amalie twirled her hair on her finger again, and looked at Daniel with an expression he could only describe as 'amazed'. She looked amazed about something. Maybe she was just fascinated with her work.

"I was mapping movement with a system we use known as quantum actuality. It takes the position a subatomic particle was last known to be in, which – in and of itself – is a rather lengthy explanation, because of ..."

"Amalie, seriously. You're losing me."

"Okay, okay. Sorry. I'm trying to keep it basic. Anyway, if you can charge a subatomic particle by its strength source, you can – in theory – control it. Needless to say, this is pretty serious stuff. If we can put little leashes on these particles and actually map out where they go when they leave this dimension, we may be able to utilize those other dimensions for other things." Amalie had become very animated, talking a lot with her hands, her face rapidly jumping between emotions as she tried to report her discoveries to the lay Daniel. Her mouth was dry, so she wet it with more wine.

Daniel sighed. "Like what?" There didn't seem to be much point in trying to follow along anymore. She had lost him long ago. Now he was beginning to wonder whether or not he could even comprehend the numbers well enough to build a program around them.

"Anything. But namely – and what you're interested in hearing is time travel," she said without emotion. She sipped from her wine glass, looking over the rim at Daniel who now sat faceless on the other end of the couch.

"Time travel. You're serious."

Amalie sighed. "If you don't believe me, there's not much point in telling you any of this. But I've already done it, Daniel. And check this out," she said, raising her glass and running her finger around the stem. "I was time traveling when you hacked into my system."

"You have got to be kidding. Do you know how hokey that sounds?"

She nodded slowly, swishing a mouthful of wine through her teeth. She swallowed. "It was two years ago that happened for me. And it's only been a few weeks for you."

"You know, you're going to have to show me all this for me to believe it, right?"

"I plan on it Daniel. Otherwise, I wouldn't be telling you all this now." Amalie got up and went to use the restroom, leaving Daniel reeling in his thoughts. *Time travel.* He was having a hard time swallowing all this. She seemed completely serious, and seemed to know what she was talking about. And if she truly worked for Royal, then it might even be plausible.

Royal Research Corporation was not only the most prestigious place in the world to get a job, but also the most difficult. Thus anyone having a Royal badge commanded a respect and a reckoning if based solely on their obvious ability to land a job there. Royal was bigger than American Airlines, richer than Microsoft, and smarter than the government. But it had few employees considering its size. Considering the global presence of the company, it had far fewer employees per capita than those other companies. Royal was extremely selective about its employees. So if Daniel had an RRC employee sitting on his couch, then it meant two things to him: number one, she was one of the smartest people he had ever met, and number two, he was in the presence of great wealth. Most RRC employees were able to retire after only a few years of service, and neither they nor their families would ever have to work again.

When Amalie returned, Daniel leaned back and closed his eyes.

"What's wrong?" she said.

"I'm sorry if I act a little doubtful Amalie. I've never met an RRC employee."

"It's okay. Like I said, you'll believe it all shortly. When you help me retrieve my Q computer."

Daniel stammered, sitting up to look at her. "Come again? Q computer?"

"Yeah. Quantum computer. We will need that, to fix the problem, you know?"

"And this quantum computer will do that for us…"

"Well yeah. That's what I was using when you erased them. That's how we get them back."

Daniel shook his head. "Okay, how the hell does it affect time at all? How does it connect to 'time'? How does it *interfere* with it?"

"Daniel, Daniel. The computer gets it bandwidth from the quantum foam, like I said earlier."

"Oh. Well, yeah. That explains everything," Daniel said nodding, brow furrowed. He was excited about getting to the point of believing her. But for now, it seemed logical as an ejection seat in a helicopter. Daniel was mentally inferior to this woman, and she was making sure he knew it.

"When all this happened, I was trying to shut the application down. But you had it hard-locked. I couldn't do anything, and the computer was sluggish. That Q computer is never sluggish."

"That's a data trap. It locks everything down so we can get what we want," Daniel said.

"Well it kept parsing and grinding, and I finally realized that the data itself was shrinking. The long block of characters kept getting shorter. Slowly but surely, parts of it were vanishing. The block would shift up and to the left as each bit got sucked away.

Those bits were mathematical representations of each second on a particular day."

"So where'd it get the numbers from?" He finally seemed to grasp what she was throwing him, and again, she finished her glass of wine, turning it up. "Those numbers were representations of seconds?" He was on the edge of the couch squinting his concentration and interest into the warm air between them.

"Yeah. From the year to the month, day, then hour, minute, second," she nodded and counted them off with a free finger. She then poured yet another glass of the now warm red wine. "Those bits you stole were little sets of seconds. All in fourteen-digit formats. Like one was 18960421034757." She pulled one finger back at a time from one hand as she rattled it off again. "1896, which is the year, 04 which is the month, 21 the day, then 03 the hour, 47, then 57 the second."

"So you think I ripped away seconds because of those numbers? Supposedly from the 1890's. Right?" Amalie nodded, staring at her wine. "Well the perpetual calendar is a man-made marker for tracking time. How would it have been put in like that?"

Amalie looked up at him. "What do you mean?"

"Supposing those are representations of individual seconds, like you suggested, why would they show up in perfect form like that from the year to the second? Man made the calendar we go by. If you were to tap into time itself, it would be a formless blob, so I would think," Daniel said.

"Well the parser is a man-made program. When it parses that particular second it displays it on our calendar automatically. That's how we built the application! It reads the second, and the conversion software makes it into a readable date."

"You amaze me, Amalie." Daniel stood up again, then excused himself to the restroom. Before he shut the door, he watched as she tipped up her glass and rolled it off her chin, then set it quietly on the coffee table leaning back into her drunkenness on the overstuffed couch cushion.

*   *   *

Walter pulled onto the highway and looked back over at Callie expectantly. "So this girl looked familiar."

"Yeah. No big deal though. Let's not talk about her."

Walter looked at her and frowned. "Wow. You're serious?" Then he shook his head. "You know, I thought I knew everything there was to know about you, Cal."

"Guess not."

The moonlight illuminated the surface of the wet road, but the trees and brush that ran alongside it were dark as pitch, and featureless as they sped past quietly. There were no other cars on the road, as everyone was either hunkered in at home for the night or already deep into drinks at the local bars.

Callie finally spoke, breaking the silence that had fallen within the truck and had become thick as syrup. "Okay, so what movie do you want to rent?" She stared out the passenger window, her breath creating fog spots against the cold.

"I really don't even know if I could stay up for a whole movie. I plan to tag one on tonight," Walter said.

Callie turned to look at him. "Oh come on! Don't be a party pooper!"

Walter sighed. "Let's just see how the night plays out." Clearly, something was bothering Walter, but he was not letting on what it was.

Callie turned her head toward the window again, staring out at the featureless nightscape.

Walter pulled to a stop in the parking lot next to Callie's Mercedes and put the Durango in park, looking over at her. "You wanna follow me back to my place then?"

"We need to go get liquor, don't we?" Callie said.

"I think I have some vodka. We could make martinis. We'd probably need to stop and get olives though."

Callie sighed and stretched her arms out in front of her, arching her back. "Mmm. That sounds good. Better drop off my car at my house though, 'cause you'll have to drive me home."

Walter nodded. "We can do that."

"Did you bring those reports home with you?" Callie asked.

"What reports?"

"The SA reports." She was referring to the statistical analysis reports of the ghosters.

"No. I could run in and get them real quick though, if you need me to," Walter said. Then he frowned. "Why?"

"Well I just thought it would be fun to look at them tonight, you know, talk them over some more."

He stared blankly at her. "You're kidding, right?"

Callie's face dropped. "No, why? Oh. You don't think that's fun. I see." She smiled, "Okay, never mind." Her eyes widened and she waved her hands defensively. "Forget I ever brought it up." She opened her door to get out.

"All right. So I'll follow you to your house then," Walter said.

After dropping off Callie's car at her apartment, they stopped at the all-night grocery store for the olives. The parking lot was almost empty. Several shopping baskets crowded the median between the parking places, and Callie got out of the Durango staring at them.

"You thinking what I'm thinking?" she said with a mischievous grin to Walter.

"Surely you don't think you can beat me…" He stopped where he was standing. Then it was on. They both dashed for the closest basket and each came off the median riding one like a scooter. They shot across the parking lot like skate boarders, and Walter was ahead of her by a few feet. The side of the entrance had a garage door built into it that could be raised to permit cart collection, and it was open. They were both headed at full speed for it.

If one rode the basket properly, and stayed low enough below the handle, it could be ridden right under the garage door and well into the basket collection area. Walter ducked low and prepared to climb the short concrete ramp that led onto the sidewalk a few feet before the door. Callie realized she was about to be beaten, so she jumped off and ran behind her basket, which was strictly against the rules. One foot had to remain on the basket at all times for it to be a fair match. But Callie did not lose easily.

She was aiming right for Walter, and passed in front of him just before his basket went under the door. She ducked at the last second and flew under the door with him hot on her tail.

"Cheater!" he yelled. "There's no way you could have caught up!"

Then Callie skidded the basket sideways and dismounted, stepping back quickly. Walter's basket slammed into the side of hers with an exquisitely loud clanging crash, and both baskets went end over end, tangling and tumbling. Callie was shocked at how loud it was, the slamming metal banging and rolling through the collection area and out into the main foyer.

Callie stood still in the hall covering her mouth with her hand, watching the baskets skid to a halt on their sides. Walter stood beside her, glaring at her. "I can't believe you cheated, Cal."

She was still covering her mouth as she spoke, "Oh my God that was loud!"

Walter said, "Yeah it was." They both broke out in laughter. They were still laughing when they entered the main corridor and Walter began picking up the baskets. Only one employee was visible and he seemed only mildly amused, staring at the two of them.

"Sorry," Callie said, waving. "I kind of lost control of it." The clerk just looked at them.

Walter came to meet her after pushing the baskets to the side and put his hand on her back as they walked into the store. "Can you tell me what aisle the olives are on?"

"Nine," the clerk replied, pointing over his shoulder, clearly not amused.

"Well thank you!" Walter said, clapping his hands together. He leaned in close to Callie and whispered, "I can't believe you cheated."

"I know. I'm a cheater dork. But I wasn't going to let you win."

*　　　*　　　*

"Aw hell," Daniel said quietly as he looked down at Amalie. She had passed out on the couch, and was quietly snoring, her lips pressed hard against her closed hand. He squatted next to her at the end of the couch and looked at her sleeping eyes.

"Oh Amalie. If only I knew who you were," he whispered. She shifted and turned her head so she was facing straight up. Daniel grabbed a blanket off the back of the love seat and pulled it across her feet and up to her shoulders. Then he shut off the lamp and walked back to his bedroom.

The lingering thought of sexuality brought back visions of Anna for Daniel, and filled his stomach with dread again. It had seemed to Daniel that it should get easier and easier to handle, but only the frequency of his thoughts had dwindled. They were still every bit as powerful now as they were the day it had happened. And often, he would cry himself to sleep in the sickness of losing her.

*　　　*　　　*

Walter's apartment was large and spacious compared to Callie's, but not nearly as well kept.

Callie often found herself picking up plates and cups and putting them in the sink for him, or wiping down counters and tables, picking up trash for him. She was obsessive to the point where she could not sit still for long, knowing there was trash or untidiness in the next room. Walter always thanked her for cleaning up, and had long ago given up on trying to get her to just sit the hell down and enjoy it for once.

As she walked into the living room she stretched and looked around. "Get any new movies you haven't told me about?"

"Nope. You were with me last time I picked one up."

"What do you want to watch?" she asked, picking up a pizza box from the coffee table and piling napkins and empty soda cans into it.

"I don't know. Like I said, I'm not really in the mood for a movie. We can just, I don't know, talk…" Walter was smiling.

Callie stopped and turned around, hair falling in her eyes, her hands full of his trash. "Is that what you want to do Walter?"

"Ah, Cal, you know I don't care. We can do whatever you want."

"Oh," she said, and blew the hair out of her eyes. "That's cool. We can talk. You fix the martinis!" She then continued on her mission, picking up trash and dishes and hauling them to the kitchen. After about ten minutes of straightening magazines and throwing clothes into his hamper in the bathroom, she finally sat down on the sofa. "There. Much better."

"Thank you, Callie." He handed her a glass.

"God I hate to imagine what a real girl is going to think when you finally bring one home, Walt."

"What, you're not a real girl?"

"You know what I mean. I don't count. I guess you have to hope she's either as tolerant as me, or as untidy as you."

"Yeah, but you're only tolerant because you love me. She wouldn't just automatically be that way. She'd have to grow to love me first."

"What makes you think I love you?" she said, taking a sip of her martini. "God how much vermouth did you put in these?"

"Why, does it taste bad?" He sniffed his cup.

Callie broke out in laughter. "Why the heck did you just sniff your cup Walter?"

"Hell I don't know. Was testing it I guess. You really don't like yours?"

"No, it's fine." She took another sip. "So tell me," she said, slapping his knee, "when do you think they will want to go public with our stuff?"

"I dunno. Just hope it's not too soon. I want to really be prepared for the speech and everything." He was running his finger around the edge of his glass.

"You really do think they're going to make a big deal out of this, don't you? You sound serious!"

"I am, Callie. I've been watching the news constantly. And no one has said shit about it yet. They are still blissfully unaware of everything. They have no idea these people even have anything in common at all."

"Well obviously, because we had to rely on parentage for our results. No one else would think of that. Well, at least they haven't. I don't think it will be long before they start thinking of it though," Callie said, and took her over-shirt off, leaving a thin white tank top beneath.

"God, Callie!" Walter said, frowning and smiling at the same time.

"What?" She looked down at her chest, seemingly unaware how revealing the shirt was.

"That thing is fucking see-through!" he said, fingering the shoulder strap. "Aren't those shirts supposed to be underwear?"

"Yes. That's how I'm wearing it! I'm hot though! You know I get hot when I drink." She looked down again. "Just ignore it."

"It's like forty degrees outside! And you're hot?"

"Yes! If it offends you then I'll put it back on, Walter," she said, fumbling with her button-up shirt again. "Besides, I didn't realize it was this revealing…"

"No, don't worry about it. If you really are hot then leave it off. Hell, take it all off!" He gulped from his drink.

"No way!" she said, slapping his leg again. "I am somewhat modest."

"Uh huh." Walter turned up his glass finishing the last bit. "Callie will you have sex with me?"

"Walter. Don't even start that with me." Callie waved a finger at him, then reached for the vodka bottle. She twisted the top off and poured more in Walter's glass for him, then grabbed the olive jar from the coffee table.

"Start what? You know, we've never talked about it. Why not?"

"You're just horny or something. I know you don't really want me," Callie said.

Walter fished a couple of olives from the jar and popped one in his mouth. "Why do you say that? Just because I've never asked you before?"

"Well yeah! That's precisely why! Oh my God. We are not going into this right now."

"Okay, okay, okay. I just had to ask." Walter sat silently for a moment as Callie refilled her own glass, then finally said, "Callie, how come we've never dated or anything?"

"Don't you think it would be awkward working with someone you're dating?" She turned to face him. "Walter, stop staring at my tits."

"Oh. Sorry. Hell I don't know. I've never dated anyone I've worked with. I just…"

"You just what?" She stirred her martini with her finger.

"I just sometimes wonder if something's like wrong with us or something," he said, raising his hand slightly.

"Like what? What do you mean?" She popped another olive in her mouth.

"Well we are both high-class, intelligent people, both attractive and well-to-do, both in good shape… But we've never even been on a date," he said staring at his glass.

"What? We go out all the time!" But she knew what he meant. She had wondered the same thing many times before. It had gotten to the point where she liked him too much as a friend to try anything new. She did not want to put their friendship at risk after all they had invested in it.

For the last four and a half years, she had worked with Walter and had grown very close to him. Neither of them had any siblings, and thus had taken to each other as such. They spent every holiday together, visiting each of the parents' houses in turn, just as a married couple would. Callie often wondered why they never dated, but seeing as how he had never brought it up, she had never pursued the thought. She certainly would not be the one to bring it up before, so it was actually a relief to her to finally be having this conversation.

They had been on hundreds of 'dates' together, but had never really called it dating, as they just assumed they would be together every weekend anyway. On Friday nights, Callie would make her way home to shower and change, then without a second thought, would be on her way to Walter's to find out what was going on that night. There wasn't a question about where she would be. It would be with Walter. She would spend her weekend days reading and putting about the apartment, but the nights belonged to Walter. They had grown so close to each other at work, and so deeply involved in their work that they had simply blocked out the entire outside world, and had failed to ever let it back in.

"We go out all the time as friends. Your parents love me. My parents love you. Why aren't we a hot couple?"

"I don't know, Walter. I think I consider you too much like a brother. It seems like it would be weird now, since we waited so long."

Walter nodded, pursing his lips. He was accepting this. In one part of her mind, Callie was hoping he would pursue it a little further; ask her out on an official date. But at the same time, she loved the way he analyzed and accepted things as they were and did not add to the entropy that seemed to envelop the world around them. She knew he would not quit easily without a reason. If he really wanted her, he would pop up at her door with roses or something. He would let her know. It was his move though. Callie definitely was not the aggressive type.

She finally spoke again, after a long moment of sipping silently. "Walter, I'm so glad we're friends."

She leaned in to hug him. He wrapped his arms around her and scratched her back. She was basically lying on him. In this way, she could feel his warmth without the commitment of something more.

"Me too, Cal." And that was the last they ever talked about it. An almost full bottle of vodka had been opened when they started the evening, and by the time they finished it, the bottle was empty, as was the jar of olives. Callie was staggering drunk and could not sit up straight, but somehow managed to carry on her intelligible conversation with Walter enough to ask him to take her home.

He did not hint around about her staying; he didn't ask her if she was sure; he simply grabbed his keys like a good boy and helped her down the stairs to the truck. Callie loved and hated him for it. She would have stayed. Maybe not any night, but definitely tonight. Tonight she would have stayed with him.

CHAPTER SIX
Awakening

aniel awoke and turned to put his feet on the cool carpet and looked about the room. The daylight crept in around the edges of the curtains. He pulled a curtain back slightly to shed some fresh light into the room and had to shield his eyes against it. It had not been this bright outside in weeks, he thought.

He pulled on some pants and a t-shirt, then made his way down the hall. Amalie was sitting up watching *Western Wagons* reruns in the living room, an afghan wound around her waist and legs. "Morning," Daniel said.

"Hey, man. You sleep long enough?" she said.

"Why? What time is it?"

"Almost noon. Do you ever watch this?" she said, pointing the remote at the television.

"Western Wagons? Hell yes. One of the best shows on TV. Well, used to be. I've seen every episode."

"Me too. I love this show." Amalie's eyes came to rest on the screen and her face grew serious again.

"Are you hungry? I can cook some breakfast."

"That would be excellent. Thank you, Daniel." Amalie stood up to go to the restroom, and swayed a little. "Ooh, wow. Remind me not to drink red wine again, Daniel."

Daniel went into the kitchen to make breakfast. He noticed the empty wine bottle on the table and realized why Amalie had been so tipsy. *Damn, she drained the bottle. Note to self: buy more red wine for Amalie.*

When Amalie finally emerged from the bathroom, she looked fresh and lively, considering she had gotten rather inflamed on the wine the night before. She had managed a t-shirt from Daniel's dresser and wore the wind pants again.

"How's it going, Dan?" she said as she waltzed into the kitchen.

"You feeling a little better?" he said as he looked over at her, stirring the eggs in the skillet.

"Yes. That is so out of character for me to get drunk and stay at someone's house. It's that red wine. If I start drinking red wine, I can't stop," she said, closing her eyes against her own smile.

"So tell me, Amalie, what is it you actually do at Royal?" he said, leaning against the counter staring hard at her.

"Have I not told you that already?"

"No. No you haven't."

She leaned back in her chair, crossing her arms. "I work in research and development. I am a physicist, and I work in R&D."

"If you were any more vague, you'd be Van Gogh."

"Well most of my projects are confidential, Daniel!"

"I see," he said, grabbing his smokes from the counter and lighting one. After a moment, he continued, "So… If you work for Royal, how come you didn't ask one of those programmers? I know they have programmers there. Probably a lot more qualified than I am."

Amalie lowered her gaze on him. "Daniel, they don't know what happened. And I'm not about to tell them. You created this anomaly, so you will help me fix it."

Daniel snorted. It still hurt his pride to have her commanding him, but he knew she was right. If he did not help her, she could easily turn him in to the authorities. "So how did you catch me, Amalie? How'd you know it was me?"

"Well, I could say I'm just that good," Amalie said. She squinted and pursed her lips, then looked back at him. "But I think it's more that you're just not that good."

Callie sat up breathing heavily, and in a thick sweat. Her nightshirt was sticking to her, and her hair was a matted mess. Her brightly lit room was cool, but under her thick down comforter, she was a furnace. Her head pounded from the vodka martinis she had drained the previous night. She put her hand on her head and cursed herself. "What the heck was I thinking?" Callie slipped out of bed and looked at herself in the mirror. *Wreck. No more martinis for a week or two.*

She let the hot shower pound down on her for nearly fifteen minutes, in a dreamy daze. It was Saturday and there was nothing on her schedule. She had planned nothing but to read for the entire weekend, which was a rare occasion. Her small apartment consisted of the bare essentials when it came to furniture. Nothing extravagant, only a modest couch set and coffee table, but on nearly every wall stood a bookcase. Every one of them was crammed full of books. Callie loved a good horror novel, which is what comprised most of her collection.

As she stepped out of the shower, she heard the phone ring. It was Walter. "Callie, I just got a phone call. Minus wants the presentation today."

"What? It's Saturday!" Minus was the director of their department at work. He had been known to have meetings and other business practices on such odd days as Saturday and holidays before, but this somehow did not seem appropriate to Callie. It seemed precocious, if she were reading it right. Walter had big delusions of grandeur about it, and she guessed he had inflated it for Minus as well.

"Yeah, yeah I know. He's itching. I think he wants to shock 'em all in the Monday morning meeting. Says he's been thinking about it since yesterday. It shouldn't involve parentage of the victims, but it does... And that's got him extremely interested."

"Well, well. Someone really is going to listen to us for once then?" she said, grinning. She shivered and stepped back into the shower to keep warm.

"Looks like it. He wants us to meet him at The Loft for lunch at around one. Can you make it?"

"Yeah, I can be there. Meet me at work then? We can ride together."

"You got it. See you there about noon thirty," Walter said, and hung up.

*   *   *

"No, you must be good," Daniel said. "There's no way anyone could have caught me. But you did. You on your quantum mechanics computer. That had to be it – that powerful computer that uses time for its bandwidth."

"Well I don't know how else to explain it, Daniel," Amalie said. "This computer doesn't use conventional processors and co-processors. It uses quantum mechanical, dimensional integration for its processing."

Daniel threw up his hands. "Who are you really?"

Amalie laughed out loud. "Who I am isn't really as important as you think it is. It's what I do that you are interested in."

Daniel did not see the difference. He watched her talk with her hands as she continued eating her eggs and bacon.

"Here's the deal. We have to get those seconds back," she said. Daniel stared patiently at her as she spoke. She looked up at him. "What, you're not going to eat with me?"

"Ate already."

"So if I can give you the information, and you can turn it into a quantum mechanical picture, then we can plug them back into the ether." Amalie held up a tiny piece of bacon and smiled before popping it into her mouth.

"The ether." He looked through the top of his eyes at her.

"Yeah. The Q computer kind of plugs into the ether, you know? That's how we access it."

"*Plugs into the ether?*" Daniel said. He looked as if he had sucked on a lemon.

"Not literally, of course. It just utilizes it. Like a ghost sucks up all the heat-energy from a room, this computer sucks up all the quantum mechanical 'nutrients' from the ether, and delegates them to specific tasks."

"Oh, dear God. Please don't tell me you believe in ghosts now. It will totally spoil my illustrious perception of you."

Amalie smiled pleasantly, but did not answer. After a few more bites, she dropped her fork and said, "Pretty cool stuff."

"Pretty incredible stuff. And how long has your company been messing with this shit?"

"Well, for as long as I've been there. The technology isn't new. I just helped refine the way we use it. But it was already in place for the most part by the time I got there."

"Well tell me about it! I want to know about it!" he said, waving his hands like a madman.

"My company has been experimenting with it for years. All we've ever done though was go into the future. That was rule number one. We never mess with the past. If you mess with the past, people will notice. Whereas if you change the future, they'll never be the wiser."

"So what was it like? Did you see sky cars and shit? Did you see the death of humanity?" He was getting excited, but still did not fully believe in the back of his mind that this was not some big show. It still seemed ultimately like a big ruse to him; he was just having fun participating in it for a while, and hoped it turned out to be real.

"No, no, nothing like that," Amalie said. "It was all very controlled and scientific. We never left the realm of our offices. And it was never anything more than a few minutes into the future."

"Oh. Well that's boring!" Daniel said, throwing his hands up.

"That's what we did, Daniel. I think it's fascinating to even conceptualize something so remote. Either way, that's what we did. Then one time I had a specific assignment in 2005. It was 2003, and I had to visit 2005 to conduct part of my experiment. And that's where I met you."

"Wow. You know this is some crazy shit you're telling me, Amalie."

"I know. Exciting isn't it?" she said, smiling widely. "You know you can't disclose anything I've told you, right?"

"Of course. I don't even know if I understand it well enough to concoct a coherent explanation. Regardless, I won't say anything."

"Good. So here's what I need from you. I need you to write a program that will turn this," she pulled a slip of paper from her purse, and handed it to Daniel, "into a digital schematic."

Daniel stared hard at the math on the paper. He did not fully comprehend it, but kept staring. Amalie stood up and looked over his shoulder, pointing at the paper. He could smell the bacon on her breath. He looked up at her, and she met his gaze, then returned to the paper.

"That represents a second, mathematically. It doesn't contain everything that happened in the second, it's just the shell. But if we can translate it into this," she pointed at another stem of the equation, "then at least we can return the seconds to their proper places." Daniel glanced at her from the corner of his eye. "In theory, of course," she said. "So I just need you to write the program that makes that translation. You can use that second as a test subject."

She then turned and slung her purse over her shoulder, and pulled her hair back behind her ears. Daniel turned to look at her. "Where you going?"

"I'm going to go take care of some things. I'll call you tonight. Think you can have it finished by then?"

Daniel nodded. "We'll see. Once I catch on to what I'm doing here, it shouldn't take long at all."

"Good. We *have to have this done* by tonight." She stretched and thanked him for breakfast, then breezed out the front door. It did not occur to Daniel that she must have been walking, as her car had been left at the Sour Apple the night before.

Callie stepped out the front door of her apartment and squinted against the sun. It was bright but cool out. She shuffled down the concrete stairs to the parking lot. Her car was cold, and her teeth chattered as she slid into the leather seat. She started the car, started the heater, and rubbed her mitten-covered hands together.

A fierce shiver shook through her as she sat warming it up. She was excited about the lunch, but nervous at the same time. Minus was always quick to jump on board with something, without even researching it first himself. He would buy into the next big thing compulsively, and regret it when he had lost his investment. However, when he did get to thinking, his ideas were sometimes so profound that it sent Callie and Walter back to the research lab with a completely new perspective on something they thought they had whipped.

Callie hoped Minus would hear them out. If they could not get him on board with their theories, they would have to start analyzing again, and probably from scratch. On the other hand, if he agreed with them, he would allow for funding into deeper, more interesting research altogether. Callie excited over the prospect again, and pulled out of the parking lot in a rush to find their future.

The roads were clear – even for a Saturday – and she pulled onto the highway switching stations on her radio. She checked her mirrors. Changed lanes. Sped up. She would meet Walter at the office. Of course, Walter would be a few minutes late, and Callie would be a few early, so she would end up waiting on him for at least twenty minutes, but today, that was okay. She had some things she could do at the office while she waited for him.

Callie instinctively turned down the radio as she approached the traffic tunnel, knowing there would be nothing but hard static as she passed under its half-mile enclosure. She rolled things over in her head, trying to gather her thoughts about the presentation. BAM!

"What the heck?" she said aloud. Her car began vibrating with a low grumble that sent tremors through the steering wheel and up her arms. Callie's heart pounded in her throat as she looked in her rearview mirror. Then another loud slam and grinding shot through the car, and chunks of black rubber flew past her windshield. The shock threw her forward against the steering wheel. She fumbled with the seatbelt, pulling it across her as she swerved badly through the tunnel. She could not get the tab into the slot. The car was shaking so badly now that she could hardly see out her windshield.

Callie gripped the steering wheel hard with her left hand as her right tried to bring home the click that would ensure her safety. Her hands were trembling badly, and the car was beginning to come apart. She was losing control, and she could tell by the way the lights on the ceiling of the tunnel were swaying back and forth, left and right as she sped along. She knew they ran down the center of the tunnel in a straight line. But for now they were swerving.

She finally found the brakes, and the car jerked hard to the right. *Oh no.* She gripped the steering wheel with both hands. Her knuckles went white. She was going to crash if she couldn't get the car stopped. Her small car jerked sideways with such great force she thought it would leave its engine on the road beside it. She swerved hard to the left and tried to keep from running up onto the curb. She was in the oncoming lane already, and thankful that the tunnel was empty. The reflective lane markers in the middle of the road played hard staccato on the car, vibrating everything in it as she swerved back to the right. Her hands were trembling even in their death grip on the wheel, and her heartbeat seemed a voluntary function, as she willed it to stay alive. *Please God don't let me crash,* she breathed out through tight lips. The end of the tunnel was within a football field. *A hundred more yards...* But the car showed no signs of slowing.

Her eight-cylinder engine screamed through the tunnel, echoing loudly through its cold emptiness. *Seventy-five yards...* If she could make it out of the tunnel, she could steer it down into the grassy ditch. Anything was better than a solid concrete wall at sixty miles per hour.

Then something else happened and the car jumped relieving itself of the hard vibration for only a second before it slammed back down on the cement and forced her head against the windshield. Her left hand went up instinctively, and as she recoiled from the impact, her right hand pulled the steering wheel slightly down. At sixty miles an hour on a curve, the car swerved hard to the right and hit the curb, slamming up onto the narrow side guard, no more than a foot wide. The right side of her car collided with the cold cement wall, sending a fury of sparks and a shout of screeching metal into the dark air. Over-correction was her final mistake, and as the car sped across the road and ran up onto the left embankment, she realized it. The left front corner of the vehicle slammed against the concrete, and her rear came around, sending the car into a hideous screaming spin of smoking rubber and grinding steel as the left rear hub tore into the cement. Callie was thrown hard against the door.

The car came barreling out the tunnel, spinning and screaming in the morning air. It crossed the road and ran up onto the sidewalk, then hit a fire hydrant. When it hit the deep-rooted hydrant on the passenger door, the car flipped over sideways, spinning roll-axis ten feet in the air. The engine died and the silent car landed on a steel guardrail, smashing the roof like a cheap wineglass under a heavy boot. Glass and plastic exploded out into the street as the car bounced off the guardrail and flipped two more times before landing on its wheels again and sliding thirty feet, sideways on loudly objecting tires and hub. It came to rest, rocking slightly, then settling completely, right in the middle of the road. Three long black tire marks and a single deep groove painted and ripped the warming pavement from the tunnel to the car a hundred yards out.

The roof was caved in so badly that the high point of the hood and trunk were a foot and a half above the high point of the roof.

*　　　*　　　*

Daniel's head lay still against the chair back, his hands resting on the keyboard. He snored loudly and his fingers twitched in his sleep. The phone shook him back to his own world and he threw his head forward, blinking rapidly. His heart beat like a bass drum in his chest; the phone had startled him. As he reached for the phone, his hand hit the computer mouse, knocking the computer back to life. His equation sat against a white background on the math processor application. He had never used the software until today.

"Hello?" he said, wiping the sleep out of his eyes. He glanced at the clock running in his system tray. It was almost eight o'clock. He had slept half his day away.

"You finished yet?" It was Amalie.

"Yeah. I think so. I got it here, but I have no way to test it. I ran it through a telegraphic command parser on the Internet, but it didn't understand the function."

"I don't know what that means, Daniel."

"What I'm saying is I have no way to test it. The parser couldn't find any errors though, so I think it's right."

"Good. Can you meet me here at work?"

"Yeah. You really work at Royal?"

"Yep. You know where the North Dallas Branch is, right?"

"It's off the Tollway and Beltline, right?"

"Well, stay on the Tollway service road for a while after you cross Beltline. It's about a quarter mile from the exit."

"Cool. See you in a few."

"Okay. Hey Daniel?"

"Huh?"

"Bring the math!" she said and hung up.

Daniel checked over his work again, and seeing nothing popping out at him, he exported it to a standard file and saved it to a memory stick. He threw on a thick flannel shirt and grabbed his keys. Within five minutes, he was out in the Jeep, backing out onto Lakewood Drive with the memory stick in his shirt pocket. The wind had picked up and was now a brutal gale against the windows of his Wrangler. The streets were wet, glistening in the cool darkness. He had a twenty-five-minute trip ahead of him, and slipped a hard-hitting CD into the player. Not only to keep him awake, but to keep him company.

Thoughts of what he was getting into still rolled around in his head. He was excited but skeptical. He was still not sure if he really believed everything Amalie was telling him yet, but knew that if it was true, he wanted to be a part of it. There was no doubt that some behind-the-scenes stuff was going on – to what end, he had no idea – but he definitely wanted to be included in it.

He had never believed in UFOs, though the allure did interest him enough to find out more about them. He had seen the videos and television shows about them, and done his fair amount of research on the Internet, but finally dismissed it all as bullshit and let it go. From that point he never cared much about it again. He had never seen anything clenching to change his mind. He figured if they were smart enough to traverse billions of miles of empty space, then what the hell did they want with us? *We can barely go to the moon!*

He did not put much stock in Bermuda Triangle mysteries, bigfoot, or anything else he couldn't see, either. Conspiracy theories, Illuminati, buried cities, dead presidents; Daniel had checked it all out. But it never held his interest – none of it – and for one common reason. Why? On what grounds would any of it be true? He did not buy it unless he could hold the product.

So why, he continually asked himself, *am I buying this time travel hogwash?* He could not decide whether it was the time travel aspect that had lured him in, or if Amalie had just seduced him. Either could be as likely as the other, he realized. She talked a good talk, but when it came down to it, it was all math. Everything she had said had been advanced applied math and physics. In order to ever apply the concepts to anything and make it useful, it would take a whole other set of beliefs. Daniel was perfectly willing and able – and for that matter, ready – to believe in the applied sciences. He just didn't know how much he believed in the 'applied' part. How can you apply temporal mechanics to lifestyle? Well, if things went the way Amalie was promising, he would be one of the first to find out.

When he finally pulled up outside the Royal Research complex, he idled slowly through the parking lot, looking for the door. There were three cars in the parking lot, one of which he recognized as Amalie's Mustang.

As he pulled around to the west side of the building, he saw Amalie poking her head out a slightly opened door waving for him to come in. He parked and met her inside. It was completely dark inside, and Daniel could see nothing but the exit sign looming above an invisible door down a side hall. Amalie took his hand and led him through the hallways until they reached a gray metal door and entered the stairwell.

"What the hell are we doing in here? Don't you have elevators here?"

Amalie turned on him, quickly putting her hand to his mouth. She whispered in his ear, "Quiet! We're not supposed to be here!" Daniel's heart suddenly sank. Here they stood in an eerie concrete stairway that ran from the basement floors all the way to the top, twenty-some-odd floors above him, and it was not even legal. The stairwell was slightly illuminated by the exit signs above every door, but no more than a single candle lights a dinner table. The white handrails were thick and cold to the touch. The only sound came from their soft steps, which echoed through the stairwell like dripping water in a cavern.

"I thought you said you worked here Amalie!" he whispered. He could barely see her two feet in front of him as she led him up the stairs. He did not want to be going, but he wasn't going to sit back and wait by himself, either.

"I did!"

Daniel shook his head. "What floor do we have to go to?"

"Thirteen," she whispered.

Dammit. Can this get any creepier? "And what exactly is it we are doing here?"

"We have to get the computer, Daniel. Would you please shut the hell up?" She had stopped halfway up a flight of stairs and was facing him now, a silhouette against the soft light of an exit sign.

"I thought you already did that!" he whispered more loudly.

"I didn't get a chance! Now come on," she commanded.

He followed blindly as they trekked up the stairs. The black placards on the walls by the doors indicated the floor numbers. The last one he had seen had told him they were on four. Then a loud bang sounded somewhere in the stairwell above them.

Amalie grabbed him and pulled him quickly toward an outer wall, covering his mouth. He was beginning to catch on. *I did.* Had she meant, "I did say I worked here" or "I did work here"? Daniel thought. She must not own an RRC badge after all. They waited for the footsteps that were sure to come. And they did. Quietly, somewhere far above, the sound of hushed steps made their way down the stairs.

"Shit!" Amalie said, and quickly yanked him toward the next door, ten steps above them. They dashed as quickly and quietly as they could, and she grabbed the steel handle. It would not budge. "Here, try it." He tried, to no avail. It was locked. A badge reader mounted on the wall by the door shone a small red service light.

"Don't you have a badge?" Daniel said, pointing at the reader.

"It's been disabled, Daniel. Come on, we have to get the hell outta here!" They turned and dashed back down the way they had come, stopping on every landing to listen for the footsteps, ever present, and growing louder. They finally reached the first floor and sprinted for the exit. Locked.

"Dammit! We're trapped in this fucking stairwell!" she cried. Daniel's heart pounded hard and fast, and his hands trembled. "What are we going to do?" Amalie stared at him like a lost child waiting for answers.

"I don't know. Wait..." he held his hand out to silence her. "Listen."

The footsteps above had vanished. But there was a new sound, more inaudible than the footsteps had been. Daniel squinted hard, trying to make out what he thought he saw. Finally he pointed. On the stair flight above them something protruded from the edge, beneath the rail.

Leaning in and putting his mouth directly against Amalie's ear, Daniel spoke as quiet as a whisper in a dream. "I think that's his foot." He could feel Amalie tremble as she moved closer against him. Her eyes were wide with fear as she looked at him.

"Holy shit. Holy shit!" Amalie whispered through heavy breathing. Daniel stood sideways on the stairs with Amalie right behind him; she looked over his shoulder toward the stairs above, at what appeared to be a foot. Her mouth was in his ear. "What are we gonna do?"

Daniel raised his hand and put his finger against her lips. "Quiet!" he mouthed.

A footstep. "Who's there?" commanded a voice.

Daniel's heart pounded hard in his chest, he felt Amalie squeezing his arms from behind. The dark protrusion on the stairs above was no longer visible. *It had been someone's foot!* There was nowhere to go but...

Another footstep. *What the hell is he doing?*

Finally Daniel made a command decision, a foreigner in this strange building. He slipped sideways down the stairs with his hands on Amalie's hips behind him. They crept quietly down the steps, one at a time, staring upward toward where they had seen the foot. Daniel had no idea what waited below, but only hoped there was a way out – or somewhere to hide.

Another footstep. "Hey! I know you're in here! Stay where you are!" the voice demanded.

"Go!" Daniel said. And the chase was on. The shadow above was now in pursuit, two flights behind, putting him directly above Daniel and Amalie. Everyone involved now knew there was no point pretending; everyone knew it was a chase. Amalie was pushing Daniel from behind, forcing him down the stairs. They came to the basement level, a T into a hallway that ran interminably into the darkness in both directions. Daniel broke to the left, pulling Amalie close behind. Machinery hummed as they ran, and fear clung to them like cat fur on a velvet jacket.

Daniel was running with his hands out in front of him, hoping the hallway would not end. With no clue where he was going, his heart pounded in his throat. A faint glow from a digital clock lit up a side room, and they swung the corner and ran through it. Then the hallway continued back to the right. They were heading back the direction they had come, but down a hallway parallel to the original. There was nowhere else to go – at least not that he could see.

Their feet scuffed on the hard floors as they ran through the warm darkness of the long corridors. Daniel could feel his way. He no longer ran with his eyes, but rather his ears and his feeling. It proved not to be enough though.

His left leg hit it first, mid-shin. Before he realized what had happened, he was flailing through mid-air, Amalie right behind him. His foot had caught the low end of an industrial mop bucket, and he was now on his way over it, his foot dumping it over. And he had been in sprint. Amalie shrieked as they flew through the air. Daniel crashed down on his knees in water and pain, and slid with the mop bucket still beneath his left leg. Amalie was right on top of him.

The bucket tumbled loudly through the hallway and Daniel heard the slam of the wooden mop handle coming down on the hard floor. Water poured across the hallway like a tidal wave, soaking his entire front side immediately. The water smelled like raw sewage as it soaked through his clothing. He was sprawled across the floor on his chest, his arms flailing as he lost control of his legs. The shock to his knees had rendered them temporarily useless. Then the broad arc of a flashlight came banging into the hallway, presumably from the security guard behind them.

"Fuck, I can't get up!" he cried. Amalie was already up trying to steady herself. "Fuck I can't get up! Help me up!" His heart was racing.

"Shhh! I'm trying!" Amalie could not get him up without falling herself, so she resorted to dragging him by his hands through the nasty water, down the hall. Daniel heard the humming and tumble of an ice machine on the left behind Amalie. "There must be a doorway near," she whispered. She was right. She slid him into it and pulled him back against a counter.

"Ow-ow-ow-ow!" He was grimacing. "I think my leg's broke…"

Then they heard a slip and a loud crack, then a split second later, the muted thump of a body hitting hard. It sounded to Daniel like a melon hitting wet pavement.

The light from the flashlight swooped through the room and across the ceiling on its way down. Then there was a hard metallic clank as it deadened itself on the wet floor. The whole incident was barely audible above the icemaker and Daniel's complaining, but it was loud enough to tell them what had happened. "What was that?" he said, already knowing the answer.

"He's down." Amalie stood quickly and searched for a light switch. "What the hell kind of place is this? There're no lights!"

Daniel spoke quietly, driving his earlier point further, "You're the one that works here, remember?" His hands were on his left knee. It had hit hard, and his ribs and chin had taken a hit as well. But the knees had hit the hardest, and first.

"Daniel I need a light! Give me your lighter!" He fished his Zippo from his jeans pocket, soaking wet with dirty mop water, and handed it to her. "I'll be right back," she said.

Amalie crept down the hall slowly, cupping her hand around the flame of the Zippo. Within a couple of seconds, she was no longer visible. She had disappeared into the darkness along with the small flickering light of the Zippo.

Daniel leaned his head back against the cabinet, trying to keep quiet, the angry hum of machinery a few feet to his right. "Amalie!" he whispered loudly. What the hell was she doing anyway? He figured she wanted to determine the condition of the chaser, but now was uncertain that it was the best idea. What if their pursuer was already back up and coming? What if he got Amalie? And what, he thought, if there is more than one of them?

A place like RRC would have tighter security than a single guy in a stairwell. If there was one, there would be another. And what about the cameras that were surely filming them? *No way it'd be this lax. There's definitely something going on.* And Amalie was probably caught by now. If she was caught, he was caught. There was no way for him to get away in his condition, without a shoulder to help carry his weight. His knee burned badly, but he could at least feel his foot and toes again. And he could move his feet, which was a definite improvement to just a few minutes ago.

Everything he knew about Amalie was pouring through his mind. *If she doesn't really work here, then we're screwed. We didn't even arrange a plan if this is a breaking and entering. I'm not even familiar with the building. How does she hope to pull this off without at least knowing something about their security?* He finally let it settle, realizing that having gotten in the building in the first place would have been a feat if she was not really employed here. *Something is definitely going on though.*

He thought he heard a yelp, and then it was silent again. "Shit. Amalie!" There was no way she could hear him above the ice machine, he realized. He would have to yell at her. He was better off remaining quiet. *No. Fuck that. I can't even move.* "Amalie!" No answer.

After what seemed like an eternity, Amalie came wandering back through the doorway and nearly tripped on Daniel's legs. She came down onto her hands quickly and whispered in his ear. "Daniel we have to get out of here," she said, and he could hear her heart beating behind her whisper.

"Why? What happened? What did you see?" He was already trying to get up. Sharp pains shot through his entire leg and up into his pelvis. Amalie put her arms around him and helped him to his feeble feet. As her face rubbed against his, he noticed she was sweating.

"I'll tell you later. We have to go."

With his arm around her, she helped him down the hallway, opposite the way they had come. In the hot dark corridor, they made their way slowly, stopping every few yards so he could rest. When they finally made it to the corner of the hallway, some hundred yards from where they had been slumped, they turned right and headed, presumably, back toward the original staircase they had come down. What good that would do, Daniel could only guess, but at least there was the hint of light from the exit signs. Here he could not see his hand in front of his face.

After a long time wandering in the basement, they came to the staircase and crawled up silently. Daniel felt the cool air in the staircase, a good fifteen degrees cooler than the stuffy basement corridors had been. On the first landing, Amalie finally spoke.

"I need to find a way out of here. If all else fails, there may be a loading dock or something that runs into the sub-basement level, but I have to find it."

"Don't you work here, Amalie? Don't you know where the hell you are going?"

Amalie snapped back, "I never had to work in the damn basement, Daniel. I work on thirteen. I've taken the stairs down once, on a fire drill."

Daniel shook his head, more angered by his injury than by her ineptness. She continued, "I'll make my way up and see if I can find a way out," and she started up the stairs.

"Wait, wait, wait!" Daniel said, shaking his hands. "Go down! There won't be an exit up there!" What good did an exit on the roof do? She had made the point herself about a loading dock under the building. It had only seemed appropriate.

"Well I still have to get the computer, Daniel!" she said, leaning toward him in the darkness.

"But your badge has been deactivated!"

"There's no reader on thirteen." And she was gone – running up the stairs and out of his sight.

Daniel sat on the cold concrete, back against the wall, on the landing between the basement and the first floor. He realized his vulnerability with a start. *Oh shit. If someone else comes, I'm a sitting duck...* Listening to the sound of her footsteps dwindling away above him, he tried to judge what floor she was on, and keep up with how far she had gone. But he couldn't. And suddenly the footsteps stopped. His eyes were wide open, staring into the black stuffy basement below. It was too dark to see beyond the T of the corridor – a small area of the basement floor. Indeed, he was a sitting duck.

Daniel waited patiently, the fire of his bum knee burning his leg and head. An abundance of patience was not something with which he had been blessed. He was bad in lines, worse in traffic, and horrible when there was no estimate of how long he would be waiting. In this case, he really didn't even know what he was waiting for. Amalie would try to get the alleged computer, then assuming she was successful, she would leave it with him and try to find a way out.

Daniel leaned his head back against the painted cinderblock wall. The pain was incredible. And it was getting worse. *Just hold on, Daniel. She'll be right back.* He closed his eyes. *Just a little while. She'll be back.* He took a deep breath. And quicker than he could have imagined, he was out.

CHAPTER SEVEN
Reconnaissance

Walter was pacing. He had been calling all day but could not get in touch with Callie. He had gone by her house, called all the hospitals in the area, and the police. None had been fruitful. Now he was back at the office, pacing behind the row of desks lined neatly across the middle of the floor. Had he called the police back later in the day, he would have heard about the car accident. But it had been his first phone call, save the calls to Callie's home, which had been unanswered. Now it was getting late. *Where the hell is she?*

He had called to cancel their lunch meeting with Minus, as Callie was indisposed. Walter had not told Minus that he couldn't find Callie – he had simply said he wasn't able to get in touch with her, and thought he remembered something about running out to Midland today to see her folks. Minus had been disappointed about it, but cooled quickly. "Okay," Minus had said. "Then be in my office extra early Monday. Six o'clock?"

Walter had said okay, and spoken for Callie as well. This was obviously all-important to Matt Minus, so he would make sure and swing by Callie's early enough Monday morning to get her up and moving in time for the meeting.

After hanging up with Minus earlier in the day, he had had to settle for the altogether less appealing truth, which was that Callie was nowhere to be found. She really would have told Walter if she was going anywhere, and probably would have brought him along if she really were going to see her parents. And certainly after agreeing to meet him at work for their meeting, she would not have taken off somewhere. Walter was patient; not the most patient of patients, but he had enough to get him by. He had waited all day for a status report from Callie. At least a *Hi, I'm okay*, but had not gotten it. And he had been patient. But now he paced, scratching his chin. *This is ridiculous.* He was about ready to give up. What more could he do but wait? He could go home and have a beer on his sofa and watch the news, waiting for Callie to call him. With nothing else to do, he left a note at Callie's console in case she happened to drop by, and left the building, turning only to lock the heavy glass door.

Daniel was awakened by the sound of a fierce alarm wailing in the night. His pillow felt hard and unyielding, his head a wreck of pain and confusion. He turned over, pulling the covers up around his neck and grabbed for a pillow to cover his head. He needed to block out these alarms, so damn loud. There was no blanket to pull up though, and there was no second pillow. His first pillow, the one he laid his head on now, he was beginning to realize, might not be a pillow at all. He finally gave in to the curiosity and opened his eyes. There was not much to see, and it was louder than a foghorn in a library. He shook his head quickly and looked around, his eyes adjusting, and realized he was not in bed. The faint red light he had presumed to be the alarm clock turned out to be an exit sign, and his hard pillow was the concrete wall against which he was leaning, head cocked to one side. *Where the hell am I? Why did I just sleep so hard?*

The alarm was still sounding when he realized where he was, then considered how long it had been sounding. Five minutes? Maybe. That sounded reasonable at least, but there was no way to tell. He vaguely remembered Amalie leaving him sometime before, but was not sure of that either. He heard a loud slam and shook himself awake. He was in a building, in the stairwell. And he was waiting for Amalie. And alarms were sounding. *What the hell am I doing here?* Daniel stood up and darted up the stairs to his right, getting only to the first one before collapsing from the pain in his left knee. *Son of a bitch!* He tried standing again, but had to grab it tightly to get it to stop throbbing. He managed this way up the entire flight of stairs, gripping his knee tightly. Once he got there, he remembered the badge reader. They were trapped in here. Hearing the faint sound of footsteps creeping slowly toward him from somewhere, he turned around quickly and peered into the darkness.

There was no one.

Above the intense sound of the alarm, he could not tell from which direction the footsteps were coming, only that they were slowly but surely growing louder. They sounded labored and determined. His memory snapped again, offering him another image of his past. The man. The mop bucket. The accident, the *cause* for his injured knee. *Oh shit. That asshole is awake and coming.* And there was nowhere to go but up. If Daniel went down, he would run right into the security guard. If he stayed here, he was caught either way. *And where the hell is Amalie?* He thought better than to turn and try to book it up God knew how many flights of stairs, chancing that he would never find an exit that worked.

Something pinged his consciousness. Alarms. Exits. *Fire alarms…* He glanced back up at the exit sign, then at the badge reader beside the door. The light on it was green. *If there's a fire, the badge readers have to step aside.* Daniel slammed through the door and into the unfamiliar corridors of the main floor. Without having any clue where he was going, or how to get back to the front of the building, he hobbled through the floor. The white strobes of the fire alarms sliced through the darkness reflecting indiscriminately across everything in their path with an eerie unkindness. Daniel headed down the hall to the left. Either way was as good as the other. Dragging along the narrow corridors, he made his way through the building, passing nothing that looked familiar.

He passed miles and miles of cubes and office doors until he began to wonder if he was going in circles. *There must be some outer circle I need to get on.* He came through another office area that looked just like every other cube farm he had ever been in, and turned to the right, pushing through a door that opened on the other side of the office. He hobbled through a bright-lit office with a long row of desks in the center and out the other side. There was a steel door just ahead of him. The exit sign above it was not lit, but he could read it. *Bingo.* And he slammed into it. It would not budge. *Dammit!*

Daniel spun on his heel and sped up his gait as much as he could muster, trying to backtrack. He was lost in an office building. At least if the cops showed up, there seemed to be plenty of desks under which he could hide. He dashed back through the bright room that seemed so out of order with the rest of the cubed offices, and back into the mix he had been in before.

After several long minutes wandering again, he passed a steel door that bore some familiarity. It blew open like a gate in a tornado and a familiar face came bounding out of it.

It was Amalie.

"Holy shit," Daniel said, covering his explosive heart with a hard hand. "You scared the hell out of me! Where have you…"

"Here, take this – we gotta get outta here!" Amalie said, forcing a heavy metal case against his chest. He followed her quickly through the darkness, limping with a grimace on his face. The pain wasn't important. Amalie was carrying a black box over her shoulder that had two other black boxes hanging from it by a belt, and she was running. They pushed through a narrow door on the right, then walked down a long curved hallway he had no memory of, then through another door, and they were out in the outer circle.

"God I'd hate to work here," he said under his breath. "Like a damn maze." They were walking presumably along the front of the building, with glass windows to their right, when they finally came to the glass door that led out into the night. Amalie pushed against it, but it did not budge.

It was locked.

"Oh shit!" Daniel said. He felt the vise of cold fear wrap hard round his spine. He felt that if he didn't keep moving, it would overcome him, and he would be paralyzed. "What the hell are we going to do now?"

"I don't know. I don't know how it got locked." Amalie was spinning around in search of answers.

"Well are you sure this is the door we came in?"

Amalie opened her eyes wide and darted her head toward the parking lot outside. Daniel could just make his car out through the tinted glass and the darkness outside. She was right. This was the door. The fourth car he had seen when pulling up was no longer there, leaving his, Amalie's, and another, presumably belonging to the man lying in the mop water. Someone had left and locked the damn door.

"Is there another way out? We better haul ass, Amalie!"

"It's on the other side of the building. It leads out to the back patio and the smoking area. That's the only other exit though, and it's always locked," she said.

"Yeah I think I ran into that one." Daniel looked up and down at the glass door that separated them from freedom, and finally stepped back and said, "Fuck it" before kicking the glass. His foot bounced hard off the glass the first time. He kicked again, this time with the heel of his boot, and the glass split neatly up the center. Another kick took the pane and dropped it on the cement outside the door. It sounded like raining steel as the glass shattered and exploded into millions of chalky pieces. Lights began to come on at the far end of the room.

"Hurry! Go, go, go!" Amalie said, pushing him along.

They stepped through the doorframe and crunched across the glass running for the parking lot. The immediate relief from the terrifyingly loud alarm inside was almost breathtaking. Daniel had almost grown accustomed to the wailing sound, and now to be free of it was a pleasure he would not have considered. He reckoned it was like the kid born with a painful illness; he never realizes the pain is there until it's gone. The only hint of the alarm now was a faint muffled version he was not sure was even real. It might have just been his memory and the echoes of the alarm in his pounding head.

They lugged the heavy equipment to Amalie's car and hoisted it into the trunk with loud grunts. "What the hell is in these things?" Daniel said, slamming the trunk.

"It's the computer. Let's go," she commanded, and they tore off out of the parking lot. Before shutting the trunk, Daniel had gotten a glimpse at the computer components Amalie had been carrying over her shoulder. It was a daisy chain of black boxes that looked remarkably like cassette carriers. Each was about sixteen inches long, five or six inches wide, and about four inches deep, but evidently very heavy. The material that housed them was black and shiny like nylon; almost identical to the soft pouches that housed those tape carriers. Between the three long boxes were short sections of nylon belt and cables. The box on the top end of the chain had a cable running out of it with a cannon plug on the end, and a nylon handle for carrying the whole getup. Though Daniel had been in the computer industry for better than a quarter of his life, he had never seen anything like this equipment, and it looked to be serious shit.

"I think you have some explaining to do Amalie," Daniel finally said.

She turned to look at him across the darkness of the car, the gauges the only light. "About what?"

"Why the hell are those alarms going off? I thought you worked there! Why didn't your badge work?" Daniel was shaking his head quickly as he spoke, angered with not being left out of the loop.

"They deactivated it because I lost my job. I think they had a feeling the quantum computer might have been a culprit in the disappearances, so they let me go."

"Horseshit! It's not like that's the only quantum computer in the world!" he said, trying to sound authoritative on a subject about which he knew less than squat.

"Actually, yes it is. There were two other prototypes in existence, but they were decommissioned a couple of years back," Amalie said, looking back at the road. Both her hands were on the steering wheel, which Daniel found himself appreciating.

"So why'd they fire you? Didn't they ask you if you knew anything?"

"Yeah, it's a long story, Daniel. But that's not the only thing that led to my termination. There were some other things going on too. A lot of it is classified though."

Daniel scoffed, then almost laughed. "We just committed a felony! We just broke in and stole a computer – probably worth thousands and thousands of dollars – and broke back out! And you are afraid you can't disclose some little secret they made you swear to?" He was trembling. "What kind of sense does that make?"

"Calm down, Daniel. I've told you everything you've needed to know so far. And I've told you everything you've asked. I'm just saying that most of what I did was classified, so you shouldn't be surprised if there is more than one factor affecting my dismissal. Go ahead and smoke if you want. Just roll the window down a little."

"You know what though?" Daniel asked, holding up a finger. "That was pretty easy, considering."

"What do you mean?" Amalie said, looking at him. The darkness framed her face mysteriously.

"Well there was only what – one guard? One guard in that whole building? And the computer was on a floor with no badge reader? And it's one of a kind?"

Amalie smiled mischievously. "That's why we had to do it tonight, Daniel. I didn't want to tell you before, because I was afraid you wouldn't go through with it. They bring the security system down twice a year for maintenance. Tonight's the night they brought it down."

"What kind of shit is that? They only have one guard there when they bring it down?" Daniel said.

"One guard? Where do you keep getting this idea there was one guard?"

"Well there's only one car in the parking lot."

"Daniel, there's a whole parking garage beneath the building. They have their own entrance. That place is crawling with security right about now."

Daniel was shaking his head. Somewhere out in the night, something was calling him to believe in this woman. He didn't know why or how, but he was determined to see his mission through. He had never been a part of something so exciting. The whole thing felt like a conspiracy – it *was* a conspiracy – and he loved being a part of it. Something that meant something. Though he knew he was now a criminal. And the mistakes he had made inside the building started piling up in his head. He had just assisted Amalie in stealing the supposed only working quantum mechanical computer in the world, and was now on the run. And he had not even worn a pair of gloves in the building. Of course, he had not known that he would be aiding her in a robbery, nor had he known she no longer even worked there. And his fingerprints were probably on a myriad of walls and doors in that building now.

He puzzled over a hundred things trying to straighten them out in his head. Then his stomach sank. The hundred things racing through his head could have been in a circus had they only jumped through hoops. They scrambled like eggs in a hot pan, dashing in and out of his conscience, then one single thought had broken the ring, and everything went silent. Everything but his heart.

"We left my fucking Jeep in the parking lot," he said, and felt the horror wash in over him as a police car flew past them silently with rack lights blazing. The fear of being caught – not the consequences, but just being caught – was the most powerful ploy against crime. And now he felt his cheeks flood with it and his ears began to burn. He had never been so afraid in his life. And he thought it couldn't get any worse. Then Amalie spoke, and it did.

"Yeah, well when I just told you that you could smoke, I looked down and remembered I don't have one of those push-in lighters."

*   *   *

Walter found himself speeding, and he didn't really
know why. His nervousness about Callie's welfare had
begun to take over functions of his body he was not
used to giving up control over. She was his closest
friend, and with her gone – missing – he was worried
sick. He realized he was going to have to accept the
fact that she was not just gone. She was missing.
Something had happened to her. It was so out of
character for Callie Simmons to behave like that,
Walter simply would not believe it.

He dashed through stoplights just before they
turned red, and flew around corners carelessly,
altogether driving like a total maniac. He had driven all
over town, and was now on his way home. At least if
he was at home, Callie could find him. He glanced
repeatedly at his cell phone every few minutes,
wondering if he had missed a call. Maybe he would
drive by her apartment on Shady Shores one more time.
As he rounded Willow Bend and approached the
intersection of King's Trail, he saw the lights of a train
in the distance. If he sped up, he could beat it…

*   *   *

Amalie looked back over her shoulder again. They
had passed several fire trucks now, sirens wailing.
Daniel had done nothing more than stare out the front
windshield into another zone. He was shaking his head
disbelieving of his incriminating stupidity. In the end

Amalie had reminded him it was her own stupidity that had dropped the Zippo and left it lying in the puddle by the security guard. And there was not much that could be done about it any rate. It was there, it was done, and he was out.

Both Amalie's and Daniel's fingerprints were on the cold steel of the lighter, so it didn't take a rocket scientist to figure out they were nailed. With the fingerprints and the initials *DMB* (Daniel Matthew Brandt) engraved on the side, there was nothing about the lighter Daniel did not hate right now. But they couldn't well go back and collect it.

Amalie had told him about the condition of the security guard, too. In the flickering light of the Zippo, she had seen the man lying in the puddle of blood and water; his face dead of emotion. He had still been breathing, but was definitely unconscious – and possibly comatose. He had fallen on his left leg, too, meaning his right leg had hit the puddle and slid forward so rapidly that he had collapsed on his left leg before he could even try to correct his footing. By the time he hit, he was already spilling blood into the cold soapy water on the linoleum floor of the basement.

The feeling of being completely sunk in their crime was eating away at Daniel's stomach. He felt like throwing up, but had nothing in his stomach with which he could part. He wanted so badly to smoke, watching his stress burn away with each ring of the cigarette. But with no lighter, and no idea where they were going, he had resolved to keep silent and try not to wake the spirits of sickness. He had a better chance of keeping his sanity if he could just get past the shock of having left his fingerprints and initials at a crime scene. He said a silent prayer for the security guard's welfare –

but hoped secretly the man would not remember any details.

The guard's condition had been an accident, surely, but it sure would look fishy with a two-million-dollar computer in the trunk. Amalie had corrected Daniel's 'thousands and thousands' estimate. Deep inside he knew – they both knew – this was not something that would just blow over. But realistically, there wasn't much they could do now, but run. And thinking about all the mistakes they had made at the scene was no way to keep their heads clear for the hard part. Inevitably, the hard part was yet to come.

After about fifteen minutes of running red lights and cutting through parking lots, Daniel finally had to ask where the hell they were going. "Back to my place. No one knows where I live, we'll be safe there."

"You said you don't have your house key…"

She looked sharply at him, then grinned. "Well, I'm counting on you to get us in there."

"Yeah, but you said you were on the third floor… Not a chance, remember?"

"I'm sure you'll figure something out. Can you think of somewhere else we could go?" Amalie seemed rather confident in his abilities considering she had condemned them earlier.

"Well, are you sure it's that safe? I mean – *no one* knows you live there?"

"Yeah. I signed the lease under a fake name." She stared at Daniel in the pale light of the sweeping streetlights. Daniel could tell she did not want to give him that name. He waited patiently to hear it though, and she finally gave in. "Amy Ireland," she said, then looked back at the road just in time to see the train she was about to t-bone.

"Holy shit!" Daniel yelled as the tires locked up and screamed at the asphalt. White smoke bellowed out from the tires as the hood slid under the striped roadblock. The car came to a stop with the arm of the roadblock touching the windshield. More important to Daniel, though, was the distance between the train and the front bumper. It was probably six feet, but from Daniel's position, it looked more like three. Amalie's knuckles were white on the steering wheel. She stared wide-eyed at the flashing lights on the cross arm, sitting directly in front of her face, just the other side of the cold windshield.

Daniel noticed her breathing as heavily as he was. "Holy God, I'm glad you looked up in time!" Amalie was frowning though, and Daniel frowned back at her, not quite understanding why. "What?" he said. Her gaze was concentrated on the rearview mirror, so he turned to look out the back windshield. There was a black Suburban not two feet behind their back bumper. All Daniel could see was the grill. And then it started moving closer. "What the hell?"

"Pull down the back seat and get the computer out of the trunk," Amalie said, calm as a lake at midnight. Daniel saw her pull up the handbrake as he leaned his seat back and twisted in the seat in an effort to retrieve the computer and its mysterious daisy-chained pack. The back seat came forward easily enough, then he scooted up in the seat, stretching his arms into the darkness of the trunk. The bump was soft enough that Daniel did not feel it, but he heard the tires skidding on the asphalt as the truck began pushing them toward the extremely fast moving train. He looked back over his shoulder and saw the cross arm was sliding up the windshield with a screech as they inched forward. He knew if the driver of the Suburban wanted, he could easily slam on the gas, and there would be no inching. There would be footing. Yarding. And they had no more than a couple of yards.

"Come on! Hurry up, Daniel!" Daniel snapped off his seatbelt and climbed full over the seat and into the back, stretching long into the trunk. He could feel the car being pushed now, its back end slightly lifted as the car tried to resist motion with its grinding brakes. He finally felt the fabric of the pack's handle, and yanked it hard through the opening and into the back seat. He then stretched back again, fingers feeling for the metal case of the computer itself.

"Let's go!"

"Hang on, I can't find it!" The front bumper was now a yard away from the screaming locomotive.

"Come on, Daniel! We have to get the hell out of here!" she screamed. The loud clanging of the safety bell tore down her screams. Aside from the slow grinding forward of the car, it was also rocking violently back and forth from the wind of the train.

"Dammit!" he yelled back as his fingers finally met metal. He yanked it through the small opening, banging it against his head as he passed it to the front. "Here! I got it, let's go!" He shoved the case at Amalie, then grabbed the daisy chain and pulled it over his shoulder and into his lap as he slid back into the front seat. "Shit, this thing weighs like seventy pounds!"

"Okay, as soon as I let go of the brakes, this car's going into the train," Amalie said, talking extremely fast. "We're gonna have to get as far away from it as we can. You go first. Take off toward the direction it's coming from, I'll follow you through your door!"

Pretty smart, Daniel thought. The train was moving from the right to the left, so when the car hit it, that was the direction it would go. And if they were running the other direction…

"Go!" The crossbar was above the windshield now and raking across the roof of the car with a loud squeal. Daniel reasoned they were not being slammed into the train because their pursuers must know about the Q computer. They would not chance losing it if they knew it was in the car. They were simply sending a message. Yet it was not relenting, and they were inching ever closer to the train. Was this a loss the bunch in the Suburban were willing to sacrifice?

Daniel pushed the door open and slung the pack over his shoulder as he bolted out of the car heading toward the train's rear end. "Hey wait!" she screamed and he stopped, turning around. "I need you to grab this!" She was leaning over the passenger seat pushing the case at him. Daniel was trying to cover his ears against the noise of the train and the clattering bell, holding the pack up high. He ran back and grabbed the case, then took off the other direction again, as he heard a door open on the Suburban.

As soon as Amalie let go of the brake, the car would spring forward like a wind-up racer. She put her left foot on the brake and threw her right leg over the console. Then in one deft move, she yanked herself out of the car and onto the asphalt, rolling free of the vehicle as it shot forward and slammed into the steel wheels of the moving train. The crash was horrifyingly loud and disconcerting. Daniel had stopped fifteen yards up the grass, and was watching as Amalie gathered her feet and took off running for him. The car was immediately lifted and flipped on its top, ripped to shreds as it was pushed down the rock-covered roadside showering sparks and glass over everything within a ten-foot radius. The Suburban had stopped and now a window rolled down, where a man shouted something incoherent at them. Another man was out of the truck now, and circling around the back.

"Come on! We have to get on the other side!" Daniel said. "Can you carry this?" he held up the case as they ran. She snagged it from him and ran past him as he hobbled along. Another shout came from one of the men, but once again it was garbled by ambient noise. Another door slammed, and muffled shouting could be heard as the men tried to communicate above the thundering noise of the train.

"Follow me!" Daniel lined himself up with the train and lay beside the track, counting the wheels as they rocketed past. The wind beside the train was like a hurricane. When the next opening appeared, he placed the daisy chain under the train onto the ties as carefully as possible, and Amalie had to grab his arm in order to avoid it being severed. Then she followed suit with the computer case. The yelling was getting closer, and Daniel thought he could make out the words *just want to talk to you!* That did not sound like a realistic option though.

"Hurry!" Daniel said, then looked up and rolled over the steel track, burning his wrist on the way. He had not considered how hot the rail would actually be. The wind had been fierce beside the train, but underneath there was almost none. It was a vacuum as the train sped past a foot and a half above his head.

Amalie, he noticed through the broken view between speeding wheels, was already out on the other side. He looked toward his feet and saw the computer and its daisy chain still on the tracks with him. "Amalie! I need you to grab these!" She nodded and crawled forward, then threw her hand under the train and grabbed them one at a time. He was surprised she could hear him above the roaring freight. Daniel was also surprised by her strength, due to how easily she seemed to be able to handle the heavy equipment.

She yelled something at Daniel, but he could not hear it. "What?" he shouted, checking the coming cars every few seconds. She cupped her hands around her mouth and shouted again, and he could hear her voice, but could not make out what she was saying. He shook his head and shrugged. *Fuck this, I'm getting out of here first.* Then he noticed Amalie grabbing the computer and its accompaniment. She was slinging it over her shoulder struggling against their combined weight.

Daniel realized it had been her steps he had heard in the stairwell when he had been awakened by the alarms. Initially, he had thought it was their pursuer coming after them again. But now he realized she must have been extremely labored by the weight of the computer as she hauled it down all those stairs. In much the same way that she was hauling it away now. *Where the hell is she going?* He looked back at the coming train and realized he had been under it for quite some time now. How long had it been? He could not tell.

Daniel began to panic about getting out. It had seemed so easy at the time to get under it. But now that he was stuck here, he was afraid to make the dive out on the other side. The train seemed to be moving a lot faster from this perspective. From the outside, its speed was evident, but not nearly as intimidating, as he could see a more broad scope of it. But from beneath, it was a rocket all around him, and he was having difficulty seeing the spaces between the wheels. He looked back at the side he had come in under and saw better light there. But on the side he needed to exit, it was almost completely dark, thus making it harder to distinguish between the blackness of the night's background, and the dark wheels ripping past. He heard rocks move on the side where the men were, and looked back to see feet running along the tracks.

Daniel finally resolved to take his chances. It was absolutely necessary for him to get out from underneath this train, especially if he wanted to catch up with Amalie, who he had last seen trotting off down the grass in the direction the train was moving. Why had she abandoned him here? Perhaps he had fulfilled his obligation to her, and he was no longer of any use. She had needed him to help her break in and steal the computer, and have someone to pin it on – leaving his car and lighter at the building – and now she no longer needed him.

If the guys who had been shouting at them were still out there, and the end of the train flew past over his head, he would be left lying on the tracks out in the open. He would make an easy target, he thought.

Daniel's hands were shaking badly, and he was beginning to get dizzy. He could count the wheels on the brighter side of the track, then take his chances rolling backward over the rail behind him, but it didn't feel as comfortable under contemplation to him. He wanted to see where he was rolling. And he was running out of time. *Time,* Daniel thought, *is not without its price.*

By the time Daniel looked forward again, he realized his chances of getting out from under the train safely had probably vanished. He could see, just on the edge of his visibility, a low-hanging coupling moving toward him. In the darkness, black against a black background, it was closing in with astonishing speed.

His eyes widened with horror as he realized it was going to hit him, no ifs ands or buts about it. There was no way he could avoid it; he could not sink low enough on the ties to duck out of its way. And he had lain there waiting too long for a good opening. Justice was steaming in swiftly, and it would tear him in half longways.

CHAPTER EIGHT
Regrouping

The darkness was more than just frightening. It was a constant nag on the conscience of its captives. The steady sound of traffic was the only source of relief to break the monotony of the silence. The sounds of ambulances and fire trucks had long since abated, but she could still see the flashing red and blue lights of the squad cars reflecting off the walls of the tunnel above. The water had been pouring in on her for the last six hours as she drifted in and out of consciousness. The rocks and mud caked on her face were cold and nasty smelling. She realized her vulnerability lying in the gutter beneath the surface of the street, and shivered every few minutes with fear, apart from the cold shivers that had been persistent throughout. But at least she was alive. Callie Elaine Simmons truly understood what it was like to have a second chance – that is assuming someone found her down in the gutter before it was too late. She hadn't the power or lungs to scream, and was doubtful it would help anyway. She had heard the echoes of machinery and saws as those above had ripped her car apart trying to find her within. How long would it take them to realize it had not been a ghost car? How long until they realized she had gotten out, and rolled to her safety into a gutter? From the sounds of the effort, it had become evident to her that the car was beyond totaled.

A draft and the hollow noise of wind blowing through a tunnel were ever present at her knees, as they were lying in the water right at the intersection of the sewage pipe. All Callie kept thinking about was Pennywise – the monster clown from one of the horror novels she had read – and every time, she shuddered. *That's what I get for reading so many horror novels. Any second, his claws will reach into the gutter and rip my life away.*

She was pretty sure her hip was broken, as she couldn't move the leg she lay on, and probably a couple of ribs, and her left arm. The events rolled through her head like a slide show as she remembered exactly what had happened. It was not a vision she was likely to forget anytime soon. She had been leaning on the door with the handle readied when the front of her car had gone over the curb on its way to hitting the wall. An instant before impact, she had pulled the handle and let the inertia do the work. The door had swung open like a shotgun, and Callie had rolled right out of it. In that split second where she had been thrown free, the car hit the wall, the door hit the front of its swing, and slammed back hard, closing as though it had been kicked by an angry god. Had she been stuck in the middle, it might have cut her in half. When she hit the pavement, she intended to roll to the edge – which she did, in fact – but had kept going. The velocity of her carriage had been badly misjudged. The Mercedes had slammed against the wall and started spinning; the terrible sound of tires screeching and wailing in the cavernous tunnel. And she had just kept rolling. Callie rolled right off the edge of the earth and into a dark cavern within the cavern.

It was a good ten minutes after the initial shock of landing that she was finally able to gather her bearings. The stars in her head and spots behind her eyes were too strong and bright beforehand. She had thought she was dead. But the confusion had dried up and blown away with the soft draft she heard whispering to her like a low howl from across a canyon. It was a haunted sound accompanying the rain that poured softly over the edge of the street and into the gutter to join her.

So alone in the dark she lay, watching the reflection of the lights dance around the dirty concrete walls. There was nothing new, no new sounds or feelings. She was bored with the thought train that had been nagging her all day; there was nothing new to think of. She was stuck and she knew it. There would be no hope of getting out unless someone was to come rescue her. And what if they didn't? What if no one ever thought she might be down there? Surely someone would notice that the car they pulled apart had no driver. Surely they would search for the driver who must have been ejected from the moving car. But what if they didn't? Callie had run these thoughts over her tired mind repeatedly, almost expecting a new reaction – or at least a different one. But this was never the case, and there was nothing she could do about it. She could not even scream. *This must be my fate. To die at the bottom of a rain gutter because no one was smart enough to look down here.*

✷   ✷   ✷

The screaming of the train overhead was loud as a weather siren, and for the last split second of his awareness, Daniel accepted the fact that he was about to die. With all the bullshit he had been through in his life, the stupid choices he had made, the ignorant way he had casually walked the wrong road so many times, this was it. *To survive all that shit, only to die under here.* But he accepted it, and laid his forehead on the rocks as he prepared to have it all ended for him. Then it happened. The ripping sensation was incredibly fierce, and he could feel himself being bodily moved like a rag doll. He thought at the brink of his awareness he could sense voices. Perhaps they were there to welcome him to the afterlife. But he could not tell what they were saying. The shaking of his head slowly made him aware that his head was shaking though. The ripping sensation finally began to creep into his mind, and he realized he was being ripped sideways – not long-ways. This was all wrong! Then he opened his eyes and realized his eyes were opening – he was not dead.

As he lay there blinking away the wonders that had inadvertently taken control of his thought process, he came to see the shape of a figure looming over him. It was not Amalie. After a few seconds, color began to fill his vision again, and he could see it was a man, and he was frowning at Daniel. "You okay, man?" his voice was deep and comforting, and though he spoke softly, it carried above the rumble of the train which now seemed distant.

Daniel looked around and tried to sit up. "No, I don't think so. What the hell happened to me?" He could not see clearly, and could not really tell where he was or on what he was lying.

"You almost got run over by the damned old train," the man said, nodding in the direction of the thunderous locomotive. "You're probably a little dizzy 'cause your head whipped around when I pulled you out. I think another second and you'da been done for."

Daniel finally found the strength to sit up, and looked around. "Where's Amalie?"

"I'm here, Daniel." Amalie was standing right behind him. "If you can get up, we need to hit the road. We are still being chased, and I don't know how much longer the train will protect us." Daniel turned to look at her. "This man's going to give us a ride."

Daniel remembered the chase that had put him under the train in the first place, then stood wearily. "Come on, Daniel! We have to go now!" Amalie had to steady him as they trotted to the car.

"My name's Walter," the man said on the way to the car.

"Daniel. That's Amalie." Amalie opened the back door and helped him inside the Durango. "You got the computer?"

"Yeah, it's already in the back," Amalie said, and the door closed.

A moment later, the front doors closed and the truck was moving. As Walter made a U-turn, he pushed in the lighter and spoke. "What the hell are you guys running from anyway?"

Amalie stared at him for a long moment, then answered, a blank look on her face, "You know, I really don't know. Thank you for driving us though."

"No problem. Do you mind if I smoke?" Walter said.

"Smoke? Oh holy God, I need a cigarette," Daniel chimed from the back. "I've been without a lighter for the last hour or two, and Am doesn't have a lighter in her car."

Walter held the pack over his shoulder for Daniel. "No thanks, I have cigarettes. Just need a light."

Walter handed the car lighter back to him, then lit his own, and they smoked. Amalie shook her head. "You smokers are going to be the death of me."

"So how'd you end up under that train?" Walter asked. "And where are we going, by the way?"

"My apartment," Amalie said, as if Walter should know where she lived, then continued. "Well, we were sitting at that intersection and this Suburban pulled up behind us and started pushing us into the train. I had the brakes on and everything, but my car was grinding forward. So we got out and ran, and they started shouting at us-"

Walter cut her off, "Shooting at you? Son of a bitch!"

"No, shouting at us. I could tell they weren't there to have a tea party though, so we dove under. I don't know who it was. I have an idea, but can't really be sure."

"Well for God's sake, if he's shooting at you, I hope you know who he was! Sounds like someone wants you guys dead! It's gotta be someone you know, right?"

"Walter," Amalie said, looking over at him patiently. "Shouting. Shouting. Not shooting. Shouting. Like yelling. But no, I don't know."

"So who are you, Walter?" Daniel asked, coming to her aid. He knew Amalie was in a tight spot, and did not want her to have to answer just on the foundation of this guy's generosity.

"Who am I?"

"I asked you first," Daniel said.

Walter laughed easily, then said, "Well, no one, really. I was sitting there at the intersection, and I saw her come out. Then she pulled out the computer, but she kept staring under the train, crawling back and forth like she was looking for something. I was beginning to wonder if she needed help. Then she ran over here and asked me for it. She said that you were still under there, so I ran up and yanked you out."

Daniel looked back behind them to see if the train was still visible. It was not. They had traveled too far already. He could see no sign of the Suburban either, which comforted him.

"As soon as I pulled you out, one of the train cars had this big ass…" He was making a shape with his hands.

"Coupling?" Daniel said.

"Yeah, coupling. Anyway, I was just wondering why you guys would get under there in the first place. But none of my business. No big deal. Just glad you're okay."

Daniel was eyeing him. Amalie was eyeing Daniel. "Thanks for taking us, Walter," Amalie said. "Hope we're not pulling you from anything too important."

"Ah, you know, not really. I was driving around looking for my friend. She's usually at home on Saturday evenings, but I haven't been able to find her all day. It's like she… disappeared." Daniel and Amalie were staring at him, as if waiting for more. "Well, not like – disappeared, you know – but, well, I don't know. She's just – you know?"

"Not really. What are you talking about?" Daniel said.

"Well, I mean I don't think she '*disappeared*' like the ghosters, but I can't find her. You guys know about the ghosters, right? The people that…"

"Disappeared. Yeah, we know about them," Amalie said. "How can anyone not know about them?"

"Yeah, well. Weird stuff, you know?" Walter pulled from his cigarette.

"Yeah. So you've been driving around all day looking for your girlfriend?" Amalie was looking at Daniel as she spoke.

Walter coughed. "No, she's not my girlfriend. But yeah. Well, no. Not all day. I mean, I've been looking for her all day, but I just started driving around looking a few hours ago."

Amalie and Daniel stared blankly at him. "What?" Daniel finally said, spreading his hands. She had been giving him a look he did not understand.

"Nothing." Amalie stared out the front window.

Daniel thought for a moment, then spoke again. "Where are we going?"

"My apartment," Amalie said, shooting him another look he didn't understand.

"I thought you didn't have your house key."

"I don't."

"Where is your key?" Walter asked.

"It's a long story." After a moment she saw he was not letting up. "I keep my house key on a different ring than my other keys. And I seem to have misplaced it. So I'm locked out of my apartment."

"Then why are we going to your apartment?" said Daniel.

"I can pick locks, by the way," Walter said.

Amalie looked at him for a moment, then said, "Good. That works out nicely. See, Daniel? He can pick locks."

"Uh huh." He leaned forward and put his elbows on the back of the front seats, taking a drag from the cigarette. "How much do you know about the ghosters?" Amalie shot him a quick look. He winked at her.

"Well, not much. They all have one date in common, that's about all I know."

Amalie looked at Walter, frowning. So did Daniel. "One date?" Daniel asked.

"Yeah. They were all descendants of someone conceived on April 21, 1896."

Daniel leaned back in his seat, perplexed. *What the shit?* Amalie returned her gaze to the front windshield. Through the darkness and the smoke in the Durango, Daniel could see her smiling smugly to herself. She was proud of something.

CHAPTER NINE
Realization

Callie awoke into another cold reality. She had passed out again. She shivered hard, remembering the accident that now seemed so distant. How long had she been down here now? It surely had to be almost eight hours, she thought. With so many different parts of her body aching and screaming, she knew she had to have broken bones. She could feel the swelling in her arm, and could not move it. And without the ability to scream or call for help, she had long ago given up the belief that she might live through this. At some point after that, she had also given up her dignity, not seeing much point in holding any longer, and had thus let her bladder release. As she lay in the cold running water that poured in from the dirty street, she shivered and bled and worried.

Humility, it seemed, was happy to be in here with her, but that – aside from fear – was her only company.

Her head had landed in such a way that it had come to rest on her left arm, by the wrist. If she could just roll off it enough to move it a few inches, she could look at the time. Her wristwatch would give her at least a clue as to how long she had been down here. It would, she thought, be near impossible to read in the utter darkness, but what the hell else did she have to do?

She rolled her head back, slowly and carefully, and onto her back. Her head came to rest on a squealing pillow, which felt for an instant very pleasant. But the squealing part came so suddenly that her head jerked forward in start, and the realization that it had been a gutter rat came over her. Without the strength to hold her head up any longer, it fell back on the concrete with a wet thump, and bolts of pain shot through her head, chasing stars. *The rats are going to eat me down here? As if it couldn't get any worse, now the rats are going to eat me?*

She shivered again, and her teeth chattered. She could not any longer feel anything below her waist. She began to wonder if she had been paralyzed. Surely not, as she could not rightly remember her back being twisted or – for that matter – even hurt at all. Callie was a strong girl, but she had no illusions. She had barely survived what surely would have been a deadly accident. Just the sounds of the saws trying to open her car had been evidence of that, she thought. But to what end was her survival? To die in a drainage gutter was hardly an improvement over the swift end a car wreck could have brought her.

And suddenly the silence was broken by voices from above; faint, but deep. Her body tingled with excitement, and the prospect of rescue. Two men, she thought. Their words were few. The water moving through the gutter drowned out what they were saying, and she could just tell they were there.

An indeterminable amount of time passed. If she could just scream, or even say something, maybe they would hear her. Were they still there? She tried to speak but her voice was too soft and only cracked when she opened her mouth. She certainly could not scream. Her arm felt like it was broken, bent up behind her head. If she could bring it down to meet the other, then she could clap… But her arm did not want to move. If it was not broken, it was definitely asleep.

Then she remembered something her mother had told her as a child. Her mother always told her, "When the world brings trouble, whistle a little tune…" So that's what she did.

Callie blew ineffectively through cracked lips, huffing and puffing like a woman in labor. She could not get a whistle out. She licked her lips and tried again, and got a slight note. Then she gulped and licked and turned her head up out of the rainwater and blew again. It came out sounding like a steam whistle on a ship. A long beautiful loud whistle escaped her lips and pierced the silence that had been nearly overwhelming.

A light. One of those big black steel flashlights, she thought. Callie could hear its metallic clunk against the concrete. She squinted against it as it broke the darkness in the gutter. It was like a nuclear blast and it burned her eyes like staring at the sun. In darkness for several hours now, her pupils had become the size of dimes.

"Hello?" Holy God, someone had found her.

*   *   *

"Well I'll be a son of a bitch," Daniel mumbled to himself. Walter met his eyes in the rearview mirror. He smiled and smoked.

"What?" Walter finally said. Amalie stared at him. "Did I say something?"

"Well, I'm just thinking about that date you said," Daniel said holding up a finger. "What was it? April…"

"April 21, 1896." Walter was frowning now, as if there was no inherent reason why Daniel should be so interested in that date. And technically, he was right. Though Daniel had never flat out heard that date before, Amalie had rattled off all its components the night before.

"So, Amalie…" Daniel said, perhaps a little loudly. But Amalie turned and put a finger to her lips. She had to remind him to keep quiet. This was classified information and they were in the presence of a perfect stranger – albeit one who seemed to have a clue what had happened. Daniel realized he had been on the verge of blurting out their little secret – the whole reason for their running with the computer. But now he leaned back and sat silent. Amalie would take over from here.

"Walter, can you tell me how you came to know that date?" Amalie said.

Walter looked at her blankly, then returned his gaze to the road. "Yeah. I work at Royal, in the SA division. It's basically our job to know numbers like that."

Amalie's eyes went wide, and she blanched. Daniel even flinched from the backseat. *Did he just say Royal?*

Walter continued. "We're basically just a statistical analysis bunch. We find commonalities, stats; shit like that. It's actually rather boring unless you just love numbers." He turned to look at Amalie and flinched. "Are you okay? You're whiter'n an albino mime in a snowstorm!"

"Sorry. Just lost my breath. So you guys were assigned the task of finding a commonality between the ghosters then, huh?" Amalie nodded slowly.

"Yeah. That's us. Why? You know something else about them?" After a thoughtful pause he continued. "I'd be interested to know more about them."

"What do you think the importance of that day is, Walter?"

"Well I have no idea. That's what I'd like to know. Why? Do you know?" he looked back at her for a moment, then drew the window down and flicked his cigarette out. The wind blew in loudly before he rolled it back up. They were approaching the Airport Tunnel, so Walter clicked off the stereo.

Amalie did not answer. Daniel was again beginning to seriously doubt Amalie worked at Royal. The rollercoaster ride that was his belief in her was on another valley. But he was still on her team. He had been relieved to see she had not deserted him under the train, after all. It was Walter's face who he had first seen, but only because Amalie had gone and enlisted his help. It appeared as though Walter might be getting an idea about what was going on, so Daniel spoke up for her. "Amalie has theories about everything, Walter. Don't get her started, or you may never hear the end of it."

Walter laughed. "Yeah I can go on and on about theories as well. I've been known to..." He trailed off as he slowed the truck and leaned forward, frowning out the windshield. "Holy shit!" He put on the brakes and slowed to see better. There were thick, dark black skid marks running all the way across the smooth concrete of the tunnel road. There was also a large gouge taken out of the concrete, as though a tire had come off. They went all the way to the opposite wall where the car had presumably hit, leaving white paint on the wall and hundreds of shiny plastic shards on the ground beneath. The skid marks were obviously from tires moving sideways. They continued off the wall and out of the tunnel about twenty yards ahead, making large loop-the-loops as the car had spun out of the tunnel at a high velocity.

A police cruiser stood parked in the opposing lane of the tunnel, half up on the curb, its lights banging silently off the walls. Two officers stood at the front of the vehicle, one on the radio. Walter was now creeping along at about five miles per hour as he peered at the evidence. Daniel noticed that Walter was now pale.

As they approached the cruiser, the officer not on the radio waved them on, but Walter instead slowed and rolled his window down. The officer shouted, "Keep it moving, please." Walter looked back over his shoulder, and seeing no other traffic, ignored the directive.

"Officer, I'm worried this might be my friend. What kind of car was it?"

The officer looked around impatiently, then approached the open window. "We've already taken the car to the junkyard. It was totaled."

"What kind of car was it?"

"I don't know. The wrecker and all the emergency crews have left already. We've been looking for the driver though. The car came out of the tunnel empty, apparently."

"Looking for the driver?" Walter said, putting the truck in park.

"Yeah. Think we just found her," the officer said, spinning to point his flashlight at the rain gutter across the road, just in front of the cruiser.

Walter's door was already open and he was running across the road, ignoring the officer's instructions to move the truck. And now there were cars slowing behind it. "Where is she? Down there?" Walter shouted over his shoulder.

"Hey, sport, you're going to have to move your vehicle. You're holding up traffic."

Daniel got out of the back seat and climbed into the driver's seat, pulling the door closed. "I'll move it." The cop nodded a silent thank you, and turned back to Walter, who was trying to see down into the gutter.

"Yeah, she's down there. We're waiting for an ambulance now," the officer said.

"Well let's get her out of there! I can take her to the hospital in my truck," Walter said, and began taking off his coat.

"I'm sorry, who did you say you were?"

"I didn't. Callie, is that you?" he shouted into the gutter. Loud whistling came banging back out at him, confirming his suspicions. "I'm here now. We're gonna get you out of there, just hold on." The whistling continued, sounding more excited now. "It's Callie. My girlfriend," Walter said, turning back to the officer.

"Well we can't move her, she might be injured!" the cop said.

"What do you think the medical techs are going to do? Leave her down there?" He dropped his coat on the ground and began scooting over the edge down into the gutter. "Daniel! Come help me get her out of here!"

*   *   *

The warmth inside the Durango was pleasant to Callie, though she was not yet benefiting from its effects. It was like running her hands under a warm faucet after throwing snowballs for three hours; the air felt cool against her skin. Nonetheless, she could feel her skin coming back alive. They had put her in the back of the Durango, where the third row seat was folded down, and were rushing her to the hospital. The back vents were blowing full blast directly on her. Some chick named Amalie was sitting sideways in the seat right in front of where Callie was lying. She kept looking back at Callie, and was holding her hand. "You're gonna make it, girl! You're gonna be fine!" she kept saying. All Callie could do was lie there and shiver.

The passing streetlights coming in through the tinted back windows did not do much to help Callie make out her company's face. With nothing but the pain running through her veins, Callie had to keep her mind off it with something. She made it a mission to see this girl's face. She could not hear what the two in the front seat were talking about, but she could hear their voices. Occasionally the woman in the back seat would pipe up and say something, and Callie could not understand that either. It was muffled through the thick seat and the powerful air.

Callie remembered being a little girl riding in the back of her mother's station wagon. She would climb all the way in the back and remove the lower parts of the sideways seats, then close herself in with the top parts. All she could hear was muffled radio and highway noise, rumbling away beneath them. One time she had pulled down too hard on the seat tops and locked herself in. They were on an hour-long trip to the shopping mall, and she had to wait until they arrived to be let out. There was no way to get her mother's attention from way in the back, closed in the kids' seat compartment. She felt vaguely like that now. Only now they were going to the hospital. Her mother had died many years ago now, but somehow Callie felt some comfort in this attractive similarity, and it eased her mind. She was deathly afraid of hospitals. The highway noise helped assuage that fear. She closed her eyes for just a moment.

Bright purple spots blazed by and noises like footsteps and talking slowly became familiar. She wearily opened her eyes and had to immediately shut them against the bright lights above her. A blurry black figure loomed above her, slightly moving back and forth as he pushed the gurney on which she lay. He noticed her awakening and smiled at her – that much she could make out. But the rest was hazy and distant. "You're doing fine, Callie. You're in a good place now, you can relax." She felt oddly like the cart was turning and the room was spinning, then the voices grew muffled and the lights dimmed. A crash shook her back to her labored senses, and she realized she was being pushed through steel doors.

Callie heard a few familiar words, but for the most part it was medical jargon. She was in a hospital. Her eyes widened, her pulse quickened, and her instincts told her to scream. The black man at her head made a nodding gesture, and the gurney came to a stop. The lights above were bright again, but seemed less concentrated somehow. She felt herself being hoisted into the air and into a softer, altogether more comfortable mattress, then a prick in her arm. Her reflexes commanded the withdrawal of her right arm, but it would not budge. She moved her head back and forth, or she thought she did, trying to gain some composure – some control of the situation. But her head was already braced in place in order to prevent further injury.

That voice again. "Okay, Callie, we're going to make you very comfortable. But I need you to answer a couple questions for me, okay?"

Callie tried nodding, and felt much accomplished, though in reality her head had barely moved. The room around her seemed to be slipping away. It seemed distant and unimposing on her space.

"Are you allergic to any medications that you are aware of?" Callie shook her head as best she could. "Okay. Have you ever been in a hospital before?" Nodding. "How long ago was that, Callie? Was it very recently?"

Callie rocked her head back and forth again. It had been almost twenty years since she had last been hospitalized, and she had prayed every night for years that she never had to experience that again. The whole reason behind her going – as if it weren't bad enough – was like a walk in the park compared to that resulting hospital visit.

Having fallen from a high tree limb, she had hit several branches on the way down. That had produced only bruises. But when she hit ground it wasn't soft grass; it had been the stone landscape around the trunk of the tree. The doctors had told her mother that had she landed in grass, she might not be in such a situation, but the hard stone had broken her arm and her hip, and busted her head open.

As she lay there in the hospital screaming with the pain of a broken child, they had set the fractures and began stitching her head – all of which she could feel. The Versed had not fully kicked in, and the surgeon had not wanted to put her under – for fear of a concussion. Thus Callie had lain there in indescribable fear and pain watching arms move over her face in a dizzying array as they sewed up her head. It took hours to get things back in place and put her in the plaster casts. Her first and only hospital visit had left a sour taste in her mouth, and she was not happy to be back. But at least she wouldn't die in a gutter. Not to mention being eaten by the damned rats.

Daniel and Amalie sat waiting in the lobby in uncomfortable plastic chairs. The inpatient lobby was definitely better suited to long-term guests. There were a few magazines, none of which appealed to either of them, so instead they talked.

"I can't believe he works at Royal," Amalie said.

Daniel turned to face her. The chair squeaked and moaned beneath his weight. "So do you know him?"

"No. It's a big company, Daniel. Lots of people."

"Well I saw you freak out when he said he worked there. Why is it such a big deal? I mean, I realize it's a secret – I guess. But why?"

"Well, for obvious reasons. I don't want everyone knowing it was me that caused the sudden ghosting of two hundred thousand people!" Amalie stretched her arms above her head then crossed them. "Besides, unless we plan to enlist his help, there's no reason to tell him. We don't even know him."

Daniel nodded. "Yeah, I know. But he seems cool enough." After a long moment, he spoke again. "It's funny, I'm beginning to believe more and more what you tell me."

"Why's that?" She looked at him with raised eyebrows.

Daniel shrugged. "Walter spit out that date like his birthday. It was the same as all those long ass numbers you were quoting last night. Right?" Amalie nodded, amused. "Yeah. It adds a lot more plausibility to your story. However weird and wild it might seem."

"Well I'm glad you're finally beginning to believe."

"What do you think…" Daniel trailed off as Walter walked into the room.

"Hey, guys," he said quietly.

"Hey," they said in unison. "How is she?" Amalie asked.

"She's recovering. Looks like she's gonna be okay. Pretty beat up though. Surprisingly enough, nothing is broken. It looks awful though, all bruised."

"I bet," Amalie said. "Poor thing."

"Yeah, her whole side's blue as a depressed Smurf holding his breath. She's smiling though. Well, she smiled when I went in to talk to her. She seemed happy to show me her 'battle wounds'."

Amalie smiled at him. "That's good to hear. How long will she need to be in here?"

"Maybe a day at most. They have to treat her for a mild case of hypothermia on top of all her bruises. Poor girl was colder'n a Popsicle in the snow. She'd been in that gutter for most of the day, I guess."

Amalie was shaking her head in sympathy. "Well I hope she gets well fast. Hey, I appreciate the ride, Walter. And I'm glad you found your friend."

"Yeah, she's been through a lot the past couple of days. She needs a bunch of rest and relaxation. You want me to go ahead and take you guys home?"

"NO!" Amalie said quickly, almost shouting, then cleared her throat. "I mean no. But we do need to get the Q computer out of your truck." *Shit!*

"The what?" Walter said, frowning.

"Computer. It's still in your truck, you know?"

"Yeah but did you call it a-"

"No. It's a laptop." Amalie stood up, stretching. Her face was flush.

"You guys are into something aren't you?" He was grinning fiendishly at Amalie. "You called it a Q computer. There's only a couple of those in the world, you know? Not that I actually believe they work."

"Actually there's only…" Amalie halted. "You know what? I really don't know what you're talking about." She was already slinging her purse and heading for the door. She had stepped off her safety ledge and was treading in trouble. Daniel was shaking his head, staring at the floor as he followed them out. Walter looked at Daniel for confirmation of his suspicions. Daniel's smirk must have crossed the Ts for him, because Walter started smiling again and put his arm around Amalie's shoulder.

"Come on, guys! What is it you're trying to hide?"

"Nothing at all, Walter. What makes you think we're hiding something?" Amalie stopped in the hall and looked seriously at him.

Walter dropped his hands to his sides and the smile left his face. "Well, you're just acting very suspect. And I heard you say Q computer! I know what that means!"

Daniel finally jumped in to rescue her, as he felt she would be cornered into talking if Walter didn't back off soon. He grabbed Walter and Amalie both around the shoulders. "Let's get outside so we can smoke, what do you say, Walter?" They started moving again.

"Do you know what a Q computer is, Walter?" Daniel said as they passed through the exit. Walter instinctively handed him his lighter, and Daniel lit a smoke.

"Well yes. It's a quantum computer," he said. He took the lighter back and lit one of his own.

Daniel opened his mouth to start talking, and then stopped. He shook his head quickly. "What?"

"A quantum computer. Though I've never heard it called a Q computer before, that's got to be what it stands for in the context, I gather."

Daniel shook his head again, playing a very convincing part. "Walter, it's a Compaq. A Compaq notebook. Nothing special about it." Daniel saw the relief spark in Amalie's eyes as she realized the rescue. Now he only hoped she had caught his drift.

"Then why'd you call it a Q computer, Amalie?"

"That's the letter on the cover. The big red Compaq Q. I call it my Q computer. It's my buddy," she said. *Yes. She had picked it up perfectly.*

Walter stood back and lightened up visibly. "Oh. Oh." Then he laughed. "I thought you... Ha! Come on guys, I'll open the truck for you." He smiled and started for the parking lot. "Here I was thinking I had some grand system in my truck!"

Daniel glanced at Amalie, whose face looked a little pale. It had not seemed like Walter was even aware the company he worked for owned a quantum computer, but it was certainly better not to take any chances. After heisting a two-million-dollar machine from Walter's company, Daniel was not ready to tell him anything.

What an amazing coincidence that the guy who saves my life happens to be an employee of the company we just robbed. Daniel decided he should get out of the theft business right now, while he was on top of his game. Only one robbery under his belt, and he had already run into enough conundrums to make him crazy. If he was not caught and arrested, he would for sure be checked into a mental clinic.

As they walked down the ramp to the lot, Daniel saw Walter looking back over his shoulder at him. "Compaq notebook," he said, shaking his head. "My God, how dumb do you guys really think I am?"

CHAPTER TEN
Rationalization

The night outside had grown even colder. Amalie had been quick to mention it was cold enough. But now it was colder. She pulled her collar up and took quick short strides, hugging herself on the way to the Durango. Walter was dashing along beside her, his cheeks comically red in the cold air. He was shuffling with his hands in his pockets trying to keep up with Amalie. Daniel was hanging back, watching Walter make a fool of himself trying to hit on a woman who had the capability of making him disappear with a blink. Daniel could tell Walter was very attracted to Amalie though. *Who wouldn't be?*

"So you guys stole that computer didn't you?" Walter stared at Amalie. "That's why those people were chasing you. Right?"

Amalie dropped the proverbial ball and let a smile creep across her lips. She shook her head slightly, but the smile meant more to Walter. He smiled back at her as they walked.

"Ha-ha! I knew it! So tell me, Amalie, what are y'all doing with a quantum computer anyway? You know how to use it?"

Amalie stopped in her tracks. "You sure are bold aren't you?"

Walter stopped smiling. "Hey, you can tell me. I'm not gonna bust you guys!"

"Thanks." She started walking again.

"Come on, Amalie. You have to let me see this thing work. I have always been curious about that stuff. Have I told you what I do?" Amalie did not answer. She kept walking. They finally arrived at the Durango and stopped. Walter stood staring at her.

"You wanna open the door so I can get my stuff?" Amalie said and raised her eyebrows.

"Uh uh. No, no, no. You have to answer me first!" After a delicate pause, he continued. "You see, I'm a statistical analyst, so we are crunching numbers all day."

Amalie cut him off. "We?"

"That's Callie and me."

"Whoa, wait. What? She works at Royal too?" Amalie said, holding a finger up.

"Yeah. We both have for the last almost five years. Why?"

Amalie was shaking her head. "What, does everyone work there?" She turned to look at Daniel. Daniel raised his hands in defense. Finally Amalie continued. "Okay so you guys crunch numbers. What does that mean to me?"

"Well, nothing as such. I mean – I'm just trying to say that I'm at least a fairly smart guy, you know. I read a lot of stuff. Hawking, Thorne, Gribbin. So I kind of have an understanding of quantum mechanics."

"Thorne? As in Kip Thorne?" Amalie was shaking her head now, her mouth twisted.

"Well, yeah. He's a theoretical physicist, you know? And," he said, holding a finger up, "might I add, a personal friend of Stephen Hawking's."

"So? What does that mean to me?"

"Well, I don't know. I don't know. I just…" Walter stood staring at her for a moment, then added, "What?"

"I didn't say anything!" Amalie raised her hands in defense.

"Well, you were giving me shit about mentioning him! He writes a lot about space and astrophysics and whatnot, but he at least has an appreciation of quantum mechanical application within the big scale. You know, the-"

"Yeah I know. The flashlight and the mirror. The spaceship in the black hole. I've read it." Amalie looked at Daniel. He was staring blankly between Walter and her. He had never heard of any of the authors Walter had mentioned, and here Amalie could seemingly quote from the books. Daniel was out of his element, and dared not enter the conversation.

Amalie continued. "So you think having read Gribbin and Thorne qualifies you somehow? Is that it?"

Walter shrugged. He started to talk, then stopped. He sighed. "I don't know. I guess I just want you to know that I kind of understand it. I'm at least well read. I'm fascinated by this stuff. Give me the chance to check it out! Please!" He was flashing his million-dollar grin.

Amalie was forced into smiling back at him. His polished white teeth and his gorgeous face got her not only smiling, but nodding. Daniel shook his head. *What is this prick trying to pull here? He think he's a movie star or something?*

She suddenly stopped smiling as if it had dawned on her. "Okay. Let me in so I can warm up. We'll talk about it in there."

Walter smiled again, then unlocked the doors with his fob, and walked around to the other side. Amalie got in and quickly turned to Daniel, who was in the back seat. "Help me out of this, Dan. We can't let him take us home now."

He gave her a neutral look. Daniel still didn't even know what the hell he was doing here. He had written the conversion program for her, but beyond that, he felt useless. He had no understanding of the science, and thus found no reason why Amalie would even keep him around. Whatever Amalie felt like he owed her for hacking her system, he felt he had more than repaid by now.

Walter opened the driver's door and got in, starting the Durango. The heat immediately came back to life.

"What do you think of all this, Daniel?" Amalie rested her chin on her arm on the seatback.

Daniel shook his head resignedly. "I don't even know who the hell y'all were talking about."

"Most people haven't. It's all nonfiction. They rarely make the bestseller lists. Though I think Hawking did." She stared pleasantly at Daniel for a silent moment, then turned back to Walter.

"So what is it you want me to tell you? Or show you, rather?"

"Well, I want to see how the computer works, of course! I mean, I did save your lives…"

"You saved *his* life," she clarified, pointing a thumb over her shoulder. "It's just a laptop, Walter."

Walter screwed up his face and leaned his head back. "Whatever. What a gyp. So you guys want me to take you home or not?"

"Nah. We can hoof it," she said and opened her door. "Come on Daniel, we've got a long walk."

Daniel closed his eyes and shook his head. *Dammit! There goes our ride.* He didn't know how long of a walk it was, but with his busted knee, the distance was irrelevant. He would be hobbling the whole way, in agony.

"Thanks anyway, man. Nice to meet you," Daniel said, reaching forward to shake Walter's hand.

Walter shook his hand and smirked at him as Amalie closed her door. "So you taggin' that?" he said, thumbing towards Amalie.

"What do you think?" Daniel said, and slammed the door behind him. *Fuckin' pig.* Amalie rounded the back of the truck and retrieved the computer and its daisy chain, handing the heavy part to Daniel. He took it unconsciously, and closed the door. *I love that guy.*

The road was narrow and shiny with rain, and had almost no shoulder. The edge of the asphalt was rough and hard to walk on, and the ground off the edge was too steep to walk on, so Daniel and Amalie trudged along down the road, in the middle of the lane. Daniel's cheeks burned with the cold and his lips and mouth were dry. They were walking against the wind, and had been trekking for nearly fifteen minutes before Daniel finally broke the silence.

"So why are we walking, Amalie?" Daniel shifted the weight of the daisy chain to his other shoulder. Carrying a bag of concrete any distance got shitty real quickly. And that's about how much this thing weighed, he reckoned. He had a very expensive, very powerful, very neatly packaged bag of concrete on a strap over his shoulder.

She looked at him. Daniel tried to read her expression, but could not. "We couldn't let Walter in on it, Daniel. He works at Royal. That's bad." After a lengthy pause, she added, "Besides, he knows too much already."

"Well I just don't understand why we couldn't let him take us home. I mean... You wouldn't have had to tell him anything, you know?"

"I don't want him knowing where I live, though."

"I see," Daniel said, but he didn't. His knee felt as though it had been closed in a vise. "How about a cab? You know, we could call a cab, and-"

"It's only a couple of miles, Daniel. The fresh air will be good for us."

"Yeah, easy for you to say. You're carrying a laptop. I'm carrying a fuckin' bag of concrete. I need to walk like I need to slam my fingers in a trunk."

"Oh, quit your bitching," Amalie said and grinned at him. Daniel didn't think it was very funny.

The rest of the way they walked in silence. There was not much they needed to discuss in Daniel's mind. He tried to keep his mouth closed to keep the stinging cold air out of his throat. It took them nearly an hour to devour the rest of the two miles, and Daniel could feel it in his thighs when they finally slowed their brisk pace entering the parking lot of the apartment complex. He sighed heavily.

"That wasn't so bad was it?"

"Hell yes, it was. I walk for nothing, Amalie."

Daniel leaned against the rail outside Amalie's apartment. He hoped she had not forgotten that they had just walked about two and a half miles, only to arrive at a place they were locked out of. "So how are we gonna get in?"

Amalie trudged her way up the last of the steps and rounded the corner to the front side next to Daniel. He was wondering how the hell he had beaten her getting there with a bum knee. As she approached the door, she stopped right in front of him and hunched her shoulders. Then she leaned forward and planted a heavy kiss on his wind-chapped lips. He was too stunned by the action to say anything.

"You don't think I'd let us walk all that way only to arrive at a place we'd be locked out of, do you?" Then she turned around and opened the door, simply turning the unlocked knob. "Oh, ye of little faith."

Amalie's apartment was horrifyingly inhuman to Daniel's eyes. Something about it screamed at him, but he could not tell what it was screaming. He had never seen anything like it. He should have expected as much, with her being so eccentric. Everything was super-modern and classy, but there seemed to be no humanity within the décor.

Her living room was ridiculously small, no more than a hundred square feet. She had a black leather couch along one wall. It was trapezoidal, rather than the standard box rectangle. The back sloped steeply from right to left, and though it looked like someone without a level had made it, it was not at all unappealing.

In the corner behind the couch was a standing floor lamp made of a steel pipe bent into a wavy line. The entertainment cabinet was polished black lacquer and took up most of the wall opposing the couch. It took Daniel a few moments to realize what it was about the cabinet that was so odd. On the left side, there were five shelves, all of which housed perfectly arranged books and magazines and CDs. The right side had a CD player with an amplifier and several stacks of notebooks, all meticulously placed. But the middle section, a square large enough to easily accommodate a 36-inch television held a simple black curvy vase full of beautiful red roses – probably three dozen.

No television.

The other wall was covered with black-framed, black and white pictures of animals – giraffes, tigers, elephants, lions, dolphins – all gorgeous pictures, but not a one of them human. Beneath these randomly arranged frames was a long cabinet filled with books. Daniel scanned the neatly arranged hardcover books and found none that he recognized. All presumably science and nonfiction, she had probably two hundred books all immaculately placed on the shelves, the spines all perfectly aligned two inches back from the fronts of the shelves. Upon closer examination, Daniel noted that not only were they neatly placed, but also alphabetized by author. He stood up shaking his head in disbelief.

"Wow, Amalie. You amaze me," he said as he walked into the kitchen to join her. Amalie was pouring two cups of cocoa. He stepped on something and it grinded against the floor in a chalky resistance to his boot. He bent over to pick it up. It was a small shard of turquoise porcelain.

"You want marshmallows?" Daniel looked up, then shook his head. "Cocoa? You know I don't drink that shit! I'm a man." He turned to go check out the rest of the apartment. He dropped the piece of porcelain into his pocket, and made his way through the common area of the apartment looking at her pictures and bookcases. There were bookcases in every room, and the same schema throughout: a lot of thought had obviously gone into the decoration, but not a trace of humanity anywhere. None of the pictures were of people.

The den – for that was the only thing he could think to call it – was down a three-foot hallway away from the living room, and was much the same as the living area. Every wall was covered with pictures of different events from history, animals, and landscapes – all black and white.

And no people.

Running completely around the room along the bottom half of the walls were the same black lacquer bookcases, all filled with perfectly arranged books. There must have been a thousand books in the den alone. All nonfiction, all alphabetized by author. Atop the bookcases in the den were several items: a lamp, a couple of artifacts, and several intricately designed clocks, all set to different hours.

"So you've read all these books?" Daniel asked over the bar that separated the kitchen from the den.

Amalie was running water over some dishes and moving about the kitchen. She frowned and stood still. "Of course. Why do you ask?"

"Well, there's a whole shit load of books, but I haven't seen one I recognized!"

"Yeah, they're all nonfiction. Science. Astrophysics, quantum mechanics, string theory, chaos math, stuff like that. I'm really into science."

"You don't say. You have more science books in your apartment than I knew existed. I've never even read this many fiction books."

Amalie stared at him. "Okay. So you don't want your cocoa?"

Daniel sighed and shook his head, then said, "Yeah, I guess I'll try it."

"Fag."

"Shush."

Amalie giggled and handed him the cup, then said, "Well, shall we get this thing going then?"

Daniel set the scalding mug down, clapped and rubbed his hands together. "Ready when you are!"

Amalie disappeared back into her bedroom for a moment, then reappeared dragging a square black table, about two feet high and as much across. It was just big enough, Daniel thought, to hold a small television, or a laptop computer. Which is precisely what Amalie did with it.

She dragged the daisy chain over and sat it under the table, and opened the computer portion – which looked like a normal laptop – on top. Amalie asked Daniel to retrieve a power strip from the coat closet by the front door. He did as he was told.

Upon opening the coat closet, he noticed more books. She had set up shelving in the closet, from floor to ceiling. There were one-by-twelve boards separated by cinder blocks running up the back of the closet, all packed tight with books. On the floor was a box full of cables and extension cords, and a power strip.

Amalie unzipped one of the soft black vinyl pouches of the daisy chain and unraveled a cable that plugged neatly into the back of the laptop, then clicked open the plastic box within the same pouch and pulled out six power cords. Each one was thick like a computer monitor cable, and all less than a foot long. Each plugged into its own port on the power strip, filling it up. She then plugged the strip into the wall outlet – both sockets – and turned on the computer.

Daniel half-expected the lights to go out, or the power to dim, but it did not. Everything seemed to be running normally.

"It takes that much power?"

"No, they're just redundant backups," Amalie responded, staring dully at him.

Daniel nodded.

"Just teasing Daniel. Yes, it takes that much power. Once we invoke the quantum computer, this motherfucker will drain every ounce of power out of the whole apartment building!"

Daniel flinched. Her use of profanity shocked him. Up until this point, she had not said a word he could recall. Daniel always thought it funny that you did not notice when someone doesn't curse in his or her everyday language. But you sure notice when they do for the first time in your presence.

"Not literally, of course. It will use a lot of power, but it won't blackout the building."

The boot was normal. In fact it ran on Windows, like every other normal laptop in the world. It did not have a brand sticker on it, but Daniel could tell it wasn't anything special. Once Amalie had gotten it to a desktop, she opened several programs that ran in the background before she loaded the TDL application, as she called it. Once these were all loaded and running, she popped in the memory stick Daniel had given her, and opened his conversion application.

"Okay, we're all set. I need you to go throughout the house and turn off all the lights, unplug any clocks or anything unswitched that's using power. We have to conserve as much as possible."

Daniel scattered about the small apartment unplugging anything making a sound and came back to where Amalie was frowning at the active matrix screen. The colors of the screen reflected in her eyes as she stared at Daniel's application up close.

"I just need to test this with a couple of numbers. Give me your birth date, including hour and minute, if you know it."

"November 14, 1978. Five fifty-two P.M."

Amalie tapped in the numbers of his birth date. Then she clicked on the insert button and they watched as the program produced an analog representation of the second on the screen in vivid green color.

"I had to fudge on the second, since your birth probably took up the entire minute, but it looks like it worked! Beautiful work, Daniel!"

"Thanks. I told you I tested it. Though I didn't know what the hell I was doing, I thought I had it right. So what is it you just did there?" Daniel leaned closer.

"I took the time you gave me, in fourteen digit format, from year to month, day, hour, minute, and second. I plugged it into your conversion app, and it converted it to a readable quantum representation of itself. Readable by the temporal delineation application, that is." Amalie pointed at the screen as she illustrated what was going on.

"Once we have all these seconds put in this format, we can then theoretically insert them back into the temporal matrix, and back out."

"Meaning what? Everyone comes back?" he asked, turning to look at Amalie – close-range.

"Well that's the thought. All righty then," Amalie said as she pulled another memory stick out of her purse and plugged it into the laptop.

"What's that?"

"I already recorded all the seconds I think you erased, so I can just plug them into your app and be ready." Daniel stared at her. "You didn't think I was goofing off with my time did you? I've been getting ready!"

She dragged the seconds from the memory stick and dropped them onto the face of his application, one at a time. They were in text file format, and as she dropped each one, the hard drive and CPU could be heard grinding momentarily, then it would spit out an analogous graphical representation. She would then save it on the hard drive. Within two minutes, she had twenty seconds saved on the desktop.

"Okey dokey. You ready?" He was. He nodded. "Okay. Let's kick in the power." Amalie reached beneath the table and depressed a rubber-covered button under the surface of the fabric on the first pack of the daisy chain. The screen dimmed slightly, then refreshed.

The quantum computer was booting.

After about thirty seconds, a dark gray box appeared in the middle of the screen with a single text box in the middle of it, ready cursor blinking slowly.

"That's it?" Daniel said, confused.

"That's what?" Amalie looked at him quizzically.

"Well I thought that sumbitch was gonna suck away all the power!" He waved his hands around. "I can't even hear it!"

"Nope. It's completely silent. But we haven't kicked it in yet, Daniel. I have to type something in the box – or, as the case is here, drag one of the seconds in – and hit enter for it to work. It's in ready mode, waiting for command." She reached under the table and pulled two thin wires out from the vinyl pouch, which were plugged directly into the Q computer. The other end of each wire had a small steel button wrapped in rubber, and an elastic wrist strap attached to it.

"Here, put this on your left wrist," she told him, and placed one on her own wrist.

"What's this for?" Daniel frowned at the device as he stretched it around his wrist.

"This is the conductor that's going to pull you into the temporal matrix. It's also our leash to get back out when we're finished. The application monitors for a particular word, which I've already programmed in. When it hears you say this word it will back you out of the program."

"Well what's the word?"

"CDROM. You want to try and choose a word you wouldn't normally say. And if you're going into the past, it's easy to choose a high-tech word that you know won't accidentally be spoken," Amalie explained. She was now opening the Human Icon Application, which would monitor their movements and interactions with the TDL application. She pointed this out to Daniel as she checked the settings.

"You okay?" she said, looking at his hands.

"Yeah. Just a little anxious. Never really done this before, you know?"

"It's okay to be nervous your first time. You know, you don't have to go back if you don't want to. I just thought you would want to be involved. You can sit here and monitor me if you want."

"No, no, no. I want to go. What's it like though? I mean, if I stayed here… What do you mean by monitor you?"

"Well we won't actually be sitting here once we invoke the app."

"We won't?"

"Well, no. Can't be in two places at once!" she said. "Well we will be right here, just not right now. And my little icon," she said pointing at a small blue icon in the HI app window, "will be all the evidence that I'm here. If you right click on it and select 'extract', it will pull me out of the program. It's not usually good to do that without the person being ready though. You can really mess someone up like that."

Daniel nodded. "This is incredible. How come this hasn't been on the news or anything? This is bad as hell!"

"Top secret Daniel. Like I told you," she said, then leaned back on her hands. "So you ready? You still wanna go?"

"Hell yes."

"All right, Daniel. It's about to get dark in here," Amalie said with absolute clarity. "Welcome to Midnight's Park." And then she dragged the first second into the text box with the mouse.

Daniel felt the slightest sensation of falling, so he stood still for a minute. The wind, however, did not relent. As he bore his face against the biting cold air, he shoved his hands deeper into his pockets and pushed on. Amalie looped her arm through his and trudged along beside him. It was an uncommonly cold April evening.

All along the street were carts full of fresh fruit and vegetables, and small shops with smoke curling lazily out of their chimneys. The wind seemed to keep to the street, where it bit their cheeks and noses. Horses and carriages strolled along through the middle of the soft dirt road, heading back toward the edges of the town. In another hour or so, the streets would be empty; the town eerily quiet, like a ghost town.

Daniel skipped through the light crowd of horses to the edge of the street to pick up a newspaper. Amalie jogged to keep up with him. As he picked up the paper, he flipped the vendor a nickel, and nodded. William McKinley was now favored in the presidential election. Amalie looked over Daniel's shoulder as he peered at the paper.

"He's gonna win, isn't he?" Amalie said, smiling.

"God I hope so." Daniel rolled the paper up and tucked it under his coat, taking Amalie by the hand. "Let's go before we get blown down!"

Together, they scuffed across the road and around the corner of a small building to the side entrance. Ducking through the wooden door, the warmth of the pub was a refreshing change from the killer wind outside. The usual crowd was around the bar, shouting and laughing, being merry. A couple turned to see Daniel and Amalie entering and welcomed them with warm hearty greetings.

"Ah, Daniel! And the lovely lady! Come drink!" Sam said, holding out two tall tankards of ale. Pale liquid sloshed over the edges of the mugs as he stood up clumsily.

"Oh, that is just what I need," Daniel said, taking the mug from him. He handed the other to Amalie, who moved to the end of the bar and sat at a stool that someone had saved for her. Daniel and Amalie rarely stayed together when they came to the Moose Horn. They liked different people, and always separated as soon as they got in the door.

Daniel sat at the bar with his elbows resting in spilled ale, and caught up on the latest gossip and news of the town. The Moose Horn Tavern was full of smoke and laughter on most nights, but on Tuesdays, it was packed to capacity. Mostly for celebration of surviving the dreaded Monday before, the townspeople would gather and drink away the echoes of the grueling workweek long before the week ended. That buffer was all some of them had to get them through the rest of the week. Wages were low for the long workdays most of them faced.

Daniel looked around admiring the crowd that seemed unburdened by their usual problems and complaints. The wives and children would all be at home awaiting their return with supper on the tables. But Daniel always brought Amalie. She was always a part of the party crowd. Daniel always included her in his excursions. He looked at her across the bar and smiled as she winked at him.

The man next to Daniel was challenging another man to an arm wrestling match. Daniel lifted his mug and scooted back so as not to have it spilled on his lap for him. The man to Daniel's right was a hulk; burly and bald, standing a few inches over six feet. Philo was one of the biggest men in the Moose Horn. It was unusual for someone to accept a challenge from him. Everyone knew it was a losing battle.

Their hands locked and the shouting of the spectators immediately drowned their grunting out. The corner of the bar had been cleared, and everyone, including the inn keep, was now in on the rally. Mugs were held high as shouts and smoke rang out into the loud air. Philo was staring dead into his opponent's eyes, his own face calm. The other man was beet-red with veins standing out on his forehead.

He was visibly in pain as he pulled with all his might. It did not appear to budge Philo's rock of an arm though. It seemed to be useless. Then Philo began pulling. And the arms went his way. Slowly they were approaching the bar, until the other man's fist was only inches above it… And the man slammed his boot onto Philo's toe, immediately turning the tables. Philo's now reddened face was stricken with anger as his fist hit the table in front of the other man.

The other man stood up laughing and shouting, as the crowd went wild around him. Most of them had presumably not seen the cheat. This was dangerous behavior, Daniel thought. And he was right. The hard left hook of Philo's arm rocked through the air and crushed down on the other man's cheekbone. And the brawl began. Within a second, the two men were on the floor socking the hell out of each other, rolling in the spit and beer with no regard for those around them. The volume of the crowd was suddenly elevated to near ear-piercing intensity as the shouting and screaming grew more and more excited.

Daniel shook his head and drained the last of the beer from his thick mug, then sat it on the bar, looking over at Amalie. She was doing the same thing, shaking her head with a smirk on her face. They were ready to leave. They did not need to sit through another brawl. These brawls seemed to take place every Tuesday like clockwork. They made their exit quietly while the shouting and spitting still filled the air. They would not be missed.

The quiet of the outside was soothing to their ears as they pushed into the evening air. They shuffled off across the street and between two buildings split by a narrow dusty alley. Trash barrels stood overflowing, some spitting flames into the air keeping the homeless warm. Daniel and Amalie scurried past them and up the creaky wooden stairs; they let themselves into the warmth of their cottage apartment through a small wooden door in the middle of the red brick wall. The apartment was small, but it provided.

Amalie slipped past Daniel and disappeared into the other room. Daniel closed the door quietly behind him, and crossed the rug to the fire. He let his coat slide off his shoulders and hung it on the back of a chair. The decorative mirror beside the fireplace caught his attention peripherally. He frowned and looked at the reflection. Something was odd about it. He could see out the side window of the apartment and into the street below. He turned to have a better look out the window.

There were few people still out, and they seemed normal enough. The crowd was at their usual bustling pace, hands in pockets heading home or crowding into the pubs and small shops along the boulevard. The horses and their carriages were all normal enough too. But it was something in the way everyone moved. Daniel picked a man on the street and watched him intently for a moment. The man took a few steps, then seemed to freeze in place completely. The foggy cloud of his breath even became motionless. Everything and everyone around the man was completely still. Then about a second later, everything blinked back into motion, but everyone had moved a few feet farther in the direction he or she had been walking. It was as if time were paused, but kept ticking in the background. When it started back up, everyone was where he would have been had time not stopped at all.

That's the weirdest damned thing. People were blinking. But he was not. *Why is it happening to everyone else, but not me?*

"Amalie!   Can you come here for a second, please?" he shouted over his shoulder.

Amalie came into the room and stood by the window with him. "What is it?"

"Watch those people for a minute."

"Which ones?"

"Just watch. You'll see." And she did.

Amalie nodded and sighed. "Okay. Okay, hang on a second," she said, walking away from the window.

"What the heck is going on?"

"Hey babe, look at the fire," she said.

Daniel glanced over at the fire. It seemed to stand absolutely still for a moment, then jump back into motion. It flickered and popped like normal, but not when it was still. Daniel squinted, frowning at the curiousness of its motion. Then the room popped and Daniel jumped back.

"Sorry about that," Amalie said, rattling furiously on the keys. "That was a little rough."

"That was weird." He sat back, looking at his hands, turning them over.

"Yeah, I think something was wrong with the temporal flow," Amalie said, staring hard at the screen.

"Where exactly were we?" He was trying to hold back his excitement, which threatened to boil up and spill over. "Or I guess I should ask, *when* were we?"

"1896. April 21, Tuesday. What you saw skipping were those twenty seconds I just reinserted. I don't think it worked."

Daniel frowned at her. "What?"

"Well I tried to put the seconds back, but I don't think it worked. That's why people were skipping." She never took her eyes off the screen.

Daniel smiled. Then his body filled with warm adrenaline and he had to stand up. "Oh my God! Did you see that shit! That was the coolest damned thing I've ever seen!" Daniel took Amalie by the shoulders. Amalie smiled at him.

"That was incredible! It's like you inserted us into the 1890s! We were in this apartment or something overlooking this street, watching people below…"

"Yeah, I remember. Aha! I think I got it. Yup. It didn't work. It was all useless. Turn on the radio, Daniel. See if you can find some news channel. We have to find out if anything happened."

Daniel plugged in the small radio on one of the many bookcases and turned it on. There was nothing but music and ads. No *'Late Breaking News'*, or *'Special Bulletins'*, or *'Attention! It looks like the ghosters are back!'* Just a normal day at the radio.

"Okay, call Anna. See if she's back," Amalie said, handing Daniel the cordless phone.

Daniel pushed the talk button. Nothing happened. "It's still unplugged," he said. Amalie walked over and plugged the power source back in. "Don't you think you should call her, Amalie? If her dad answers – which he will if they're still gone – he will recognize my voice."

"Oh yeah, good point." Amalie took the phone from him. "What's her number?"

Daniel sat on the couch, reeling with what he had experienced. It seemed like a dream now that he thought about it. Amalie switched off the quantum computer, but left the laptop running. She stood up stretching, and joined Daniel on the couch. The call to the Nicholas household had been fruitless. Anna and her mother were both still gone.

"Pretty serious stuff, huh?" Amalie said, patting his leg.

"Hell yes! That was the bee's knees! But what did you say just before we went back?"

Amalie frowned at him. "You need something to drink? I do." She stood and walked to the kitchen, pulling a bottle of Rolling Rock from the refrigerator. "What did you ask me Daniel?"

"I asked what it was you said just before we went back."

"Oh. I said welcome to Midnight's Park." Daniel stared at her. "We at the company call it Midnight's Park because when the Q computer is on, everything around you goes black.   Not an ounce of light anywhere. It's like nothing else exists."

"How is that?" He was still trembling with the excitement from the experience of being placed in the late nineteenth century. It had been too real to deny; he was a true believer in Amalie and her doctrine now – whatever doctrine that might be.

"It just sucks up all the energy from every dimension around you. Every single available resource is put to use by its core."

"I still can't believe how real that felt. It was unlike any dream I have ever experienced," Daniel said.

"Well it was real, Daniel. Congratulations, you have just traveled back in time over a hundred years!"

"I need a cigarette." Daniel put a cigarette between his lips but waited to light it. "You don't mind, do you?"

"No, go ahead." She stood up and stretched again, then turned to face Daniel. "Well, we're going to have to find another way to do this." Seeing him sit there with the cigarette, she turned and fetched a book of matches from the cabinet, then tossed them at him.

"What are you talking about?"

"I thought just reinserting the seconds would fix everything. Well, except that the bulk of the seconds didn't actually get reinserted. It's like we put the seconds back with nothing in them. Like book covers with no text in the middle," she said scientifically. There was no science for temporal mechanics yet. She was inventing it. She could describe it any way she wanted, and probably set the benchmark on operational lingo. "So we have to find another way to reinsert them."

"I see. But how do we do that?"

"Well, the only thing I can think of to do is to go back. We go back to that Monday before. Like April 20, or even the 19th, of 1896. Then we just stick it through until the day after. All we really need to do is start briefly before those twenty seconds take place, and stay until they are finished."

"So if we go back and live them, you think they will never get taken away, right?"

Amalie nodded, pursing her lips.

Daniel came to the realization that he was into something completely new. Virgin science. The excitement pulsing through his veins was so fierce it made him dizzy. He wanted so badly to call someone and tell all about the experience. Anyone. Just to let someone know he had been back in time. It really could be done.

"You know what's weird though? I don't remember being inserted there. But I remember it seemed like I had just always been there. I had memories of going to that bar every Tuesday night. It all seemed so normal," Daniel said.

"Yeah, funny how that works, huh?"

Daniel looked down at his shirt. It was dirty from being under the train, and everything he had done that day.   But otherwise it was a perfectly normal flannel shirt.   And his jeans and boots were perfectly normal too.

"I wasn't wearing these clothes back then was I?"

"Well surely you were."

"But I distinctly remember wearing a coat!   Where is that coat now?"

Amalie raised her eyebrows.

CHAPTER ELEVEN
Explanation

Walter held Callie's hand as he talked to her. She was staring at him through wide glassy eyes, thankful to be alive, but still horrified by the memory of the wreck. Her feet were cold, but at least she could feel them.

"Thank you for being there for me, Walter. Thank you for saving my life." She smiled at him. He had been there for her through thick and thin.

"Sure thing, sugar. I'm glad you're okay. Glad you didn't break anything."

"Yeah, me too," Callie said, fingering the remote to change channels on the small television that hovered over her bed on a crane arm. "So who were those people with you when you rescued me?" She was having trouble finding anything appealing on the television. It had been muted, and she had been only half-watching it on and off for the last couple of hours, drifting in and out of sleep.

"It's the weirdest damned thing. I got stopped by a train, and I was the only one sitting there at the intersection. I put it in park and I'm just sitting there counting cars. Chilling, you know?" He put his elbows on his knees, resting his chin on his fists.

"So I'm just minding my own business when I see this chick roll out from underneath the train."

"Nuh-uh!" Callie said wide-eyed.

"Yeah! It freaked my shit out. But there she was, crawling back and forth like a maniac, looking under it like she'd left something behind."

"Oh my God! That is so weird!"

"Well she reached back under and grabbed some stuff, then after a minute, she came running up to the truck and asked me to help her. Her friend was still stuck under there. I told her she could put her shit in the back of the truck if she wanted. It looked heavy."

"Someone was stuck under it? Oh my God, Walter!" Callie looked as though she had lived through it herself.

"Yeah. Turns out, I got there just in time. Cause I reached in and pulled this guy out and not a second later, this big ass..." he was making a shape with his hands, but seemingly could not find the word.

"Coupling?"

"Yeah. This big ass coupling ripped through where he was laying. It would have killed him, no doubt."

"Oh my God!" Callie said again, covering her mouth. "So you saved two people's lives tonight, Walter!" She grabbed him by his chin and shook his head lightly. "I'm so proud of you!"

"Thanks." He was blushing.

"So you gave them a ride then. Were they helping you look for me? Why were they under that train?"

"Well that's the weird part. They were running from someone. And as it turns out, I guess they had stolen the computer they were carrying."

"They were carrying a computer under the train?" Callie said frowning.

"Yeah. That's not even the best part. It was like a notebook with three separate compartments that were belted together. And get this: that girl called it a Q computer."

"A *Q computer*?" Her eyes widened again, and she grabbed Walter's shoulder. "A quantum computer?" The smile had dripped right off her face, leaving the realization in its place. Callie knew something.

Walter smirked and nodded. "Can you believe that shit?"

"Oh my God! They stole that from Royal!" she said, sitting straight up in bed.

Walter lost his smile. He frowned. "What? How the hell could you possibly know that?"

Callie was looking around the room for her clothes. Her rested mind had finally put it all together. She needed to get out of here, and fast. Her head was rushing like she had stood up too fast, though she had not even gotten out of the bed yet. She knew it was the Versed making her groggy. She would have to fight through it.

Walter was still staring at her. "How do you know it came from Royal? I didn't even know Royal had one."

"Walter, that girl was Amalie London! She used to work at Royal. She got fired a few years ago for disclosure!"

*   *   *

"So the coat got left behind because I took it off, didn't it?" Daniel said. He crushed his cigarette out on the top of an empty soda can Amalie had retrieved for him.

"Yep. Anything not actually *on your person* when you eject doesn't come back with you. Had you been wearing it, you'd have a hundred-year-old coat right now."

"And the newspaper! I'd still have that newspaper too!"

"Yep. You sure would."

"Wow Amalie. You totally amaze me."

"You flatter me, Daniel. I'm just doing my job."

"Yeah well-" Daniel started, but the phone rang, cutting him off.

Amalie turned and stared at the phone sitting on the arm of the couch until it stopped ringing. Then she stood up and walked into the back room. "I need a shower," she said. "And some coffee."

Daniel agreed.

It was a relief to his dirty skin when he finally stepped into the shower. The water running down the drain was nasty and brown. His body was caked with mud, blood and sweat, and he smelled something awful.

Amalie had laid a fresh towel on the toilet seat for him, and gone to use the other shower while he cleaned up. When he stepped out of the shower, he noticed she had also put some clothing there for him. So it was that the night before she had borrowed his clothes, and now he would have to wear some of hers. *Fate is not without a sense of irony.* The wind pants she had set on the counter were fresh and crisp, and looked like they had never been worn. They were too big for Daniel, so he imagined she could not even wear them. He had to pull the drawstring as far as it would go. The shirt was a Sarah McLachlan concert tee about five years out of commission. Oh she's going to enjoy the hell out of putting me through this, Daniel said to himself.

"You ready to go get some coffee?" Amalie said, wringing out her hair in the living room.

"Sure. Thanks for the clothes. I'm glad I wasn't wearing this when we went back," he said, pointing at the shirt.

Amalie looked at the shirt and smiled. "2000? Yeah. They probably wouldn't have even thought it was a year though."

"So how many times have you gone into the past, Amalie?"

"Not too many. Only a couple, really. And not that far back. I much prefer the future though."

"Well that wasn't an unpleasant past."

"I know, but I don't belong in the 1890's. I'm too fascinated by technology. Maybe I'll take you forward sometime," Amalie said.

"Cool. I'm on board with that."

"Let's go get some coffee though. Gotta have my caffeine fix."

The wind nearly blew them back into the apartment when Amalie opened the door. She had taken her spare key from the kitchen drawer and was ready to lock the door. Daniel had called a cab while Amalie was shutting down the computer. Having lost her car to a train wreck, and leaving his Jeep in the Royal Research parking lot put Daniel in a sour mood every time he remembered it. That, on top of Amalie leaving his Zippo by the unconscious body of the security guard, was an arrest waiting to happen.

He continually tried to remind himself not to think about any of that. He was now on the inner circle. He was now a member of an elite group who had the power to control time. He could go back and make things right. He was beginning to understand why Amalie never worried about anything. He also seriously doubted that she was being honest about not traveling often. He was already addicted after the first trip. Daniel could not wait to get back in front of that computer and check out more stuff. More places, more times.

When they got to the bottom of the stairs, the cab was waiting in the parking lot. "That was fast," Daniel said.

"Yeah, I don't think I could have waited too long out here," Amalie added.

Daniel paid the cabbie and hurried Amalie into the warmth of the coffee shop. The Haunt, the sign simply read. The interior was mostly like an all-night café, but had a step-down area in the front where the owner, a man called Hatcher, kept a collection of his favorite books. You could buy or borrow them, or sit at the counter and have coffee with him when he was around. The place was always busy, as it served a lot more than food and books. It served soul.

They moved quickly for the back section, where Daniel always sat. There were a few people around, the usual crowd, Daniel noticed. Some of them he knew, but he was in no mood to chat with them right now. The only thing he wanted to do was talk about their next trip. As Daniel and Amalie breezed past the table of his friends, they shouted out to him. "Hey Dan the man, what's up?" He smiled and nodded at them, slapping their hands as he walked by.

"Can't talk right now, fellas. I'll hit you up in a while." They had been ready to ask all about this fox he was with, and shook their heads as he walked away.

Daniel and Amalie moved to a booth by the window and were quickly approached by Toni, the server. She already knew what Daniel would have, and thus brought a pitcher of coffee and two mugs. She spoke in broken English, and was very friendly.

"Hello Daniel. Your friend have coffay tonigh?" Daniel looked across the table at Amalie. She nodded at Toni and said yes, please, and Toni filled their mugs.

Daniel sat with his back against the wall, where he could keep an eye on everything. He never liked to sit with his back to a crowd. From his position, he could see all his friends, and they were, of course, eyeing his companion. It was obvious they were very curious about her. And it was sure to Daniel that they had never seen someone quite so striking waltz into the coffee shop, much less at this time of night.

Amalie set her purse on the table, then slipped out of the booth and headed to the restroom. No sooner did she disappear into the restroom than did Fitz, one of Daniel's closest friends, jog over to the table to get the lowdown. Fitz was short for Fitzsimmons, his last name. He stood just over six feet tall and had semi-long hair and brown eyes. He was not good looking, but something about him was intriguing and genuine.

"What's goin' on, DB? We haven't seen your ass round here in a few weeks, man."

"Yeah, I have been kind of out of it," Daniel replied.

"Right? Well we've missed you around here."

"Yeah I took a couple of weeks off work and shit. I've just been dead inside."

Then Fitz said, "So what's up man, who's the chirp anyway? She's kinda fine! Me and the boys are tryin' to decide what team she plays for. I'm puttin' her on the Cardinals."

"Nah. Red Sox," Daniel replied.

Fitz looked at him questioningly. "Really? I need to get a better look then."

"Yeah, she's finer than fishin' line split down the middle. I just can't figure her out. She's crazy as hell. But check this out," Daniel said, leaning forward on the table. "She's definitely the smartest chick I've ever met."

"Well that's a bold statement, Dan. She smarter than Prissy?"

Daniel breathed in deeply. He shrugged. "Yeah, I think so. Ultimately, I think if it came down to some run-off, she'd have her – hands down."

"Impressive. If she can beat out a Yankees pitcher, she's got something goin' for her. So who the hell *is* she?" Fitz said. He tilted Amalie's coffee cup to look in it, then pushed it toward the center of the table.

"That's the weirdest part man. I have no idea. She just like appeared. I met her the other night outside the nevele neves, and I've been with her ever since," Daniel said without thinking.

Fitz opened his eyes wider and held his head back. "What happened to you and Anna? Y'all okay?"

Daniel responded quickly, as he realized what he had said, "Nah, man, that's not what I meant. I have been *with* her ever since, but we haven't done anything."

"Haven't done anything? Uh huh." Fitz looked about the room, then toyed with her coffee cup again.

"Serious man. It's been strictly business. But I'm telling you, this has been the most *fucked-up* couple of days in my entire life. But nothin' happened, dude. That's for sure."

"Strictly business? Bitches like that ain't about business. Unless you mean…"

"No, dude. She's not a pro," Daniel said quickly. He took a sip of his coffee and leaned back in the seat again.

Fitz nodded. "So you and Annabelle doin' all right then, right?"

"No man, she ghosted." Daniel sipped his coffee again, suddenly trying to look calm.

"Oh shit man, I'm fuckin' sorry. I had no idea, dude." Fitz took Daniel's hand on the table.

Amalie returned and stood at the end of the table smiling at Fitz as she waited patiently to have her seat back. "Sorry," Daniel said. "Mike, this is Amalie. Amalie, Mike." Amalie shook his hand and reclaimed her seat as Fitz stood up and excused himself, bowing out of his conversation with Daniel. He gave a semi-salute as he backed away from the table. *To be continued.*

Amalie sipped from her steaming mug of black coffee, staring at the table. Daniel smiled at her, still boiling with excitement. He wanted to talk of nothing but their excursion, but knew Amalie had other things on her mind right now. He needed to calm down a little and let her bring it up again.

"So tell me about your family, Amalie. Are you from Birminghamalie Alabamalie?"

She didn't smile. "I grew up in an orphanage. I never knew my parents."

"Sorry."

"That's okay. It's no big deal. When I was five or six, I became aware that something was amiss," she said, squinting her eyes. "I somehow conceived the notion that I was supposed to have regular parents. I don't even remember how I stumbled onto that knowledge. But I did.

"I had a sponsor though, and for the most part, he treated me like his daughter, but there was never any affection. All he did was school me and train me. It's like all I ever got to do was study and stuff. There was no fun, no toys, no excitement. Just school. I was often told I was too bright to simply let all my intelligence blither away into oblivion. Whatever the hell that meant."

"Well aren't you happy for it now? I mean, look how far you've come," Daniel said, shaking her wrist on the table.

"Yeah, I guess so. I try not to think about it too much. I'm happy with what I do, but it would be nice to have parents to call home to. I used to think that someday everything would be normalized. Everything would somehow come together for me, and it would be okay then. It simply failed to materialize. Then this job offer came along and I kind of let myself forget about it."

"Where did you go to school?" Daniel lit a cigarette.

"It was a small private school in Nowhereville, Minnesota."

"No – what college?"

"MIT."

Daniel was in awe. Here he sat with perhaps the most brilliant woman ever to have walked into his life. He suddenly felt as though he did not know how to act. He felt as though he needed to start acting more serious, or more mature somehow. It would take a lot to impress her.

"Wow. So you are a regular bad ass then, huh? You have your master's and shit?"

"PhD, actually. Particle Physics. Applied Astronomy, with a minor in cosmology. But the astronomy was just for fun."

Daniel's eyes widened and his jaw dropped. "You're a fuckin' doctor?"

"The Ph doesn't stand for 'fuckin,' Daniel."

He snorted. "Wow. So how the hell does cosmology fit in to all that science?"

"I'm not following," Amalie said, looking seriously at him.

"Well you said particle physics and astronomy, but you have your minor in cosmology. How does makeup fit in there with all that science?"

"Makeup? Daniel, that's cosmetology. This is cosmology. The history and structure of the physical universe."

Suddenly Daniel felt like a fool. "Oh. Yeah."

Toni returned to the table to make sure everything was okay, and the coffee was still warm. The crowd was starting to thin out, leaving only the die-hard all-nighters who were ever present within these walls after dark.

Daniel and his friends were often called fixtures, as they had their own tables, and basically kept the place in business. For years they had been coming every night, ordering meals and coffee and staying all hours of the night.

Amalie leaned in and spoke again. "So I'm thinking. If we go back and..." she trailed off as someone rapped on the table with a closed fist. Their privacy was gone. Amalie looked up to see four men standing at the end of the table. They were a group of Daniel's friends who had just arrived. There was no keeping this bunch away from their table. Croucher and Jeffrey slid in beside Daniel and Amalie, respectively. Nicky stepped over the back of the bench and into the seat next to Amalie's other side, while his brother Donnie stepped up onto the table itself and walked across to the spot next to Daniel. This was not out of the ordinary. They all had assigned seats, and they got to them by whatever means were available.

A series of handshakes and greetings followed, as they all were introduced to Amalie – the newcomer. Toni slid four new mugs onto the table and set a fresh plastic pitcher of coffee directly in the middle, where a dusty boot print marked the route to Donnie's seat. Toni stood with her hands on her hips as she asked everyone how they were doing, and if anyone needed menus.

Croucher ordered his usual, without the need of a menu, and the rest said they didn't need anything. Jeffrey was a big man, so he always sat on the outside. He immediately put his arm around Amalie and stared at her. The questioning would begin shortly. Amalie smiled pleasantly back at him, and beat him to the punch.

"Annabelle couldn't be here tonight, so I am sitting in for her."

Jeffrey nodded and smirked, then adjusted his glasses. "No problems here, m'lady. Always nice to be in the presence of a Pirates catcher."

"Angels," Croucher corrected.

Nicky shook his head and chortled. "Fuck that. Blue Jays. And she's the shortstop."

Amalie looked wide-eyed at Daniel, shaking her head slowly.

Daniel shrugged and waved her down. "Nothing. Just baseball talk."

"Well if I'm suddenly playing for a baseball team, it'd have to be the Yankees," Amalie said, raising her chin to Jeffrey.

The whole table erupted with a series of "whoas and oohs". When it died off, Donnie finally spoke. "Well you're on the Yankees in my baseball card collection," he said, a little too sappy.

Croucher reached behind Daniel and slapped Donnie on the back of the head. "Bitch you couldn't hire a batboy, shut the hell up." More laughter followed as the whole group picked on Donnie before letting it go. Amalie still stared listlessly at Daniel, clearly having no idea what they were talking about. She was just happy to be the center of conversation for a bit.

Jeffrey grabbed her shoulder and dug his fingers into it, a sort of welcoming massage with his massive hand. She flinched visibly, a silent *Oww!* etched on her face before he finally stopped. "Glad to know you, Amalie," he said. He then turned forward and started filling Daniel in on the previous few nights' happenings. Nothing profoundly interesting, the same old usual non-events and coffee drinking. But it was ritual. Amalie seemed comfortable with putting off the private conversation she had been having with Daniel and enjoying her new acquaintances. She had been accepted quickly.

A couple of hours passed in which there was much intense conversation, which was common among the Coffee Crew. But this time they had a physicist in their presence, so the debates were much more heated. They discussed things such as time travel, black holes, parallel universes and dimensions, and a whole slew of other fascinating anomalies.

Amalie had not let on to the group that she was an applied physicist. She had simply counter-pointed everything that had been said with accurate scientific explanations, and shrugged off all the odd looks this had provoked. They were in awe of her intelligence, without ever realizing exactly what – or who – she was.

Jeffrey said something about how it was not possible to travel back in time because of the effects it would have on history. Amalie had simply answered, "Actually, if you consider the many worlds theory, the past is still alive and booming right here next to us, just in another dimension."

Jeffrey frowned, then asked what the hell she was talking about.

"Well, think about it. If you take the many worlds theory – you *are* familiar with said theory, are you not?" A couple of the guys nodded, but the rest simply frowned, and asked her to clarify. "What the hell kind of physicist enthusiasts are you if you haven't heard of that theory? It's an essential slice of the grand pie we call quantum mechanics!"

Jeffrey answered for the group, "Well, darling, not all of us actually finished high school."

"Oh yeah. Sorry. Anyway, the many worlds theory states that instead of the wave function collapsing every time there is a fork in the road, the universe splits, creating actualities from all the eventualities present." This provoked more frowns. More confusion. She sighed and slapped her hands down on the table. "Okay. Let's start over. Have any of you heard of Schrödinger's cat?"

To this, Jeffrey nodded, as did a couple of the others. Nicky was sketching on a torn sheet of paper, too busy to pay attention to the current conversation. "Yeah, I have," Jeffrey said. Croucher added that he had as well.

"Great. The principle suggests that you can't observe the state of the experiment without altering the outcome, right? So before you open the box, there is a period in which the cat is neither dead, nor alive. It is also both dead and alive simultaneously. These are the eigenstates. When you open the box and observe the cat, the wave function collapses and therefore you have set in stone one of those eventualities. You with me so far?"

"I think so," Croucher said. "Isn't that the Heisenberg Principle though?"

"Nope. His principle was about not being able to effectively measure an object's speed and position simultaneously. In order to measure its position you must shine a light on it, which in turn heats the particles up and alters its speed and position. This theory is beside that, but the same basic factors are at work, no less. An object, a measurement, and a state of unknowing. Merely observing the cat has changed the state of its being."

"Well what does the Heisenberg Principle apply to then?" Croucher asked.

"Movement. Watch a car go by. You can measure its speed or its position, but not both. If you know its speed, you can't be sure exactly where it was when you measured it," Amalie said, and sipped from her mug. "Likewise, if you know its exact position at one point in time, you won't truly know how fast it was moving right then and there.

"Anyway, so instead of the wave function collapsing when the box is opened, the universe splits, which creates a world where the cat is alive, and another where the cat is dead. So for everything that has ever happened, instead of thinking about it as a wave function collapsing, think of it as the universe splitting, and each eigenstate stays in existence. Becomes a reality."

Donnie shook his head quickly, "What the hell are you people smoking, man? That is some deep shit!" Everyone laughed.

"You'll have to excuse Donnie. He's a realist," Jeffrey said, reaching across Amalie to pat Donnie's arm. Amalie smirked and nodded.

Daniel said, "I think you lost me at the part about the eigenstates."

"An eigenstate is a potential reality before the wave function collapses," Amalie said. "A wave function is how you measure quantum particles. Without getting too detailed though, for every probable place that particle could exist in the next nanosecond, there exists an eigenstate. When the wave function collapses, or becomes reality, it brings about the most probable eigenstate. For instance, think of yourself, and every place you could possibly be in the next second and a half. Now keep in mind, this works on a macro level – so it involves everyone else as well. But let's focus on just you. So in the next second or so, you could be standing there beside the table, or sitting on it, or sitting over here by me, and so on. Let's say you could be in any one of ten places in the next second and a half. Those potential places are called eigenstates.

"Now, the Schrödinger's Cat theory suggests that when the object in question is actually observed, the wave function collapses, and the *most probable* eigenstate becomes reality. And in this case, the most probable is that you will be right there where you are now. So, snap!" she said, snapping her fingers, "the wave function collapses and there you are, right where you were."

A few of them clapped, and Daniel smiled. He hadn't really caught on to what she had just said. "Yeah, I got it."

Jeffrey took over, saying, "So what you said then, is that instead of the wave function actually collapsing, that the universe splits right there into as many eigenstates as existed for his possible location?"

"Exactly," Amalie said with a smile. "So every millisecond, ten or fifteen new universes are created *just* because of Daniel! That obviously doesn't include the infinite number of others created by everyone and everything else alive out there. Just between the six of us, there are ad infinitum others created, because it is exponential when more than one person is interfering with the potential outcome. But trying to do the math on that is chaotic."

Jeffrey shook his head now, and Daniel leaned back against the seat putting his arms around Croucher and Nicky. He was pleasantly impressed with her brilliance, and smiled smugly when Jeffrey asked him, "Where did you say you found this woman?"

"Well, good news, Jeff – she is single," Daniel said.

"Kick ass," Jeffrey said.

"Woo hoo!" said Croucher.

Amalie smiled, then took a sip from her coffee. "Single is a little ambiguous, no? I am singular, but single seems a little out of place when describing a person."

"What are you talking about?" Croucher asked.

"Well, even if someone is married, technically, they're still single, right? It's like-" she suddenly trailed off and looked up. There was a tall man standing at the end of the table in a long coat and a fuzzy hat. Hello, Amalie. I have been looking all over for you." The man had a bandage over his nose, and a frown on his face.

"Can you excuse me a moment, guys?" she said. Jeffrey stood up to let her out, and she brushed off her blouse as she stood. "I'll be back in a minute."

Daniel stared at the stranger who put his hand behind Amalie's back and quickly led her out the front door. As soon as she got up and left, the questions flew like rocks. "So what happened to Anna?", "Dude, are you nailing her?" and everything in between. He just smirked and drank his coffee.

After an hour of wondering and waiting, Daniel got up to walk outside. The door swung open again, and he felt the cold draft blow in. Expecting Amalie to walk through the door, he prepared himself for what he would say to her. But it wasn't Amalie who came around the corner.

It was Priscilla.

He had not seen her in almost six months – and even then it had only been a short sighting. Now here she stood in the corridor of the coffee shop. *My God.* It amazed Daniel how quickly his world kept being turned and twisted around.

Priscilla was tall and slender, with long, dark brown hair and green eyes, and everything about her spoke of class. The way she walked looked as though she floated on air, and her voice was soft and sexy. Anyone she met took an immediate liking to her. She had moved to New York three years ago, and had moved back about six months ago. They had always said that if she ever moved back they would surely be together again. And that was that. But her return had been unexpected to both of them, and Daniel had already been two years involved with Annabelle. The only agreement that remained between him and Priscilla now was that if neither of them were married by thirty years old, they would wed.

She was smiling, engaged in conversation with a friend of hers when she came around the corner, and the instant her eyes met Daniel's, the smile went away. She touched her friend's arm and said, "Go get us a table, Edie. I'll be there in a minute." She then looked into Daniel's eyes and straightened her head. She was as surprised as Daniel by the encounter, as she rarely made it to the Haunt anymore.

"Hi, Daniel."

"Hi, Pris. How's it going?"

"I'm okay. You?"

"Fine. A little distraught right now, but all in all, I'm okay."

"How's Anna?"

"Gone. She ghosted with the rest of them."

Priscilla's hand flew up over her mouth and her eyes widened. "Oh my God, Daniel! Oh my God, I am so sorry! Come here, baby," she said, putting her arms around him. His eyes burned as he fought back the pressure of tears. It did not take long though, before tears were wetting his cheeks.

Daniel had nothing to hide from Priscilla. He never had. She knew everything about him – a lot more than Annabelle did. He had been sparse on his details when telling Anna of his past, thinking it was more than she could – or would – tolerate. In addition to that, he wanted to feel as though he was helping her maintain some sense of her purity. So he had always just kept quiet with her, only telling her what she needed to know. And likewise, she never asked. It was his way of starting over.

It was different with Priscilla. If something happened, Priscilla was one of the first to know about it. And she always reciprocated. In light of his new relationship with Anna, he and Priscilla had decided to carry on their relationship as just close friends. She was more like his sister now than anything, despite the fact they had not seen each other in months.

"Come on, Daniel, let's get out of here. We should go talk. Let me go tell Edie we're leaving and drop off this book." Daniel had no compunction about leaving with her, as Amalie had walked out with the stranger almost an hour ago.

Daniel wandered up to the front door, looking through the glass in an effort to see Amalie outside. He could not. Daniel was now hoping she would see him leaving with Priscilla. It would even the score for him. He was a little jealous of the stranger's ability to simply waltz in and whisk her away from him so effortlessly. Whoever that man was, he commanded a part of Amalie that Daniel could only imagine.

Daniel made his way up to the center counter, where Hatcher was leaned across it on his elbows, engaged in a conversation with a couple. "What's up, Mister Brandt?" Hatcher said, extending his arm. Daniel grasped his forearm and shook it.

"How goes it?"

"Adequate, thank you. Need prose?"

Daniel shook his head. "Not tonight, bud."

Hatcher nodded and returned to the couple next to Daniel.

Priscilla scooted up and slid a book across the counter, not wanting to interrupt, then turned and looped her arm through Daniels as he stood to walk away.

"PM," Hatcher called aloud."

Priscilla turned back. "Yes?"

"How was it?" he asked, holding his hand up in the air.

"It was everything you said it was, Hatcher. We'll have to discuss it over coffee though. I'll come back and see you."

"Very well. Good journey."

Daniel and Priscilla walked out into the cold air. She wrapped her other arm around his stomach and hunkered in close to him as they fought the bitter wind on the way to her car.

"How's Edie gonna get home now?"

"She'll ride with Jeffrey. He said he'd take her, since she didn't want to leave yet."

She opened her passenger door for him and Daniel got in, shivering in the warmth of the car. Priscilla ran to the other side, and buckled her seatbelt as they sped off. No sign of Amalie anywhere. Daniel was almost disappointed. He wanted badly for her to see him leaving with Priscilla.

Priscilla's apartment was small and sparsely furnished, but warm and homey. She took off her black leather jacket as Daniel sunk into the brown suede couch. She offered him a drink, which he refused, then she turned the gas up by the fireplace, sending roaring flames high into the air above the gas logs. Daniel immediately felt the heat from across the room. At his feet lay a Chinese dragon rug, spread under the dark wood of a badly clashing African coffee table. The eclectic furnishing gave the room an odd sort of random consistency in and of itself.

The walls were plain white, with a few Dali paintings and movie posters strung about. It was very modern looking, and save for its small size, completely classy. And everything down to the magazines on the coffee table was immaculately organized and stacked, giving the air of a lobby for an affluent business office. Priscilla finally came back into the room, having removed her black blouse, opting for an altogether more comfortable – albeit more revealing – dinky yellow tank top. She was also now short her bra. *Why in the great green shit do women do that?* He turned his face to the ground in order to avoid the inevitable gaze that would surely betide. If ever someone wanted to know the exact shape and size of a woman's breasts, he needs only see her in a dinky yellow tank top, sans the bra.

She sat cross-legged, facing him on the couch and took his hand in both of hers. "How are you holding up, Daniel?"

"Well, I was actually doing quite well until I told you about it. I am in such a weird ass situation though, Pris. I just don't know what the hell to think."

She looked closely at him, squinting slightly. "You'll have to elaborate, Daniel."

"Well, okay, check this out. A couple of days ago I met this chick at the nevele neves, and have been with her ever since."

Priscilla was not hip to the lingo. She stared blankly at him. "Nevele what?"

"Sorry. 7-Eleven. Backwards, it's nevele neves. So I met her there, and she said she needed to talk to me. We got to talking and just never separated. It was weird."

"So she's stolen your heart from Anna then."

"Nah. Not really. What makes you say that?"

"It's a normal way to deal with grief, Daniel. It's emotional displacement – and it's okay." Priscilla squeezed his hands.

Daniel shook his head. "It's weird. I do like her. She's bad as hell. And part of me wants Anna to come back, but the other part wants to stay with Amalie. But I don't think I like her that much."

"Amalie? Her name is Amalie?" She put her hand on his knee.

"Yeah," Daniel said, and lit a cigarette.

"Well, I don't see what you're confused about, Daniel. Sounds like you found a great girl. Anyone who can capture Daniel's attention like this has got to be worth the time," Priscilla said, smiling. After a brief pause, she said, "What are you afraid of, Daniel?"

Daniel didn't think he was ready to tell Priscilla about the time travel yet. The possibility of bringing Anna back, along with the rest of the ghosters still seemed pretty remote to him anyway. He still didn't really believe that part himself. While he was now a firm believer in the ability to travel temporally, he didn't know how they were going to bring back those who had disappeared.

"Well, I'm thinking Anna might be back."

"Oh, Daniel, come here. I'm so sorry," Priscilla said, and pulled him close again, hugging and kissing his head. "You have to let her go, baby. There's nothing you can do now."

"But there is, Pris. There is something I can do," Daniel said, pulling away.

"Denial is a powerful stage, Daniel. But we have to accept the things that happen to us."

Daniel did not respond. He decided not to go into it right now. Maybe there were some things he had to hide from his best friend. He wanted to tell her everything, but the secrecy he had sworn kept him from it.

"So where is this girl now? Are you sure you don't want a drink, Daniel?"

"Yeah, sure. Why not." As she poured him a glass of wine, he said, "She left with some guy at the coffee shop."

"Uh oh. What guy?"

"I don't know. Some dude with a bandage on his face came in and whisked her away like a prisoner."

"What did she say?"

"She said, 'I'll be back in a minute'. So I waited an hour, but she never came back. Then you showed up." Daniel stretched his feet out on the coffee table.

"Hmm. Mystery chick has a cloak and dagger relationship." She put her arms around him and kissed his cheek. "I'm sorry things are so rough for you, Daniel."

"What are you talking about, 'cloak and dagger relationship'?"

"Just seems weird that she would leave with some guy like that. He sure knew where to find her though, right?"

"Yeah, that is weird. She obviously knew him though," Daniel said. He crushed his cigarette out in the orange ashtray on the coffee table and leaned back on the couch, folding his arms behind his head.

"So you have kind of treated this like a problem you hope will disappear if you don't think about it, haven't you?" Daniel was happy to be talking to Priscilla about his problems, as he knew she would have it all figured out if she got enough information. She was good at people.

"Yeah, I guess so. I'm just so sick of all these games and shit. I am so ready for all this to come to an end and everything to be normal again. Why the hell did you ever have to move, Prissy?"

"Oh, Daniel, this isn't about me." She set her drink on the table and put her hands on his leg again. "If you need me, you know I'm here for you. But don't get so mixed up that you think you miss me. That isn't right."

"I *do* miss you. I always have. I started seeing Anna because I thought you were gone forever. But I always used you as a basis of comparison for her. And of course she never matched up."

"You shouldn't say that, Daniel. Of course she did. She has a lot of great qualities. She is a beautiful girl."

"Yeah I know she's beautiful, but that's not the point. You heard of the Liberty Bell, right?"

"Umm, yeah. What in the world-"

"Doesn't serve a lot of purpose for how beautiful it is, you know," Daniel scoffed.

"Oh my God, Daniel! I think that may be the cruelest thing you have ever said. You know you don't feel that way. You have a lot of unchecked aggression. You are being angry with her so that when it sinks in you won't be so lonely and upset. You would rather blame her for everything. It makes the getting over her easier," Priscilla said, stroking his hair as she spoke. "It's a natural stage in the healing process, but you really should watch what you say, regardless. You will regret it later. You can't possibly be that full of anger toward her."

"It's not about her, Priscilla," he said, sighing.

"What is it about then, Daniel?" Priscilla was shaking her head, appearing to Daniel to become defensive against his attitude.

"Look, let's back up. I'm just lonely, Pris. I got this other girl running around playing with my emotions, making me think of Anna, I'm missing her every day, then you come waltzing in." He was waving his hands around a lot. "I just... I just guess I haven't really realized how much I missed you until I saw you again."

Priscilla put her arms around his neck and pulled him to her breast, where she tried to comfort him. "I'm so sorry, Daniel." She kissed his head again. "Boy, you've had a rough couple of weeks, haven't you, sweety?" She pulled him tight against her.

Daniel had a desperate need for company and affection, so extreme, in fact, that he could hardly stand to be beyond the presence of a woman. Sexual or not, he felt he simply could not exist without being near one. Priscilla was exactly what he needed right now. She was the perfect woman at the perfect moment.

CHAPTER TWELVE
Motivation

allie found her clothing on one of the guest chairs in her room, covered by an extra set of sheets. She had enlisted Walter's help holding her up as she made her way around the room, sure she would crash to the floor like cut timber if he were to let go of her arm. Unsteadily, and "shaking like a scared Chihuahua," as Walter had said, she bent over the chair and unfolded her pants. They were stained brown and nasty smelling from lying in the storm drain most of the day.

"Walter, what am I going to do? I can't wear these out of here! They're still wet!"

"Callie, I really don't think you should be leaving yet. You could relapse with hypothermia, or-"

"Get over it, Walt. I'm a big girl. As long as nothing's broke, I'm getting out of here." She suddenly stopped as if something had paralyzed her. "You didn't give them my name, did you?"

"Well of course! They had me fill out all kinds of forms since you were out."

"Okay, okay. Fine, they'll just have to bill me." Callie stood up straight and pulled her hair back into a ponytail, using a band from around her wrist. Her purse was still presumably in the wrecked car, in the back of some junkyard now. "Meanwhile, what am I going to do about clothes?"

"I don't know! What do you want me to do, Callie?"

"Will you go get me some fresh clothes? That's the only way we'll be able to get out of here!" Callie looked at him pleadingly.

Walter stared at her saying nothing for a long moment. "Damn it, Callie, you know I don't approve of this."

"Okay, your objection is noted. Now go to my apartment and fetch me a pair of jeans and a sweater," she said, slapping her hand against his chest. "Oh, and make sure and get a pair of panties for me. They're in my nightstand drawer. But don't look at them!"

"Callie, what the hell has gotten into you?"

"Just go!"

He sighed heavily then helped her back to bed. "Okay, I'll go. But if you get sick again, I'm going to whip your ass, Callie."

"Fine! Permission granted. Now go on!" she said, pulling the tight covers back up to her chin.

Walter shook his head and blew out the door like a gust. "I'll be back in a while." He closed the door behind him as he left.

*   *   *

Priscilla had turned off the lamps, letting the fire suffice for ambient light, and had turned on some background music. Daniel told her all about the last couple of weeks, Anna's sudden disappearance, and how he had been dealing with it all.

Priscilla was understanding; not talking, but instead listening and offering words of encouragement only when he asked her questions, rhetorical as they were. She was an excellent friend, and had been an excellent girlfriend at what point she had been one to him. Daniel poured out his heart to her, every event that had taken place in the last few months, and covered every base he could think of. Except the time travel. He still was not ready to be sure about that. Priscilla had only listened, nodding and smiling at him. She was so beautiful in the firelight, and this weighed heavily on Daniel's emotions. He missed her badly, only not having realized it until she had so smoothly blown in with the breeze earlier in the evening.

He was not sure how he felt about Annabelle at the moment – his emotions all in a tangle. He would have to start getting over her someday, and now would be as good a time as any, he reckoned. If he were to start off on a positive note with Priscilla, it sure would make the getting over her part easier. He still felt a shock every time he thought about Anna.

Having thought about and talked about nearly every second of his life covering the last few months, Priscilla finally rounded on him, bringing the topic back to light on that mysterious character about whom he had almost forgotten.

"So tell me, Daniel, who exactly is Amalie? You said you met her at the 7-Eleven. Something about her was magnetic enough to bind you to her for more than twenty-four contiguous hours. What was it about her that imprisoned you? Her passion?" She held up quoting fingers and said, "Im Gefängnis Ihrer Neigung." All this bought her was a blank stare. "It means 'In the prison of your passion'. It's German."

"Nah, I don't really know. It's easier to say who she isn't than who she is."

"Do tell, Daniel. Now you have my curiosity!"

"Well she said she was a physicist-"

"Yeah, whatever."

"No, really. She all but proved it to all of us at the table. Well, all of those of us with the capacity for understanding what the hell she was talking about."

"What the hell are *you* talking about? What did she say?" Daniel was happy to see he was not the only one excited by Amalie's elusive personality. More precisely, he was happy to see it could affect a female as well. It was easy for men to fall prey to her incredible aura.

"Well, she started talking about quantum mechanics and theoretical physics and shit. Like alternate realities and universes and such."

"That isn't hard to talk about. I could go on about the basics of theoretical physics all day without having scratched the surface of what it's really about. But I have a degree; I don't know if that matters." Priscilla frowned.

"Well, I know I can't talk about it all day. She said she has her PhD in physics and astronomy. Said she did the astro part for fun. Regardless, she wasn't just talking about the basics though. She was saying some shit that had my head spinning about eisengates and wave functions and all this other technical stuff. It was pretty serious."

Priscilla frowned hard, then said slowly, "Eigenstates, you mean?"

"Yeah. That's what I said."

"So you believe her then."

"Yeah, I don't see why I shouldn't. She's got no reason to bullshit about it."

"Well, I guess. It just sounds a little far-fetched for anyone who lives around here."

"What about you? You've got a degree. You're intelligent."

"Daniel, you're a smart guy. I'm not going to tell you how to watch out for yourself. Hell – you're probably better at it than me. Just be careful, babe."

Daniel was sharp as a knife, with common sense in abundance. He was not well read, but intelligent. He could not tell someone where Austria was on a map. He could not tell someone what the Pythagorean Theorem suggested. He could not tell someone what World War II was fought over, nor could he tell someone where it took place. It simply didn't matter to him and his everyday life. Like so many others, he took a lot of things for granted, especially his world history. He was the victim of the same mind disease that infected 99% of all Americans. A severe case of apathy.

But Priscilla was right. He had not really thought through who Amalie really was. She was certainly suspicious. He had let his emotions run his mind. Who wouldn't find it intriguing to hear a beautiful woman talking at length about physics and applied sciences? Being dumbfounded by a girl he found so appealing was a turn-on indeed. Priscilla did the same thing for him – to him – but she tended not to get as technical, as detailed. She was all in all a little more modest than Amalie seemed to be.

Priscilla had graduated magna cum laude with a double major in Psychology and Music Theory. An odd combination, many had said, but it was truly what her heart desired. She had always gone for and gotten exactly what she wanted, never settling for something less. Her music had been on the side, but she had taken it no less seriously. She had played the violin since before she could read. She was quite good at it, having played all over the world in a magnificent series of symphonic reproductions of her favorite classical gods: Bach, Beethoven, Chopin, and Mozart, among a few others. After several years of it, she finally gave up the touring to stay home and concentrate on her career.

Priscilla was a juvenile psychologist, and for such a young woman at only twenty-eight, she seemed so advanced and mature to Daniel. But the crowd she ran with was not indicative of such a profession. In most cases, people of money generally ran with people in their own monetary league. Not Priscilla though. Her circle of friends never changed no matter what social status she attained. She was true. And Daniel always adored that about her. While he made pretty good money himself, his income was dwarfed by her salary, which was close to double his own. He never worried too much about her abandoning him as much as he feared she would stop hanging out with his friends and him at the Haunt. Time had put his mind at ease though, and they only became better friends – all of them.

"So do you want to go back to the coffee shop? Wanna go dancing? Wanna go get drunk at a sleazy bar? Wanna go back in my room and have cheap, meaningless sex? What do you want to do?" It had never been 'meaningless' for them. Even though it was technically indifferent, it was not quite as meaningless to him as maybe it should have been. Had she never been more than a Friday Night Friend, he would have never labeled it anything but meaningless. But she meant a lot to him, thus the sex had its attachment as well.

They had been friends for a long time, even before they had dated. And their friendship had always had perks. They had both realized long ago that sex was a fantastic anti-stress agent, beside the fact that it was so much more. But it had never adversely affected their friendship, even when she had been involved with another man, because they were both of the opinion that it really didn't change anything. She had still made time for Daniel, being of the mind that it wasn't new territory, and it didn't change her feelings for either of the men, so there was no need to end their occasional intimate encounters. Neither of them were ever emotionally overcome on account of the sex alone.

Now Daniel was having more and more of a hard time keeping his eyes off her chest, which he was by now sure she was trying to show him. Tight dinky tank tops on women who hardly wore bras were fine by him. But tonight he had tried to maintain connection with her eyes in an effort to avoid derailing his self-control. After the last two days with Amalie, the sexual tension had risen to almost a boil – at least on his side of it – and one look would surely send him into a dark room to take care of business. He was aching now. Only a man would understand his predicament. Women, he knew, would blab all day long about how they did not need sex to survive. But men – he also knew – did. The relief of release is a force not to be underestimated.

Not only was he sexually stressed at that moment, but he was also confused about what to do about Annabelle. Or what not to do, as might have been more the case. He had loved Anna for a long time, and was to marry her next year. She was to be his wife. Was she gone for good? Could he get her back? And if so, would it be the same when she returned? Would they pick up where they left off, or would they go their separate ways? He wondered if her disappearance would somehow affect her feelings for him.

On top of his love for Anna, he was beginning to sense strange feelings for Amalie, whom he barely knew. Then of course, there was Priscilla. Again. He had been fine until she had breezed into the coffee shop and knocked him off his high horse. When it rains it pours, he thought. Now, if he could just have them all… All at once, no less… His mind was beginning to wander dangerously. In his condition, he could break at any moment.

She turned and lowered the flame on the gas logs, then stretched her arms above her head, pushing her chest out in a long-winded stretch. And that was the final straw.

"Yeah, that sounds good," he said, breaking the long silence. "Your room will be just fine."

Walter ran up the stairs to Callie's apartment and let himself in. The air was stifling hot as he stepped into her living room. "Whoa, shit!" he said, and searched for the thermostat in the dark. He finally found it, and it was set to HEAT / ON, at the highest temperature. Walter knocked it back to about 75, then flipped it to AUTO / AUTO so as not to run her out on the electric bill. Feeling his way back to her room, he retrieved a fresh pair of jeans and a sweater as instructed. He grabbed panties from the nightstand drawer and began searching for a bra. After shuffling through every drawer in every chest in her room, he spun around harrumphing. "What the hell? Bitch ain't got no bras?"

He checked the laundry room, the washer, the dryer, and the shelf above them – all to no avail. Callie had no bras in her apartment. He guessed the only one she owned was crumpled up in the chair beside her bed at the hospital. He shook his head, then smiled as he grabbed up the clothing and let himself out of the apartment. He noticed he was sweating as he turned to lock the door behind him. It was a full thirty degrees cooler outside, and felt like someone had poured a bucket of ice over him after his being on fire. He let out a long breath, and took in fresh air, panting for its coolness in his lungs.

Walter made it back to the hospital uneventfully, and folded the clothing up, shoving it into his pants and under his shirt, trying to hide them from view of anyone who might see him inside. The place would surely be a little quieter as most of the patients were asleep, so most of the nurses could have gone home for the night. At least this was his theory.

He was wrong.

There were at least five nurses at the nurses' station eating and talking, checking charts, doing the normal things that nurses do at nurses' stations. Walter smiled at one as he walked by, and he caught her eye. She followed his gaze around the entire walk from the entrance to the ward hallway. She finally let a smile creep across her face, then turned away quickly, blushing. Walter stopped just the other side of the hallway door, peeking back at her, and just in time to see her open her eyes wide and cover her heart with her hand. She was telling another nurse how gorgeous he was.

He grinned and hurried down the hall to Callie's room. He passed no less than two nurses on the way down the long hallway. When he got to her room, there was a nurse taking Callie's vitals and giving her some medication. He stood there watching Callie look back at him silently, then backed out into the hallway to let the nurse finish.

The room was hot and dark, the clock on the stereo the only luminance. The stereo hummed at a medial volume, not loud enough to cover their heavy breathing. Daniel lay on his back with Priscilla snuggling up to his chest, on her side. A thin layer of sweat covered their bodies, and the heat between them was enough to burn a candle by. Daniel slowly stroked her shoulder.

Shortly after she had grabbed him by the hand to lead him into the bedroom, he had reached up and taken hold of the back of her shirt. She spun into his arm as he lifted it above her head, her breasts bouncing pleasantly into his view. He had then pushed her onto the short bed. She had not been able to see, and thus had screamed, then exploded into laughter as she hit the bed and Daniel landed on top of her, his mouth immediately seeking out her chest. They had started an engine that was now forced to travel the length of the track, however long that was to be.

The lights had stayed off, and the radio had sung throughout, slightly masking their moans and heavy breathing, and marking the moment forever with an array of songs that would bring only fond memories of the event to mind in the future. In the thick darkness, she had forced Daniel onto his back, his hands on her flat stomach and her soft breasts as she strode her way into beatitude upon her human charter. They had remained silent for the entire duration of their engagement, only whispering their feelings and thoughts into the steaming air.

In the end, she had turned up the radio and held his hands tightly to her chest as she grinded him into the soft satin sheets, her posture perfect silhouette staining his wide retinas with the subtle image of her ascendancy. Daniel could do nothing but oblige – she was holding the reins. They came together, then she collapsed to his side where she still lay silent and motionless.

Daniel finally spoke, softly and quickly, between gasps, "I think I could stay right here, like this, all night. What time you planning on heading back to the coffee shop?"

"I'm in no rush, baby." She was panting as well. Daniel was glad of her answer. He wanted to relax, to hold on to the feeling that enveloped him where he lay. He had found purchase in her presence, and was at ease of mind and body for the first time in weeks, having her baby him into a complete and total calm, unbound by anything tangible but the smell of her sweet perfume and the feel of her burning body against his own. In this calm, he felt he should never leave. He was scared of what was outside of it. His life outside had become so complicated it was beyond calculation. It was beyond any scientific evaluation, beyond any reasonable explanation. Yet he knew it would be there awaiting his return. He shrugged off the thought of it and pushed it under the rug of more pleasant thoughts. He was so at peace here. So relaxed, so content, so free. And in this freedom he no longer looked for a door. He wanted no way out. And as his eyes drifted heavily closed, he felt Priscilla's hot kiss on his neck, then he slept more soundly than a baby.

*   *   *

Callie lay as still as possible as the nurse took her blood pressure. She had a thermometer under her tongue, which had beeped almost a minute ago. The nurse, it seemed, was in no hurry to relieve her of it. Every couple of minutes, she saw Walter pop his head around the doorjamb and raise his wrist, dramatically checking the time. He would look hard at his watch with huge eyes, his face only an inch or two away from his wrist, then look at Callie with a deranged face and wander off again, as if he were the only patient in a mental ward. She closed her eyes hard and bit the thermometer in an effort to still the laughs that threatened to sweep through her aching, swollen abdomen.

After what seemed like an eternity, the nurse finally took the thermometer from Callie's mouth, and scribbled the reading on her chart. Callie's cheeks were locked and aching now, from holding in the thermometer for so long. She sighed with relief and the nurse gave her a dirty look. *Oh shut up.* Callie rolled her eyes. She was beginning to lose her patience. She was antsy to be back out in the real world, free from this horrid hospital and its rude nurses.

Finally, the nurse hung the clipboard on the wall above the bed and walked out of the room. She said nothing to Callie. Callie took this to mean she was getting better. Walter stuck his head around the corner again just as the nurse was approaching the door, and straightened up quickly when he saw her. The nurse flinched visibly, and Callie had to laugh out loud this time.

Tremors of pain, like hammers banging her bones, shot up through Callie's ribs and into her chest. She had to wrap her arms around herself and calm herself down. Despite the pain though, Callie could not quit smiling. Walter looked awkwardly at the nurse and apologized as he scooted past her into the room.

"Visiting hours are over, son, you need to wrap it up," she said as she walked out of the room.

"Yes ma'am," Walter said. He stood still, waiting for her to disappear from sight, then dashed to the bedside to help Callie get up.

Callie threw her arm around his shoulder and got to her feet.

"Do you feel any better?"

"Yeah, a little. Just a little drowsy, but I'm okay," she said. She let her hand slide down to Walter's forearm and steadied herself as he set the fresh clothes on the chair beside her. "Okay, be a good boy and look away." Walter did as he was told.

"Wait, first untie this for me." She pointed to the knot in the back holding her gown together. She had no idea her rear was entirely visible. Walter got his first look ever at her rump in its full glory.

"Wow, Callie, that may be the nicest ass I've ever seen." Callie turned quickly on him, frowning.

"What?" she said too loudly.

"Your gown is…" he started, but did not need to finish his sentence. Callie's cheeks were already red with embarrassment. "Sorry," he said, untying the knot. Before he turned his head away to let her dress, he slapped her butt lightly.

"Walter, you asshole!" she whispered. She had realized she had almost yelled before, and now overcompensated the correction of her vocal volume. As Walter looked away, she let the gown drop to the floor and stepped into her underwear and jeans, then had to let go of him to put on her sweater. When she let go, Walter turned quickly to make sure she wasn't falling, and saw her swinging the sweater over her head. She had no idea that he now stood looking at her bare breasts.

"Okay, you ready?" she said, and looked around the room.

"Yeah, sure." He was smiling.

"What? What are you smiling at Walter?" She was not.

"Nothing. Let's go."

"You go out ahead of me. Make sure it's clear. Did you find a secret way out or anything?"

Walter turned letting his hands fall to his sides. "Yeah. You know these hospitals have all kinds of secret exits for patients that don't want-"

She slapped his shoulder. "Fine, just go! Just don't walk us by the nurses' station." She took his arm again. "You're going to have to help me walk a while, so don't go too fast."

Out in the hall, it was quiet and relatively dark. All the nurses had disappeared from the hallway, presumably into the rooms of their patients, or back up to the front to commune. Callie threw her arm around Walter's shoulder and they hurried down the hall, opposite the way he had come in. They swung wide around a corner and saw a nurse coming, but she was staring at a clipboard in her hands as she walked, so they pulled back quietly around the corner.

"That was close. Let's take it a little slower next time," Callie whispered.

"Why are we trying to sneak out of here, Callie? You know you can just walk out, right?"

"Because, dumb stupid! Whoever put me in here might be looking for me!"

"That doesn't make any sense, Callie," Walter said, frowning.

"Just shut up and do as you're told!"

"Okay, whatever," Walter said. While Callie was walking softly and hunched over like a spy, Walter was walking normally with his hands in his pockets. She grabbed his arm before he walked out into an intersection of hallways.

"Peek! Walter, you have to peek!"

Walter leaned over and peeked around the corner. The nurse was gone. "It's clear, Columbo," he said.

Callie slapped his shoulder, looking hard at him with a mean face. "What's that mean?"

"You're acting like a fucking detective. Why don't we just walk out of here?" he said, holding his hand toward the next hall. Callie put her finger up to her mouth and shushed him, frowning again. She was taking this seriously.

Out into the hall she dashed, slipping as quietly as possible past rooms with the doors wide open, as Walter walked casually by them, occasionally waving at the patients inside. But every time Callie would look at him, he would hunch over, acting like he was creeping, and put his finger up to his mouth. "Shhh!" he would whisper. There were TVs on inside some of the rooms, and in others, patients were visible walking around, but most of them were silent and dark, full of medicine-induced slumber and comatose silence.

They passed the room occupied by a nurse and saw her leaning over the bed. They were clear. They came around another corner and saw an exit sign halfway down its length. Being on the fourth floor, Callie guessed it was probably a stairwell. That would be painful on her ribs. She hoped they would find an elevator just as easily.

When they were halfway to the exit door, they heard footsteps and voices. Immediately, Callie grabbed Walter and pulled him against the wall beside an open room, and turned him to face her. He shook his head and smirked as two nurses – one male, one female – came around the far corner. Callie leaned casually against the wall with her arms crossed. Walter stood with his arms crossed and sighed, then said, "Wow, look at the time!"

Callie made another face. "Behave!" she said forcefully, but quietly.

"Okay, okay." He raised his hands in defense.

Walter glanced at the approaching nurses and raised his chin at them.

Callie was trying to make a face at him again, but he ignored it. The nurses approached, laughing and talking and Callie was sure they were going to walk by without saying anything. At the absolute last possible second, the male nurse stopped the other by the arm as he turned to address Callie and Walter.

"Ma'am, you should probably return to bed. We don't want you to catch pneumonia."

"Yeah, good idea. I was just on the way back in. Thank you doctor," Callie said.

The man had started walking away, but stopped when she said this. "It's nurse, ma'am."

"Nurse. Sorry. Goodnight, nurse." He frowned at her and then continued on his way down the hall. Callie thought it odd that neither of them even seemed to notice Walter was standing there. Walter was shaking his head and smirking at her again.

"The lengths you go," he said.

"Shut up, horrible actor!"

Walter laughed out loud.

"I still have my medical band on, Walter. I forgot to take the darn thing off."

Walter looked down at her wrist. "Oh my! I knew we would forget something." Callie was still looking down the hall. The nurses rounded the corner, and Callie grabbed Walter's hand and dragged him off again. Without thinking, they busted through the exit door they had seen earlier, and Callie remembered wanting to find an elevator.

"Walter, I can't go down the stairs. My legs and ribs will kill me!" Her words echoed like clanging steel in the concrete stairwell. Walter tried to smile at her, but was clearly growing tired of the charade she insisted on perpetuating.

"Fuck it, I'll carry you," he said, and had her hoisted over his shoulder before she had a chance to object. Unfortunately, a fireman's carry was no alternative to her walking on her own, and she shouted out in pain. A ring of fire shot through her abdomen as her ribs creaked against his shoulder. The shout scared Walter so badly he almost dropped her, but was able to right himself and set her down on the top step.

"I'm so sorry, Callie. I didn't even think about that! Are you okay?" He put his hand on her ribs just to the outside of her breast.

She knocked his hand away like a pesky fly. "Yes, I'm fine!" We need to find an elevator, Walter. I can't walk down these stairs, and you sure as heck can't carry me without killing me."

"Okay, sorry," he said again, raising his hands in defense. "You wait here. I'll find an elevator."

He turned and walked casually out of the stairwell. She heard his footsteps dwindling down the hallway, and then they stopped momentarily. Within thirty seconds the footsteps were heading back for the door she waited behind like a prize on a game show.

The door swung open and Walter reached in with his hand. "Come on, I found them." And they were moving down the hallway again.

She was having trouble keeping up with Walter's naturally long strides. With pain tearing through her like a saw, she felt like she was running. Callie was trying to be a trooper. She was not very good at circumventing the system – whatever system that may be. She had never broken the law, and had certainly never been to jail. So even going against the hospital rules, which said a patient had to be formally discharged, was uncomfortably awkward for her. She was invigorated though, and began to believe her flight was responsible for pumping the adrenaline into her veins now, and was washing her free of the medicinal hangover she'd been suffering.

They swung around the corner at the end of the hallway, and it dead-ended in a bank of elevators.

Callie ran up and slid to a stop by the buttons, then pressed the down call. Walter came walking up a few seconds later, hands in his pockets. They stood staring at each other, Callie sweating and out of breath, and Walter cool as clay. Callie's feet were like ice blocks, and she thought about giving Walter a hard time for not remembering to bring her some dry socks, but then thought better of it. He had, after all, been nice enough to go get her some fresh clothing. The dirty clothing, she remembered, they had left in her room on the chair. Maybe if nothing else, the nurse would see them and assume Callie was only in the restroom or something. It might buy them some time.

Standing there, she began to smile wildly at Walter. "This is fun!" she said, then they heard her name being called through the hallways. Walter's face dropped and he shook his head.

"Shoot! Did you hear that?" Walter nodded. And the elevator dinged. Then the doors slid open smoothly, mechanically. A doctor inside the car looked up long enough to make eye contact with Callie before returning his gaze to his notes.

Callie and Walter both turned to face the door as it closed, thinking better of waiting for another car. It would look too suspicious, she thought. They were almost home free. The light for the second floor was lit, so she pressed the button for the first floor. After a few seconds, the elevator swished smoothly down and came to a swift stop on two. The doctor got off without ever looking up.

Then they heard it. Over the speakers in the floor as well as the elevator box, *Attention all personnel. We have a code Adam, repeat a code Adam, fourth floor. Please check all patients moving about.* The doctor had stopped just outside the door and was now looking up at the intercom as if to see the source of the voice. At the last second, he turned back to the car, but the doors were already closing.

Callie let out a loud sigh as they came together. "I told you, Walter! We have to sneak!" She stood staring at him for a minute, but he only shrugged. "What will they do if they catch us, by the way?"

"Us? You're the one running. I don't have to be here. They'll probably put your ass in a papoose and inject you with barbiturates," he said, dead serious.

Callie's face went white. "What?" She covered her suddenly stopped heart with her hand.

Walter could not hold it back though, and broke up. Callie jumped at him, slapping his shoulders and chest as he wailed loudly. "Oh my God! You should have seen the look on your face!"

"Shut up Walter!" she said, still slapping away. He was ducking and guarding in the corner of the elevator, laughing so hard he couldn't breathe.

"Oh man that was perfect. I wish I had a camera!" The doors opened. They both straightened and stepped into the hall. "Oh shit. Hang on Callie. We have to get this damn thing off," Walter said, pulling on the medical strap around her wrist. "If you walk through that front door with it on, it will self-destruct!"

Callie looked at him for a moment, wondering if he was being serious. She caught on pretty quickly though and rolled her eyes. "Owww!" she yelped, and yanked her hand away. "Those things don't just pull off, Walter!" She slapped his shoulder again.

"Will you stop hitting me?" He took her by the shoulder and led her down the hallway as she fumbled with the bracelet. "People are coming! Pull your sweater cuff down over it!" She yanked and tugged on the bracelet, stretching it as far as she could to slip her hand out. She finally got it off, and dropped it in a trash bin as they rounded a corner.

There were two nurses coming toward them, but they walked right by, never looking up from their conversation. Callie guessed they either had not heard the announcement, or were just too caught up to care. Either way, the exit doors were twenty-five yards in front of them, directly ahead. Beyond the doors lay the darkness of night, and all the freedom Callie could ever hope for.

*   *   *

The sweet, soft sound of violin music filled the air, illuminating the small rooms with its beauty. Daniel awakened to it, the music barely audible to him from the closed bedroom. Lethargically, he climbed out of bed and wandered into the living room where Priscilla was playing a sad melodic piece. The digital disc player behind her accompanied her music with a cello. She had a series of these instrumental karaoke disks she could play along with, each with different accompaniment instruments. The acoustic reproduction of a concert played from a digital concert disc was realistic enough to have the neighbors poking out their front doors looking for the band in the street.

Priscilla's eyes were closed, her head swaying slightly as she pulled across the strings. She was wearing a long black dress that covered the soft velvet player's stool entirely, and the candlelight created shadows that danced about the walls and projected elegant contrasts on her cheeks.

Daniel stared, brows furrowed as he listened intently, not wanting to miss a note she played. He loved being in her audience. It was such a dreamy experience to hear her recreate such gorgeous harmonies on such a simple instrument. She played a Stradivarius antique, an heirloom left to her from one of her aunts who had died long ago. Like wine, the violin's harmonic aura grew more and more superior with its increasing age.

He leaned back on the couch, his hands on his face, stretching as he still fought with the sleep that kept trying to reclaim him. His stomach ached and growled. He was famished. He had not eaten since – well, he could not even remember the last good meal he had eaten, short of a ton of sugar in his coffee the night before. It was a wonder he had gotten any sleep. When Priscilla finally opened her eyes and noticed him sitting there, she smiled broadly and finished the piece with a long pull across the strings, then set her violin on its stand and stood up, straightening her dress. Daniel complimented her playing and asked if she was hungry. She said that she was, and she knew a great little place to get some lunch. It was then that Daniel realized he had slept past noon.

Callie sat up sharply, breathing heavy as bricks. Her hair was stuck to her cheeks and her ribs were aching something fierce. She lifted her hand to rub her face and realized a remote control was clinched in her fingers. The television was still on, as it had been all night, but the sound was so low she could barely hear it above Walter's snoring. She looked down at him on the floor, leaning against the couch. He had one hand behind his head, fingers wrapped around Callie's ankle. Callie looked around the room for some sense of what time it was. There were no clocks within the range of her poor eyesight. She thought of her glasses and guessed they must still be in her purse, in the wrecked car, in the back of some junkyard. She sighed, and threw her hand up to cover her mouth. *Oh my God.* Rubbing the sleep from her eyes, she stretched her back and felt her sweater pulling at her chest, where it was stuck like masking tape. The thick afghan she was swaddled in had brought her to a simmer, and she was soaked with sweat. She shook Walter's hand and noticed it was cold as ice. She rubbed it, trying to restore some of the circulation. *He'll be hurting when he wakes up.* She peeled his fingers off her ankle and shook his hand hard. He didn't move. His arm was completely asleep.

"Walter!"

He did not so much as twitch.

"Walter," she said again, leaning close to put her mouth against his ear. His snoring was extremely loud at close range. She giggled and kissed him hard on the cheek. His eyes popped open like mousetraps. He swung his arm forward, but had no control over it, and it flopped comically to the floor like a dead fish.

Callie sat back laughing. She stretched again. Her mouth tasted horrible and her breath was potent. She finally stood up and dragged herself to the bathroom to pee and gargle. She looked at her face in the mirror and shook her head. *God I look like hell. I smell like hell. I feel like hell. I must be hell.* She pulled her sweater off and looked at the reflection of her chest and ribs in the mirror, touching them feebly with cold fingers.

Her bruises were hard and dark, and covered her entire left side. She looked as though an angry abusive boyfriend had beaten her. She was happy to notice the edges of some of the bruises were already yellowing though, and wondered how long it would be until she looked normal naked again. Not that it mattered, as there was no one she needed to impress at the moment, nor would there be in her near future, she presumed. She had not had a boyfriend in forever, and didn't see herself running out and finding one anytime soon, and certainly not to get naked for.

She opened the cabinet at her knees looking for some Scope but found nothing but men's magazines and toilet paper. Callie shook her head and closed the cabinet. She found the Scope behind the mirror and poured herself a mouthful, then sat on the toilet swishing it.

Walter knocked and spoke through the door. "You almost done in there? I have to piss like a racehorse."

Callie could not answer, because of the mouth full of wash. She sat on the toilet, her sweater in her lap, with her knees together like a little girl. All she could do was moan, but it was not loud enough.

"Callie? You okay in there?"

"Mmmm!"

"Callie if you don't answer, I'm coming in there! Don't play games! You're scaring me!"

"MMMMMMM! MMMMM!" she cried, uselessly. She leaned over and tried to reach the sink to spit, but it was too high. And she couldn't stand, as she was in mid-stream. Quickly she fumbled with her sweater, trying to find an opening. But it was too late. The door was open and Walter was looking at her. Callie sat upon the throne, her cheeks puffed out like a chipmunk, covering her chest with the sweater as best she could. Her eyes were open wide and she was humming like a maniac. "MMMMMMM!"

Walter looked up at the ceiling and backed out into the hall, shaking his head. "Dammit, Callie, you scared the hell out of me! Next time knock on the counter or something!"

Callie still stared wide-eyed at him, then waved him away frantically with her elbow still held tight against her chest. She needed to spit badly, as the mouthwash was burning her mouth like fire now. Walter finally got the point and pulled the door closed.

"Hurry up in there, Cal! I got to piss!"

Later, Callie and Walter sat in the kitchen sipping coffee, staring at each other over the rugged little breakfast table. The sun was shining brightly through the window, its blinding rays seeking a spot right in Callie's eyes. She shifted in the chair and leaned her head against her hand, trying to block out some of the light.

"So what are you going to do when you find her?" Walter said.

"Well I don't know. I was hoping you could help me figure something out. We should probably take the computer away from her. Get it back to Royal. I don't know how she got in there and got that bad boy, but we're all in danger as long as she has it."

"What do you mean, 'danger'?"

"Well based on what I've heard about the computer set, there's no telling what it can be used for. I have no idea what she could possibly want with it, but I bet whatever it is, she's trying to get back at RRC for firing her," Callie said, sipping from her mug.

"Well that sounds like an idea," Walter said, pointing at her.

"Huh?"

"You said you had 'no idea'. Then you spouted off a pretty good one."

"Shut up, Walter."

"I don't get it. How can you use a computer against…"

"Think about it, Walter! It's a quantum computer. A computer that utilizes quantum state particles also undoubtedly has the capability to manipulate them. She may be making a quantum bomb or something."

"A quantum bomb?" His mug was suspended between the table and his mouth.

"Yeah, I don't know. It's just a thought. She could be making an antimatter bomb or implementing cold fusion or something. Who knows? But we have to stop her. I know that much." She took another sip of her coffee, staring at Walter over the top of the mug. His jaw was still slack.

"Wow. Whoa! This is some cool shit, Callie." She stared at him. "I mean, it would be bad if she blew us all up, but it's cool as all hell."

Callie rolled her eyes, shaking her head.

Daniel ordered the steak and eggs, knowing the small café would not prepare him a strip steak, but rather a dried up, stiff, cardboard excuse for a sirloin. Still, he longed for the red meat. Priscilla ordered a club sandwich and the soup of the day – a thick brown broth with large chunks of vegetables and meat. It smelled wonderful to Daniel, who watched her eat it, clutching his stomach. The main courses would be brought out shortly, so they had been assured.

Priscilla was talkative, her topics bouncing around from the current gossip to how good her soup was, and how nice it had been to travel all over the world, and how much she missed it. Daniel asked her if she would consider going back to it, to which she replied no, and that she loved her job as a juvenile psychologist way too much. "Oh, you should see these children, Daniel!" She worked with children who did not have a fighting chance left to their own devices. Most of them loved her like a mother, but some were such royal pains in the ass that she nearly couldn't stand working with them.

The food arrived, and Daniel sat back staring at his steak. It was lackluster. Most steaks when fresh off the grill have a slight sheen to them. This one seemed to have soaked up all moisture that would have been, and disposed of it entirely, and probably at the expense of taste. Daniel sawed into it with his dull steak knife, and after sawing for a good half minute, finally separated a piece of the tenacious meat. It pulled away like tough salt pork, fibrous and dry, and defied taste when he put it in his mouth. After smothering the rest of the steak with steak sauce, he was able to tolerate it.

Priscilla asked, "Is it good?" munching on her own sandwich. He nodded briefly, and washed the dry meat down with a quaff of his sweet tea. "So this physicist chick… What was her name again?"

"Amalie." He was sad that Priscilla had chosen to bring her up again. He thought he had told her enough about the mysterious Amalie the night before.

"I keep thinking Anna for some reason. I knew it wasn't Anna, but the name keeps popping up into my head. Anyway, so tell me about this Amalie chick. Why is it you spent so long in her company? Was your love for Annabelle abated by her beauty? Did she speak in soliloquies? Did she put her tits in your face? I know you're a big breast man, Daniel," she said, pointing her sandwich at him.

"A big breast man? I have never liked big breasts. Well, I don't dislike them as such, but I prefer small ones."

"That's not what I meant. You are a big lover of breasts. A breast fanatic, if you will."

"No, she didn't put her tits in my face. Don't be ridiculous. She just – what were my other choices?"

Priscilla laughed. "She just seems to have swept you off your feet. While I wouldn't say you were a loner at all, I've certainly never known you just to run off with someone you didn't know, not even reporting to home. So what is it with her, so powerful and alluring that would steal you away from the one you love? Can she move her hips like me?" She smiled and stuck her arms out in front of her, fingers snapping, wiggling her hips in the plastic seat.

Daniel shook his head. "You know, I really don't know what it is about her that drew me in."

"Well, what does she look like?" He was treading on thin ice as it was, not being able to tell her why he could no longer report to home, or why he was hanging on to Amalie like a fleeting thread.

"She's hot. She's hot for sure. She is definitely one of the best looking women I have ever seen."

Priscilla pouted her lips as if she were jealous. "That's what I assumed." She finally smiled. "So does she play for the Yankees?"

"Red Sox," Daniel said, looking up at her again.

Priscilla nodded thoughtfully. There might have been a little pride in her smile, as she learned she had maintained the top position in the league. "I had bet that she either made some grand entrance and immediately whipped her shirt up and buried your face in her cleavage, or she was just extremely hot."

"What the hell is all this with her putting her tits in my face? You think *every* woman does that? It takes someone with no shame, and a bundle of nuts to raise her shirt and flash a stranger. And besides, she didn't make any entrance. It was a 7-Eleven, for shit's sake." He prodded his stiff steak with the fork, frowning intently at it.

"You think I'm a slut don't you?" Priscilla said.

Daniel shook his head, widening his eyes at her. "Why the hell would you think that?"

"Because of the way I introduced myself."

"No. Well, no. It was a little curious, but no, I didn't think you were a slut. I'd definitely never been approached like that before though," he said, and popped a bit of steak in his mouth.

"That was the whole point. Your friends had said you were a breast man, so that was my approach. Regardless, I know Amalie must have been something special to attract you like that."

"Whoa-whoa-whoa, back up there, turbo," he said, holding his hands up. "What was that about my friends?" He was pointing his steely fork at her.

"You do remember where we met, do you not, Daniel?" She looked at him through the tops of her eyes, her head leaning forward.

"Of course. In the Haunt."

"Come on! You know all this already!"

"Umm, no I don't, Pris. I have no idea what you're talking about."

She sighed heavily, then sat back, putting her palms flat on the table top. "I had been staring at you for most of the evening. When you finally got up to go to the john, I slid over and asked Croucher what it took to get to you. He kind of looked me up and down, as if measuring me up – you know how Croucher looks at you, his mouth open like he's either gonna curse or puke…?" She waited for Daniel to nod. "Anyway, he told me you were a wild and crazy guy. And if I like wild and crazy things, you might like me. He also told me you were a breast man, though. He said 'Show him your boobs and he'll probably marry you.' So I did."

It was true. She had walked up to him shortly after he had returned from the restroom and stood at the end of his table. He looked at her and smiled, then she promptly said, "Hi, my name is Priscilla Martin. I sure would like to get to know you," whereupon she lifted her blouse, and flashed her breasts at him, asking, "Do you think I have a chance?"

Daniel had been so shocked – as had all his friends – that he could not even answer. He simply sat there staring at her, mouth locked open like a fish out of water. The only refuge he had from complete idiocy was the fact that his actions were pluraled by his companions. Especially Croucher, who had not thought she would actually carry through with it. He sat dumbfounded with his mouth open as he tried to review what had just happened.

Priscilla had finally said, "What's a matter boys – you never seen boobies before?" and sat down. She looked directly at Daniel and continued talking as if nothing had ever happened. "You know, I like music too," in a nodding reference to his Dave Matthews Band t-shirt, "and so much, in fact, that I never turn my stereo off at home. I also play the violin."

Daniel had finally recovered some of the muscle control in his jaw, enough to close his trap, then shake off his daze so that he could speak. "Uh, yeah. I umm, I really – I like music too."

"Yeah, I think we covered that," she said. She was very witty, he had realized from the beginning. She challenged him with every word that came from her thick lips. She then smiled and patted his leg under the table. "So tell me about you." It seemed to have launched from there, and then simply failed to ever land. The rest of the night was a tight engagement in lengthy conversation that stimulated both mind and body for Daniel; every word out of this woman's mouth had been right, and Daniel knew immediately that he could 'get to know' her, as she had so eloquently suggested.

He now faced her, renewed of the old memories, and nodded slowly. "So you had done some research before you ever approached me."

"Since when have you ever known me to dive into water without putting a foot in it first?" she asked, one eye squinting.

"Yeah, but flashing your tits at someone in a restaurant… What would have happened if I didn't like you?"

"Come on, Daniel. I knew you would at least give me the time of day then. And besides, you know I don't think breasts are any big deal. They're just another body part. Hence my immodesty," she said, waving the last chunk of her sandwich around as she spoke. "I just really don't care, you know? What did I have to lose?"

Daniel shrugged a give-up shrug admitting that once again, she was right. She was far from being reticent, and that about summed it all up. They had once been in the discount store together, looking for something, and she had noticed a man checking her out from the corner of her eye. She had then proceeded to wrap one leg around Daniel's waist and started kissing him heavily, her tongue lapping his lips and face in plain view of the spectator – just for effect.

Another time, they had been in the music store, standing face to face in discussion. Daniel had looked over her shoulder and noticed a guy checking her out. Knowing she would play along, he reached around and gently lifted her skirt up, showing the stranger her bare butt, clad in nothing but a thong, the equivalency of dental floss. Priscilla had looked over her shoulder and made eye contact with the stranger, then winked before turning back to Daniel.

Daniel had always been in love with her personality. She was the essence of a man in a woman's body; quick and sly like a man, yet tender and sensitive as a woman. She was willing to do just about anything, not just to get attention, but more to drive home a point. She was also the only woman Daniel knew who was wild enough to ride around in his Jeep topless. He had carelessly whipped his shirt off in the summer sun, sweating from every pore. In order to 'fit in', she followed suit, just as carelessly tossing her shirt into the back of the Jeep and stretching her arms to emphasize her new freedom. She had not been wearing a bra that day, but it would not have mattered anyway. The amount of attention she got was enough to be considered a road hazard. People had honked, and almost every man who drove by screamed, yelled and hooted. She just smiled lightly, minding her own business. She was one of the boys. Croucher sat in back, shaking his head. Her actions were not out of the ordinary. She had always been like that.

Priscilla said, "Besides, I wanted to stick out in your memory. I didn't want an ordinary introduction. I wanted you to remember that day you met me for the rest of your life." She stuffed the last bit of sandwich in her mouth, then sucked the mayonnaise off her thumb. "That's how I came to pitch for the Yankees, am I right?"

He nodded. Since all his buddies had been present for the flashing, they all knew first-hand what team she played for. And seeing how the pitcher was the most desirable position on the team, that's what they gave her. It was therefore possible for two women to play for the same team, but they would unlikely take the illustrious coveted position from her without some fair amount of argument. And since some of the guys never actually *saw* tits that great on their own, Daniel doubted her position would ever be in jeopardy. Priscilla was much hotter than most of the girls he and his friends ever ended up with.

The waitress brought the check and Priscilla laid a twenty on the table as they scooted out.

"Yeah, you were drafted on the spot for that one." He shook his head as they walked to her car. He stopped short, frowning, his arm shielding his eyes from the sun. "Where the hell is my car, anyway?"

"I'd assume it's at the Haunt, Dan. Just being in my presence voids your memory. God, I have an amazing effect on men."

"You're telling me," he said, folding into the hot leather seat of her sedan. "Actually it's in the RRC parking lot."

Priscilla stared at him for a moment. "What the hell is it doing there?"

"That's where Amalie works," Daniel said as if it should have been obvious. "She wanted me to meet her up there for something. I just left it there. No big deal."

Priscilla stared at him for a moment longer, before finally letting it go.

"Hey Pris, can I ask you a big favor?"

"Sure, hon. Anything."

"You think I could put up at your place for a couple of weeks? It's not real safe at my place."

"Daniel, what's going on?" she said with a sudden seriousness in her eyes.

"Nothing," Daniel said, shaking his head. "I just need to stay out of the house for a while. Is it cool?"

"Of course, Daniel. Is everything okay?"

Daniel nodded, closing his eyes. "Yeah. It's fine. I promise." He could not lie to her with his eyes open.

Callie sat on the sofa with her legs crossed, watching television, waiting for Walter to get out of the shower. She stared unenthusiastically at a horribly buff woman advertising an abdominal exercise machine that required no work at all. The consumer strapped it around his or her waist and turned it on, and the electrical impulses would trigger the muscles to contract up to seven hundred times in just ten minutes. Laziness, she noticed was now a preferred way to get in shape. *Elegant.*

Walter finally came out of the bathroom in fresh clothes, drying his head with a towel. Callie looked up at him and turned off the television. "Do you have a company directory? One that might have, say, Amalie's address in it?"

"No, not if she got fired years ago. If I do though, it's probably in that pile of shit on my desk," Walter said, drying his ears.

"That's what I was afraid of. Well could you look for me please? We need to find where she lives."

"Well, couldn't we just look it up on the Internet?"

"Yeah I guess we could. It might be a little more up to date, too. Good idea. Go look it up on the Internet, Walter," she said, pointing down the hall to his office. Walter turned to look down the hallway, then turned to face her again.

"Why don't you look it up, you lazy bitch?" Callie threw a couch pillow at him, missing by more than six feet. The pillow plowed harmlessly into the wall by the entry hall. Walter looked over at where it had hit, then looked back at her. "Nice shot." He turned and walked down the hall to his office.

"You remember her name, right?" Callie said, standing to follow him down the hall.

"Amalie something." He sat down behind the desk and moved his mouse around.

"Amalie London."

Walter found the name on people search, the only London in the area, and scratched the address down on the back of the business card. "So are we ready? Or do we want a plan of action?"

"Nah. I think we should just show up. Take a look around the place. If anything, she may think we're there to thank her for being there for me last night," Callie said, tucking her hair behind her ears.

"Uh, she was kind of forced to be… But okay."

"Let's just see what happens."

Walter opened Callie's door for her and helped her up into the Durango, then ran around to the other side. As he got in and started the engine, he looked at her. "You know where this place is?"

"Quail Valley Apartments. I think they're over across from the water company on Shady Grove Road." She looked at the chicken scratch on the back of the business card. "I don't know how you read this scribble, Walter."

*   *   *

Daniel was hunkered down in the back seat of Priscilla's car, ducking below the level of the windows. After circling the block a couple of times in surveillance, Priscilla dropped him off at the end of his street so he could run home and shower and change clothes.

"I'll call you later," Daniel said as he got out of the car.

"You want me just to go home?" Priscilla said.

"Yeah. I need to get some shit together. I'll call you to come get me later." He shut the door and Priscilla drove off dejectedly. He hated not telling her the truth, but knew it would be better to keep her safe, just to leave her out of it all. He crept through the alley and down a long row of trees, then hopped the back fence and entered through a window he always left unlocked. After walking through the entire house on eggshells, he was finally satisfied that he was alone, and in no danger of being ambushed by the cops. If they were watching his house, he had not seen them, and they most likely had not seen him sneak up to it, so he would be safe – at least until a car came to a stop in front of it. Then they would get suspicious.

His mind was now eased from the full night's sleep he had gotten, and he felt relaxed and calmed for other reasons entirely. Tomorrow he would be going back to work. He was not terribly excited by the prospect. Maybe he would call out for another few days. Daniel pulled his keys and change out of his pockets and dropped them on the dresser. The shard of porcelain caught his eye. He had forgotten about it, and was surprised it had stayed with him through a change into Amalie's wind pants. He turned it over in his fingers a little, admiring it. Something about it fascinated him. It was like a fidget stone, smooth on the sides, but rough and chalky on the edges.

Daniel turned in the shower, letting the steaming water bang him from every direction. He did not want to get out, but made it a quick one, hoping to be in and out of the house before anyone had a chance to start thinking anything. He would get out and get dressed, then pick up some stuff he would need, and stay away from the house for at least a few weeks. That should be enough time to either let things blow over, or at least try to fix those things.

He pulled the towel from its place draped over the shower door, dried his face, then stepped out onto the cool tiles of the bathroom floor. Removing the towel from his face, he blinked and jumped back as he realized he stood face to face with Amalie, who was standing less than six inches from him, smiling like a giddy little girl.

"Oooh! Slippery clean!" she said, rubbing her fingertip across the skin of his shoulder. "I like!"

"Well hello there, Amalie." He could not wait to ask: "So who was that tall dude with the broken nose you left with last night?"

"That was Blakely. He works with me. He said they have us on video all over the building. We have to move. I didn't leave with him, though. We just went to his car for a while."

"I see. Well I gave up waiting for you and left after about an hour, myself."

"Yeah, I saw you leaving with a woman."

Daniel's heart jumped for joy when he realized she *had* seen him. When he had left the night before, he had been secretly wishing Amalie were standing outside specifically so she would see him leave with Priscilla. Two could play at this jealousy game, he thought.

"Oh yeah," he said, feigning forgetfulness. "Yeah, we went to her place to talk for a while."

Daniel was hoping Amalie would say, "Really? So just who was that lucky woman?" But she did not. Instead, she just nodded understandingly. He was so caught up in trying to make her jealous of Priscilla that he had entirely failed to notice the reasons for which she was not asking such things. These reasons being respect for his privacy, as well as just plain keeping her nose out of business in which it did not belong. She was altogether being polite.

Amalie said, "Yeah, that's what your friends said. They said she was an old friend and there was no telling how long you would be gone with her. So I just stayed there waiting for you and talking with your friends for a few hours. They are great people, Daniel! I just love your friends."

Had Daniel been a battleship, then he had just been sunk. It had all been for nothing. She knew. She knew where he had gone, she knew who he had been with, and she knew Priscilla was a long time friend of his now. Daniel felt like an idiot. And now he stood dripping on the tile of his bathroom in the presence of the only woman in the world right now who knew his intentions better than he knew himself.

"Yeah, they are a great bunch of guys. I'm glad you like them."

"Yeah," she said. She smiled softly, breathing through her nose as she looked up at his wet dripping hair. She had taken the towel from his fingers and was now concentrating on drying his hair for him.

It was a sensual experience having her dry him from head to toe. And even in his naked state, he somehow felt at ease with her looking him over. He had nothing to hide from her anyway. She was not making it a sexual experience, though it could have easily tilted that direction. "You want to try something different?"

Daniel's pulse raced. "Sure," he said as calmly as he could muster.

"You will really have to trust me bunches Daniel. You sure you can do that?" At that moment, he reckoned Amalie's smile could buy her a ticket to anywhere in his mind.

"Ready when you are." She clapped briefly, grinning as she ran into the other room. Daniel watched her down the hallway as she fingered through his CD collection, looking for the right music. He could not see her choice, but as soon as the slow melodic bass line came to life, he recognized it as Peter Gabriel. Music to live by, he thought. Music to love by. She knows how to choose 'em.

She came back into the bathroom and told him to kneel down in front of the counter. He did as he was told. And then from behind her back, and as calmly as if she were about to put on makeup, she brought forth a pair of scissors and started cutting his hair. He breathed in sharply through his nose as he felt the cold steel against his head.

"Um, Amalie? What the fuck are you doing?"

"We need to cut your hair Daniel. You don't want to look like that guy on the crime video, do you?"

Daniel sighed, but vowed himself to keep still and let her finish. She had a good point, but moreover, it was already too late to object – stopping now would leave his head messed up. He was in her hands now.

The soft sound of the steel scissors continued as she slowly made her way all the way around his head. It felt so different to be short the weight of the long hair that had come down to his shoulders. And as he stared at the hard floor upon which he knelt, he saw long locks falling away, leaving him with only inches of his hair.

She finally laid the scissors atop the counter and started blow-drying and combing his hair. She then squirted some gel into her palm and lathered it, then spread it long over his short hair. Running her fingers through it, she tousled and teased it until it looked exactly the way she wanted it to look. And after many long minutes on his knees, she tapped his shoulder having him come to his feet. He stood face to face with her as she had him bend his head forward slightly, to put the final touches on it. He looked deep into her eyes as she looked at her hands in his hair, a look of determination on her face. He loved being this close to her. Then her eyes finally met his, and she smiled.

"Okay, have a look." He did. The difference was shocking. His hair had been long and straight, healthy and beautiful. Now it was short and messy, sticking up every which way. It reminded him of that Walter guy's hair. Had she wanted him to look like Walter? It had much style to it, but it would definitely take a while to get used to. Still, he could immediately see why she would like it. He looked back at her, shaking his head.

"What the hell? Are you trying to make me look like Walter?"

"Oh, Daniel, steal my heart!" she said, eyes wide open. "You look like such a hunk! It makes you look buff too. Your arms and chest and everything already look bigger." She ran her finger down his arm. He looked again into the mirror, and had to admit to himself that he actually quite liked it. He nodded, running his tongue along his teeth, then looked back at her.

"Cool. Looks good. What next then?"

"Well, there's this little church downtown that will do a wedding on short notice…" she said, staring at him seriously. Then she finally smiled. "Just teasing, Danny. You look ever so good though. I liked your hair the way it was, but now you look awesome! I love it!"

"Well I'm glad you knew what you were doing."

"That's actually the first time I've ever cut anyone's hair."

"What if you would have screwed it all up? I was your experiment?"

"Well just look at yourself in the mirror!" she said. "You look ultra-good. If I messed it up, we could always have buzzed it for you." Daniel looked again, and finally decided he really liked it. He would miss his hair, he thought, but it did – after all – look pretty damn good. What would his friends say about it? He could see it now: Croucher would say, "Man you whipped bastard! You let a bitch trim your stitches?

She pulled a Delilah on your Samson ass." He could hear it as though Croucher had already said it.

"Can I ask you a question? Completely off subject?" he turned and said to her.

"Sure, Daniel. Anything."

"Have you brainwashed me or something? Cause I don't really feel a damn thing about Anna. I hate to say it and all, but I keep thinking about how I'm not thinking about her at all. The only reason my mind settles on her is to remind myself that I haven't been thinking about her."

"Daniel, the last thing I want to do is replace her. Brainwashing you would be the farthest thing from my mind." She looked at him with puppy dog eyes. "You know," she said, nodding slowly, "it might have something to do with where you stayed last night."

Daniel felt himself blush. *Great. She knows everything.* He reckoned the guys might have told Amalie that he and Pris used to be a couple. "Okay, whatever. So are we ready to go fix this thing?"

"Go get dressed Daniel. We'll go for a walk, and I'll tell you what I've been thinking," she said, patting his shoulder.

When Daniel finished dressing, he looked in the mirror and jumped, still not used to seeing his hair so short. This would take a while to get used to, he reminded himself. Amalie had sat on the far side of his disheveled bed, facing the wall, hands in her lap. She watched the wall so as not to see Daniel dressing, as if it was something she had not seen now.

After walking all the way around the block, they approached the volunteer park and came to rest on a park bench. Ducks scattered down into the creek, as they got comfortable. Even in the winter months, it was hot outside, and Daniel wondered if the weather would ever make up its mind.

Daniel leaned back against the picnic table, and wiped the sweat off his brow. "I'm gonna have to take another shower now. It's hot as hell out here."

"That's okay. Maybe I will take one with you this time," she said. He let it slide. But he knew one of these times he was going to hold her to it – 'it' being whatever she happened to have said.

"Yeah, yeah, whatever. So start talking, woman. Tell me what you came up with."

"Well Blakely told me they were looking for me, they know we stole the computer. Fortunately none of them know where I live. I keep two apartments. One that they know about, then the other where I go to be alone," Amalie said. "So we have some time. But not much. We will have to hurry."

"So did you tell him what you were doing with it?"

"Yes. I had to. I didn't tell him everything though. I didn't tell him we had already used it. I just told him what I had to."

"Well is he gonna turn you in?"

"To whom? They already know I have it. They had the plates run on your Jeep, and they know who you are too. Chances are, they've already come by your place looking for us. It's best that we stay away from there."

"Yeah, I need to be avoiding that place like the plague," Daniel said. A squirrel ran across the open field and disappeared into the trees before the creek. He watched until it was out of sight.

"So, Amalie… You said something before about only ever messing with the future? Why is that?"

"That's the only way we can be sure not to mess something up. You could begin to understand the effects of taking Hitler out of the picture, or saving Lincoln or Kennedy from assassination, you know."

"Ah," Daniel nodded. After a moment of silence, he spoke again. "You know, you sure are different."

"How do you mean, Daniel?"

"Just – well, take your job for example. You mess with time. You must admit that's pretty extraordinary. I never dreamed I'd actually see a quantum computer. Much less use one."

"Yeah. Well that's my job, and now they are coming after us to keep me from letting it out. If I get caught using the Q computer by someone other than them, the secret's out. They won't let that happen. So they are trying to stop us. And apparently they went after Callie too."

"Callie? You mean that blond girl in the hospital?"

"Yup. They put her there."

"What the fuck?" Daniel said, his face bitter with confusion. "That doesn't make any sense."

Amalie shrugged and sighed.

"She was apparently one of the engineers who designed the application, and they're about to go to press with what they know about the ghosters. They think she'll talk for some reason."

"So that was Royal in the Suburban last night?" Daniel said.

"Of course. You didn't think they would let us waltz out of that building with a two-million-dollar machine did you? Theft has its cost."

"I didn't think we'd get run into a train! Ooln's Beard!"

Amalie stared at him blankly for a moment. "Ooln's... Whose beard... What?"

"Ooln's Beard. It's an expletive. I got it from a book. You know, if I had known I might get killed I wouldn't have followed you into that building."

"Let's not forget, you owed me this, Daniel. Had you not hacked my damn system in the first place, we wouldn't be dealing with any of this." She sighed. "You know, they want me dead now. I'm their nemesis."

Thoughts of prison swept through Daniel's mind. His stomach tightened. "I want you to take me to get my Jeep, Amalie."

"They're going to be all over the place there, Daniel. Besides, it's probably been impounded by now. Burt is doing what he can to fend them off for a while, but he can't hold them back for long."

"Who the hell is Burt?"

"Blakely. Burt Blakely. He's on our side, Daniel."

"F Burt! I don't give a shit about him! I just want my fucking Jeep and my life back!" Daniel stood up and faced her. "Dammit woman, when will this end?"

Amalie stared at the creek. She was breathing heavily. Her eyes were glassy. "Soon, Daniel. We'll fix it all, and everything will be back to normal."

Just two days ago, he was fine. Granted he was dealing with Anna's disappearance, he was at least not in any trouble. Now he had no car, he had been forced to avoid his house, and the police were looking for him for breaking and entering, and burglary.

"Well the sooner that happens, the better. I'm not good at this stress shit," Daniel said, holding out his hand. He helped Amalie up from the bench. They walked across the grass back to the road.

"I know you're worried about things, Daniel. But I promise you all of it can be fixed. And once we return everything to normality, you won't remember any of the bad stuff."

"I sure as hell hope not," Daniel said, looking at the sky. Amalie stared at him as she held his hand. They came to the end of the alley that ran behind his house. "Where'd you park?" They were still at the end of the alley. "How'd you get here?"

"I acquired another car, Daniel." She pulled the keys out of her pocket, dangling them from a stretched finger. Daniel smirked.

As they approached the fence separating them from Daniel's backyard, Daniel stopped again. "Okay. Why don't you run on out, and let me take care of some shit I've got to do. I'll catch up with you later tonight. We'll make our fix then."

Amalie looked up at Daniel again, tilting her head. "What's more important than-"

Daniel put a finger to her lips. "Never you mind. I'll be there."

Amalie looked confused, disappointed. "Okay then," she finally said, sighing. Daniel stood with his arms crossed as she got into her car – parked in his driveway – and pulled the door closed. Her window was down.

"Thanks for the haircut, Am." Then he snuck into the house to call a cab.

"Holy shit!" Priscilla screamed as she realized who she was looking at. It had initially taken her a moment to register. She had opened the door and stared vaguely into the countenance of someone she had thought was a stranger, without the slightest air of recognition or care in the world. Then it had hit her like a three-ton safe. She stepped out onto the porch and spun him around, looking at him from all angles, mouth hanging wide open.

"Oh my God, Daniel! You look fantastic! Holy shit!"

When he had finally been observed from all angles, and he came to rest facing her again, he stared unenthusiastically into her eyes and said, "Are you done yet?"

She finally took her hands off his shoulders, but only to cover her mouth with them. "Holy shit, I cannot believe it! You look so fucking gorgeous! I could take you in there and fuck your brains out right now!" she said, almost shouting. Daniel's eyes widened. "What in the name of the elephant made you decide to cut it off?"

"I didn't. Amalie did it. I got out of the shower and she was standing there. She – look – can we not talk about her right now? I came to ask if you had eaten lunch yet."

"Oh. My. God," she said, three separate sentences. "Yeah. Let me get my bag. Holy shit!" She disappeared into the small apartment. She was still talking as she retrieved her purse and finally reappeared, but he could not hear anything she said except the occasional phrase that she had already said before. She pulled the door closed and locked it, still talking.

"You know, you're gonna have to come back here afterwards and have serious 'lights-on' sex with me. You know that, right?"

"Yeah, sure. Whatever. Does it really look that good?"

"Yes! Oh my God!" As they walked down to her car, she ran in small circles around him, viewing his haircut from every angle, once again. The whole time Daniel had known Priscilla his hair had been long. And at some point long ago it had been longer than hers. She was obviously not getting used to it as quickly as Daniel had.

"Hang on. I need to get my camera!" she said, then turned and ran back toward the apartment. Daniel's arms dropped at his sides and he sighed heavily, impatience audible in his breath. He pulled his smokes from his pocket and went to lean against her car to have one.

After a brief moment Priscilla reappeared and snapped him from every angle with her digital pocket camera, logging each click with a comment. "You are so gorgeous. Holy shit." When she had satisfactorily photographed every possible hair at every possible angle, she shoved the camera in her purse and smiled giddily at him.

"You are so crazy," he said as she unlocked her car.

Then everything stopped. Priscilla was silent. She looked around, confused, then turned to face him again. "Daniel, where is your Jeep?"

"I have no clue. Probably in the impound."

"Impound? Like the jail for people's cars?" She pulled her shades down to look at him.

"Yeah. Forget about it. Let's go. You drive." She did.

They pulled out of the parking lot and onto Beltline heading north for no particular reason. Beltline ran all the way through Dallas and the surrounding everywhere, seemingly in every direction. One almost could not drive through Dallas without crossing it at least once. A friend of Daniel's had once told him he took it all the way around to see where it went. It had brought him full circle to starting point, and had killed three and a half hours of his day.

Daniel stared lazily out the window as the buildings and businesses blew by, vaguely aware of what Priscilla was saying. Generally he was very attentive to her, but he had a lot on his mind and couldn't find the mind to concentrate on her words. Then she turned onto a dirt road that connected to Mill Street, which would lead out by his house. He recognized the path.

"Where are we going?" he asked.

"Well I don't know. I guess I was subconsciously heading to your house, but…"

"Holy shit, stop the car!" Daniel shouted. He was practically sitting sideways in his seat with his face against the glass.

"What? What is it?" She pulled into the rocks on the side of the road.

"Park. That's my car back there!"

"Are you sure?" she asked, bringing her car to a stop in a hardware store parking lot.

"Hell yes, I'm sure. That's my damn Jeep back there behind that chain link fence! Mother fuckers!" Daniel was already out of the car. "Hey," he said turning around, "you have a coat back there?"

"Yeah. Why?" Daniel did not answer. He opened the back door and grabbed her long leather coat and turned back, jogging back to the fence where he had seen the Jeep. Priscilla was quick behind him, trying to keep up.

"Well do you have the keys? How much will it cost to get it out?" She had no idea what his intentions were, or she would not have asked the latter.

"Of course I have the keys! It's my fucking car!" Three feet from him, just the other side of the mesh, stood his old dusty trusty Jeep.

"What are you doing, Daniel?"

"Go get in the car. Meet me back at your place," he said, and threw the coat over the barbed wire that ran the top of the fence, then scaled it swiftly. The coat protected him from the barbs as he swung over and grabbed hold of the sleeve on his way down. The coat dropped off with him, and he was safely on the other side. He wadded it up and tossed it back over the fence to Priscilla, who frowned at the way he was treating her five-hundred-dollar leather coat.

She finally stepped back a few feet as she realized what was going through his head. Within the moment, he had the car started, and was backing up. He stopped about fifteen feet back, then Priscilla watched in amazement as he put it in gear and floored it, coming straight for the fence. She stepped back a few more feet and prepared herself as best she could manage.

The Jeep came crashing through the chain link, bringing down the poles on either side of the area through which he crashed. The metal made a sickening squeal as it scraped across the front of the hood and the crash bars before being smashed to the ground in a useless heap of wire and knots.

Daniel brought the car to a halt directly beside Priscilla, and without a word, she was swinging herself up into the passenger seat. Daniel floored it again, and they were throwing gravel. The yardmaster was finally out of the small building and shouting, shaking his fist at the fleeing car while Priscilla looked back at him smiling. Then she waved. That was what Daniel loved about her.

He pulled up next to her car at the hardware store and stopped quickly. "Hurry!" he said, and was off again. Shortly, she was in his rearview mirror, both hands atop the steering wheel. Daniel's heart raced with excitement as he hauled ass down the service road and back to Priscilla's house. It was nice to have at least part of his life back.

When they pulled into her parking lot, he came to a squealing stop beside the trash dumpsters and waited as she pulled into a space and dashed to his car. She was moving quicker than he had ever seen her move. *Good girl, Pris.* Within the minute, they were back on the highway, heading west.

∗ ∗ ∗

"Okay, here we are," Walter said, pulling into the Shady Grove apartment complex. "What number is it?"

Callie was frowning at the business card. "You tell me. I can't read your chicken scratch," she said, and held the card up where he could see it.

He squinted at it for a moment, then smiled. "Oh. 312. You can't read that?"

Callie screwed up her face. *Always the character.* She looked up at the building in front of them and saw the placard that read the building number, and the apartment numbers it housed. "Okay, must be the next building down," she said. "Just park over there."

Walter looked where she was pointing and frowned at her. "Oh yeah, nice and inconspicuous."

"We're not trying to be inconspicuous, remember?" Callie said smartly. She loved beating him. It didn't matter if it was a game of checkers or a math problem; she loved being the one to win. She was not terribly competitive by nature, nor did she necessarily like to see Walter being beaten. But if someone was going to beat Walter at something, she liked it to be herself.

Walter parked the truck and they got out, meeting at the back bumper. "All righty. Let's go knock on the door." They headed for the stairway.

Walter knocked politely on the door. After waiting several long moments, he knocked again, a little harder. He turned to look at Callie, who was staring quietly at him. She had intentions she had not yet let on to him. She guessed he was beginning to figure them out though, as he pounded a third time, then reached down to try the doorknob. The knob itself looked as though it used to be brass, but now stood lusterless and patchy, as if someone had used sandpaper gloves to open the door.

It turned easily and the door swung open with a lengthy creak. Callie tightened her shoulders against the sound. The hinges were in bad need of an oiling. The apartment was dark and cool, and smelled fresh like flowers or incense. Callie sniffed and smiled. After a brief glance around the cramped apartment, she gathered no one was here.

Walter walked back into the bedroom as Callie went in the den area behind the kitchen. There was a large desk made of particleboard and veneer standing against the back wall, overloaded with papers and books, with a small monitor right in the middle of it. Callie glanced under the desk to have a look at the computer. It was a standard mini-tower clone, nothing special. Definitely not a quantum computer. Standing in one of the thin mail slots on the desk was a stack of envelopes, and after shuffling through them Callie discovered they were bills. She picked up a handful and pulled one out, checking the name on it. Amalie London, it was. They were definitely in the right place.

"What'd you find?" Walter said from behind her. Callie jumped like she had been shocked with a cattle prod. She spun around and dropped the stack of envelopes.

"Oh my God! Don't do that to me!" she said, punching Walter on the shoulder.

"Sorry. Didn't mean to scare you. You nervous?"

"Darn it, Walter! Here, help me pick these up." There were ten or eleven on the floor, spread wide like they had been thrown in the air. Walter bent over to help her retrieve them, and having picked the first one up, held it up and stared at it, frowning.

"What?" Callie said, looking up at him. He turned the envelope where she could read the address. She read it aloud. "Amy Ireland. Who the shoot is Amy Ireland?"

Walter rolled his eyes and dropped his hand. "Callie, you cannot use 'shoot' as a noun. Not ever."

She closed her eyes and shook her head quickly. "Whatever. Who is it?"

He shrugged. "You tell me." He picked up a few more envelopes, then fanned through the rest of them on the floor. "But it looks like half of these bitches are made out to her."

"Okay, so Amalie has a roommate," Callie assumed aloud. "Funny, this apartment didn't look that big."

"It's not. It's one bedroom." He turned and walked back into the back of the apartment.

"Where you going?" He did not answer. After a moment, he returned.

"There's only one toothbrush in the bathroom. So unless they're really close, she ain't got a roommate," Walter said. He stood leaning against the wall now, with his arms crossed.

"Well what does that mean?" She was sure something was amiss, but could not figure out what she was being told.

"Don't you think it's kind of strange that the two names on those bills are Amalie London and Amy Ireland? I don't know about you, but to me that looks like a pattern."

Callie frowned hard at the floor, then picked up the bills again, looking at them carefully. "Hey wait, the ones for Amy have a completely different address on them," she said. She stood up quickly, holding the envelopes in front of her. "Where is... Where is Saddle Creek?"

"What is that? An apartment complex?" Walter said, stepping toward her.

"Yeah I guess. Apartment 303. Saddle Creek Circle."

"I don't know. Why the hell would she bring those bills to this apartment?"

Callie already knew why. "She's keeping another place. Assumed name. She's living a secret lifestyle."

"What a weird bitch!" Walter said, and threw the stack of envelopes on the desk. "I knew something was weird about her. I knew she was hiding some shit!"

"Well she must be hiding something pretty big to be keeping a whole other place for it," Callie said, then straightened all the letters and stacked them nicely back in the letter slot on the desk. She searched quickly for a notepad and pen, then wrote the new address on a sticky sheet and put it in her pocket. "Well that was too easy."

He nodded and sighed. "Well let's go get her ass!"

"Yeah, but Walter, it's in another town entirely. I have to get food first," Callie said. "I'm hungry as a horse."

"What? The action is just getting started! You wanted to sneak all around the hospital! Now we have some real cloak and dagger shit, and you say you're hungry?"

"This is not up for discussion, Walt," Callie said, walking away, one finger held up above her shoulder.

"All right, fine. We'll stop at the Mexican joint on the way." They breezed out the front door, pulling it closed quietly behind them.

*   *   *

Priscilla was sitting sideways in her seat, staring at Daniel, face locked in a huge smile.

"Woo hoo!" she shouted. She took his face in her hands and kissed his cheek loudly, speaking each kiss as she pulled away, "Muah! Muah! Oh, I can't get enough of it, Daniel!" As if he couldn't tell.

"God, get over it, Pris! Damn! I don't look that good!" She furrowed her brow and nodded her disagreement. "You know you look pretty hot yourself," he said, matter-of-fact. She was wearing a long light skirt with a barely visible large floral pattern, the same color as the skirt, only a different texture. Her blouse was light as well, an almost see-through pale green, but had strategically placed pockets that prevented any snoopers from seeing anything too pretty. She wore it with the bottom two buttons open, so when she sat it split up to just below where her bra line would be – had she been wearing one – and her pierced navel was visible. Her tanned belly was fully exposed giving her the overall appearance of someone on vacation – someone completely relaxed. She had her dark hair pulled back tightly and high on her head in a small simple bun, and covered with an Easter hat.

"Why thank you, kind sir," she said, smiling. She had removed her shades from her purse, and now looked like a tourist, the large frames covering her entire eye sockets and brows. It was almost comical, but not to the point it outweighed the beauty of the whole package. She looked like the personification of elegance and class, sitting here in his front seat. "Let's go fast, Danny!" She held tightly onto her hat with one hand and turned the stereo up to beat the howling wind as they ripped down the access road and pulled onto the highway, exceeding the speed limit long before they had passed the first sign.

Priscilla leaned over and cranked the stereo up to almost a deafening loud.

On they drove. "Where are we going, anyway, Daniel?" He doubted she really cared. The moment was perfect. The weather had finally broken that day, giving them a break from the nasty rain that had plagued them for the last couple of weeks.

"I figured we'd go see Pappy," he said.

"Yes!" Pappy was the owner of a small burger joint out by a private airport. Daniel had stumbled onto it inadvertently when he and a friend were out cruising one night and they had gotten lost. They had been trying to find their way back out to a main road, and drove right past it. The small wooden sign above the front door very simply read, "Pappy's Burgers".

Daniel and Croucher had then traveled back the next day when it was open and eaten there. It was the best burger he had ever tasted. He had taken Priscilla there on a few occasions, and she had liked it not only because of the great-tasting burgers, but also the atmosphere. It screamed of family ownership, not corporate table service.

The road had gotten worse since he had last been there. The potholes now stretched all the way across it in some parts, and in the places where there were not potholes, the pavement was pushed together into long bumps cracked along the tops, and altogether it made for a completely and totally uncomfortable ride. Daniel was thankful to be in an off-road vehicle. They plowed over the bumps and through the troughs at high speed, bouncing and jumping all over the road, Priscilla hanging onto the oh-shit handle for dear life, screaming. The smile never left her face though. Daniel knew she lived for this ride.

As they came around the last curve, the grass was too high to see over, and there was no vantage at which they could see anything coming. Daniel swung wide and turned his wheel sharply as the Jeep slid hard into the dirt shoulder sending a cloud of dust and dirt into the air. It was then he realized the road was blockaded just ahead, and there was no time to stop. The bumper slammed through the wooden sawhorses like toothpicks, where tiny splinters and massive chunks of wood exploded into the air and rained down on them as they hit one final pothole before approaching the edge of what used to be a bridge, but was now a sharp cliff about forty feet high. The tires locked up and slid on the dirty pavement, rocks and glass covering their path. The edge was approaching quickly, and there was no sign of stopping. The noise of the sliding rocks under his tires was audible even above the loud music.

Priscilla was now holding tightly to the bar just above the glove box, eyes wide with terror, face flushed of all color. Everything seemed to be happening in slow motion. Daniel's heart seemed to have stopped beating entirely, and his spirit screamed with horror for an exodus from its body's looming demise. The smoke from the tires was thick and white as they skidded toward their fate in the creek far below. And only feet before the front tires left pavement, Daniel threw the shift lever into reverse and popped the clutch sending the tires squealing backwards against their trek. A loud bang and a whirr ground down before smoke and rocks shot and spat out in front of the vehicle over the edge of the cliff. Then the blaring stereo and screaming woman in his passenger seat fell silent as a tomb as the engine died and the car fell still. Daniel had unwittingly turned off the ignition in the heat of panic. When the smoke cleared, the silence was broken only by the sound of dirt and pebbles raining into the creek below. They both sat, staring out into empty space, reluctant to say anything, and much less, to do anything.

Daniel was finally the first to get out. He walked to the front of the vehicle and looked down at the tire. Had it rolled another inch, it would have gone over. The front half of the tire hung precariously over open air, the contact area resting at the exact edge of the asphalt. Small rocks and pebbles still drizzled off the edge of the eroding asphalt. There was no room to walk in front of the car. The front bumper hung two feet out above the chasm where a bridge used to cross. It looked as though it had been washed down by high rains, and it had happened very recently.

Looking across the chasm, he could see fragments of the concrete bridge lying at an angle in the water, only part of the structural beam still attached at all. A large slab of concrete lay jutting out of the water, and the bottom part of it was black as soot. It looked as if there had been a fire on it. Priscilla finally came around the back of the car and joined him near the front, staring out into the void. Neither said a word. They were both too shocked and surprised to even be alive.

The breeze was the only sound aside from the quiet lull of running water deep in the creek below. As they stared down at the dark water, Daniel finally had the realization that someone must want him alive. Someone must be watching over him. He squatted and dropped onto a knee, lighting a cigarette. Something about this view was inspirational to him despite its eerie wickedness. Priscilla stood behind him and put her hands on his shoulders. He just stared across the emptiness to the other side, smoking, and taking it in.

After a long moment of silence, Daniel flicked his cigarette butt far out into the void. Then he said, "You remember that guy we used to run with – his name was Darrell – he had the freak haircut and the shiny shoes?" Priscilla said that yes, she thought she did. "I think this is how he died. He went over a cliff in his truck."

"I don't remember hearing about that."

"Yeah, he was driving home from work on one of them windy mountain roads and had to swerve or something. So when his tires left the road, he just sailed off the side of the mountain."

"My God. I can't imagine the horror of going through something like that. Knowing you are going to die."

"No doubt. Knowing that all providence lost, life is just taking its final course, and there is nothing you can do to stop it. You have to sit there and watch it unfold. Not like being shot in the head or dying in your sleep or something. You have to watch it happen."

"Hopefully it happened quickly for him," she said.

"Yeah. But still, I can think of worse ways to die."

"Like what?"

"Drowning. That would be the worst in my book. Being stuck underwater and knowing you were about to have to take that final fatal breath. Knowing that that next breath would be of water, not air, and that would be it. F that. I don't even like to think about that."

"Well, actually, I have read about that though. They have talked to people who've drowned and survived it. They said there's a euphoric feeling when your lungs fill with water, and they forgot all their fears and stuff and actually enjoyed it."

"Enjoyed it? Must be a serious high to forget you're dying," Daniel said.

"I think the worst way to die would be by burning."

"Yeah, I hadn't thought about that. Ah, yeah, that would suck. Still, just think about if we had gone over this cliff here," he said, tossing a pebble out into the creek. "You said you couldn't imagine it. I think you can. It almost happened. But had we gone over and survived the fall... Then we would have to deal with drowning in it."

"Uh huh. Don't think we would have survived that fall though. That's a pretty good drop," she noted, looking over the edge, holding tightly to Daniel's shoulder.

"Yeah. Kind of glad my trusty old brakes here kicked in."

"You mean your reverse gear," Priscilla reminded him.

"Oh, shit, yeah. I forgot about that. I hope I didn't kill my transmission." Daniel stood and walked around the back and peered under the Jeep. Nothing appeared visibly wrong, so he rounded back to the driver's side and got in, about to start it.

"I've started it in reverse before but this is a little too close for comfort. I think I want to push it back first. I don't trust this predicament," he said, standing behind the wheel to look out over the edge again. He could not see anything above the hood, but the trees on the far side. It looked as if the world simply came to an end right beneath his car. Technically, it did. "Okay, I'm gonna pop the brake, and put it in neutral. You push me back from the edge. Just a couple of feet should be fine." Priscilla rounded the car and put her hands on the roll bar, preparing to push.

As soon as he popped the brake, the Jeep rocked forward on its axles, then settled back, swinging in its position. It was discomforting, and his face went white. It matched his knuckles on the steering wheel. He looked back at Priscilla, eyes wide. "That was bad," he said. She nodded thoughtfully.

"Okay, here goes," he said, and took his foot off the brake. For a moment, the Jeep did nothing. "Push, Prissy. Push hard!"

"I am!" she said, grunting. "It's not fucking moving!" Her words were beaten by frustration.

"Hang on, Pris." Daniel dropped low on the edge of the seat and stuck his foot out of the Jeep. He pushed back with her as hard as he could. It was ineffective, so he hopped out and shoved wholeheartedly against the driver's side of the roll bar. It rocked, but the wheels did not turn. "Let's rock it."

They tried this, letting it rock for momentum. There was, of course, the danger of it rocking too far forward and rolling off the edge. They were slightly arrogant in their hold on the bars, considering this potential, and having not planned for it.

While it was doubtful the Jeep would end up in the creek below just on this rocking momentum, it would still be near impossible to get it back up onto the road if the front tires went off. The possibility did exist that the whole car could go overboard though, based on how tall the tires were, and the vehicle's stance upon the axles. The angle at which it would be sitting if the front tires went off would be fierce.

"Okay, shit. This isn't working. The tranny must be fried after all." He stood back, scratching his head. Priscilla crossed her arms and frowned, looking to Daniel for answers. He knew she hadn't the foggiest idea about cars. She probably didn't even know what a 'tranny' was.

Daniel squatted again, staring at the Jeep, and lit another cigarette. "You know," he finally said, "the only way to tell if the transmission is really hosed is to push that sumbitch forward. If you can't push it forward either, then the transmission is effed up."

"If you say so, Dan. I don't know the first thing about cars. I don't even know what a transmission is." Daniel just looked at her and smiled wanly. He was not going to start training her.

"But I kind of don't want to try that, what with the ditch in front of us and all."

"I can see your reasoning there," she said, nodding.

He scratched his head, pacing. "I just don't know, Prissy. This is weird. Why won't it roll backward? What could possibly be keeping it from rolling back?" There were no rocks behind any of the tires, nor were any of the tires in trenches, he noted as he walked around the Jeep again and again. And according to the pitch gauge, they were level, so it was not an uphill push.

Daniel screwed up his face and looked at Priscilla. "My dad's transmission went out one time. You could push it but it would click like a wind-up toy, and it would stop either direction after about a quarter turn." He stopped and took a long drag from his cigarette, then stared at the ash. "If I could even push it a quarter turn, it'd at least tell us something."

"Daniel, if you push it a quarter turn, it goes off the cliff."

"There is that possibility. I think it will lock and catch before I can push it an inch though." He squatted again and Priscilla came around behind him. She put her hands on his shoulders and rubbed with her thumbs.

"I wish I could give you some ideas, Daniel. I can't even change my own oil though. Heck I have to have the guys at the filling station put air in my tires," she said. Daniel looked over his shoulder at her.

"You can't put air in your tire?"

"Yes, silly I can do that. I just can't make the gauge thingy work." It sounded as if she thought there was some nobility in being able to do the former, without the latter.

"You are too funny, Pris." He scratched his chin and sighed. "Well I think pushing it forward would at least set my mind at ease about the tranny. I'm just bettin' that son of a bitch won't roll a click." He looked at his cigarette and screwed up his mouth.

Daniel finally stood up, flicked his cigarette long and far, then conceded to his plain lack of other options. He walked around to the back and shook his head, putting his hands on the back of the car. "It's the only way to tell," he said, and then promptly pushed the Jeep off the edge of the cliff, down into the creek forty feet below.

CHAPTER THIRTEEN
Situation

Walter and Callie were seated in the non-smoking section in a booth by the window at Sancho Salsa's, Callie's favorite Mexican restaurant. Callie leaned back in her seat, stretching her arms behind her head. She sighed and closed her eyes, shaking her head.

Walter was looking at her when she opened them again. "So what are we gonna do if we walk in there and see the computer sitting on her desk? You plan on just picking it up and walking out with it?" He was munching on chips and salsa as he spoke.

"I don't know. What do you think we should do? I guess we could always call the cops or something," Callie said, taking a chip and staring at it. She then wiped off the excess salt and bit into it.

"Nah. Forget that. I'd rather just take it from her and return it. Be the heroes, you know? Dammit! That thing was locked in my truck too! If I would have just realized earlier that they stole it! I could have blackmailed the hell out of 'em!"

"Blackmail? For what?" Callie said, frowning.

"I don't know. Whatever. Who cares? It just pisses me off." He slammed his fist on the table. "I didn't catch it until too late. I let her trick me into opening the truck thinking she was going to be going for a ride. She said she was cold and we could 'talk about it inside'. Which we didn't. She just got in, warmed up, then got out and took off with the computer." He took another chip, dipped it, then popped it in his mouth. "And I fell for it all."

"Don't worry about it, we know where she lives, Walter. We'll get it back." Callie smiled at him, then looked up as a couple appeared at the end of the table. "Oh my God – Stuart! Beth! What are you doing here!" she said, standing up quickly.

After hugs and hellos, Callie introduced Walter to her friends, and he shook their hands. Callie had not seen them in over five years, and excitement pumped through her veins.

"Well we're sitting over there in the big booth if you wanna come join us," Stuart said after a few moments of catch-up talk. He pointed to the booth in the corner, where two other couples sat waiting for them. A couple of them waved at Callie as she looked over at them. She recognized all of them as old friends.

She turned to Walter. "Can we go sit with them Walter?"

He nodded and shrugged. "Sure. I'm in no rush to save the world from the quantum bomber."

* * *

Hands on hips, Daniel stood staring at the dust cloud. "That has to be the single stupidest fucking thing I have ever done in my life." Priscilla stood staring wide-eyed over the edge, mouth slightly open, but said nothing. Gazing upon the single stupidest thing Daniel had ever done in his life, she had nothing to say. Finally, her eyebrows rose and the edges of her lips twitched slightly, and then from her belly, the hardest laughing she had ever experienced.

Daniel still stared quietly, shaking his head. He looked over at Priscilla who was wildly amused, holding her hands in fists, laughing, and eyes closed toward the sky. He grunted once, then looked back at the dust cloud. It was then that he slowly came to laughter, and was quickly overcome by it almost as much as Priscilla. She still stood in the same position, whereas he had to bend over to catch his breath. They both laughed so long and hard that they almost forgot what they were laughing about to begin with.

He finally came to grips with his hysteria and approached the edge of the cliff, looking down cautiously. There at the bottom on the rocks, lay his broken, mangled Jeep. Smoke and dust still blew hazily about the wreckage. "Shouldn't there be an explosion or some shit?" he asked seriously. "I thought for sure it would blow the hell up when it hit."

"I think maybe you have seen too many movies, my friend. Though I must admit I was a bit surprised myself," she said. "But that, Daniel, sad as it sounds to say, was comedy gold."

"Yeah, it was pretty stupefying. I can't fucking believe I just did that," he said, shaking his head, and wiping the sweat from his forehead. What the hell are we going to do now though?"

"Well, if we can get back into town somehow, I will buy you a brand new Jeep, Daniel. I'm sorry I laughed. But it was funny to me, watching you push it over the edge."

"No, no, don't worry about that, I can get myself a new one. You know, of all the regrets I have about my life up to now, my biggest regret is that no one was here video taping me doing that," he said, pointing repeatedly at the chasm. "That would have been America's funniest."

"I absolutely have to agree, Dan." Priscilla was red in the cheeks, and her eyes were glassy. That was the deepest she had ever laughed, and undoubtedly the most expensive punch line ever.

Daniel smiled right back at her as she laughed in continuous small spurts, until she finally crossed the few feet between them and took him in her arms. She kissed him hard on the lips and neck, somehow very aroused by the situation. He kissed her back intensely, and held her for a few minutes, until the excitement died away.

After scaling the cliff wall by way of a rope someone had tied to a tree, Daniel gathered all the important things he could get out of the car and tossed them up to Priscilla. He grabbed all his CDs and his shades and the quarters from the money holder. He left everything else to be scavenged. Upon rejoining her atop the cliff, they began their long trek back to the city, on the hot road, just slightly north and to the left of the middle of nowhere.

"What brought you back, Prissy?" They walked an easy, patient pace. There was no need to rush and waste what little energy they had. There was no telling how long they would be walking.

"I have been back. I just haven't had much time for coffee in the last few months. But I have been here."

"I tried calling a few days ago, just to catch up. I got a 'disconnected' message." He mocked the recorded voice that had spoken on the recording.

"Yeah, it changed when we got that last batch of new area plus codes. Then it just quit working. I have a new number now though. Not that you need it. You have always just dropped by. I wouldn't want to endanger that."

"Some things are just too personal for plastic, you know?" he said. She nodded, smiling. After a few moments, he continued, "You know, we sure have been through a lot of shit together for only having known each other for…"

"A few short years? I know. I think the same thing sometimes. I am so glad we are such good friends." She put her arm around his waist and laid her head on his shoulder. He leaned over and kissed the top of her head as they scuffed along the unkempt road.

Just atop the hill Priscilla stopped and pointed ahead to the side of the road, where a deer stood staring at them. She whispered, "Hey, look at the deer."

He looked up and put his arms up as if holding a rifle. "Pow." He raised his arms as the kick would have knocked him back at the shoulder.

"Aww, you can't shoot him! Look at how cute he is!" The deer bolted across the road and into the trees, gone forever. "How can you shoot a deer? They're so cute, and harmless."

"I couldn't. Tried once, but couldn't."

"What do you mean you tried once?"

"Well I went deer hunting with a friend of mine once. He and his dad go all the time. They loaned me a rifle and everything. But it was tripped out, because everyone went separate ways. I was afraid I was gonna get shot." He cleared his throat and lit a cigarette.

"You sure have been smoking a lot lately, Dan," she reminded him, sounding maternal.

"Yeah, well I just pushed my car off the edge of a cliff. Give me a break, would ya? So anyway, they were all up in their own deer blinds, and I was up in my own, way across the deer lease from them. I was in there all day. But I was determined. I was trying to be a professional deer hunter and shit. So I sat up there all morning waiting for a deer to walk into the clearing."

"How did you go to the bathroom?" she asked, brow furrowed.

"I didn't. I didn't have to. This thing is tight though – the blind I was in. It was hidden well up between these big ass trees. I could barely even see it from the ground. It was like the size of an airplane bathroom, with a cushion in it, and a sliver for a window on one side. Clearly made for one medium-sized man."

"So you sit up there all day and just hold it if you have to go?"

"Yeah, I guess. But I didn't have to." He cleared his throat and continued. "I remember there were a bunch of dead yellow jackets in there from the previous summer, so I had to get them all out before I could sit down. And spiders. Son of a bitch, those were some big spiders."

"Yuck. So if you pee, you're just shit out of luck?" Priscilla said.

"Good fuck, woman! You're still stuck on that?" he said as he took a drag from his cigarette. "I guess. I guess if you had to go, you could climb down and go find a bush or something. But I didn't. I remember I was hungry though." He took another long pull from his cigarette, then continued, pointing his fingers as if to illustrate where the blind was. "So I'm up there, like fifteen feet in the air in this tight ass blind, freezing my nuts off, rifle in hand, waiting for a buck to enter my line of sight. I remember my fingers were numb – it was so cold. It was the opening weekend of rifle season – like the beginning of November. And I kept having these visions of sitting by a fire and eating this huge plate of – well, what the hell ever. I was so hungry I could have eaten the ass end out of a menstruating skunk."

"That's lovely," she said, furling her lips. Daniel laughed. "So did you finally see one?"

"Yeah, about six o'clock. I was starting to get antsy, thinking about Christmas coming up, seeing those fiery visions and stuff. I was cold and ready to go the hell home. Then he walked into the clearing. Like a nine point or some shit. He was huge. A big score, he was. I pulled my ought-six around to my shoulder and lowered like a storm on his ass. He never saw me coming." Priscilla's eyes widened with excitement as he continued, "I lowered my scope right on his face to watch him coming. He was like thirty yards out, and I was cool. I was a cool customer, didn't make a damn sound. I was downwind of him too, so that helped. But check this out: he stepped right into the middle of the clearing, like ten yards away from me. I could feel my adrenaline pumping hard. My rifle was already cocked. I was ready. All I had to do was pull. And he looked right up at me. Just like that." Daniel moved his hand up to illustrate his point.

"Oh my God! He saw you?"

"Yeah. I was hidden as hell too. Had a little Smokey hat on and stuff. There was probably only six inches of me showing through that little window. But he looked up. I was almost right above him and he looked right up and looked me in the eyes."

"Well surely he must have seen you before," she said, crossing her arms as they walked.

"No! I was silent as… Well, I was silent. I didn't make a peep. You should have seen it though. He just slowly raised his head, like he already knew I was up there. It was like he realized I was betraying him and he was disappointed or some shit. He looked me in the eyes for a long while. I pulled my eye away from the scope and stared right back at him. He didn't blink or nothing. Then finally, he just looked back down at the ground and walked off." Daniel coughed, then nodded, looking at Priscilla. "It was like he knew I couldn't shoot his ass. He didn't even run away. It was the weirdest thing. I swear he knew I was there."

"Well, of course he did! He saw you up there!"

"No, I mean, it like – occurred to him – when he walked into the middle of the clearing. It occurred to him that I was up there, so he looked. I can't really explain it better than that, but I sure as shit couldn't shoot him after that. I could have, but I couldn't do it. And oh boy the guys gave me hell about it. Supposedly, he was like the biggest buck on the lease."

"That is too weird. So you made like some weird psychological connection with this deer then. That is too strange," she said, shaking her head. "That's a pretty neat story. You tell it well."

Daniel frowned at Priscilla, then shrugged. "If you say so."

They rounded the final bend of the bad private road, and crept up onto the blacktop that was maintained by the city. It was nice to be back on good solid road. Not ten seconds after they had reached the good road, cars started zooming past them.

"Okay, I guess this is where we start hitchhiking," Daniel said. "Actually, why don't you let me hide in the tall grass and you hike your skirt up a little. That'll stop traffic."

Priscilla spun round on her heel and faced the oncoming vehicles, and proceeded to raise her skirt above the knees. The first car in the line pulled over just ahead. They looked at each other smirking, but nothing needed to be said. She had fantastic legs and superior presentation. Thus, they had a ride.

The inside of the pickup smelled like weed, and as Priscilla scooted to the middle, she snapped her fingers, smiling wildly, singing along with the loud music that blasted inside the cab. Daniel climbed in behind her. The driver hardly seemed to notice them. He was staring out the driver side window, resting his chin on his hand, slouched way down in his seat. From the outside, the truck looked like any normal pickup, but inside it was a concert hall, complete with the darkness and the thick cloud of pot smoke. The Tejano music blasting from the speakers spoke loudly against the quiet of the walk they had made through the private airport.

As the door shut behind Daniel, the driver pulled back onto the road and carried on as if they had never been picked up. Daniel peeked into the back seat and noticed for the first time that the truck was full. There were two ladies in the back with another guy, who were all wearing shades and passing a pipe. Daniel nodded at them and turned to face the front. Not one of them said a word to either of the newcomers. It was as if everyone just wanted to mind his own business, and wanted nothing but the same in return. Of course neither Daniel nor Priscilla minded. It beat the hell out of walking.

How odd, Daniel thought, *that the truck is full of people, but all the passengers are riding in the back seat kissing their knees.* They were sitting with their feet on the speaker box. It had to be uncomfortable as hell. It was as if they had expected to pick up two hitchhikers. Or maybe they had hopped in back when the truck pulled over. It just did not seem that was the case.

Throughout the duration of the trip back into town, no one spoke to them, nor did they proffer the pipe. Daniel would not have accepted it anyway – nor would have Priscilla – but he thought it rather rude of them not to even offer. When he mentioned it later, Priscilla had slapped his shoulder and said, "Daniel!" as if that explained her whole outlook on the situation.

Once they finally reached the edge of town, the driver pulled the truck over in a very conspicuous effort to evacuate the two hitchhikers. They stepped out onto the grass and said thanks and saluted the driver before closing the door. Daniel's ears were ringing.

They walked the short distance up to the next gas station where Priscilla phoned a friend who lived nearby. The conversation was quick, Lisa was eager to help, and would be there in "a jiffy".

"You know what I forgot to do, Pris?" Daniel said after she hung up.

"What's that?"

"I forgot to grab clothes and stuff. I have to go *back* to the house," he said, holding his hands out to his sides and dropping them impatiently.

"You know, Daniel, I'm worried about that. Can you not tell me what's going on?"

"I got into some trouble and I may have the cops looking for me." Priscilla tried to cut in but he held his hands up to silence her. "It's no big deal. Trust me. It's gonna be fine. I just need to wait it out for a couple of weeks."

"Daniel, these things don't just blow over!" Priscilla said, taking him by the shoulders. "You think if they don't find you for a week or two they'll just give up on you? They know where you work, undoubtedly."

"Priscilla, I don't want to talk about it."

"Don't want to talk ab-" Priscilla stopped in mid-sentence, turning to face the street. She was shaking her head. She finally turned to face him again. "What can I do, Daniel? How can I help you if you don't tell me what's going on?"

Daniel could not think of a way to tell her that he could fix it. If he could get back behind the Q computer, he could make it all disappear. But he couldn't tell her that. "I'm sorry, Pris. I just..." he trailed off.

"Daniel, you know if you stay with me I could be arrested too. That's harboring!"

"Not if you don't know about it, Priscilla! That's why I wasn't going to tell you about it!" he said, taking her by the shoulders.

Priscilla obviously did not like it though. She stood staring at him, biting her lip and shaking her head. "I love you Daniel. That's the only reason I'm doing this for you. I am completely against it though."

"I know. And I'm sorry to put you through this. I'll be out before you know it." He did not want to get her in trouble, but he needed a place. There was simply nowhere else he could think of that would suit his needs. His mind was covering all the bases for him. He could stay with Croucher or Jeffrey – assuming he didn't mind putting up with the pigsty – but then his *wants* wouldn't be met. He was not just thinking shelter. He was thinking comfort.

Lisa dropped Daniel off at home first, so he could pack the stuff he had forgotten to pack earlier. Priscilla said she would be back with her own car in an hour to pick him up. Daniel had told Lisa to stop at the house at the end of his road, acting as if it were his own. Then he waited until they drove off before sneaking around the back to the alley and down to his house. He was getting good at this incognito shit.

Lisa took Priscilla home directly, and accepted her invitation to come in for coffee and chat. But as they pulled into the parking lot, a strange woman approached the car and smiled, recognizing Priscilla. "Maybe you better let me handle this first," Priscilla said. "I'll call you later."

They said their goodbyes and Priscilla exited the vehicle, having a pretty good idea who the woman was. As she shook her hand, the displeasure began to growl in her stomach.

"Hi, I'm Amalie London, a friend of Daniel's," the woman said, confirming Priscilla's suspicions.

"Priscilla Martin." She already did not like this woman. Priscilla had never felt challenged by another woman when it came to men, but somehow she felt instantly inferior to Amalie. And it pissed her off. She had earned Daniel's friendship, respect, and love. She had refined it over a period of many years. Then this knockout model-like princess with a degree in physics and a slight accent walks in, and Daniel is already talking about her like a new girlfriend.

She maintained her direction for the door, with no intention of stopping for a conversation with the strange woman, but Amalie trotted behind her, catching back up. "Umm, Priscilla, I was hoping I could talk to you a little bit."

"Uh huh," Priscilla said, still walking.

"Are you okay?"

"Just fine." She reached the door and dug through her purse in search of keys.

"You look a little stressed out or something, is all."

"Yeah, well today has been burdensome – just the other side of annoying – and I'm ready to call it quits."

"Do you want to talk about it?"

Priscilla stopped. "What, with you?" She let the disdain ring through in her words. "Not really. No offense, Amalie, but I don't even know you," she said, her voice cracking. She finally retrieved the keys from her purse and unbolted the door. The warm air blew out around them.

"You sure you are okay?"

"Scratchy throat. Besides that, I am physically without noticeable ailment beyond the fair lack of slumber and usual allergenic bother I have begun to accept as proprietary function. I sang and played the violin for a friend and noted my resonance was foreboding as a coming loss to my voice entirely. But that's okay. I sound sexy when I'm hoarse." She stepped into the apartment and pulled the door against her cheek. "So did you come to take my blood pressure? Make sure I'm gonna make it?"

Amalie smiled – again the fake smile – and shook her head. "No, I'm just here to talk about a friend of yours. May I come in please?" Priscilla stood there staring at Amalie for a long moment, head resting between the door and the jamb. She finally gave, sighing, and walked away from the door, letting it swing open. Amalie pushed it closed quietly behind her.

"Oooh, I love your table! Is that African?"

"Yeah. My mother bought it for me."

"Wow. This is really nice in here. Cozy!"

"Uh huh. So I'm sure you came here for other reasons than to comment about my furniture and the oblique décor."

Amalie sat on the edge of the sofa, and carefully set her purse on the coffee table. Priscilla looked at her, standing with hands on her hips. She thought Amalie looked as though she were walking on eggshells – on the verge of a nervous breakdown.

"I need to find Daniel," Amalie started.

"What does this have to do with me then?"

"I'm sorry?" Amalie widened her eyes.

"You heard me. What do you want with me? You want to help Daniel, but you are sitting on my sofa."

"I don't understand, Pris-"

"Don't play stupid, Amalie. I know who you are. You think coming over here with that glow on your face is going to buy you some respect? It doesn't work that way. I love Daniel. I'm not going to let you fuck him around. And if you don't start talking straight, and cut the bullshit, I'm going to ask you to leave. What is it you want from me?" she said.

"Okay, Priscilla, I'm not here to fight with you. I just need your help finding Daniel."

"Daniel is not mine to control, Amalie, and the quicker you realize that, the better off you will be. If he doesn't want to speak to you – which I wouldn't blame him for – then you have to respect that. There isn't a thing in the world I can do about that. There's nothing I would *want* to do. I won't force your doctrine down his throat. That's his to decide."

"I understand, and I would never intend to force anything on him. But he was supposed to meet me at my place, and never showed up. And he's not at home. I don't know where he's gone, but I know he won't go home," Amalie said.

"Once again, I ask you: What does this have to do with me?" Priscilla was getting short, and rapidly. Amalie did not answer, but looked down at the floor, sighing lightly. "I don't want to be rude," Priscilla lied, "but Daniel's fiancée vanished a few weeks ago. He's a little vulnerable right now, so he doesn't need – he doesn't need…" Priscilla stuttered, waving her hands in Amalie's general direction.

"I understand completely, Priscilla, but it's not really like that. I'm not trying to take advantage of him."

"Then what are you trying to do?" Priscilla said, only half-interested in hearing the answer.

"I'm trying to help him get Anna back."

"What? What the hell are you talking about?" Priscilla stopped waving her arms.

"I know why the people ghosted. I assumed Daniel had told you about what was going on, but I think we can bring them back."

"Look. I don't have a degree in Physics, but I know what it means when someone is gone. They all vanished. That's it!" Priscilla huffed.

"It's not really that simple," Amalie started, but Priscilla interrupted again.

"You know, I didn't know her well, but I liked her a lot. Anna was one of the most genuinely sweet and caring people I have ever met. But she's gone! And it doesn't take a rocket scientist to figure out that you can't bring her back. Let it go! If you're telling Daniel you can bring her back, you need to stop. This is a cruel joke, Amalie!"

At this, Amalie nearly shouted. "It's not a joke!" She looked full on at Priscilla, glare in her eyes. "I know you don't like me. You have made that more than obvious. But I am not here to steal Daniel away from you. I'm not here to ruin his life. I am here to help him. I am here to make it better."

"Oh brother. Will you stop already? You can make both of our lives better if you just desist and disappear." Priscilla maintained her firm. She could not back down now. They had both risen to raised voices, and sunk to insulting chatter. All they needed now was a fistfight to complete the scene.

"Which is exactly what I plan on doing as soon as I finish my work here!" she shook her head and hands as she grasped for explanatory words. "I will disappear, never to be seen again. Guaranteed!"

Priscilla breathed deeply, closing her eyes and fighting back the fight that stood just around the corner from her patience. "Amalie. What do you want from me?" she said slowly and surely, eyes closed throughout.

"You know, forget it," Amalie said. "I wanted you to help me find him. I need him... We started something the other night, and I need him to help me finish it.”

Priscilla’s face softened and her eyes welled up. The realization that it had actually come to love between Daniel and Amalie was nearly too much to handle. She had begun to feel special again. There was a chance they might even get back together now. With Anna gone, and no one in her own picture, there may be a fighting chance that they would actually follow through with their original commitment. And now it comes out. He’s sleeping with Amalie too. Priscilla breathed deeply again, and blinked away the emotion, damming the reservoir.

“If you could just tell him I was looking for him, I would be happy,” Amalie said, collecting her purse. She straightened her blouse, and headed for the door.

Priscilla stood sharply and turned, grabbing Amalie by the arm. “Why don’t you tell him yourself?”

Amalie looked her in the eyes, and Priscilla noticed Amalie’s eyes were glassy as well. Amalie licked her lips and spoke slowly and thoughtfully. “There is one thing you have over me in this situation. I know you love Daniel. I’m happy for you. He’s a great guy. I’d love to have someone like him. I may not have known him for years, but if you truly love him you know it doesn’t take years to fall in love with him.

“But when you wake up in the morning, you will still have him. For the rest of your life you will have the pleasure of his company. He will always be your friend. And that’s what you have over me. When I wake up in the morning, I have to squint my eyes against the burning sun and remind myself that I will never ever see him again as long as I live. Ever.

“So while it’s fair for you to be angry with me, or hateful toward me, and even jealous of me… You could pay me the one small respect of allowing me this darkness. This ship I steer follows nothing but sadness and sorrow-filled waters. So please, for the love of peace, allow me my darkness."

Priscilla blinked again rapidly and frowned. *What the hell is she talking about?* As the door closed quietly, the absence settled, and Amalie's words began to sink into Priscilla's pain-filled mind. And as if she had been commanded, she fell to her knees, wrapping her hair up in her hands, soaking it with her own tears.

After a long sob, she sat up and leaned back against the edge of the couch. She could not understand why she was crying so much. She guessed part of it was her own situational stress, and the rest was sympathy for her best friend. Perhaps she was disappointed. She should have known better. *He's always been like this with women.*

She sat staring at the clock on the wall, letting it all soak in while salty tears ran into her mouth. She refused to wipe them from her cheeks. Something about Amalie had sparked some sort of recognition, somewhere deep within her. It was not necessarily her face. Perhaps it was her voice. Maybe Priscilla remembered talking to her at some point – over the phone or something. She didn't think that was it either. She was about to let it slip away, to forget about it. It was probably nothing. Then something clicked, and she began squinting as she tried to pinpoint it. She felt it was on the edge of her memory – slipping away, and she had it by the tail. Something... Something familiar... What was it? She dropped her face into her hands, concentrating. *Amalie, Amalie, Amalie.* She let the name roll through her head a few more times. *Amalie, Amalie...*

That was it. It was her name that was familiar. With a quickness that startled her, Priscilla was up off the floor and dashing into her bedroom.

CHAPTER FOURTEEN
Reckoning

aniel sat up and ran his fingers through his hair. He had fallen asleep on the couch watching TV earlier. At some point, he had wandered into the bedroom and collapsed on his bed. Now it was nine o'clock. He lit a cigarette, sitting on the edge of his bed. His short hair disheveled, and in need of a shave, Daniel was rugged and beaten down by the hard weekend. So much, in fact, that he had been careless about staying in his own house. He had fallen asleep and stayed there, too tired to care about the consequences. He had bruises on his chest and legs from the running and dodging and diving under trains. As he sat on his bed smoking and replaying the events in his head, he wondered how it would be different at work when he went back. That was when Priscilla came waltzing into his bedroom. This in and of itself was no surprise, as she often showed up unexpectedly, walking in without knocking. At least it had been like that when she and Daniel had been a couple.

But this time she was on a mission.

He sat confused on the edge of his bed in nothing but his silk boxers. "Here, wear this," she said, throwing a thick button-up shirt at him. "We have to go and stop her, Daniel. She's dangerous. What she intends to do could damage our way of life in a way we cannot conceive."

Daniel looked up at her, lost. "Damn, Pris. Slow down a little, okay?"

She stopped in mid-step and turned to look at him. "No, Daniel. We don't have time to slow down. You need to speed up. We have to catch her, and we need to go now."

Daniel shook his head. At least someone has a plan, he thought. "Can I assume you're talking about Amalie?"

Priscilla rounded on him, her eyes narrow and her finger in his face. "Yes. I'm talking about Amalie."

Walter looked over at Callie and they stared at each other through a drunken haze. They had been at the large booth for the last several hours now, drinking margaritas and Mexican beer with Callie's old friends, catching up. Both of them had seemingly forgotten about the mission at hand, and Walter had been okay to let it slide to the back burner, as one of Callie's old friends was giving him the eye. The cutie directly across from Walter with short red hair and gorgeous eyes had been showing him her blazing smile all evening. And it seemed the more drink she got in her, the more eye he got out of her. She was flanked by females, and the only other men at the table were accompanied by women of their own. This woman was single, and she was singling him out.

Callie had caught up on about five and a half years of lost time, and had been thoroughly enjoying herself as well. She had not paid much attention to the drinks, she just knew they kept coming and she kept dutifully putting them away. Her evening had been filled with smiles and laughs, and old stories coming back to life. She had finally looked at her watch about thirty minutes ago and realized it was time to start slowing it down. She began drinking only water, and knew her bladder would soon be talking to her. She finally passed around a small scrap of paper and had everyone write his or her phone number and e-mail address on it. She wanted to keep in touch now that she knew they were back in town. She gave her number to a few of the others as well.

Now she looked at Walter and put her hand on his leg under the table. "You about ready to go?"

His eyes widened, then he smiled. He jerked them to the left, as if to indicate a direction. Callie followed his cue and looked across the table. Cute little Thevi was staring thoughtfully at Walter. "That's Thevi. You like her?" Callie said in his ear.

"Uh huh. I think she may be my wife soon, Callie." Callie could smell the liquor on his breath.

"Okay, Walt. Have you even said a word to her yet?"

"Uhh... Well, no, not yet. But the night's still young, you know..."

"No, it's actually not. We need to get going. We still have to find Amalie. Remember?"

"Oh nooooo, Callie!" he slurred. "Your dedication to duty will be my dying regret."

"Well get her number, Walt! There's always tomorrow!" Callie said. "You have exactly two minutes. I'm going to the ladies' room, then we have to hit the road."

Walter stood up and let her out. She said her goodbyes to everyone and excused herself to the restroom as Walter stood stretching at the end of the table. When she got back, he was still standing there, so she took matters into her own hands. Callie held her hair behind her ears and leaned in closely to speak to Thevi.

"I think Walter over here likes you."

"Well tell him I like him too," Thevi said.

"Well I'll let you tell him. Can I get your number for him though?"

"Sure!" she said and scribbled it on the piece of paper Callie already had ready. She was a professional when it came to hooking Walter up.

"Thanks darlin'," Callie said and patted her on the shoulder as she turned to leave. She waved bye one more time and they made their way out.

"What kind of a name is Thevi, anyway?" Walter said.

"I think it's Czech. Why? You like it?"

"Yes. You got her number for me?" He looked like a schoolboy.

"Yes," Callie said, handing him the scrap of paper. "I always do your dirty work." She was shaking her head as they walked out the door and into the night.

Walter opened her door for her, and she thanked him as she climbed inside. When he got in, she turned to face him. "You all right to drive?"

He nodded. "For the first few miles, yeah. Beyond that, I guarantee nothing. I just don't know where we're going."

"That's okay. I asked Beth where Saddle Creek Apartments are. She gave me detailed directions. It's about forty minutes away." They pulled out of the parking lot and headed south on Beltline. *The interconnectedness of all things, through Beltline...* Callie thought.

* * *

"So why are we on this sudden mission to stop Amalie? And what are we to stop her from doing?" Daniel asked, holding tightly onto the handle bolted to the support beam in Priscilla's sedan.

"Well, when I got home, Amalie was there waiting for me. And she said some stuff that really bugged me out." She turned and merged onto the highway.

"Like what?" Daniel stared at the gauges of the car as she sped along.

"Well for one, she said was going to fix it. She also said she knew what happened to the ghosters."

"Wow. That is some spooky shit, Priscilla. We must find her and stop her now!"

"No, Daniel, for real. She was talking weird saying shit like 'this ship I steer sails through quiet waters' and all this gibberish. It didn't make any sense to me, but it got me to thinking."

"Okay. I'll bite," Daniel said.

"She said I'd still have you when I woke up tomorrow, and that she wouldn't. I don't know what the hell she was talking about, but she said she thought she could bring Anna back."

Daniel waited patiently for her to get to the point.

"So anyway, her name started sounding familiar to me. It's like it finally just clicked and started banging around in my head. Then suddenly I had it! I remembered where I'd heard her name," Priscilla said, and touched Daniel's leg. He looked at her hand, and she continued. "So I started rustling through magazines looking for an article I'd read in Popular Science. It was a column about RRC doing some experiments with temporal delineation. Somehow, some of their 'top secret' projects had leaked, so they came clean with this one, trying to downplay it. Pop Science set up an interview, and they were talking about their experiment with temporal delineation. They had employed the use of a Quantum Computer."

"Yeah?" Daniel said, feigning surprise.

"So I knew I had heard her name before. I knew it. So, I got this…" she said and stretched her arm into the back seat, bringing forth the magazine, folded open to the column in question, "idea. I remembered having read something about RRC and failed experiments with time travel. Earlier when you said she worked at Royal, I felt a click, but couldn't place it. Well I just did." She slapped the magazine on Daniel's lap.

He turned on the map light and read the column. Just as Priscilla had said, they were talking like none of it was working. They felt on the verge of a huge discovery, but couldn't quite untangle the meshed fabric of space-time. Close to the bottom of the column, there was a statement taken from 'former RRC employee, Amalie London'.   Daniel looked up, confused. He lit a cigarette.

"What the fuck? Former employee?"

"Yep. That's her name right? Amalie London?"

Daniel nodded.

"Look at the date of the magazine," Priscilla instructed. Daniel unfolded the magazine and looked at the cover date. June 2003. Over two years out of date.

"Well I'll be damned," he said quietly, taking a drag from his cigarette and holding it in.

"It was all a bunch of bullshit. A cover-up."

The buildings along the highway were cold, silent and gray. Daniel looked at them with a cool distance. He felt disconnected, sitting in Priscilla's passenger seat. She had been there for him through thick and thin. They told each other everything. But now he was stuck with his insider information on time travel, and couldn't say a word to her about it. He could not tell her about his experience. He was utterly alone.

"Where are we going, by the way?" Daniel asked, flicking his cigarette out the window. The cold air was loud rushing into the car until he rolled the window back up.

"Amalie's apartment. I looked up her address after she left."

"She doesn't live there. She keeps two apartments. If you want to see Amalie, hit the Birdsong exit, and head up toward the mall."

"That's odd. So tell me, Daniel. If she no longer works at Royal, why were you there the other day with her?"

Oh shit, here we go. Now comes the inquisition.

"What are you hiding, Daniel?"

"Why are you chasing this? What you are telling me is that you believe she can time travel or some shit, right?"

"I know it, Daniel! I know it!" Priscilla said, taking the exit. "They've all been doing it for at least two years! No telling how much they've fucked up."

"Well who cares? Why don't we just forget about her?" Daniel lit another cigarette. He tended to chain smoke when he was nervous. "Who cares if she can time travel?"

Daniel instructed her how to get to Amalie's secret apartment, and shortly, they arrived at the complex, and pulled into a narrow space. She turned to face him on the seat. "Daniel, this is serious shit she's messing with. She's going to try to bring back the ghosters!"

"Good! Great! That's what I want! I want Anna back!"

"Wait-wait-wait!" she said, raising her hands. "After I read that article, I started checking out stuff on the Internet about the effects of the ghosting. I came across a bit about that bridge." She was talking extremely fast.

"What bridge?"

"The one we take to Pappy's," she reminded him. He nodded. "I started trying to find out when it happened, and I found a newspaper article about it. There had been an explosion on it that caused it to go down."

It wasn't high waters.

Priscilla continued, "They found all this stuff in the truck, these parts of a bomb and stuff, and these blueprints."

"Blueprints to what?"

"The federal building in Dallas." She stared at him for a moment, expecting him to know what she was talking about. He did not. "Daniel, that man was going to bomb the federal building! He had it all mapped out and had outlined the structural weaknesses. All he had to do was park in front of the building, and walk away."

"I don't get it," Daniel admitted, flustered.

Priscilla suddenly got out of the car and headed for the building. "You going to tell me which one she lives in?"

Daniel slammed his door and jogged up behind Priscilla on the sidewalk. "Third floor. 303. But what does any of this have to do with that bridge? Weren't you gonna tell me something?" His mind was racing with thousands of ideas, but none of them fit together. It was like having thousands of puzzle pieces, but each piece was from a different puzzle entirely. He wanted to stop her and get it all sorted out – tell her the truth – before they saw Amalie. As of now, it would be every man – or woman – for himself. He saw a skirmish on his horizon. They jogged up the steps.

Priscilla walked right through the door, no knocking, and no questions.

In the kitchen, Amalie was on hands and knees with a roll of paper towels, trying to soak up scalding coffee. Priscilla came in and crossed her arms. "What the hell are you doing?" she asked, looking down at Amalie.

Amalie looked up, shocked to hear Priscilla's voice. "Hi, Priscilla! I am trying to clean up-"

"What the hell are you doing here Amalie?"

"Oh, I live here. What are you doing here?" she said, almost smiling from the floor.

Priscilla breathed in deeply and stared her down, hard.

Amalie stood to face her, the friendliness sliding right off her face. "Did you come to your senses yet,

Pris?" she said with a smirk. Daniel entered the kitchen and stopped short. He was surprised by something.

"Damn you, Amalie. You have no idea what you are about to do here," Priscilla said, shaking her fist at Amalie, brown hair falling from its locks and hanging in her face. Daniel looked on, frowning. But he was not frowning at the standoff. He was frowning at the busted mug on the floor. Daniel looked on as a love to both of these women, not knowing whose side to take, or why they were against one another at all. He still had not figured it out. More to the point, Priscilla had not had time to fill him in yet.

"I have no clue? I know exactly what I am doing," said Amalie. She stood dropping the soaked paper towels from hand to hand. "I'm making preparations to finish up here so I can go on with my miserable life!"

"I can't let you do this, Amalie."

"You can't stop me, Priscilla," Amalie replied. She suddenly had a thick growl in her voice. "You can't stop time."

"Wait, wait, wait," Daniel said, stepping between them, staring at the mug on the floor. "Amalie, can you explain to me where you got that mug?"

Both women stared at Daniel, frowning. Amalie answered, speaking slowly, as if dumbfounded by his apparent oblivion to what was taking place around him. "Um, yeah, Karma Kafe. Why?"

"Uh, Daniel? What the hell does the mug have to do with anything?" Priscilla asked. Daniel just stared, trying to make heads or tails of something. Anything. He was clueless.

"The mug came from Karma Kafe?" Daniel pulled the shard from his pocket that he had found the day before in this very kitchen, and held it up in front of the girls' faces. "Then where did this come from?" None of them seemed to be impressed.

"I don't follow, Daniel," Amalie said. She sighed.

"I found this here the last time I was here. Right here on the floor. It matches your mug." The piece clearly did match the coffee mug, and looked as if it had come from it.

"Yeah, it certainly appears so," Amalie said, straight-faced. She gulped. "But I still don't follow your lead here, Daniel."

"Yeah, what the hell are you talking about?" asked Priscilla.

"Look." Daniel bent down and wiped the coffee away from the scene with his hand and found the grind mark on the linoleum where he had stepped on the piece of porcelain. "See that? That's where I stepped on it yesterday and ground it into the floor. Yesterday."

A look of realization washed over Priscilla's face as she caught on. "That is a little odd, Amalie," she said. She was smirking. It looked to Daniel as if she expected it.

Priscilla looked hard at Amalie. "You screw this up too, Amalie? This would only add more merit to my story, Daniel," she said, turning to face Daniel. "If that piece does belong to that mug, then you have just witnessed one of Amalie's fuckups."

Daniel scratched his head trying to come to grips with the situation. He knew time travel to be possible – he had lived it – but he was perplexed by this conundrum that had swept in and taken him by surprise. He believed in what he was seeing, but with a standoffish faith that could easily be swayed. He did not think paradoxes like this would be possible. In some way, he figured time would have a way of correcting itself in order to keep any flaws from becoming visible. Especially in the case of something as trivial as a coffee mug. "If this fits, then I have to seriously rethink what I know about time."

"That's exactly the point. If it fits, then she's exactly who I thought she was, and she's been messing with time all around us," Priscilla said, turning back to Amalie. "Go ahead, Amalie. I want to see you put it back together."

The mood in the room changed. It was as if the hot summer day had just been picked up and moved into the arctic region. A cold front had just blown in and turned everyone's sweat into icicles. It was quick and sharp, and everyone felt it alike.

"There's no point, Priscilla. It's the same mug. You're right. My mistakes are showing."

"Ha! I knew it! Miss Amalie here is a time-traveler," Priscilla put a fingertip in Daniel's chest.

Daniel's pulse quickened. He knew it was about to come to blows between the two women, and all he could do was try to keep out of their way. It did not seem terribly important to hide what he knew anymore, but at the same time, he did not want to offer the information at this stage. Amalie should catch on, he thought, and keep him hidden in the side wing of her little project. She should know the delicacy of his situation.

"You can't do this, Amalie," Priscilla said.

"I have to, Priscilla." She suddenly looked uncomfortable. "Can we please go outside?"

"Why? I think it's nice in here," Priscilla said, folding her arms.

Amalie pointed her head toward the front door, but her eyes jerked back toward Daniel. So Priscilla spoke again, "Ah. So you don't want Daniel to know what you are doing. If you don't tell him, I will. Go ahead. Tell him."

"You know, Priscilla, I think he knows a little more about this than you realize." When Daniel remained silent, Amalie finally rounded on him. "You want to help me out here, Daniel?"

Dammit! Daniel closed his eyes and tilted his head back. He sighed heavily and shook his head. No more hiding. "Don't get me involved in this. I'm just along for the ride," he said, turning to walk into the living room. But Priscilla was smarter than that. He realized as her hand caught his arm that she had seen it in his eyes.

"Not so fast. Talk to me, Daniel," she said softly. "Have you been hiding something? Are you an accessory to this madness?"

Daniel looked her straight in the eyes, baring as much disappointment as he could muster in his colorful gaze. "Pris, just let it go. I don't even know why we're here."

"Bullshit! You've been helping her the whole time! You've both been running all around, changing shit to make it happen the way you want it to. The way she wants it to!" Priscilla yelled. "Isn't that right?"

Daniel could not speak.

"Daniel, you know she's wrong. And guess what? I saved Callie's life!" Amalie touched her finger to his chest.

"You did what?" Daniel said, confused.

"Who the hell is Callie?" Priscilla cut in.

"A girl we met the other night. Two days ago she was in a severe car accident, and she died. But I took a little trip here and fixed it. I saved her life. So don't tell me I don't know what the hell I'm doing!"

Daniel winced as she said that. "I don't understand…"

"Cut the crap, Daniel. Priscilla knows you've been back with me. Whose side are you on anyway?" Priscilla was frowning at her again. It looked as though a vein might burst on her forehead at any moment now.

Daniel spread his hands and let them fall to his sides. "Doesn't mean I understand what the fuck is going on!"

Priscilla sighed deeply, then finally said, "Let's all just sit down and have a little pow-wow. I think we all need to hear everything."

The three of them sat down at the table, scooting in, chairs whining as they slid across the linoleum. Daniel had walked around the table and sat facing Priscilla at the long side, while Amalie held the end.

"Priscilla, I work – or rather worked – for Royal Research Corporation. We've been experimenting with temporal manipulation in the future tense using a Quantum Computer. This has been going on for the last several years. I recently stole the computer so that I could try to bring the ghosters back. That was our first experiment with the past. If you mess up the future, no one will ever know. But anyone can see the differences if you change history. You have books telling you what's already happened."

Priscilla smirked and looked at Daniel. "I knew it. And you've been helping her," she said shaking her head. She looked disappointed.

"I can't tell you any more than that," Amalie said.

"Bullshit. You're going to go in there and fuck with the past again, so this conversation will never take place anyway. So get on with it."

"What I was going to do, Priscilla, before you came and took over Daniel's life, was bring back those seconds he had stolen." Then she turned to face Daniel. "I guess you haven't told her any of this."

"What the hell are you talking about 'took over my life'?" he shook his head. "And no, I haven't told her anything. I tried to maintain your 'code of privacy'," he said, stressing the quotes like an ethic.

Priscilla was shaking her head wildly, and waving her hands. "What the hell are you talking about? Those *seconds he'd stolen*?"

Amalie sighed and looked down at the table. "Thank you, Daniel."

Priscilla looked at Daniel again. "Has everyone lost their freaking minds? Daniel, how can you not care about what's going on here?" She shook her head again, then waved her hands as if to wipe away the problems in front of her. Then she scooted her chair back and stood. "Look, you can't go through with it, Amalie."

Daniel and Amalie stared at her. She had the floor. To Daniel, it seemed perfectly logical to want to fix what they had messed up. Why not? If two hundred thousand people vanished because of their unfortunate meeting, then by God, they need to bring them the hell back. There was nothing left to discuss here. He and Amalie needed to get to work. Why the hell was Priscilla so against it?

"Daniel, you remember I told you about that explosion on the bridge?" Priscilla finally said, still standing.

Daniel answered, "Of course."

"That was what prompted me to come here. I read about that on the Internet this evening. That car that blew up on the bridge belonged to a ghoster," Priscilla said, pausing, waiting for someone to speak. But no one did.

Daniel thought about this. She had told him earlier about the bridge, but had not gotten to the part about the driver having vanished. Now he was beginning to see the point. A van loaded with C4, heading for the fed building in downtown Dallas. It didn't take a genius to figure out what she was getting at.

"I'm sorry, you lost me there, Priscilla," Amalie said.

"Well, Daniel and I were on our way out to Pappy's this afternoon when we came upon a small bridge that had been seemingly washed away."

"Pappy's?"

Priscilla ignored her and continued, "Well I got curious about the bridge so I looked up the report on the Internet. And come to find out, it wasn't washed away at all. It had been bombed. The investigation said there had been a van carrying half a ton of TNT, and blueprints of the Federal Building in Dallas. Funny thing is, they never found a trace of the guy's body."

"What guy?" asked Amalie.

"The driver. And he had clearly intended to blow up the Federal Building. But he never made it that far."

Amalie twirled a napkin on the table. She obviously was not entertained by Priscilla's theories, nor was she intimidated by her threats. Daniel stared at her for a moment. And with a sudden spark of clarity like a fresh-cleaned window, Daniel's mind skipped a beat and sent a wave of realization through his body that made his fingertips twitch. All at once a whole new dawn settled in. All at once he realized why Amalie was so eccentric. *No wonder she can't keep any friends! No wonder she has no pictures of people on her walls! She's addicted to time travel! She can't stay in any particular time period long enough to make people like her!* And furthermore, she couldn't stay there long enough, because they'd find out what the hell she was doing and force her out.

Priscilla was still talking. "There was no trace of him. Not a thread of his clothing or anything. He had disappeared."

"This is deep," Amalie simply said. "But still – what does it mean?"

Priscilla patiently answered. "My mother – along with twenty-thousand other people – works at the Federal Building in Dallas." She turned to look at Amalie again. "You need to call it off, Amalie."

Amalie looked at Priscilla with an eye of hatred and spoke like she wasn't there. "She wants to sacrifice two hundred thousand people for twenty thousand."

Daniel frowned. "You're saying you think if we bring back the ghosters that guy will still make it to the fed building and blow it up?"

"Yes, Daniel. Obviously that's what would happen."

"Well couldn't we stop him? I mean we already know about him and his plan! We could foil it easily enough!" Daniel saw the potential to be made heroes. All they would have to do was blow out his tires. Arrest him on the spot.

"Daniel, if she brings them back, we won't have any memory of it! It won't have happened! We won't even remember this conversation right now! It will never have happened!" Priscilla said, jabbing the tabletop with her fingertip.

Priscilla then leaned forward and put her hands flat on the table, looking Daniel deep in the eyes. "Daniel, there is no choice here. I am sorry for you, I wish Anna was back too, but we are talking about thousands of people here in that one building alone. There are ten or fifteen other buildings that could go down with it. Remember the horror of nine-eleven? This is horrifyingly real."

"Oh, and Anna disappearing isn't?" Daniel leaned back and folded his arms. Tears began to burn his eyes. The thought of Annabelle crept back into his mind, and with more intensity, as she seemed so close now. It seemed so plausible that she could be brought back. Her long brown hair, her beautiful blue eyes. He missed her voice. He missed her dainty little hands running up and down the ivory keys of her grand piano. He missed her emotions. "Why the fuck are you looking at me anyway? I'm not the one with the time machine!"

"She knows I can't do it without you, Daniel," Amalie said quietly.

Priscilla leaned forward and kissed Daniel on the head. "Daniel, you need to take a break. Let's walk out front and have a cigarette. You need to think on this," she said. Daniel sensed she was getting maternal again, as if she thought she could change his mind.

"I don't need a break. I know what I want. I don't concern myself with the future. If that's what happens in our future, then so be it. It's not my fault. But I know what the hell happened in my past. And I know Annabelle isn't in it anymore. And if anything, I think that should be returned to as close to normality as possible," Daniel said, staring at the table. Then he smiled and surprised himself by saying, "What's that saying? 'The future's not ours to see'?"

"Daniel, look at what's important here!"

"Are you saying Anna is not important?"

"Yes, of course she is, Daniel, but you have to weigh the alternatives here!"

"Hey," he said, standing sharply. "It's my fault those two hundred thousand people disappeared, Priscilla! I caused that catastrophe!" he said, jabbing his own chest with an accusatory thumb. "Two hundred thousand people! And that includes Anna. I caused her to disappear. Don't you see what this means to me?"

Priscilla stared at him for a moment, not saying anything. Her brow was furrowed. She reached across and touched his hand, which Daniel quickly pulled away. "Daniel, how could you have caused this?" she said, in almost a whisper.

"Imagine the guilt I'm dealing with, Pris. Two hundred thousand people."

"And countless others," Amalie chimed in. "These are just a few of the quirks we have to repair. There are millions. People all the way back to 1896 who have ancestry in that lineage. There are probably half a million empty caskets buried in fifty-year-old graves."

Daniel pulled his cigarettes out of his front pocket and lit one, standing up. "I miss Anna, Pris."

"I do too, Daniel! But this is something we can prevent," Priscilla stood up straight.

"Bullshit! You know, you didn't even know her!"

"I knew her well enough to miss her."

Daniel pointed two fingers at her, cigarette between them, "You have no idea what it's like, Priscilla." Then he turned to walk out of the kitchen.

"But I will if you don't stop this woman!"

Daniel had stopped in the doorway, and now he turned slowly to face the women again. "Sorry, Pris."

Suddenly, Priscilla frowned again and walked toward Daniel. Then she turned back and looked hard at Amalie. "Hey, Daniel, that Popular Science magazine was two and a half years old. How did you cause this three weeks ago... If she got fired from Royal almost three years ago?"

Amalie looked at Priscilla with no expression. Then she said with equal blankness, "We only ever experimented with the future, Priscilla. He – we – erased those seconds in one of my trips into the future. So when we returned to present time, which was whatever year that was, it eventually just came to be."

Priscilla squinted and raised her eyebrows simultaneously. "You messed up the past – in the future?"

"Yep."

"I see," she said, then looked at Daniel. "Daniel. Please. Come with me. Let's get out of here. I'll love you forever."

"Anna already does."

Priscilla pulled her head back on her neck, looking appalled at Daniel, as if he had just insulted her badly. He realized with a wash of adrenaline that he had just broken her heart. *Ah. She's fallen back in love with me.* Daniel took a long drag from his cigarette, then stared at the ash on the end.

"Let's do it, Amalie," he said. "I want my girlfriend back."

The whole conversation had taken about fifteen minutes. Words and insults, pain and pride were present, and all in great abundance. Every emotion had been present in the kitchen. Daniel had looked at both women and initially been confused about whom to trust. Which one of them really knew what was going on? Which one of them really knew what needed to be done, and – more importantly – what was really at stake? Daniel, being the least witty of them all, had been able to figure out pretty quickly that time itself was not to be reckoned with lightly. But he also had come to the conclusion that if you screwed up time by traveling through it, then you need to fix it by traveling through it. Simple math in his mind, it was. You dig a ditch, you have to fill it with its own dirt.

All in all, he didn't quite understand Priscilla's major bitch with the whole thing, though he did see how she would initially have been so upset. If it were his mother who worked in the fed building, he was quite sure he would have felt the same way. But after a brief explanation of how time really worked, he would have been talked into believing that just as easily as it had been messed up before – it could be repaired. And no one would ever know the difference.

Priscilla, unfortunately, did not see it from this angle. So Amalie should not have been surprised by Priscilla's reaction. For it had come down like this: Amalie had been arrogant in her power trip, knowing she had Daniel's full support again. She had taken this arrogance to a new level when she walked out of the kitchen, letting her fingers slide across Priscilla's shoulder.

"Don't take it so hard, Pris. You'll never be the wiser."

Priscilla turned and grabbed Amalie by the shoulder, spinning her round like a rag doll. Amalie's face was filled with confusion and shock. She looked down at Priscilla's hand on her shoulder, then sudden as a slam, that same hand reared back, then came up and socked Amalie in the cheek. Amalie crashed to the floor, hitting the chair on the way down. Priscilla stood over Amalie shaking her finger like an angry mother. "I've never in my life met anyone as selfish and arrogant as yourself. I hope you burn for this, Amalie."

Amalie looked up at Priscilla, rubbing her swollen cheek and shook her head. A wild, crazy look came over her face, then she spoke words that sounded as though they'd been pulled directly from the deep freezer. "I know your future, Prissy."

Priscilla's cheeks burned with anger and her lips trembled tightly. But she couldn't speak. She thought she had never been insulted so badly in her life. In order that she might preserve some sense of dignity, she turned and stormed out of the apartment, slamming the door as she left. It was not the worst insult by words, but rather the way Amalie had spoken them. Because she was smiling when she said it.

CHAPTER FIFTEEN
Reiteration

Callie was laughing so hard her stomach was beginning to ache. They had pulled into the parking lot of Saddle Creek, and now sat in the cooling Durango, trying to pull themselves together. "Maybe," Callie said, "we shouldn't have drunk quite so much."

"Yeah, I'm feeling it now. My head's starting to hurt a little," Walter said, rubbing his forehead. "But I guess if we're gonna do this thing, we better go ahead and get moving. Otherwise, I'll fall asleep here in the parking lot and miss all the fun."

Callie nodded, then frowned as a light appeared at the top of one of the landings. A door had opened, and a woman emerged. Now she was running down the stairs. Callie leaned forward to have a better look.

"Is that her?" Walter said after a moment. He had caught Callie's gaze and was now staring intently out the windshield as well.

"You tell me. I've only ever seen her in the darkness. It looks like the right apartment though."

"What's the number?" Walter said, looking for the scrap of paper.

"303," Callie said. The woman was now off the stairs and heading directly for them. "What's she doing?"

"I don't know. Did she see us?"

Callie did not answer. They both sat in silence, watching the woman approach in the darkness of the parking lot. The streetlight across the parking lot was not powerful enough to illuminate the entire picture. It silhouetted the woman as she approached rather quickly. Finally, she became visible, and Walter whispered across the seat to Callie, "No, it ain't Amalie."

The woman got into the car right next to Walter's side of the truck and started it. She barely gave it time to warm before she was backing out and pulling onto the road. Walter sighed. "I don't know who the hell that was. But it wasn't Amalie." He pulled a cigarette from a package above the visor and lit it. "I think Amalie's a little shorter than that. And prettier."

Callie looked thoughtfully at Walter for a moment, but said nothing. They let the silence settle back in for a few moments, not quite sure what they were waiting for, but not motivated enough to get out and climb the stairs to the unknown.

Walter finally leaned his head back against the seat and closed his eyes. Callie chose this as the time to get moving. "Let's go," she said, putting a hand on his leg. Then she opened her door and stepped out into the cold.

*   *   *

As they sat before the computer again, Daniel took Amalie by the hand and looked her in the eyes. He was trembling slightly: partly with fear, and partly with nervous excitement. He wondered if this was a trip anyone could ever get used to taking.

"You sure you're gonna be okay?" he said finally, breaking the silence. Amalie's cheek was dark blue already, and swollen like she had a lemon in her mouth.

"Yeah, it's just a bruise. She's got a pretty good punch, that Priscilla."

"Well fortunately I never had to find out." He looked down at the floor in front of him and picked up the thin wire, stretching the band around his wrist.

"You ready then?" Amalie said, adjusting her own strap.

Daniel nodded. "I trust you."

Amalie smiled at him. "Good." The Human Icon monitoring application was running, and as the strap settled on Daniel's wrist, a small image appeared in the dialogue box next to one just like it already there waiting. The first image represented Amalie.

"How do you tell which is which?"

"What, besides just the color coding?"

Daniel looked back at the strap again, and noticed the wire leading to it had a red stripe down its length. It matched the color of his icon on the screen. Amalie's wire had a blue stripe on it.

"There's another in the pouch, too," she said, pulling out a wire with a green stripe on it. Then she right-clicked the image that represented her and typed in her name. "I can also label the icons like this. But it's kind of useless, 'cause we could just swap wristbands and the monitor would never know."

"Pretty cool stuff," Daniel said, nodding. "Let's do it."

"K." Amalie dragged a date into the quantum dialog box, then looked at Daniel as she let go of the mouse button. The guy across the street was waving at Daniel as he pulled the tarp over his wagon, closing shop for the night. Daniel waved back and shouted something about the weather. The road was almost entirely covered with snow. There were a few thin tracks through it, no wider than a couple of inches, and horses everywhere. People dashed from place to place, tucked low into their coats as they hurried home for the evening. Daniel crunched through the ice to the side of the road and up the wooden stairs to his apartment, where Amalie awaited his return. As he pushed open the creaky wooden door, she smiled at him from the hearth of the fireplace.

"Shhh. Angie's asleep," Amalie said, smiling. Daniel set the thick paper bag on the table and crept into the sitting room to squat beside her. He ran his finger over his daughter's fragile forehead.

"She looks so peaceful," Daniel whispered. Amalie's eyes beamed at him. Daniel stuck his hands out toward the fire, shivering in his wool coat. "Dorothy sends her regards."

Dorothy was the clerk at the Wells Fargo just up the road. The Wells Fargo was the only bank in town, and Daniel stopped by most days, on his way home from work. His job at the mill was taxing on his mind and soul. All he felt like doing when he got home was to lie back on the cushions and relax until dreamy sleep would envelop him. He always seemed to have weird futuristic dreams that seemed perfectly reasonable while he was asleep, but he could never seem to explain or understand when he was awake.

Some of the things he dreamt about he could not even find names for. They seemed so advanced he doubted he would ever live to see anything like them in his lifetime. Maybe his daughter or her children would. Upon awakening, he would wonder what the next century would bring. It was right around the corner, and everyone was readily excited about it. The nineteen hundreds would be the dawn of a new era.

*   *   *

Callie knocked this time, and again, with no answer, they decided to try the knob. As it turned out, it had been the same apartment they had seen the woman walking out of earlier, and the door was still unlocked. When they pushed it open, it was completely dark inside. Callie walked in ahead of Walter and flipped the switch by the door. But nothing happened. There was a single candle standing atop the entertainment cabinet, and it only partially illuminated the room. With the weak flickering light of the candle, they stood in the entryway waiting for their eyes to adjust.

It became apparent pretty quickly that they were alone.

Walter pointed at the small black table standing in the center of the room. Underneath it sat the three vinyl pouches he recognized from the other night. Callie looked closely, squinting against the darkness, and realized there was a notebook computer sitting on the table, and it was running. The screen seemed to be blank when she looked directly at it. But when she would turn her head, she could vaguely see images from the corner of her eye.

"Where the hell are they?" Walter whispered.

Callie shrugged. She then made a waving motion with her finger, instructing him to go check the other rooms. He walked down the hallway a short way and flipped another light switch. Again, nothing happened. Callie was bending over the table trying to get a better look at the computer. Walter tapped her on the shoulder.

"I'm gonna go get my Mag Lite from the truck," he whispered. She nodded.

As he crept out the front door she looked around briefly, then frowned. *All the power's out except for the computer.* She put her hand on her chin and turned quickly as she heard Walter pounding down the stairs outside. She shook her head and bent over, looking under the table. Beneath it were the three pouches, and behind them, a power strip with all six sockets filled up.

Oh my God. Callie followed the cord from the power strip to the wall and saw it was plugged into both sockets on the wall. *This thing is using all the power.* She stood up quickly with another thought. She frowned again, then chewed her bottom lip. The gears in her mind clicked and whirred as she began to grasp what was happening. Then with a sudden impulse, she reached over and knocked the mouse with her hand. It slid across the small table and the screen jumped to life with color. *A quantum computer using a screen saver.* She shook her head. *I can't wait to tell Walter about this.*

Callie squatted level with the screen and looked at the programs running on the desktop. In the middle of the screen was a simple gray box with a long number in the middle of it, and the number was growing every second, like a clock. Only the number was fourteen digits long. Below that, another program was running just above the task bar. The title bar of that window read 'HI Monitor'. In the middle of the box were two icons, each shaped like the head and shoulders of a person. One was red, the other blue. A red dotted line surrounded both the icons and the dots seemed to be moving clockwise around them. *Action.*

Callie moved the mouse pointer over and hovered it over the blue icon. A square caption box appeared that read 'Amalie'. She jumped back with a start and nearly kicked the table over, and covered her heart with her right hand, staring wide-eyed and ghost white at the image on the screen. Callie finally understood what it was that Amalie was doing with the quantum computer. Amalie was not using it to make a bomb. She was time-traveling.

*   *   *

The next day, Daniel walked to the dentist's office to keep an appointment. His tooth had been bothering him for some time. As he sat in the chair, the dentist asked him about his family as he prepared his tools. "How's Amalie?"

"Oh you know, she's doing great. Still tired a lot of the time, but she's getting by," Daniel said.

"And little Angelina?"

"She's getting big, doc. You wouldn't believe! You know, she's starting to speak intelligibly. Like full sentences and everything. Not a day goes by that she doesn't just completely amaze me."

"Well that is just fantastic," the doctor said, holding a needle up to the light. "Okay, Dan, just go ahead and get comfortable. I'm going to give you a little anesthetic here, then we'll be halfway done." That was about all Daniel remembered of his trip to the dentist. It was true, they had been halfway done, and the anesthetic did its job well. Daniel's entire face felt numb, and he was happy to have gotten it taken care of. He knew as soon as the anesthetic wore off though, he would be in pain city.

As he walked home wearily, he thought about his life and how things seemed to be happening so quickly. Amalie and he had gotten married two years ago, and had been blessed with a beautiful baby girl. They had not tried but for a couple of months, and then that one brilliant day, Amalie had come home glowing.

Daniel would never forget the look in her eyes. She had been so beautiful, pumped full of happiness and excitement. She had come in the front door with a huge smile on her face. The fire had been reflecting in her eyes, her white teeth beaming at him as he put down his paper. Her cold cheeks matched the red scarf around her neck. Daniel was sure he had never seen anyone so beautiful in his life. She was absolutely stunning.

"I just got back from Doctor Kirby's, Daniel. Guess what?"

"Tell me!" he had said, unknowing how warm the room was about to get; how his heart was about to speed up and pump hot blood through his body as he danced excitedly around the room with his wife.

"We're going to have a baby!" She shook her fists as she smiled widely. Daniel jumped up out of the rocker and ran to be with her. He held her tightly against him, kissing her head and her cheeks. It was the most exciting day of his life.

That was two years ago. His daughter was talking and walking now, developing a personality, stealing his heart more and more every day. Daniel had never been more in love with someone in his life. He smiled as he thought about these things, and kicked a stone up the road. The anesthetic was already beginning to wear off. He felt the familiar tingle in his cheeks, signaling the end of the cakewalk.

Just around the corner was the staircase to his apartment. Daniel stopped and sat down on the third step, staring out into the street. Amalie had told him he needed to quit smoking. Last time Angelina had caught bronchitis, the doctor had said the smoking could be causing it. Daniel had stopped smoking effective immediately. Now he sat outside sometimes just thinking about it. She had told him, "I bet I can get you to quit smoking, Daniel." Then she had gone and had a baby. It had worked – he was no longer a smoker.

Walter slipped quietly back into the apartment and Callie was waiting by the door for him. She grabbed him quickly by the shoulders and led him over to the computer, pointing and panting with excitement. "They're time-traveling, Walter!" she said, still whispering.

"What? Who is?"

"Amalie. Someone else is with her though. Look, look, look," she said pointing at the screen and dragging him closer. "See those little icons?" Walter nodded. "Those represent people. And those people are in a sub-atomic state right now. They've been pulled into the quantum foam." She stared at Walter.

"How do you know?" he finally said.

"Look. Watch this." She right-clicked on the Amalie icon and a whole series of options showed up including one that said 'Statistics'. She clicked Statistics and a summary box popped open on the screen. Among the indices in the summary were 'Tenure of Expression – 14:31 m.s.' and 'Temporal Region – 1896.20.04.11.01.57'. Callie watched Walter as he stared at the summary box.

"What's that mean?"

"Tenure of Expression would obviously mean how long she's been in. Looks like almost fifteen minutes. Temporal Region, I assume is what time period she's in right now. That's a date, and it matches the one in the middle of the screen exactly."

"1896? Oh, oh, I see. April 20, 1896, 11:02 in the morning."

"That's what I get out of it," Callie said.

"So what do we do?" He squatted to her level and leaned against his fist on the floor.

Callie's face softened and she smirked. Then she raised her left hand, and from her index finger dangled a strap with a thin wire running from it, that disappeared into the nylon bag under the table. "Put this on. You're going in, Walter."

"What? What the hell is that?"

"You see, my theory is this." She pushed her legs out in front of her and came to rest on her behind, giving her knees a break from the squat. "She took somebody with her and she's trying to bring back those people who ghosted."

"I'm not following you." He sat back and frowned at her.

"Remember that date our logic program found?" she said, raising her eyebrows.

Walter nodded.

"Look at the date on the screen. It's the day before our date. She's gone back to investigate why those people ghosted. Though I don't know why she went back to the day before."

Walter shook his head. He reached in his shirt pocket for a smoke, and lit up, despite his being in someone else's home. "How in the fuck did you figure all this out, Callie? Do you know something I don't?"

"No. It just has to be. Why else would she have broken into Royal to steal the computer? I just bet she thought she could fix it all. Go back and be little Miss Temporal Vigilante."

"I don't see how she could possibly do anything about it though. Not by going back to that date anyway," Walter said, then took a drag, blowing the smoke sideways.

"She can't. She can't do a darn thing," Callie said, shaking her head. She was smiling now. "So I figured you could go in and check it out real quick. You know, just to see whom she took with her. Who got suckered into going back."

"Whoa, this is some heavy shit. I can't believe she's time-traveling. How'd you figure this out?"

"Come on Walter, we don't have time for this! Do you want to go or not?" Callie said, shaking him.

"Daniel. I bet it's Daniel."

Callie looked at him oddly. "Daniel who? Who's Daniel?"

"That guy who was with us when we took you to the hospital."

"Ohhhhh, okay. Well do you want to go see what it's like in the late 1800s?" She had a mischievous look on her face as she held up the wrist strap with the wire on it. Walter stared at her for a long time, not saying anything. His face was void of expression.

"You can go spy on them for a few minutes, then I'll pull you out. It'll be fun, Walter!"

"How can you pull me out?" Callie could see his hands trembling. He was nervous. She could not blame him. She would be nervous too, she knew. *That's why he's the one who needs to go back.*

"Right-click, extract," she said simply.

Walter started nodding. Then he smiled. "My extraction from a temporal delineation expression all comes down to a fucking Windows command. That is priceless." They both had a good laugh, then he added, "Yeah. Yeah, okay, that sounds like fun. I'll do it." He took the wristband from Callie's finger and slid it over his hand. A green icon appeared in the box next to the red one, but the red dotted line was not dancing around it.

Callie smiled at him, then spoke softly. "You ready?"

Walter nodded. Callie right-clicked the green icon and selected the 'Insert' option. And Walter promptly disappeared.

Daniel sat on the stairs enjoying the morning air. Beside him he had a paper bag with some groceries in it, including a box of marshmallows. He intended to teach his daughter how to roast them when he got inside. Leaves blew by lazily on the dirt alley beneath the stairs, and moisture blew in his face from the melting snow on the roofs.

He heard the door open above and behind him, and Amalie's soft call. "What do you want for dinner tonight babe?"

Daniel shrugged. "We still have that turkey in there, right?" He looked over his shoulder at her. She was leaning out the door, wearing nothing but a smile. With a start, Daniel sat up straight and looked back at the road to see if anyone was around. No one was.

"What's wrong Daniel? You don't want anyone to see this?" she said, and stepped out onto the landing. She shook her hips and twirled around, smiling and wooing. Daniel stared in awe at her. Normally she was reserved, almost shy. Now here she stood, naked and shaking her boobs on the porch, dancing a jig in the forty-degree air, smiling all the while. Daniel could tell she was cold by the way her nipples stood out like bullets, but not by the way she acted. She was hot.

Daniel heard a sound back in the street. Something had gone *crack*. He looked back at the road in time to see someone duck around the corner. *What the fuck?* And he was up and running. He took off down the narrow dusty alleyway toward the road, not knowing whom he was chasing, or even why. The sun was reflecting off the glass in the windows across the street. Daniel squinted against it as he approached the corner of the building.

As he rounded the corner, Daniel saw him. A tall slender man with a dark coat was running down the street, looking back every few seconds. Daniel sensed a vague recognition, but could not be sure at this distance. The man kept running, and so did Daniel. The messy black hair on the man's head looked dirty and unkempt, but somehow its disheveled state seemed deliberate.

Daniel was out of breath, but kept running, pushing himself. *What the hell am I doing? Why am I chasing this guy?* Daniel's mind was working faster than his legs. *Well he saw my wife naked, that's why. Fuck that. I'm the only one who gets that privilege.* Around another corner and down a side street they dashed. Daniel was nowhere near gaining on the man. He knew it. And this street was busier than the last. Horses walked about and people scurried through the mud and puddles. Daniel saw the man hurdle a fruit cart adeptly. Daniel did the same thing. His foot caught the wood edge though, and now there was fruit all over the side of the road. Daniel slammed into the mud with a loud splat.

The woman in charge of the stand was swatting something at him, presumably a fly shoe. "Look what you've done! You ignorant thug!" She was hitting him on the back and shoulders hard with the swat.

"I'm sorry, ma'am!" Daniel said, ducking. He reached in his pocket and fumbled for some cash. Finding none, he took off running again. "I'll make it up to you! Sorry!" Little did he know, that would be the last time he ever saw her. The next time he thought of her, he would be a hundred years away.

The wet road splashed under Daniel's feet as he ran, fast as he could manage. He had completely lost the man now, but some spectators were standing aside the road pointing. Daniel thanked them as he ran past, waving a hand at them. He swung around the corner a few seconds later, and ran directly into the business end of a snow shovel.

The room was spinning when he woke up. It was also moving; sliding past him from head to toe. He lifted his head wearily, chasing the light across the ceiling. His arms were stuck above his head and he could not bring them down. His wrists were hurting, and he was disoriented. He let his head drop back to the ground – carpet; it was carpet he was lying on – and stars shot through his mind as his head hit. Then something popped into his vision. Something blocking out the moving light. He raised his eyes and studied what it was that loomed above him.

It was a man. The room suddenly stopped moving and the figure let go of Daniel's wrists. Daniel realized the room had not been moving: it had been Daniel that was moving. He had been dragged across the floor, and no doubt, now had carpet burns from his neck to his ass. "Where am I? What the hell happened?" Daniel asked to no one in particular.

"Get him onto the bed. Grab his feet," a man's voice said. Daniel felt himself being hoisted bodily into the air, then dropped onto a bed. Then the voice finally addressed him directly. "You're okay, dude. Just lay back and relax. Try to get your bearings."

"You could help me by telling me where the hell I am." He tried to sit up again. Hands held him down.

"Relax, man. You'll be all right. You'll have all the answers soon."

"Why don't you go get him some water or something. You're being a little rough with him, Walter," a pleasant female voice said. It took Daniel by surprise, and he sat up looking for its source. Shortly, he felt the bed move as someone sat down beside him.

Then the voice spoke again. "Go ahead and try to get comfortable Daniel."

The woman reached out and put a hand on his forehead. It was cool and soft. "How do you feel?"

"I don't really know, to be honest," Daniel said, and raised his head. "Oh, shit. Wow."

"What? What's wrong?" she asked, concern in her eyes.

Daniel shook his head and laid it back on the pillow. "Nothing. You're just hot." The woman sitting beside him was extremely attractive to his weary eyes. Her blond hair was cut so short she could barely tuck it behind her ears, and her mouth was slightly open, her thick lips pouting. She wore thick-rimmed glasses that tried to mask her beauty, but Daniel saw right through it. She was hot in a librarian-after-hours sort of way.

"Hot?" she said.

"Yeah." Daniel raised his head again to look her in the eyes. "You're gorgeous, really. Those glasses don't fool me."

"Thank you," she said, and smiled. "These glasses are brand new. Just got them today."

"Nice."

"You're very sweet. You know, my whole life no one has ever told me that."

"Wow. Well you haven't been around the right people then. Who are you?"

"My name is Callie." She took Daniel's hand as it lay on his chest and shook it.

"It's a pleasure to meet you, Callie. But who are you?" He sat up on his elbows, successfully this time, and was able to get a look around the room. It was small and cramped, and every wall had a bookcase on it. "God, where am I, a library?"

"You don't know where you are? I don't expect you to remember me, but I thought you would know where you are, at least."

"No. I haven't a clue," he said. He leaned in a little and smelled of Callie. "Whew Callie, you smell like alcohol. You wouldn't happen to have an extra drink on you, would you?"

"No, sorry. I smell like alcohol?" She tried lifting the top part of her dress to her nose to sniff. "I don't smell it."

"You've been drinking though, haven't you?"

"Yeah I had a few before I got here," she said, looking down at her lap.

"Aha! Before you got here! Where is 'here', Callie?"

"We are in Amalie London's apartment. Do you know Amalie?"

Daniel nodded slowly. "Yes, she's my wi-" he stopped himself. "She's a friend of mine. I think." Callie stared at him through an odd eye. "Callie, can I ask you a really, really dumb question?" He took her hand again.

"Sure, anything," Callie said, tightening on his hand.

"You're going to think I'm retarded. But can you tell me what year it is?"

Callie laughed easily. She sounded relieved. "Sure, Daniel. It's 2005. Don't worry, I don't think you're retarded. You're back in the present day. Everything's okay now." Callie squeezed his hand and smiled at him.

"So you know what was going on then…" Daniel said, and then tried to stand up as Walter walked into the room. Callie successfully held him back. "What the hell are you doing here?" he said, clinching his fists.

"Hey, Daniel. Sorry about the shovel thing. I didn't know what else to do. But anyway, that was over a hundred years ago," Walter said and laughed. Daniel did not.

"Walter, will you leave us for a few minutes?" Callie said, looking at her shoulder. She did not even turn to face him.

"Sure thing. I'll just be outside smoking," Walter said. Daniel was surprised at how cool he seemed about leaving. He had been ready to stand up and sock Walter's lights out for that shovel trick. "Dude, I really am sorry about hitting you, man." Then Walter left the room.

Callie looked back at Daniel. "Sorry about that, Daniel. We had to get you out of there. I really don't think you belong in the past," she said, rubbing his hand.

Daniel thought suddenly that he recognized her. "Wait. Are you the girl we took to the hospital the other night? You got in the wreck, right?"

"Yeah that was me," she said, biting her bottom lip.

"How do *you* feel? Walter said you were all bruised up and shit."

"Yeah. My side is almost totally brown and yellow with bruises. Well, bruise. It's like one huge bruise. It goes from here to here." Callie illustrated by putting a finger just below her breast and another just above her hip. "It looks horrible."

"Ooh, you poor thing. Can I see?"

"Ha-ha, very funny." But she smiled. Daniel liked her already. He shrugged.

"So you guys work at Royal too, right?" he said and Callie nodded. "Did you work with Amalie?"

Callie shook her head slowly, deliberately.

"So what's going on, then? I mean, why are you here?" He was beginning to feel an ounce of worry in the back of his stomach. It seemed to be building. Something was tingling his sense of fear. Nervousness. Apprehension. He couldn't quite place it. But it was there, and creeping up on him.

"Well it's a long story, really. We actually came to stop Amalie from doing whatever she was going to do with that computer in there," she said, pointing her thumb back over her shoulder.

"Wait a second. You don't know what she was doing?" *Still creeping.*

"No. We don't. We just knew she planned on misusing the computer. We had to stop her."

"So where is she then?" He was beginning to worry something had gone wrong.

"Well she's… I need to…" Callie started.

"Where is she? Where the hell is Amalie?"

Callie flinched. "It's okay, Daniel. She's okay. Just stay calm, okay? I don't want to feel threatened."

"Threatened? You feel threatened?" he scoffed. "I'd never hurt you Callie. I've never hurt a woman in my life." He lay back on the pillow. "So tell me what happened, Callie."

"We came looking for the quantum computer. We didn't know what she was using it for; we just knew she had it. She stole this computer from Royal Research, Daniel."

"Yeah I…" he started. "Okay, go on."

"Well, when we finally figured out what she was using it for, we saw someone was in there with her, so I sent Walter in to find out who it was, then he said you chased him." She was still holding Daniel's hand. He liked that she had not let go.

"Well I chased him because he ran. My wi--
Amalie was standing on the-" Daniel stopped again.
"He just showed up and I chased him down to find out
what he was doing. I just…"

"Are you okay, Daniel?" Callie said, putting her
hand on his forehead again.

He came up on his elbows again. "She hasn't told
you what we were doing?"

"No. She hasn't," she said, looking at her lap again.

"We were trying to bring back the ghosters."

"That's kind of what I figured."

"Well, we thought if we could just stay through that
entire day, just *live* those seconds, they'd never have a
chance to disappear," Daniel said.

"Sorry, Daniel, I don't follow. What seconds?"

"Amalie said those seconds had been erased. She
had been messing with the Q computer back when she
worked there. They were doing some project and I hac
—well, she erased them from existence or something."
He saw Callie's eyes open wider with recognition and
she nodded slightly. "What?" Daniel said.

"That makes sense. So she erased seconds from the
quantum stream then," she said.

Daniel nodded. "Yeah, something like that. I don't
fully understand it all. I just know she thought if we
went back to that day they were erased from and
actually lived through those seconds, they'd like come
back or something."

Callie was shaking her head now, her eyes closed.
She pulled her hair back and tucked it behind her ears
with one hand, still holding Daniel's hand with the
other. "That's not how it works. I would think she
would have known that. You can't physically rebuild
missing matter. If she destroyed that matter then it's
gone. I don't think it can be done."

"God. Where were you when we needed you?"

"There is one thing I think we could try…" Callie said, pouting her lips out and putting her finger to them. She stared intently at nothing. Daniel finally rose up and sat up straight, looking directly in her eyes.

"It didn't work then, did it? Where is Amalie?" He saw her flinch again. Her eyes were suddenly wide open again, and she was looking for an answer in his eyes.

"We're working on that right now, Daniel. As we speak."

Working on that. "Working on what?" Daniel said. His sense of nervousness was suddenly overwhelming, and he felt claustrophobic in the small room. Callie was looking the other way, her cheeks awash with color.

"Working on bringing her back."

Daniel tried to get up, but Callie held him in place. He felt lost – as if all hope was gone. With Amalie – whom he had been looking to as sort of a savior for Annabelle – trapped back in the past, everything seemed sunk. The light at the end of his tunnel had just been snuffed out. Sick fear crept up in his stomach, and he felt like he had to stand.

"Callie, you're telling me Amalie is still stuck back there?"

"Daniel, I'm going to do everything I can to get her out of there. But she got herself into this mess when she stole the computer. I need you to stay calm, and let me go in there to see what I can do." Callie looked at him for a long moment, squeezing his hand. She looked a little nervous herself. "I think I have a way to fix this whole thing. If that happens, you realize none of this will ever take place, right?"

"Yes." Daniel gulped. He tried to calm himself. Somehow, he would make it through this. Callie seemed to know what she was doing. She seemed to be in control. With her behind the wheel, maybe there would be hope after all. Maybe even more hope than Amalie could have sewn.

"And if that happens, Daniel, I will try to come find you. I will look for you, and I will check up on you." She relaxed her posture and swallowed. "I might at least be able to help you attain some sense of peace."

"I don't know what you mean," Daniel said.

Callie sat silent for a long moment, then smiled weakly. "I'm sorry things have turned out like this, Daniel. I'll find you in a week and see how you're doing."

Turned out like this... He felt dizzy again, and hot. The claustrophobia, along with the unknowing of what was truly going on had suddenly swept in and taken control of him again. "Turned out like what? What do you mean, Callie?"

Callie stood up and let go of his hand, straightening her dress. Daniel noticed she was sweating. She looked back at him briefly. "Try to relax, Daniel. Give me a week, okay?"

"A week? What the hell is a week? What am I supposed to do in here?"

But Callie was already closing the door, and she was on the other side of it. He tried to stand, but his head filled with swimming sickness, and he toppled back onto the bed, trembling and disoriented. *Give me a week...* What was Callie talking about? Was he supposed to stay here in this room for a week? Where the hell was Amalie? And what about Anna? Would he know if Callie had been able to fix everything? His dizziness enhanced. He was sweating profusely, and probably dehydrated. It was not long before his worry handed him off to sleep.

After a long while – he could not tell how long as he had drifted in and out a few times – the shutting of a door awakened Daniel. He sat up straight and adjusted his eyes, but they would not focus. It was dark and hot. He could tell he was still in bed, but was no longer sure if it was the same bed. He was not even sure now whether or not any of what had happened had been a dream. His mind raced as he tried to make out what was real and what wasn't. He felt as though the boundary between reality and his dreams had somehow been moved a few inches, if not erased.

"What's up, man?" It was a man's voice.

Why the hell is he leaving the light off? "What's going on?" Daniel asked, trying not to sound stressed. He could feel his stomach tightening again, picking up where it had left off earlier. His apprehension seemed to be thickening, but he still could not pinpoint what was making him uncomfortable. He ran his sleeve across his sweaty forehead.

"Not much. Just wanted to come tell you bye, man. We probably won't see each other again," Walter said.

"What are you talking about? Why is it dark in here?" He suddenly felt hotter, as though he had an instantaneous fever outbreak.

"Oh, no reason. But I think Callie found a way to fix Amalie's fuckups." He sounded like he was getting closer.

"What does that mean?"

"It means all this shit's going away. This will never have happened," Walter said. "That's too bad, too, Dan. I think Callie likes you. A lot."

Daniel's heart was racing, and he didn't know why. He normally excited over the prospect of a new woman. But now he knew his excitement was not about her. In fact, it felt like a negative excitement, and he knew it was going to be more than butterflies in his stomach. "She likes me, huh?" he said, trying to sound casual, but his voice was shaky.

"Yeah. Shit man, I've known her for five years now, and she ain't never talked about a guy the way she talks about you. She's good as they come, too, Dan." Daniel suddenly felt the foot of the bed sink. Walter had sat down. And when he spoke again, Daniel could tell he was facing away. "If you somehow make it out of here with some memory of her, you should find her, Dan. If she liked me, I would have taken her away long ago. But we're just friends. C'est la vie."

"Yeah she sounds like a great girl," Daniel said. He now felt bile rising in his throat. He coughed and sat up straight, covering his mouth. *What the hell is that?* Something was banging at the edge of his consciousness. It was begging to be let in.

"Yep. She's a hundred percent pure, bud. Virgin snow, too," Walter said, and stood up. Daniel felt the bed lurch up sickeningly. He knew it had only barely moved, but it felt like an earthquake to his weak stomach.

"Ah, well. Maybe in the next life." Walter sounded like he was smiling. "Take care of yourself, man." Then he walked out of the room. The door clicked shut behind him.

Daniel sat frozen in the hot darkness. And quick as lightning, the sweat cooled on his forehead and chest. He could not move a muscle. The air around him felt suddenly cold. It would have been relief had he not been sweating before. Now it seemed the droplets would freeze on his skin.

Without a sound, realization flooded into his head. Everything he had known to be true for the last three weeks was suddenly wrapped up in a tight tangle and drawn right before his eyes. It hung suspended and motionless in the darkness before him like a silhouette of his consciousness. He knew what was going on now. The cold air around him became suddenly colder, and the darkness dimmed a notch. It had been completely dark, but with a sudden click, it had become absolute, like he was blind. The sweat on his forehead burned against his skin. It was ice.

Daniel could feel time slipping away from him. It felt as though he were growing extremely tired, and very rapidly. He felt his consciousness being ripped quickly away, and he fought hard, moving his eyes all around trying to save himself from this evil fate. He was alone, and scared as hell. He had never been so useless in his life. He felt his bladder let go and his legs went warm, then immediately they grew cold as it froze around him. He could not even hold his damn bladder.

His breathing was getting slower. His eyes widened with horror. *Damn you, Amalie!* That was all he could think. *Damn you for bringing this into the world!* Temporal manipulation was all very attractive until you were just outside the circle. His pulse bore a turtle pace now, and his blood felt cold in his veins. He finally let himself fall back onto the bed and stared irresolutely up at the ceiling, which he could not see. He could not feel anything anymore, and knew this was it. It was here. Whatever *it* was, it was here now. Here to take him away. Daniel's eyes rolled back and came to a close.

Then even the absolute darkness was gone. And there was nothing.

CHAPTER SIXTEEN
Justification

The sound of the fountains filled the air. It was a pleasant sound, and Daniel was relaxed by it. He had been victim to a weird feeling for most of the day, one that he couldn't quite place. It was nothing he worried about, but a nagging at the back of his mind that he could not quite remember how the day started. It was like one minute he was asleep, and the next, he was walking with Anna.

The events of days previous were untouched; he could remember them in perfect clarity. And he could remember three days ago, he had heard on the radio about a bomb going off downtown on the street right outside the Federal Building. It had collapsed the entire building, as well as three buildings around it. The whole superstructure the block was built on had been compromised. Thousands were feared dead. With the superstructure damaged, some of the roads and smaller buildings had finally caved in, trapping thousands more in the subways and tunnels.

A few hours into the rescue, about a quarter-mile-worth of Commerce Street had collapsed, crushing and destroying almost thirty rescue vehicles including ambulances and fire trucks, police cars and wreckers. Almost half of the rescue workers were lost along with the rest of the victims, and now most of the city had come forward to volunteer. Daniel and Anna had gone and given blood the day before, after waiting in line for nearly four hours. He was proud of the way the people had come forward when they were needed. It was sad to him that it took a tragedy to bring everyone together, but it was no less encouraging in the end.

And he could remember it unscathed.

Daniel could remember two days ago as well. The cleanup and rescue was still in full scale, and would be for the next several months, he was sure. But two days ago, a convoy of trucks had rumbled into town like thunder. Over four hundred trucks from surrounding cities and states had come in to assist with the cleanup and hauling off of the debris. Throughout the day they had streamed in steadily, and on into the night. Some of the volunteer workers were going on two full days of work with no sleep or food. People were so motivated by the rescue effort they forgot their personal pains. One such man had spoken to a television camera saying, "Well we got people stuck down in that subway that can't even move; much less eat. So I have no intention of eating or resting until I've at least pulled a few of them free."

There were no skips in Daniel's memory about any of that.

And he could remember yesterday with the same clarity as looking through a window at it. His recollection was absolute. Yesterday, the President had addressed the nation and offered prayers of support and hope for the victims and their families. And he had done it from the center of the catastrophe. He had flown into D/FW International Airport on Air Force One, and stomped right out to the center of it all to speak to the nation. He was one of them. One of the people. Daniel was proud to have him as president, even though he had not voted in the election. General apathy, standard issue – one share.

Daniel had watched the speech on television, and had found himself nodding to what the President said. He was nodding in agreement and empathy. And he could remember it vividly as it had just happened.

But not today.

Today was the only day giving him trouble. Had he lost consciousness? Had he lost part of his memory? Daniel was beginning to wonder. He had talked with Anna briefly about it, but she had been able to offer no consolation, just odd looks and a tilted head. She simply frowned and said, "That's strange." He still wasn't worried, but profoundly curious about what had happened. Just that few minutes of incoherence, not knowing where he had come from or where he had been. As the day wore on, he thought less and less about it, finally coming to the conclusion that nothing was really wrong – whereupon he dismissed it entirely.

He had been under stress lately at work, with the new company merger and all. Well, that was what they wanted him to call it. He thought of it as more of an acquisition. Simply put, Royal Research Corporation had bought DataTrack. There was really no other way to look at it in Daniel's mind. RRC had more money, and that was the name that would remain. Besides, how could it be a merger when half his company would be laid off? That's not convergence – that's a conquest.

Aside from the stress, Daniel could think of no reason not to enjoy his day off. Everything was fine now, sans the national tragedy that lay in the wake of the assault on the fed building. The sky was a hazy autumn blue, sparse clouds strewn across its vast surface, and just the right amount of sun shining down upon them. In the west, there were tons of thick beautiful clouds, but somehow they did not seem threatening at all. Anna sat with her mouth wide open as Daniel pitched ice into it. He mostly missed, and mostly because she would start laughing too hard for him to get good aim. He sat on the opposite end of the wooden park bench from her, and they were turned sideways to face each other. The sun was well on its way into the horizon. It felt like early spring, with a nice breeze blowing through.

The park was mostly empty, scratch the few people passing through on their way home from a late study session at the nearby library, or work. The fountain in the middle of the park was spraying a light mist into the breeze, which made the air cool and pleasant. It was set with six or seven nozzles that would randomly shoot off at different angles in succession, so it gave the impression that it was one stream of water jumping from place to place in the fountain like an excited porpoise. The mist would dissipate into the air leaving small rainbows that faded, as the next stream would spout off.

Daniel could not think of an evening he had been this relaxed in years. He could think of no place he would rather be, and no one he would rather be right here with, right now. Anna was full of laughs and natural color enhanced by the setting sun, and he doubted he had ever been as happy in his life as he was sitting on the bench right now, looking at her.

They had been sitting on the same park bench for over an hour. Earlier they had walked downtown to see how things were progressing. Daniel had written a check to donate to the Red Cross, and felt happy about that as well. He felt he had done as much as he could, short of climbing into the rubble to try and free some people himself. He doubted he would be any good at that, as he was out of shape and had smoked too long. He had quit smoking suddenly a few days before, but didn't really know why. He knew Anna had always wanted him to, but he never really had the desire. It had just happened.

As Daniel reached into his near empty wax cup and fetched another small chunk of ice, he looked up and caught sight of a new silhouette coming up from behind Annabelle. He squinted against the sun in an effort to make out the face of the newcomer. As she came closer, he was finally able to see her face. Her features were soft and subtle, but not unattractive. Daniel wondered who she was.

She wore a long black dress that seemed thin as chiffon and soft as silk. It blew lightly in the breeze, almost angelic.

Daniel was surprised by her simple beauty, but being drown in the presence of his true love, thought no more of the stranger than a passing picture in a magazine. She was elegant, but insignificant. Sophisticated, but feckless. There would always be women to look at. He could sit in front of a fish tank for hours, and never go fishing.

As she neared the bench, she slowed her step and smiled at Daniel. Did she know him? He certainly could not remember ever meeting her. And he never forgot a face. He was immediately aware that her dress was the only clothing she was wearing, as it clung to her like a paintjob on a new Chevy. In the way that it hugged her hips, he could see no panty line. He could also see the exact shape of her small breasts under it and had to look away quickly.

Anna turned to look up over her shoulder, and smiled back at the strange woman. Daniel noticed her head movement and reckoned Anna had noticed the stranger's lack of undergarments as well. Anna was old-fashioned. She never went without a bra, and certainly always wore panties. Daniel didn't mind her strict devotion to it, but much preferred the easy breezy carefree spirit of a woman who didn't bother. Some women, he thought, really didn't need bras, and he loved when they made it obvious they weren't wearing one.

"Hello. My name is Callie," the woman said, offering her hand, and Daniel shook it. She did not offer to shake Anna's, nor did she even appear to look at Anna. Even when Anna spoke.

"Hi, I'm Anna, and this is my fiancée, Daniel," Anna said, and looked at Daniel and smiled. It still shocked him to hear that word, as they had not even been engaged a day yet. He guessed it felt every bit as odd for her to say it.

"Would you like to sit down?" Daniel swung his legs off the bench and patted the place between Anna and him.

"No, thank you. I'm just passing through. I think you might have dropped this back there, though," the woman said as she pulled a thin scrap of paper from her purse and held it between her slender fingers. Her fingers touched his hand ever so slightly as Daniel took the scrap from her. Her touch seemed a little unnecessary, and he shot her a quick glance, but she simply stared at his hand as he took it.

Daniel squinted and unfolded the paper. It was almost a perfect square, creased neatly down the middle. Written on it in Sharpie-style black marker were two words. It very simply read:

MIDNIGHT'S PARK

Daniel frowned at the note, then turned it over to see if he was missing something. He wasn't. The rest of the paper was beautifully blank. He turned it over a couple more times, trying to make sense of it, then looked up at Callie, puzzled.

"Uh, this isn't mine. I've never seen it before," he said, and handed it back to her. He noticed her lips pulled tightly together as she took the note back, seemingly disappointed. "Are you okay?"

"I'm fine. Just thought you dropped it, is all."

"Nope. I didn't drop it. Did you drop it?" he said to Anna. She shook her head. She did not even need to see the note to know it was not hers. Callie never so much as looked at Anna when she answered. It was apparent to Daniel that this was no mistake. He was not a fool; this woman was trying to pass him a note. She was trying to tell him something, and had written it in as few words as possible so as to specifically prevent Anna from catching on had she actually read it.

Daniel had caught on quickly. Had Anna not been there, this woman would have sat down and talked to him. About what though, he had no idea. He had never heard of that park, and was sure that whatever meaning it had to this woman, it didn't have to him. She must have simply mistaken him for another man.

"Well, I'm sorry to have bothered you. Have a nice evening," Callie said, looking down at the note. Daniel wondered what her eyes looked like behind those dark shades. If he could have bet on it right then, he would have guessed they were shadowed with disappointment. He frowned at this and wondered why. He wondered what she really wanted with him. Then she turned and walked away, only pausing for half an instant to look at Daniel again. Her faint smile was for him. He caught it and smiled back.

"You do the same," he said. *Texas Rangers. Pitcher.*

And Callie was gone.

Somewhere in the distance, thunder rumbled.

As the breeze blew the mist about, Daniel blinked and looked at his watch. Nightfall would be here soon. The peace he now felt inside seemed to have come about so suddenly, though he didn't know of its source or its reason. He just accepted it and carried on. It was as if everything was right, for the first time ever. He really didn't care to question why, nor did he know whom he would ask if he were to question. He nodded and let himself be taken with it.

Daniel was with the love of his life. No one else in the world could make him feel the way Anna did. He was so in love with her it sometimes hurt. There was no reason to question any of it. He smiled at Anna and looked out over the parking lot. He heard the slamming of the car door and saw Callie disappear into it. Then she started it and backed out, driving away and out of his life forever.

"That was weird," Anna said, finally breaking the silence.

"Yeah. We were the only ones she approached about the note."

"What do you mean?"

"It looked like it was meant to be a message."

"Why? What'd it say?"

"Well not by what it said. Just by her presentation," he explained. "It said Midnight's Park."

And then it clicked. Like an empty revolver, it clicked. The thought steamed in over Daniel so suddenly and fully that he felt physically heated by it. Burning clarity pulsed through his arteries with lightning speed as he came to the realization of what he had just seen. It had only taken him physically saying it to bring forth the memory.

"Oh my God," he said, and suddenly stood up, spinning quickly on his heel to look for Callie. She could not have gone too far, yet. But she was gone. Nowhere to be seen. The white Mercedes she had been driving was already out of the parking lot, and probably on its way to the freeway.

"What? What is it, Daniel?" Anna said, standing to meet him. "Are you okay?"

"Oh my God." His vision seemed to be clouding quickly, not with tears, but a fog of confusion and perplexity. It was a fog he had not known, but instantly recognized. It was wrong. Whatever it was that was happening was wrong. "Holy God. What in God's name have I done." It was not a question. It was an answer.

"Daniel, you are really scaring me! Tell me what's the matter! Are you okay?" Anna tried to pull Daniel back down onto the bench. He would not budge.

Memories ripped through his head like razors, and he tried to put them in order. Shards of evidence presented themselves for brief instances, so quick and untimely that he didn't recognize them. But he knew what they meant. Daniel spun again, looking all around, searching for something. He had just been handed a thousand jagged pieces of a puzzle and now had to put them together. Somehow, he knew what the final picture was. That nagging sense of forgetfulness he had experienced earlier was starting to make a little more sense.

Thunder rumbled again, this time a little closer – a little more intent on being heard. Daniel's eyes darted around the edges of the park in search of something specific. And at last, he found it. With less time than it took to click in his mind, he was walking toward the cemetery, just behind the park.

"Daniel, where are you going?" Anna trod along behind him, struggling to keep up with his long strides. He did not answer, just kept walking. And she shouted more loudly, "Daniel, you are scaring me badly! Will you please tell me what's wrong?"

"Not now!" he finally shouted. Coming to the edge of the cemetery, Daniel hopped over the short decorative fence and trotted up the first row, scanning the names on the headstones. He saw nothing he recognized. He continued down the soft green path, looking at every name on every headstone as they rushed by. There was no order about them. All plots were seemingly random – of no visible sequence. The only common factor was that all their inhabitants were dead. He skipped back to the second row and did the same thing, once again coming up dry. Then he turned and headed down the third, now running as he looked at headstones like an excited freak. His mind was racing with his heart, and his head felt full of blood, hot between his ears, as if his brain were pumping the blood to the rest of his body. He could hear the warm rush with its every beat, swishing softly within his mind. And behind that, the closing in of the storm. Thunder boomed loudly just over the skyline of buildings to the north, echoing and rumbling the ground.

Anna ran behind him, now in tears and panic. Daniel could hear her crying behind him. She was way behind, and finally had to take her heels off just to stay on the same row as him. The sun looked as though it had suddenly been shoved into a closet, as dark maddening clouds covered it and shouted their anger at the world below. Lightning streaked across the sky and cracked loudly, shaking the ground. Daniel could feel the sweat clinging to his forehead, and turning cold by the breeze as he ran down the aisles, forgetting he was out of shape. He had seemingly forgotten he had been a long-term smoker, and was not used to running. But it didn't hamper his efforts. It seemed to be no ailment. And as he turned onto the fifth row, he slipped on the slick grass and his feet came up in front of him. He landed hard on his rear, and sat up quickly, hopping to his feet.

But he didn't move.

He had found what he was looking for. He had landed next to the tombstone for which he had unwittingly been searching. The name on the headstone was oddly familiar, but simultaneously strange and eerie. Complex confusion and unparalleled discomfort settled in over him like lead as he stood again, facing the headstone. And the thunder clapped like an atom bomb going off over the hill. It rumbled loudly in his ears drowning out the cries of Anna, who was still running to catch up. He felt the first few droplets of rain spatter on the back of his neck as he stood staring at the headstone. "God, I thought so," he said to himself.

The grass around the base of the headstone had not been cut in some time. It grew in small sprouts around the granite like weeds. There were no flowers, and there was no hump, like some of the more recent graves. It looked as though no one had visited this plot in a long, long time – if ever. With this he felt a sudden disgust, but at the same time an inexplicable peace. It was the same peace one might feel after a tornado has ripped through and demolished his house, but knowing he had survived. It was not a happy peace. Lightning tore into the dark sky and an ear-splitting clap of thunder shook the ground again, stopping his heart for an instant. Then the soft patter of rain rippled the grass.

Anna was there with him now, bending over and out of breath. Her dress was sticking to her sweaty body, and her face was glowing in the low light. Dark spots were visible on the dark fabric as the rain became more consistent, more intense. Daniel stood staring wide-eyed at the headstone. His heartbeat was still wildly excited and his breathing was heavy and wheezing. He stepped forward and put his hands on the headstone, and let himself slide down, his hands brushing along the face of it as he dropped to his knees in front of it. *Why?* His eyes looked to the sky, but closed as the rain began to hit them. It picked up and within an instant, he was drenched. It was very loud now, rustling through the tops of the trees and pounding on the stones.

"Annabelle, I want to ask you one question. I need a simple answer please," he said with as much calm as he could control.

Anna looked at the headstone, then back at him. "Sure. Anything, Daniel." She was still out of breath, and had to sit down beside him. "What is it, baby?" Thunder boomed from the heavens, muting all other sound.

Daniel turned to look at her. Her face was so pure. So gorgeous. It shined with the brilliance only true love could bring about. Only someone who had been all the way to love and back would radiate as she did right then. With shining raindrops running down her cheeks, she looked in one instant both sexy and innocent. And at a glance he had the memory of every time they had ever made love. Every time he had ever danced with her and held her against him. Every time he had ever kissed her naked body and gazed upon it with wanting eyes. He remembered instantaneously every time he had ever slept with her warm body against his own, fit together like spoons, and every time he had ever kissed her mouth – with such passion and intensity he had forgotten the world around him. *Might all thee worldly bury me tonight.* All these thoughts rushed through his mind in a sickening frenzy, chasing each other like children in a playground.

He shook his head again. "Oh my God. I think I'm gonna be sick," he said, and had to cover his ears as the sudden shock of thunder interrupted the evening. There was not a dry inch on his body now, as the rain beat down on him like a waterfall: hard and steady, unyielding.

Anna put her hand on his shoulder. "What is it, baby? Daniel, are you okay?" When he did not answer, she began to panic again. "Oh my God. I need to get help," she stood and turned to look around. But no one else was there.

"Holy God, I can't believe this is happening," Daniel said. His hands were trembling and his mind was running a hundred different directions all at once. He felt bile rise in his throat and his eyes squinted shut against the burn. He swallowed hard and put his hands on his knees, leaning forward against the current of nausea that threatened to push him back. "Anna, come here." The rain ran down his hair and stung his eyes.

She knelt beside him in the grass again. "What is it, honey? What did you want to ask me?" She was breathing harder. Through the dull gray darkness that hovered among them, Daniel saw a new kind of recognition in her eyes. A new kind of familiarity. One perhaps she would never understand.

"Annabelle, what was your maternal grandmother's name?"

"Oh my God, Daniel, are you okay?" she said, putting her hand on his shoulder again.

"Answer the question!" he shouted, looking at her through angry eyes.

"Her name was Angelina! Daniel, her name was Angelina! Why?"

Like a tidal wave, his fears and worries came crashing in over him. Like the weight of a galaxy, the realization slammed in on him. All his worst fears had been confirmed. Daniel was dizzy with incomprehensible sickness and rage, battled by emotions he had never known could coexist. He felt detached and removed from the body that sat there in front of the headstone, pulling grass up by the handful. He felt disconnected from himself, as if watching his body stand up, spinning and shouting at the sky, the words dying softly in the nearby trees. Without echo; without effect. He didn't feel himself shouting *NO!* at the top of his lungs, crying out to a God he scarcely believed in. It all seemed a hazy blur to him, as if his body was a distant ship and he were stranded from it.

Daniel Brandt didn't feel his heart beating; he didn't feel the tears that stung his eyes and the pain that filled his face, but thought he could see it from a bird's eye view. He was vaguely aware of Anna still staring dejectedly at the headstone, her eyes darting back to his dispirited body. He knew she would not understand what it all meant. He knew the name would never make sense to her the way it did to him. And as he wandered off into the night, detached and abandoned by his soul, he left Annabelle standing in confusion and tears, soaking with rain, staring at the meaningless headstone she would never comprehend. It read:

AMALIE GRAY BRANDT

AUGUST 6, 1871 - APRIL 21, 1900

REST IN PEACE

When Daniel walked away that night, he walked right out of her life. There were no goodbyes, no hugs and kisses, and no last words. He had just wandered right off the face of sanity, never to be seen or heard from again. He had left Anna to ponder her thoughts, her intuitive speculations, and her genealogy. He had not been able to look her in the eyes again. For those eyes were his own. And man was not meant to look with fervor into his own eyes.

www.ingramcontent.com/pod-product-compliance
Lightning Source LLC
Chambersburg PA
CBHW021438310726
48971CB00005B/1406